THE PERSISTENCE
OF VISION

LISA GERY

Underdog Publications

LisaGery.com

Published in the United States by Underdog Publications

First paperback edition

Library of Congress Control Number: 2018913738

ISBN 978-0-9980431-0-4 (Paperback edition)

ISBN 978-0-9980431-1-1 (Ebook edition)

Cover photography copyright © 2018 by Martha Gery

To Mom,

for knowing

&

To Mr. Charles Byler,

for believing

"The moaning and groaning,

The sighing and sobbing,

Are quieted now,

With that horrible throbbing

At heart: —ah, that horrible,

Horrible throbbing!"

—Edgar Allan Poe, "For Annie"

THE PERSISTENCE OF VISION

PROLOGUE

I remember life before the fire. In those days, Main Street was a carnival of activity. Foot traffic pounded the brick sidewalk, lingered in the doorways, flowed and ebbed like blood through a beating heart. I would stop on the corner, under the tall porch overhang of Yuler's Cigar Factory, and watch it all swirl around me. The sweet smell of tobacco lingered on the warm air, and I would wait there until my father returned with the object of his quest: a brightly colored, foil-adorned box of cigars from the factory shop.

In the days after the fire (or "The Tragedy" as it was referred to in the newspapers and by those who couldn't bring themselves to utter the terrible word for fear the very mention would ignite the embers once more) the cigar factory was closed and didn't reopen for two weeks. They had lost so many of their workforce that they could not operate.

I never realized how much I liked the smell of the tobacco that drifted faintly through the town, especially on warm summer afternoons, until it was gone, overpowered by the acrid smoke of burnt brick and timber and flesh. *That* smell permeated every building, no matter how tightly you shut the windows; clung to the curtains and the black bunting on the doorways that marked the houses of the deceased. As you left the town limits the smell mercifully dissipated, but the black crepe adornments did not.

Evansville was a shining jewel in 1908; a bustling hub of industry and commerce wrapped in a quaint, small-town package. Large enough to foster growth and expand the town into the farm fields surrounding it little by little, and prosperous enough to line the side streets with spacious Victorian homes, laden with ornate trim and boldly painted details. And yet, despite this growth, it was still secluded enough that generation after generation of founding families settled there, their lives and their businesses intertwined, the fabric of their lives becoming one cloth.

But perspective can change in an instant. Jewels can lose their shine, and even a stone can be broken.

After a night like August eighteenth, you could be considered fortunate to lose half your family — only half. Blessed that you weren't among them. Lucky you didn't lose them all. You would see ash in the street and wonder what it consisted of. Even the air was tainted but you had to breathe it in anyway, and you tried not to let yourself think about the details or contents of anything.

Guarded. Always guarded.

I remember life before the fire, but sometimes it seems so long ago that I think I might have dreamed it.

In Union Cemetery, on the top of the highest hill, there is a monument. A tall marble angel, sturdy and graceful, holds a wreath bearing the fateful date. Her head is bowed as she looks down at the granite platform on which she stands and reads the twenty-six names engraved on its base. This peaceful hill is where they brought the ones who would never find rest — the twenty-six out of one hundred and eighty-two who perished in the fire and were never identified. Once everyone they could account for was buried in their family plots, they brought who was left — and what was left — to the mass grave at the angel's feet. Never claimed; never whole. Recognized only by the process of elimination.

When it rains, she weeps, alone on the hill where no one can see.

I sit here often and look out over the town. In the days after The Tragedy I realized if you could get high enough you could rise above the smoke and the horror. Hidden here above it all, nothing could touch me. The angel and I kept vigil over the ruins, waiting for the earth to settle and the walls to fall and new ones to rise.

"You can never start over—you can't erase the past," I said to her on the day they rebuilt the theater and opened its doors. "Nothing will ever be the same."

She didn't respond. She didn't need to. It was simply a statement of hard-learned truth.

ONE

It was a sweltering, humid afternoon in mid-June, and the baby wouldn't stop crying. He screamed and fussed in protest of the heat, the way I wished I could have myself if it would have helped at all. I struggled to balance him on my hip, carrying and bouncing him in an attempt at distraction, as I tried to finish sweeping out the living room with one free arm. My husband, Henry, was at the train station picking up his cousin and would be returning any moment. It was an inopportune time to realize I no longer loved him.

The realization had come to me the night before, if I was being honest with myself, but it was such a subtle thought as it crossed my mind, like a message of no real consequence that had been conveyed many times before, that I did not realize it was a revelation until that moment, as I waited for Henry to return and found myself wishing he would not.

I swept the dust out of the simply furnished room and onto the front porch. Setting Henry Jr. on the rocking chair, where he continued to pound his fists and cry, I swept the dirt into the yard where, in the absence of any real grass, it would inevitably be tracked right back into the little white wooden house with black trim. I propped the broom against the railing and sat down on the step, trying to focus on the sound of the birds singing in the oak trees and not the crying little boy next to me.

Hubie, as we nicknamed him as an imitation of his attempt to say his own name and to differentiate between him and his father, had been born with a scowl. In times when his countenance was neutral his forehead crinkled warily over his narrowed eyes, his lips pursed in perpetual disapproval. My mother teased me that he reminded her of Father after he came home from work in the evenings—a tired old man worn out by the day's demands. Indeed, the pointedly un-childlike concentration I saw in his eyes unnerved me sometimes, as though he already knew that life would be arduous and he could do naught but cry and rail against the injustice of it.

At just over one year old, he had not begun to outgrow his fitful disposition and I was beginning to suspect it was a permanent flaw. He was cranky when you played with him or when you let him be to entertain himself. He screamed when he was hungry (and it seemed he was always famished) but met every food with equal disdain. He slept no more than two hours at a time—which meant that I had not slept for more than two consecutive hours in over a year.

But this was not supposed to matter. I was a mother, and this was to be expected. By everyone but me, it seemed.

What I had expected was a child who would smile and laugh, cling to my apron and regard me with even a fraction of the affection I bestowed upon him. A husband who would return home enthusiastically each night and complete the tranquil scene of a young family just starting out; who would hold me in reverence as the mother of his child and his industrious and capable wife. A home that would be a haven and an expression of our family; a sturdy place that would host family and friends and reverberate with joy.

Sometimes even I can't believe I was ever such a dreamer.

Four years after I stepped into the world of matrimony with Henry I would have settled for a child who slept through the night even once a week and a husband I conversed with during the daylight hours.

It wasn't that he didn't work hard to provide for us in every way he knew how. No one could ever accuse Henry Bartolet of being lazy. He was up before dawn and didn't stop moving until he crashed, like a battering ram, into bed at night. He was built solidly, at twenty-four years of age, from years of hard labor that began early on his father's farm. With the constant expansion in town, there was no shortage of work to which he was well suited—construction. This is where he excelled. He was strong and reliable and willing to work, and had developed a reputation that made his employment from project to project a certainty. Long hours, odd hours, easy or back-breaking; he did not say no. He was straightforward and knowledgeable, and generally well-liked in his field.

Because of his aptitude, he had recently received a promotion from common laborer to construction manager on the latest, and arguably most highly anticipated, project the town had seen in years — the construction of the Walt Theater. With this new job came greater responsibility, longer hours, and higher pay.

This was our point of contention. This was also where his cousin Daniel entered the picture.

The argument that was spoken — yelled — over the past few weeks was that the extra hours his job demanded would take him away from the repairs that needed desperately to be done to the house and the barn. Henry's resolution was that Daniel would come stay with us for the summer and perform the work in exchange for room and board.

The argument that was silent — seethed only in my mind — was that the extra hours his job demanded would keep him away from his family, the only ones he could seem to say "no" to. Daniel's arrival was not a resolution in any way to this, and his company was not particularly welcome. He was willing to work for us because we would be kinder bosses than the ones he had at the textile mill in Philadelphia. At barely nineteen, he lacked the fortitude needed to face the responsibilities of adulthood.

As I sat on the front porch that day awaiting their arrival, knowing both arguments had been lost the moment Daniel got on that train, the revelation that I was no longer in love with Henry hit me suddenly and brought my train of thought full circle.

If I didn't care if he never came home, there was no more reason to argue about his long hours and perpetual absence. There was no more reason to argue about much at all, truly, if I no longer loved him and did not care. It was a liberating notion.

The confrontation between us that was the catalyst for this realization, which had occurred the night before, was something I was trying hard not to think about. Replaying it in my mind now would only upset me, as I was already quite certain the same scene would repeat itself again tonight in our bedroom.

But the moment I felt the freedom that came with untying myself from my emotions, it rang false. I could tell myself I no longer cared, but I knew it was a lie. Perhaps it would be easier if I no longer loved him, but the weight in my heart at the distance that had grown between us forced me to admit it wasn't true.

I was so lost in thought that it took me a moment to realize the baby's crying had stopped. When I looked over I saw him sitting remarkably still, staring intently at a small yellow butterfly that had landed on the arm of the rocking chair. He reached his chubby finger toward it and gestured enthusiastically, never taking his eyes off it and never making a sound. A gentle breeze fluttered across the porch, sending a welcome waft of cool air over us, parting the stifling humidity. The branches of the oak trees that lined each side of the lane out to the main road rustled, their dry leaves sounding like a round of applause as the birds sent up another chorus of song.

For a moment I could breathe again. I soaked up the quiet scene, wrapping it around me like a veil. I closed my eyes and leaned my head against the railing, barely noticing the heat of the wood that had been baking in the sun all morning. Hubie sat quietly, sated by the soft wind that cooled him and gently rocked his chair.

The stillness was broken shortly thereafter by the sound of hooves coming up the lane. Henry had returned.

I stood and removed my apron, draped it over the back of the rocking chair, and smoothed the wrinkles out of my white shirtwaist blouse and long black trumpet skirt. I left Hubie beginning to doze in the chair, not wanting to disturb him until absolutely necessary. Their noisy arrival would do the trick without my touching him.

As soon as the buggy came into view, the figure sitting next to Henry began waving to me. I waved back, trying to make my smile look genuine. Like it or not, our household had just grown by one for the next few months. I told myself that perhaps it wouldn't be so bad having some company around during the day. He was certain to be a better conversationalist than Hubie, at least.

They pulled up to the house and Daniel jumped down and immediately started toward me. Henry whistled sharply and gestured behind him, and Daniel turned and pulled his trunk and tattered violin case out of the back of the buggy. The large brown trunk looked heavy but he carried it easily up to the porch as Henry tapped the reins and turned the horse toward the barn.

"Annie!" Daniel exclaimed, dropping his belongings at the foot of the steps and ascending the first stair to wrap me in an enthusiastic hug. With two steps between us we were the same height.

"Daniel!" I gasped as he squeezed the breath out of me, laughing. "My goodness, look at you! When did you grow up?"

He grinned and released me. "I was, what, fifteen when you last saw me? A lot can change in four years."

"Has it been that long?" I wondered aloud. The last time we had seen him, or any of Henry's cousins, had been at our wedding. I felt guilty that we had let so much time lapse without keeping in closer contact with them. The years that passed so fleetingly were written plainly in his features.

When last I saw him, Daniel was a gangly child. Only four years younger than I, but his maturity had come slowly. He had seemed on the precipice of adulthood but unable to break through—average height, unlike his tall elder brothers; his arms and legs thin and untoned; his cheeks round with boyish chubbiness. Now his dark brunette hair had been cut short, his face was thin and his chiseled cheekbones prominent, and he walked with the presence of a man who was confident in his own step.

But still I could see it, in his smile and his voice—the boy who pulled my braid while his cousin stole kisses from me when we thought no one was looking.

I offered to carry his violin case but he waved me away and picked up his luggage himself. I picked up Hubie, who had been observing this new stranger intently but calmly, and he buried his head shyly against my shoulder. It was only then that Daniel acknowledged him with a pat on the back and a "Hey, little one" before we walked into the house and I showed him to his room.

The fact that he had been so happy to see me and only politely interested in my son shouldn't have made me smile. I should have been offended that he hadn't immediately asked, "Is this my little cousin Henry?" and asked to hold him, fawning over him like everyone else did. But I couldn't remember the last time someone had come to my door and looked only at me.

The afternoon was growing late. I excused myself and carried Hubie into his bedroom across the hall and laid him down for a nap. His eyelids were already fluttering closed by the time I left the room.

I sat on the wooden chest at the foot of the bed that held extra blankets for winter while Daniel unpacked his belongings into the dresser and chatted amiably about the train ride to Evansville. Although he was excited to get out of the city, the travel had been long and hot, and he was looking forward to washing up and resting before dinner.

I doubted there would be any rest in his future once Henry finished tending to the horse, but I held my tongue.

The door downstairs slammed shut and the heavy sound of Henry's black boots reverberated up the stairs. Before they reached the second floor, Hubie was already whimpering from the other room. My chest began to tighten. I noticed beads of sweat on the back of Daniel's neck as he bent over the dresser drawers and was overcome with the heat and staleness of the air in the room.

"It's terribly hot up here, isn't it?" I asked suddenly, flitting to the window and pushing open the white lace curtains. I unlocked the window and pushed up against it but it didn't budge; the wood had swelled so much from the heat that it was stuck shut. I leaned my shoulder into it, shoving as hard as I could, and it slid open stiffly just as he turned to see if I needed help. A length of wood lay on the sill, which I used to prop it up. The ropes that held the weights in the wall which provided balance for the windows to stay open had broken before we bought the house. One more thing Daniel would have to fix this summer.

Henry appeared in the doorway. "Hubie's crying."

"I hear him," I replied, leaning out the window and wishing for that cool breeze to come back again. "He was sleeping till you woke him. He'll settle himself."

"He rarely does," he returned.

"He'll settle himself," I repeated, without turning around.

He hesitated. "Very well," he finally sighed. "Daniel, I want to show you some of the repairs I'd like you to start working on tomorrow in the barn."

"Yes, sir," Daniel replied, shutting the dresser drawer before following him obediently down the stairs.

As the noise of their departure ceased with the slam of the front door, I was left alone in the house with Hubie's nasal-pitched cry. He spoke few words but had many different cries which conveyed his mood more acutely. I was entirely too familiar with this one. This elongated, grating whine told me he wasn't hungry or soiled or hurt, he was simply tired and unhappy and was not going to stop expressing it until he was either good and ready or completely exhausted, regardless of any action or inaction from me. It was also the fastest route to a splitting headache I had ever experienced.

I retreated from the second floor to the relative peace of the kitchen, where everything was quieter if not cooler and I would be largely undisturbed. Final preparations for dinner would keep me occupied until the evening meal, at which point I could no longer hide from Henry. We had been civil although terse since the decision to send for Daniel and, in light of our company, I had no idea what to expect when we were all seated at the dinner table.

Our home was a paradigm of moderation. Its size was neither large nor cramped; its details neither too ornate nor completely lacking in charm; its location settled between the depths of farm territory and the fringes of town. It was situated on the main road out of Evansville, just far enough that the rolling hills obscured even the tallest buildings and the chimney of the nearest neighbor was just barely visible farther down the lane. The house was simple but sufficient; three rooms downstairs and three above. Each bedroom had its own small closet, which was a luxury I had not expected, and the walls were covered each with a different floral wallpaper. Downstairs, the green and pink cabbage rose paper was peeling and the plaster chipping away near the doorways.

The kitchen was my favorite place to be if outside was not an option. The walls were not papered, but paneled with off-white beadboard which made the room feel light and open. Three large windows graced the room; when opened in the summer the crosswind drew the heat from the stove out fairly well, and brought in the fresh smell of earth and pear trees in the early morning. Our home was furnished modestly but in the kitchen Henry had insisted I not be timid in expressing what I desired.

"Anything my doll wants!" he had exclaimed lavishly as we stood in the mostly empty house the week before we were married, hugging me tightly to him with a kiss upon my forehead. And so our kitchen was furnished with a sturdy new coal stove, a Leonard Cleanable Refrigerator, and fine granite ware pans to cook in that were much easier to handle when full than the heavy cast iron ones.

Although these conveniences did ease some of the labor of my daily duties, the work was still drudgery, and hardly enjoyable. I certainly didn't prefer the kitchen because I enjoyed standing over a boiling stove when it was ninety degrees out, even if there was a breeze. To be honest, it was still hell. But the kitchen was rarely intruded on by guests or other family, and in the moments of stillness, the space felt like my own.

I had just taken the roasted chicken out of the oven when I heard Henry and Daniel come back into the house. Quickly stepping into the doorway, I called out, "Wash up for dinner; it's ready!"

"Yes, ma'am!" Daniel responded, and the door closed again as he and Henry stepped back out to the water pump to wash their hands and faces. I set the table with the blue filigree patterned plates my parents had given us as a wedding present and arranged ceramic bowls of green beans and baked potatoes around the platter of chicken.

Upstairs, Hubie was sitting up in his crib, playing with a small stuffed dog, swinging and shaking it by its long black velvet ears. I hoisted him and his puppy onto my hip and carried him down to the dining room. He babbled happily, content from his nap.

Henry and Daniel were already seated at the table when I returned. In clothing alone they looked like twins sitting catty-corner from one another; white dress shirt, brown trousers and suspenders. The typical attire of a working man. There the similarities ended. Henry was sandy-haired, broad-shouldered and deeply tanned. During the winter he had grown a beard but shaved it off when the weather grew warm. I was glad; I preferred him without. He was handsome in a simple way that didn't necessarily strike you until you got to know him.

When he was a child his locks had been tight, beautiful curls that, sadly, relaxed and disappeared as he grew. Hubie had inherited this from him, and my ocean blue eyes. I prayed that his curls would remain. Our son was a beautiful boy. I had no doubt he would grow into a striking young man.

I took a seat across from Daniel and set Hubie in his high chair beside me. We bowed our heads and Henry said grace. Practiced from years of recitation, the words tumbled out quickly in one breath.

"Dear Lord, bless this food for our bodies, to nurture us and keep us strong. In Jesus' name we pray, Amen."

I sighed quietly and reminded myself that God had perfect hearing, and the gesture must surely count for something.

"So, Henry," Daniel began, serving himself some green beans, "how is your father? I haven't seen him in a few years now."

"He's getting by. I wish I could say he was better. He sold the farm and moved out of town shortly after Annie and I married; he didn't want to hire help and once my brothers and I were gone he couldn't manage it. He's living with William now, in Stowe, not too far from here."

"Is he ill?"

"He has a bad hip. He walks with a cane now." Henry took a potato and passed the dish to Daniel.

"I'm sorry to hear it."

Henry shrugged. "He could be worse. I'm thankful he's not."

"It's good of your brother to take him in."

"That's what family does," he said matter-of-factly. "William was glad to have him. But what of you? Tell us of Philadelphia."

Daniel twined his fingers and chuckled. "Well, where to begin?" He paused. "It's loud. And dirty. It does me good to breathe this fresh country air. I'd rather spend a thousand days working out here than one more in that damned factory. Oh, pardon," he excused himself, glancing at me apologetically.

"Where were you working?" I asked.

"Mayfield Textile Mill. Deplorable, it was. Absolutely deplorable." He piled his plate high with food. I wondered when he'd eaten last.

"All factory work is hard work," Henry said as Daniel dug into his dinner and was momentarily silenced. "But it's an honest day's wage and an opportunity for anyone to earn their way. If you don't have a trade, you have to start somewhere. You can't expect to just walk into something better."

Daniel swallowed. "I understand that—"

"Do you?" Henry interrupted, setting down his fork with a clatter.

Daniel looked up in surprise and I glanced away, suddenly intent on feeding Hubie. The room felt still, as if everything had frozen with the tension.

"Yes," he replied, refusing to escalate. "But you have no idea of the working conditions—"

"I've worked a factory job. I know what it's like. I also know how sorely disappointed your parents are at your lack of ambition and this playboy lifestyle you seem intent on pursuing. You forget your responsibilities and your station. Our family works hard for what we have. It doesn't come another way." His voice dripped with self-righteousness; there could be no arguing with him. I braced for the spectacle that would ensue if Daniel did not recognize that.

Thankfully, he did. "I think you misunderstand me," he said.

"I pray you don't misunderstand *me*," Henry countered, still meeting his gaze directly. "You are here for our mutual benefit, and because you are family. But I will not expect less from you because this is so. We have a deal, you and I, and if you do not uphold your end of it I will put you out. Understand?"

Indignation glimmered in Daniel's eyes and twisted his lips into a sneer, but he held his tongue. "Yes, sir," he said, returning Henry's glare evenly.

No one spoke for a long time. Finally I said, "So, Daniel, how is your mother doing?"

"She's well, thank you," he said with a strained smile.

"Perhaps we could have your family for a visit later this summer. It's been forever since we've seen them."

My suggestion received a slight nod from Daniel and a sideways glance from Henry. We ate in silence after that.

Occasionally I glimpsed at Henry. He didn't look angry; just stoic. Daniel's expression was unreadable, a move I didn't doubt was intentional.

It wasn't that Henry's rant was untrue. Most of what he had said were things that had been in my own mind since Daniel had come up in discussion. Whenever I tried to delicately voice any of it, however, Henry glossed over his shortcomings. I was genuinely surprised to see he placed more weight on these concerns than I realized. Still, I disliked his approach. There was no need to condemn the boy the minute he stepped foot into our house. Henry could be stern, but he was very rarely rude. It made me curious as to what may have transpired in the barn that I wasn't aware of.

After dinner Daniel offered to entertain Hubie outside while I cleaned up. I gave him a brightly painted tin top that Hubie liked to play with and they went out onto the front porch. I gathered up the dinner plates, warmed a pot of water on the stove to wash them with, and filled the two copper basins in the dry sink. To one I added soap flakes and the dirty dishes; the other was for rinsing. I was standing at the sink, immersed in my task, when I heard footsteps behind me and felt Henry's arms wrap around my waist.

He kissed me on the cheek. "Dinner was very good," he said softly.

"Thank you," I replied, perplexed by his sudden affection.

He pulled me away from the sink and turned me around to face him, and kissed me gently on the lips. "We've never entertained an overnight guest before. Seeing that he'll be here all summer, I don't want his presence to interfere with any of our...time together."

I began to blush when I realized what he was referring to. "I can't believe you're even thinking of that," I spluttered. "We have a *guest*."

"Who is residing in *my house*. We will go on as we normally do. Discreetly, of course. But we will not rearrange our lives for him."

I wanted to protest but nothing that came to mind had enough logical weight to sway his mind from his firm declaration. The excuse I had planned to use tonight—"But we have a *guest*"—certainly wouldn't work for the duration of Daniel's three month stay, but I had planned to try to use it for as long as I could.

I knew the damage to his ego I would cause by rebuffing him. I nodded and said nothing.

I turned back to the sink to continue with the dishes, and after a minute I heard him walk away. I didn't ask how he would entertain himself for the evening. There was always something waiting for his attention, just as there was always something waiting for mine.

We both stayed busy in our separate corners of the house until nightfall, when the evening quieted and the distractions fell away and it was time to turn our attention to each other.

Daniel retired for the evening shortly before we did. Henry went on ahead of me to our room as I stopped and knocked on Daniel's door. He opened it just slightly, leaning so I would not see him in his night-clothes. In the dim light of the candle he held his face was obscured by shadows.

I held out a wad of cotton to him. "Hubie cries at night," I explained. "I would suggest plugging your ears with this. It helps."

"Thank you." He took it and pulled off two small pieces. "Is this what you do?"

I laughed quietly. "Who would tend him if I was getting a good night's sleep? Henry uses it. It helps him. He's also getting used to sleeping through certain noises, though."

He stuffed the cotton into his ears. "That should do it. Thank you."

I nodded and pulled the door shut, and heard the squeak of the floorboards as he climbed back into bed. Then I proceeded down the hall to my own room.

Henry was waiting, looking out the window with the oil lamp burning low on the dresser, the flickering glow making the gold leaves and circling tendrils shimmer amidst the gray-blue blossoms on the walls. He turned when he heard me enter.

My stomach twisted into tight knots and my heart began to drum frantically at the sight of him. I slipped out of my dress and hung it on the hook in the closet, feeling exposed as his eyes wandered over me. Then he was behind me, kissing the base of my neck, and the thoughts I had been shoving persistently away all day came back. It was last night all over again.

In the past six months we had barely made love three times. As our bickering over the methods of rearing Hubie and his distraction with work grew, his physical interest in me waned. But last night he had reached for me, and said the last words on earth I expected or wanted to hear: "I believe it is time for us to have another child."

When I didn't respond, staring at him in stunned silence, he had continued, "Hubie is a year old now. It's time for him to have a sibling. I know he didn't come as quickly as we had hoped, and only the Lord knows how long until we are blessed with another." He waited for my response, searching my eyes for some hint of a reaction.

I shouldn't have been surprised. We were young and healthy and there was no physical reason why we wouldn't have many more children. I didn't know a single family who had only one child, unless tragedy had befallen them. It had never even been a consideration to keep our family this small.

I had been burrowed in self-denial, and now it felt like he had punched me in the stomach.

Two crying children who could not be contented. The torturous sickness and nausea of pregnancy with a demanding child screaming for my attention. Feedings all through the night in addition to Hubie's wakings. I might very feasibly never sleep again.

Tears had begun to well in my eyes immediately, betraying my outward composure. "I think it's too soon," I whispered, not trusting my voice.

"But that's just it! It is exactly the right time. Nine months from now Hubie will be past this frightful stage. If we are lucky a baby could be here by next summer. If not, perhaps by Christmas. That's quite a long time; we can't wait forever."

"How do you know he'll be past it?" I asked, unable to hear anything else he said.

"All children can be difficult. Especially those with a willful temperament." He saw the first errant tear fall from my eye, and pulled me into his arms. "Hush, now. You're just tired, poor thing." He kissed me on the forehead. "You are doing quite well with him. I know this hasn't been easy. What we need to do is move forward. Haven't we always prayed for a healthy family, a house full of children? That is our future! Everything was new to us with Hubie, but now it will get easier. We'll learn as they grow. This won't be such a big change; you're already a mother now."

My throat tightened and I couldn't speak. He was right; I was already a mother. So how could I tell him now that I didn't want to be again? To say that would be to say I didn't want my son, and I could not say that. I loved my son—just not in the way I expected to. From the moment of his birth there had been a disconnection, a fray in the cord that bound mother and child, somewhere in my brain that I could not overcome. Try, desperately as I might, I could not summon joy at tending to his needs or find fulfillment in raising him. The ability to feel joy had slipped away from me, it seemed, replaced with a growing certainty of my own inadequacy—and as long as there was breath in my body I could not bear the shame to utter that terrible truth aloud. I locked it deep inside myself, where it could harm no one but me. The look of horror I imagined on Henry's face if he ever knew haunted me into silence.

To say that I *couldn't* be a mother, on the other hand, was an admittance of failure. We each had our role to play and they had been clearly defined from the beginning. He provided for us and I provided the "us." It sounded harsh, but I had signed on. I had become his wife and the mother of his child. I had taken my place in this family willingly, and now the burden was mine to carry.

I had longed for him to reach for me in this way for months; not for procreation, but out of passion. I needed the reassurance of his touch that would tell me he still craved my presence, despite the hours he spent away and the sniping remarks we each were apt to sling. I wanted his actions to silence the voice in my head that whispered, *You're a failure as a mother and he knows it.* But this was simply a means to an end; a conjugal duty rather than a passion.

There had been no way to explain the way I was feeling without also saying things I didn't mean. There were no words to make him understand things I didn't completely understand myself. Confused, conflicting thoughts that would only cause more damage if articulated than left silent.

I had acquiesced, staring motionless out the window into the starry night as he loved me, withdrawn inside my mind as he took control of my body. My thoughts raced around and around, chasing themselves in circles without conclusion. I weighed his argument against my own fears, against the promises I had made him and the vows I had taken. But I could not make myself want this.

In that moment, as I concentrated on the flecks of light in the blue velvet sky and tried to imagine what they would feel like beneath my fingertips, the distance between us did not feel like a revelation, but rather a slow, creeping grief at the death of something beautiful.

Now, after one day of trying to keep the obsessive carousel of apprehension at bay, we were alone again, and there was no hiding from it. He pulled at the laces of my corset and I shuddered in spite of the heat.

He ran his hands down my now bare back and my mind began to spin dizzily. My thoughts were no longer a safe place I could run to and close myself off.

I couldn't spend another night locked inside and suffocating.

I turned to face him and kissed him hungrily, forcing my consciousness silent with action. He responded enthusiastically, wordlessly. I lost myself in the effort of passion, refusing to dwell on the implications of the act. I ran my hands through his hair, clenching his locks and pulling in frustration. I dug my fingernails into the flexing muscle of his neck, scratching my resentment into his skin and letting him think it was excitement. I wanted to break him into pieces that matched the broken ones inside me. It was so much easier to lie to him with my body than it was to lie to myself.

Afterwards, as he lay sleeping, the world was still and quiet again. I stared out the window and counted the stars, tears spilling down my cheek as I waited for the brief mercy that was sleep to come and take me. Eventually it did.

TWO

As the first pink light of dawn slipped through the lace curtains Henry was pulling the cotton from his ears and stretching his brawny limbs, throwing the sheet back and climbing out of bed before I could force my eyes to open or my knees to uncurl from my chest. Hubie had had an especially fitful night, I suspected due to the excitement and upheaval of Daniel's arrival, and I had been hyper-vigilant about quieting him to ensure our guest's first night was not an unpleasant one. I greeted the morning sun with one slitted eye and a groan I was too exhausted to even vocalize.

A body never truly accepts a continued dearth of rest, but it adjusts in interesting ways. Eight hours of night seem to pass in a wink, while eight hours of day can take years. Your limbs begin to weigh more than your torso. Objects shift in the corner of your eye as your vision fights to remain working and the peripheral is the first to be sacrificed. Basic motor functions remain while agility falls to the wayside. Congeniality hardens into curtness as it just requires too much effort.

When we first married, I was charming, graceful, and small-waisted, with energy that could put a hummingbird to shame. Where did that woman go?

I could hear Henry dressing—the snap of his suspender, the thud of his boot—but I felt immobilized, as if my body had become one with the mattress during my brief slumber. I played through the upcoming day's tasks in my head, searching for one thing that would motivate me to rise. Then, with a smile, I remembered.

Moving quietly around Henry as he washed his face in the basin on the dresser I pinned my hair up into my signature chignon style, took my long, lacework-adorned white cotton dress from the closet and laid it out on the bed.

"Little fancy for housework," he noted of my attire.

I slipped into my corset and turned my back to him, and he habitually began to tighten the laces.

"Yes, it is...but Emma is calling on me today."

I couldn't see his face but even behind my back I suspected he was scowling. He wasn't fond of my childhood friend. He never disclosed the reason for his disdain but I believed it had more to do with a dislike of her husband, whose father owned Yuler's Cigar Factory, than it did with her. After all, he had never been capricious about her before she married.

"It will just be the two of us and the children," I added, hoping it might please him that Robert would not be in his house.

"Very well." He finished tying the laces and placed a quick kiss at the base of my neck before leaving the room, stopping to rap loudly on Daniel's door before heading out to the barn to feed the horse. I quickly finished dressing and hurried downstairs to fire up the stove and prepare breakfast.

Daniel was on his way out the door just as Henry was coming back in, which was timed from years of practice with my announcement that breakfast was ready.

"We rise early and get to work," Henry informed him. The smell of the food seemed to distract him and he refrained from chiding Daniel further as he took a seat at the table.

"Yes, sir," he said, taking his seat from last night.

I laid out plates of scrambled egg, steaming bacon, and two cups of black coffee. Daniel's eyes grew wide as he surveyed his plate. He stole a sip of coffee before Henry began to say grace and clutched his fork throughout the prayer, launching into his food the moment he heard "Amen."

"Today you'll start on the roof repairs for the barn," Henry stated, summarizing what he undoubtedly had explained in detail the previous evening.

Daniel nodded, took another sip of coffee, and gnawed on a piece of bacon.

"Did you sleep well?" I asked him as I coaxed a forkful of egg into Hubie's tightly clamped mouth.

He struggled to swallow a mouthful of food. "Very well, thank you," he said finally. "Cotton worked like a charm. And you?"

I smiled wanly. "Well enough," I said.

The rest of the meal, like dinner before it, was mostly silent. After we finished eating I set Hubie in a corner of the kitchen and gave him a large mixing spoon to play with. He swatted the floor and the walls with it, occasionally examining it or holding it out toward me with a grunt as I gathered the dishes and cleaned up.

"That's a spoon," I told him as I worked. "Can you say spoon?"

"Ah!" he squealed, smacking it against the beadboard.

"Spoon."

"Ah!" *Smack. Smack. SMACK.*

I felt a twinge in the back of my head, but at least he wasn't screaming.

Henry strode into the kitchen, kissed Hubie perfunctorily on top of the head and me on the forehead, and continued out the back door. Not long after I heard the crunch of wheels on the dry, dusty lane that led out to the road.

I carried the basins of sink water out to the back porch one at a time and dumped them over the railing, standing for a moment to watch Henry leave for work and feeling something like emptiness settle in the bottom of my stomach.

Hubie waddled over to the doorway and flopped onto the floor. *Smack. SMACK.*

"I hope you stay in a good mood, little one," I said to Hubie as he threw the spoon down and began to crawl away in search of something else to amuse himself with. "You're getting playmates today."

The faint sound of hammering caught my attention before I left the porch to chase down my inquisitive son. Daniel was on the roof of the barn, shirt sleeves already rolled as high as they would stay, wiping his brow between swings. The sun was shining brightly without a cloud in the sky. There was no breeze.

I smiled a little to myself, not in maliciousness but in cognizance, as I wondered how long our new house guest would really last.

A few hours later the double honk of a horn signaled the arrival of Emma's otherwise silent hunter green Baker Victoria electric car. I hurried outside to greet her, knowing she would have her hands full.

She parked the long, graceful vehicle in the lane by the side of the house and stepped out, a baby already attached to her hip. We exchanged tiny squeals of delight as we embraced, awkwardly around the side to avoid crushing the child. She was every bit a quintessential Gibson Girl—stylish, beautiful, and discerning. Her pale pink, moderately bustled dress cinched sharply around her tightly corseted wasp waist. She looked like she had stepped out of time from a cooler day; her nose was freshly powdered, betraying no hint of sweat or exertion, and her dark blond hair was pinned up in a perfect bouffant underneath her raspberry silk hat with grandiose striped osprey plumage. Gold filigree and crystal drop earrings dangled in the sunlight. I wondered if they were real diamonds. Judging by the size of the one Robert had put on her finger, it was possible. Not that it mattered in the slightest. I loved her just the same, and was happy for their success. But my lack of audacity to ask such a question fanned the curiosity.

The little boy on her hip watched me intently as I picked up his sister, a curly-haired toddler in a white crepe de chine dress with deep pink satin edging, and set her on the ground next to her mother. She grabbed for Emma's hand instantly, hiding her face shyly in the folds of her mother's skirt.

"Have you forgotten me already, Katie?" I asked, stooping down to her height. She peeked at me cautiously, and burrowed closer to Emma's legs.

Emma laughed and patted her on the back. "Where's our little Hubie?" she asked as she turned and retrieved a wicker picnic basket from underneath the black upholstered bench seat.

"He's inside, safely stowed in his playpen. Shall we retrieve him?" I took the basket from her so Katie could resume her clinging.

"Let's. I'm famished."

We entered the house and I picked up Hubie and two flimsy coverlets we didn't use on the beds much anymore. With picnic basket and children we left by the back door, heading away from the barn and down through the field towards a wide grove of trees that lined the property. The high, dry grass snapped and rustled as we trampled through it, sending flutters of moths and gnats into the air in our wake. The rhythmic sound of Daniel's hammer hung in the air, fading as the distance grew with no wind to carry it.

"Is that your cousin?" asked Emma, glancing backwards but seeing nothing as Daniel was on the far side of the roof.

"Henry's cousin."

"Well, that makes him yours, too."

"Not really. Cousin-in-law sounds too formal. He's just Daniel."

"So…" She dropped her voice, even though we were far enough away that it was ludicrous to think he might overhear. "What's his story?"

I shrugged. "Don't know. Don't know that it's any of my business, anyway."

"Oh, come now," Emma teased, her eyes glittering with the hope of gossip. "He must be running from something. Do you think it was scandalous? Do you think he got a girl…in trouble?"

"Emma!" I scolded lightly. "Why must you speculate him into something so inappropriate? He's my *family*, for goodness' sake."

"You didn't consider him family a minute ago." She was grinning.

"Close enough. You shouldn't make presumptions. As far as I can tell he just doesn't like working."

"Is that it, now?" she mused.

And just like that she had tricked me into spilling the dirt.

"You keep those lips buttoned!" I warned her. "I never said *anything.*"

"You never said anything," she intoned, glancing sideways and smiling from ear to ear.

"I mean it!" I said with a laugh. "No gossiping!"

"No gossiping." But she looked as though she might burst already.

"Fine," I acquiesced, glancing around as though someone might leap out of the grass to eavesdrop. "What I've heard from Henry's aunt is that Daniel would prefer to spend his days in the city socializing and carousing than working at the textile mill. He lost his job and has no interest in procuring another."

"Ooh, how scandalous," she salivated. Her voice dropped to a whisper. "Is he a playboy?"

I blushed. "Goodness, I don't know. I doubt his mother would be divulging such details to us if she even knew."

"Do you think he could be?" She seemed lost in her own daydreamed narrative.

"How would I know that?"

"Well, is he handsome?"

I blushed harder.

"Oh, my! Hold your silence, Annie, I have my answer nonetheless!"

We were both giggling by the time we reached the edge of the trees. We picked up our pace as we entered the welcome shade and quickly came to the edge of a creek. There I set Hubie and the picnic basket down and spread out the faded yellow blankets; one right near the water's edge for Emma and I to stretch out on, the other behind us for the children to play on. The canopy of oak leaves shielded us from the unrelenting sun, letting only slivers through to play off the running water. We dipped our hands in the icy water and took them quickly, still dripping, to the children's faces and arms, spreading the sweet coolness onto their skin. Katie and Ronald laughed. Hubie cried, then seemed to consider its effects and eventually pointed toward the creek for more.

Katie was old enough to eat her sandwich with little assistance. She still refused to speak, pointing instead and whispering to Emma when she needed to communicate. I tried not to take it personally. She didn't see me often, after all. I might be her mother's best friend, but I was little more than a stranger to her. I wished that wasn't the case, that we could all spend enough time together that she would know me as her Auntie Ann, but I knew it couldn't happen. A stolen day from responsibilities was a rarity for me. I didn't have hired help like Emma did.

After we fed Hubie and Ronald, Emma took some small wooden alphabet blocks from the picnic basket and spread them out for them to play with. Then we removed our shoes and stockings, dipped our bare toes in the blissfully cold water, and ate our sandwiches.

As I listened to the children babble quietly to one another, I closed my eyes and let the muscles in my shoulders and back relax. My toes slid back and forth over a patch of smooth stones stuck in the mud of the creek's bottom. A sparrow began to sing in a tree nearby. The water caressed my feet and the stones massaged them. Back and forth. Back and forth.

I realized I was dozing off when my chin hit my breastbone.

Emma was watching me. I took a bite of my sandwich, which was resting loosely in my hand on my lap, and pretended nothing happened.

"You look tired, dear," she said finally.

"Oh, I'm fine," I assured her with a smile that felt familiar.

"Did Hubie darling give you a rough night?" she pried.

You have no idea.

He wasn't the only one.

"A little," I admitted.

"Well, you must have done a good job. He seems well-rested and happy today." She watched him stacking blocks with Ronald while Katie picked dandelions off the edge of the blanket.

"Yes. Surprisingly so. I think he thrives off my exhaustion." I said it in jest—obviously she would know I was joking—but I forgot to laugh. She looked at me oddly. I chuckled. She didn't. I turned my attention back to the creek, feeling the jovial mood that had hung over our afternoon quickly slipping away.

"I remember he gave you a hard time those first few weeks," she said carefully, waiting for my response to gauge it before she continued.

The silence was long, and stubborn.

"Henry wants to have another baby," I blurted out. I hadn't intended to tell her but it was the only thought in my mind at the moment and it came tumbling out in my haste to change the subject before I could think of anything else.

It worked. "Really?" I could see the glow in her face without looking. "Oh, isn't that wonderful?"

"Isn't it?" I echoed, unable to muster a more steadfast reply. I finished the last bite of my sandwich.

"Just think—this time next year, Hubie could have a little sister! And when she gets older, Katie would finally have a girl playmate when we bring the boys together! Isn't that exciting?"

"Isn't it?" The color was draining from the trees. I tried to blink them back into their proper perspective.

"Little girls' dresses are the cutest things. I've been so excited for you to have a little girl—oh, but I suppose I'm getting ahead of myself!"

I nodded, the lump in my throat too large for me to vocalize an agreement. I nodded and smiled and stared straight ahead.

I noticed her shifting uncomfortably from the corner of my eye. I could almost hear the questions she conceived, deemed inappropriate, and discarded. Finally the silence was broken by a rustling noise and the smell of tobacco smoke.

She had my attention again. "Emma Yuler! Does Robert know you started smoking?"

"Of course he does. Who do you think gave me the cigarettes?"

They were from his factory, of course. He would be a hard one to hide it from.

"Would you like one?"

I shook my head. Henry would not be pleased if he found out. And he didn't need more reason to dislike Robert for providing them.

"When did you start this?" I asked her.

"When that poor woman in New York was arrested for smoking in public! Apparently it's fine for men to do it, but not us. Robert and I were in New York City one weekend—where he got me this lovely hat, you see, it's from Moreau's—and we heard all about it. And I was simply outraged."

"Is that a law here, too?" I could remember hearing of no such law. I would think Henry would have an opinion on it if there were one, and I would have heard about it.

"No, they repealed it in New York, too, after quite a public outcry. And that's just the point. We women have to look after each other, to protect each other. I decided to take up the cause, regardless of who likes it!"

I felt an unexpected pride swelling in my chest for her, and I shook my head in awe. "I have to admit, you've surprised me. I never would have expected you to stand up like that, to try to…put the men in their place!" I chuckled at the thought of petite little Emma, up on a soapbox with her cigarette held high. "What did Robert say when you put your foot down? Was he terribly cross about it? When did he finally give in?"

Her bravado receded a little as she glanced away from me, taking another drag. "Oh, he doesn't mind. He rather thinks they're cute and dainty compared to his cigars."

I could feel my smile fading although I tried to hide it, so I looked back out at the creek with a sigh. I supposed rebellion is much more convenient when your husband doesn't mind.

Once the children began to grow tired we gathered up the remains of the picnic and returned to the house. We tucked Hubie and Ronald into the crib together for a nap and made a bed of blankets on the floor next to them for Katie. Then we tiptoed downstairs to the kitchen and began to prepare dinner. They wouldn't be staying for the meal—Emma had to return home to Robert, for although their cook would take care of the preparations, he did not wish to eat alone. We prolonged our time together by cutting up vegetables for a stew and talking as we worked.

For Emma, cooking was a treat; something she had learned as a girl but had little practical use for as an adult with house girls to take care of the work. She chattered about Katie's shy streak and Ronald's first word and how much she'd like to have another baby and, with giddiness in her eyes, that it would probably happen in the next year, so how exciting it was that I had similar news!

I made the obligatory affirmations and coos but my mind was far away. I couldn't stop thinking about those first few months—not weeks—after Hubie's birth when he had "given me a hard time." When he refused to take my breast to feed, no matter what I did or how much I begged him. When my mother came to stay with us to help with him, and the absolute terror I felt when she left and we were alone. When he cried, seemingly all day and all night, for two straight weeks, until I was bloodshot and delirious with the lack of sleep. When the fatigue finally took its toll on Henry and he ordered Hubie's crib out of our bedroom and down the hall. Or the days when it was only him and I in the house and I would sit beside him and cry as he cried, letting myself wail just to drown out the sound of his incessant screams. Or the time I walked outside, down through the field, and sat by the creek for hours, letting him cry alone in the house and thinking that if anything should happen to him while I was away that it wasn't really my fault...

I kept her busy, continuously pushing vegetables toward her to cut up, hoping that she wouldn't see the darkest of memories written on my face or the guilt that hung itself around my neck like a noose.

There was a pause in the conversation. I laughed and smiled broadly, shaking my head in mock disbelief and handing her a potato. She beamed and began to chop. "So then she says, 'Mama'…"

I slipped away from her again, back to the creek where the only sound was a lone sparrow.

THREE

The following Monday brought bright, high clouds and a glorious drop in humidity. In the yard behind the back porch was set up a low table approximately thigh-high which supported two wooden tubs—one with steaming, soapy water; one with cold, clear rinsing water—and a wringer. Baskets of Henry's work shirts, Hubie's tiny outfits, and my skirts sat on the ground waiting to join the baskets at the other end of the table that were filled with fresh, wet linens ready to be hung to dry. That journey would take most of the day.

I had started with the bed linens and moved onto Henry's shirts next since they were all white and I could use the soap with the stronger lye mixture which would pull the stains out better with less scrubbing. When that was done I would have to dump the tub and heat a new batch of wash water with the gentler soap I had mixed up last night for the darker clothes.

My hands were calloused, rough and used to the abuse of the scrubbing board, but they still stung and ached as I alternated between the hot and cold buckets. I sang out loud to distract myself and pass the time and also to entertain Hubie, who had his spinning top and his stuffed puppy and was playing on the porch.

Daniel was on the roof of the barn again, his hammer occasionally falling into time with my song. We hadn't spoken much since his arrival. Henry had worked late the first day of Daniel's stay, as was usual, and ate alone when he came home. Daniel was so exhausted from the long day in the sun he could barely keep his eyes open through the meal, so I essentially ate alone as well. Afterward he thanked me for the food and stumbled up the stairs immediately to his room, asleep in his work clothes before Henry even returned.

Over the weekend Henry kept him busy and he seemed studious, quiet, and eager to please.

I was contemplating going inside to prepare lunch when I heard a howl of pain, a loud scrape, and a short scream followed by the crashing sound of tin and something more solid hitting the dirt.

I grabbed Hubie and ran to the barn, my heart thudding all the way into my stomach. From the peak of the roof the fall would easily be high enough to kill a man. A shorter fall from lower down could still snap his neck if the landing was awkward. Not to mention what he may have landed *on*.

I didn't see Daniel anywhere so I began to circle the barn, hurrying before I had a chance to fear what I might find.

He was on the far back side, lying prostrate, half covered with the tin shingles he had been replacing. He was drenched in sweat, his hands and forehead smeared with dirt, but I didn't see any blood. I hastily set Hubie, who was beginning to wail with confusion, on the grass and knelt beside Daniel.

His eyes were wide and he was gasping for breath, wincing with pain. None of his limbs seemed twisted in unnatural fashion and he seemed alert, so my worst fears were immediately put to rest.

"Daniel," I said, afraid to touch him but looking him over for signs of injury, "where are you hurt? Can you move?"

He coughed and clutched at his chest, rolled to one side and struggled to sit up. I braced his arm and helped him. Tears glistened in his eyes and his face was red from strain. "My foot," he finally gasped, and as I followed his gaze I saw the long crooked nail sticking out from the bottom of his right boot.

"I stepped on something sharp near the edge of the roof. Next thing I knew my other foot slipped out and I was on the ground."

I had caught my dress on loose nails like that in the barn before. Some of them were almost six inches long, and thick. With his boot on, there was no way to tell how much of it was buried in his foot.

"We need to get you up to the house," I told him. "I've got to pull that nail out of your foot, and I can't fix you up properly out here."

His face went from red to white.

"Are you hurt anywhere else? Do you think you can hobble if you lean on me?"

He rubbed the sweat out of his eyes with the least dirty part of this forearm. "I think I can manage," he said. He surveyed the scattering of Henry's tools, which had fallen off the roof with him, and reached for the hammer.

"Leave it," I said. "We'll clean that up later."

"I can't leave his tools lying about," he insisted, reaching farther for a pair of pliers.

I took the hammer from him and set it back down on the ground. "We will clean this all up before he gets home," I promised. "But we need to take care of you first. Hubie? Come see what your cousin Daniel has! Come look at this tool! Can you carry this tool for mama?"

Hubie crawled over and took the pliers from Daniel's hand, happy to have a task.

"Now I need you to walk with us and bring that with you. Come on!"

I coaxed him to his feet and then helped Daniel to his. He planted his left foot and took my hands as he rose stiffly upright. "Good idea," he said.

"Well, I can't carry you both," I said with an intentionally lighthearted smile. There was no need to tell him yet that the pliers were actually for him. With his right arm around my shoulder and Hubie stumbling along beside us we began the slow, shuffling march to the house.

"Ugh, God, I can feel it inside my foot. What if I damaged something? Do you think I punctured something vital?"

"You'll be fine. It just hurts. You don't feel any blood pooling in your boot, do you?"

"Um, no, I don't think so."

"Then I don't think you punctured anything vital. We'll get it out and bandage you up and you'll be fine. You'll just have to be gentle on it for a week or so."

He sniffled. "I interrupted your washing," he said guiltily.

"Stop that," I chided. "I'm just relieved you didn't break your leg. I don't know what I would have done."

He leaned heavily on me, hobbling on his heel, and his weight pushed me off balance. I stumbled but regained my footing. I didn't recall the house being so far away just ten minutes ago...

"Henry will pitch a fit. He knows I'm clumsy. He'll have no use for me."

I sighed. "If you keep on whining you can walk back to the house yourself," I warned him.

We finished the trek in silence.

By the time we reached the house I was exhausted and Daniel was whimpering from the pain of the blood rushing to his foot. Just inside the back door he dropped to the floor on his knees, and, as I was too weak to catch myself, took me with him. He rolled onto his back, moaning and raising his leg to relieve some of the pressure. I stayed crumpled on the floor for a moment, trying to catch my breath, my sweaty forehead pressed against the floor boards. I could feel a band around my head beginning to tighten and pound.

"Annie? Are you all right?" Daniel panted.

With a deep breath I forced myself up. "Yes. I'm fine. Let me gather some things and I'll take care of you." I grabbed Hubie, relieving him of the pliers, and placed him in his playpen in the living room. Scurrying upstairs, I hesitated in the hallway, contemplating what I would need to tend to Daniel and wringing my hands as I tried to stop them from shaking. I tried to reassure myself that I knew what I was doing and would not injure him further. Then I assembled the items I would need and returned to the kitchen.

Daniel was sitting up against the wall when I returned, quiet but clearly in pain. I spread out my tools on the floor beside him—a bundle of rags, a roll of bandage, some herbal salve, and a bottle of laudanum. Then I added the pliers to the pile.

"Pliers first?" he asked, his voice shaking.

"No. Medicine first." I took the bottle and measured out a dose of the bitter liquid onto a teaspoon. He swallowed it, grimacing and coughing as he did. Then I measured out a smaller dose for myself.

"What will this do?" he asked, wiping the remnants from his lips.

"It dulls the pain," I explained, knocking back my spoonful expertly, like a man takes a shot of whiskey. I dropped the spoon into the empty sink basin and resealed the bottle. The throbbing in my head began to subside almost immediately. "It dulls everything." I picked up the pliers and knelt before him, balancing his foot on my lap and untying his bootlaces. He shifted nervously, steadying himself.

"Now you be a good boy and just—" I hooked the pliers onto the nail and pulled it straight out with one swift yank. He screamed in a pitch I've never heard a man hit, but the sound was quickly choked off by a low, gurgling sound as he bit down on his fist and squeezed his eyes shut.

"Hold still." I finished. I dropped the twisted, bloody nail and pliers to the floor, pulled his boot and sock off quickly and readied myself with a handful of rags, allowing the wound to bleed for a minute to help flush out any dirt since the blood flow was surprisingly minimal. The puncture was in the pad of his foot, just below the second toe.

When the blood increased I rubbed the top of his foot reassuringly as I put pressure on the bottom. He grunted and breathed deeply but didn't make another sound.

"How are you doing?" I asked.

"Never better," he said, his voice strained. He wiped the saliva from his hand and craned his neck half-heartedly but couldn't see the injury. The nail hadn't gone all the way through his foot. "How bad is it?"

Judging by the amount of blood that was running down his foot, it wasn't as bad as I had feared. "Not terrible. How bad does it hurt?" I asked.

"Not as much now, but I think that's due to what you gave me. I don't feel the pain in my back at all now."

"Good."

"Yes…I feel so much calmer now, too."

"Yes, it will do that." My own anxiety was pleasantly quelled as warm, relaxing waves undulated through my limbs, steadying my hands and slowing my breath. I no longer feared that Daniel was in pain or that I would hurt him worse. I was lulled by the quiet certainty that he would be fine and the worst was over. I couldn't tell where this knowledge came from, but I believed it and took solace in it.

"Why do you take it?" he asked openly.

"I get headaches," I replied. "It makes them go away."

"I bet it does."

After a few more minutes I didn't see any more fresh blood staining the rags so I carefully peeled them back and examined his foot. The dark purple puncture was fairly small, the edges clean and not jagged. I smeared it with salve and began to carefully bandage it.

"Try not to walk on it much today. I'll go clean up your tools."

He was already shaking his head before I had finished. "I have to—"

"Rest so that you might be of some use tomorrow. Unless you want to ask Henry to take you into town to see the physician in a few days when you can't walk at all."

His eyes narrowed.

"Don't be stubborn, Daniel. Be a good patient. You can go back to work tomorrow and he never has to know."

He couldn't argue.

I took the pliers and hurried up to the barn, gathering up the tools and shingles that were scattered in the brown grass. The ground shifted continuously beneath my feet, making the task more difficult than I had anticipated, and a tingling numbness that seemed to seep from my skin deep into my muscles made the prospect of lying down to take a nap much more desirable than pushing my body through this arduous task. I forced myself to continue methodically, scanning the area completely for signs of metal. Once everything was safely stored back in its proper place, I made my way as fast as I could back to the house. My stomach was beginning to growl and churn now, and I grew concerned about the effect the medicine would have on Daniel's empty stomach.

Once in the kitchen I pulled out a loaf of bread and some cold meats and hastily threw together some sandwiches. Daniel tore into his immediately, and by the time I had retrieved Hubie, he was almost finished and ready for another.

After we had devoured our sandwiches and a pitcher of lemonade, I cleaned up the kitchen and boiled a large pot of water. Daniel stretched out on the back porch, his back against the house, and tried to coax words from Hubie as I mixed the next batch of soapy water and began to soak Henry's pants.

After about an hour, Hubie began to irritably rub his eyes so I took him inside for a nap. I brought the picnic blanket down with me and handed it to Daniel, who thanked me and used it as a cushion to lean back against. I gave him another small dose of laudanum and took some for myself as well. It dulled the ache and fatigue in my muscles from laundering.

The still silence was peaceful, and neither of us spoke for a long time. I didn't feel his eyes on me as I worked; he let them flutter closed for a time, then stared out over the grassy field. The splashing and wringing of the clothes made a warm, quiet sound.

"It's so different out here than Philadelphia," he said eventually. I didn't reply. I had no basis for comparison.

"It's so quiet," he mused. "No ears out here...no eyes. No one to watch you. No one to see you for miles. No one to listen in on what you're thinking."

That struck me as odd. "How would anyone hear what you're thinking?"

"Sometimes it feels like they do. Like the whole world can hear your secrets… like there's no place deep enough to hide them."

I glanced up at him. He was looking at me now, but he didn't look troubled. His eyes were tranquil, as if this heavy fare were no different than discussing the weather.

"You keep your thoughts in your head and there's nothing that needs to be hidden," I said matter-of-factly, the warm serenity that had enveloped me fading around the edges as the medicine began to lose its grip on my placidity.

"They're still secrets. Even if you never say them out loud."

"Well, they don't get you in trouble that way."

"That's where you're wrong. They write themselves on your face. They give you away in the things you don't say."

I shot him a scathing look. What was he hinting at? How dare he be so bold? "And what do you know about secrets?" I snipped.

He smiled. "That would rather counteract my previous statements, wouldn't it?"

I scrutinized him, frustrated that I was unable to discern his intent from the placid and somewhat bemused look on his face. "What is your purpose?" I asked bluntly.

His smile faded. "Have I offended you?"

"That certainly seems to be your intention." I rinsed the pants vigorously and threw them into the basket.

"Not at all. I was simply thinking aloud. I intended no implication…although your reaction certainly makes its own."

"Well, who doesn't have secrets?" I asked.

"My purpose exactly, and nothing more. I did not intend to speculate on yours. I was simply musing on my own."

His eyes were concerned now, and eager for forgiveness. I softened. "I apologize. I didn't expect you to speak so candidly with me."

"If it offends you, I'll refrain."

"No," I answered quickly. "Don't." I sighed as another small wave of requiescence lapped at edge of my consciousness. "I'm so used to the incoherent babbling of babes during my days alone that I fear I'm unaccustomed to insightful conversation." I tried to smile. "Please, tell me of Philadelphia."

The same statement had ignited a tirade from Henry at dinner the first night. I wanted him to have the chance to be heard.

"What part of it would you like to know? Would you hear of the filth that lies in the corners, or of the lights so bright they blind you to it?"

I chuckled, thinking him sarcastic, but he awaited my reply, his question in earnest. "Well, as it is washing day, let us avoid talk of filth. Tell me of the lights."

"The lights." He closed his eyes and rested his head back against the blanket. "The lights are everywhere, in many forms. Comradery, music, drink, companionship...distraction is everywhere. There is just so *much* of everything—people, wagons—the city teems with motion. How can you be lonely when you are so utterly surrounded?"

"That sounds a bit stifling," I admitted.

"It is," he agreed, opening his eyes and staring at the ceiling. "In the most glorious way. Growing up on the farm was such isolating drudgery. But then, to be buffeted with such recreation and attention was intoxicating." He sighed. "I would take again my first six months there. Going out in the evenings with the lads from the mill. Acquiring my taste for fine Irish whiskey. Learning new dance steps in the music halls. Utterly surrounded...by satin and sequins and velvet..." He trailed off, his eyes closing again, and I feared by the looseness of his tongue that I might have given him too much opiate.

"Surely you're not the playboy they've whispered you to be," I probed, shamelessly hoping he was tipsy enough to divulge further.

"Am I? For indulging the companionship and fair beauty that would gladly have me? Or for imbibing with the lads until the toil of the day disappeared from our minds? Which sin undoes the hours of filthy, treacherous work more thoroughly?"

"Certainly there was less filthy and treacherous work to be found. I can't imagine, with such congenial company, why you would want to leave the city."

He opened his mouth to speak, and I saw his eyes tighten with a moment of lucidity. "Perhaps there was," he said, his tone shifting from musing to careful. "Perhaps I just no longer found myself suited to strenuous labor."

He didn't have the wherewithal to concoct a convincing façade, and I saw right through his deflection.

"I think there is more to it—"

"No, there is not. I know what you think of me, Annie," he said quietly, his hands folded in his lap. "I'm grateful for your hospitality in spite of it. And you are exactly right. I left the mill for selfish reasons. I was lazy and self-indulgent."

I knew if I attempted to delve into his psyche that he would be stalwart. His jaw was set, his eyes wavering but determined to retain control of his senses.

I emptied the basket of dirty laundry into the hot tub and began to wash the last few pieces. "When I was a young girl my brothers and I had a dog, Cooper. He was given to my oldest brother, John, but he belonged to all of us. He was a fairly large dog, already grown when we got him. He was a member of the family for us. He would sit under my chair and I would sneak him bits of bacon at breakfast. I think that's why he always seemed to like me best. That, and my brothers played rougher with him than I. We had him for many years, *many* years.

"One day he wasn't under my chair at breakfast. I looked for him everywhere. After a few days of searching John told me that he had run away and that he wasn't coming back. I didn't believe him. I kept waiting for him to come home, imagining I heard him outside, waking up in the middle of the night to go out again and look under the porch.

"Then, about a week later, I was searching around in the back corner of the barn when I found the shovel...and it still had blood on it. And I knew what John had done. I took that shovel to my brother and it took everything I had not to swing it at him. I screamed at him, 'How could you do this?' He wouldn't look at me. He just kept saying, 'He was mine. I had to.' I didn't speak to him for a month. I hated him deep down for a long time after that. It wasn't until I was much older that I really understood why he had done it. Cooper had been very sick — he must have been closer to dying than I realized, being a child, and John had seen him suffering. He could have asked my father to do it easily with the gun, but we all would have known when we heard the shot. He hid it from all of us, even my parents. I hated him for keeping it a secret, for letting me search, for doing it the way he did, but eventually I realized that it grieved him as much as it did all of us, probably more so, and he kept his silence because he was trying to protect me. Sometimes a lie is necessary…merciful…when the truth is so ugly."

Daniel didn't speak, but when I looked up I saw him nod. He leaned his head back against the wooden siding and closed his eyes again, listening contentedly to the continuous sound of my washing.

By the time Henry came home for dinner, Daniel had retired to his room to hide his limp. I sat at the table with Henry while he ate, struggling for topics to converse about. The day before he had been set off about the inadequacies of certain members of the labor force at the theater, inflamed by an article in the newspaper, but tonight he was withdrawn. I couldn't speak about any of my day's events, save for the actual washing itself, so I mentioned it in passing and instead gushed trivially about Emma's recent visit and how fresh she had looked in her pretty new hat and how quickly her children seemed to be growing up. He listened politely but I suspected he wasn't truly paying attention, which was fine with me. My mind was so many other places I couldn't be sure I was making sense anyway. I was simply filling the silence.

The rest of the evening followed a familiar routine—clean up dinner, put Hubie to bed, read in the living room, and retire. As I went through the motions I continued to puzzle over Daniel. The more I played back his words in my head the more my curiosity grew. By the time I opened my book of poetry to read I decided to continue our conversation over dinner the next day and see if he would reveal any more. By the time I lay down to go to sleep I decided to ask him outright.

In the middle of the night, as I walked in circles around Hubie's room, rubbing his back and whispering to him to stop crying, stealing glances at Daniel's door across the hallway, I decided to leave him alone.

FOUR

"What shall we do for Independence Day?"

I looked up from my plate at Daniel, who had posed the question in between eager mouthfuls of baked potato and ham. Hubie had apparently decided he wasn't eating meat today and screamed as if scalded every time I touched it to his lips, so I had acquiesced to feeding him bits of potato for dinner. I hadn't been paying much attention to Daniel in the process, and his question caught me off guard. He raised his eyebrows as if expecting a quick, predetermined answer.

"Uh...nothing that I know of."

"Nothing?" he floundered. "What do you mean? What do you normally do?"

"Nothing," I replied again, taking a bite of ham for myself and thinking how nice it was that it hadn't gone cold yet.

Daniel was perplexed. "Don't you at least ride into town and watch the fireworks? Or see the parade?"

"There are no fireworks. There is a parade but it's very small. Henry doesn't find it worth going into town for."

"Don't tell me the 'safe and sane' movement has reached Evansville. They've banned fireworks in countless cities because of it, and it's hogwash."

I could hear his eyes rolling without looking at him. "Do you have any idea how many people are killed each year in those celebrations?" I asked him.

"Not many," he muttered obstinately.

"Too many," I countered. "Fireworks are far too dangerous. Children get maimed. Fires break out. And for what? It's not worth it."

"There is an element of danger to everything in life," he argued back. "You can't legislate it away. Shall we outlaw automobiles next, to protect the fragile citizens from ever having a smash-up?"

"So according to your logic, the laws *shouldn't* be there to protect us? Would you prefer anarchy?"

"That's rather extreme, isn't it? Are those my only options?"

We stared each other down until he broke into a grin and I relented with one of my own.

"Seriously," I insisted, "these laws are important. People are killed every year, and it *is* getting worse. I imagine you would feel differently if you had lost someone you love, or if you had a child to protect."

"Perhaps I would," he relented. "But the matter remains that holidays are meant to be celebrated, and we must find a way to mark the occasion."

"I suspect you have been out of the city only a few short weeks and have already exhausted your taste for peacefulness and solitude," I guessed boldly. "And now you are craving the bustle and spectacle once more."

He grinned. "How quickly you see through me. Perhaps I do. But it is more than that. We could all use a day of new scenery, of fun, a break from constant work."

I fed Hubie the last bite of potato and laid my fork down. "I agree, for the most part. But I'm still not sure about the fireworks."

"I'll bet Hubie has never seen them. Would you deprive your boy of such a wonder?"

"He'd probably just scream in terror."

"Oh, I don't know about that. I think he'd be mesmerized. Especially if we were just far enough away that the noise wasn't terribly frightening—and the distance would provide a measure of safety for everyone. Maybe we could even pack a picnic and make a nice evening out of it."

I sighed. He did paint an appealing picture. "Where would we find fireworks, then? I told you Evansville doesn't have a show."

He rose from the table and shuffled into the living room, still limping mildly from his foot injury, and returned with yesterday's newspaper. Folding it open carefully to the selected article he plunked it down on the table in front of me. There was a large advertisement for the "Independence Day Spectacular" in the city of Reading, a short train ride away. The listing promised a parade, a baseball game, and a reading of the Declaration of Independence in the park, with the finale being a fireworks show. Directly below the advertisement was an article discussing the city's efforts to reduce fires and accidents during the coming holiday, which, I saw at a quick glance, dealt mostly with restrictions of the sale of fireworks and firearms.

"I don't know, Daniel," I hedged. "I don't think Henry will be keen on going into the city."

"Reading is only a city by the most technical definition of the word. It's nothing like Philadelphia. I have a friend from my school days who lives there. We could meet up with him and go partake in some of the festivities, and when dusk comes we can have him drive us out to the fields to watch the fireworks, away from the crowds."

I drummed my fingers on the table and studied the newspaper. Of course it sounded appealing to get out of the house for a day, but there were still risks involved. Less with Daniel's plan than there would have been otherwise, but still...

"I'd be willing to consider it," I said at last, "but *you* have to convince Henry."

"Done," he said happily, as if we had just reached a business deal. I knew it wouldn't be as simple as that, but decided he could learn that on his own.

As it turned out, I underestimated Daniel's charm and persuasive appeal. I wasn't privy to the techniques he employed, but he must have worked the angles with Henry expertly, because one morning after breakfast Henry walked into the kitchen and said, "Daniel has proposed we spend Independence Day in Reading with a friend of his. He has a runabout; we could easily avoid the crowds if things become too raucous. I think Hubie might enjoy the fireworks. Would you be agreeable?"

He looked puzzled when I broke into a smile and sighed good-naturedly. "Yes, that would be fine," I told him, stooping with a dishrag to wipe Hubie's mouth and hands clean. *A deal's a deal*, I thought as he walked away to tell him the news. *Daniel should be a salesman.*

July 4th was a clear and beautiful Saturday. After a large, hearty breakfast I packed a knapsack with flannel diapers, Hubie's stuffed puppy, and a picnic blanket, and then set to work making sandwiches and packing the picnic basket. Feeling festive, I dressed in my summery white cotton gown and wove navy ribbons into my scarlet geranium-adorned hat.

After Henry and Daniel tended to their morning chores we all rode into town to the train station. Hubie stared with wide, cautious eyes at the massive train cars as we waited while Henry secured our tickets. When the whistle blew, he yelped and began to cry. And then he didn't stop. I rocked and patted him, tried to engage him in the passing scenery, and begged him to settle, all to no avail. The tiny veins in his forehead raised with the exertion of his bellowing, his face turned red and slick with mucus, and his clenched fists trembled with agitation. I could feel the eyes of the irritated passengers on me, and after ten minutes I wanted to throw myself under the wheels.

"Give him to me," Henry finally snapped, snatching him out of my hands and rising from his seat to walk down the aisle with the baby, who was now full-on screaming "NO!!" as he carried him farther away from me. Daniel, who sat across from me, smiled encouragingly, trying to pretend all was normal. I buried my face in my hands.

Henry returned eventually, flopping into his seat and handing our tear-stained mess back to me with a sigh. The separation which had worsened his tears seemed to make the reunion sweeter because he wrapped his arms around my neck and, although he continued to sniffle, buried his head bashfully and quieted down.

"My father would never tolerate a tantrum like that," he muttered.

"He's just willful," I said protectively, but also a little condescendingly. "Isn't that what you always tell me?"

"He's undisciplined."

"He's one! He doesn't understand."

"Well perhaps he needs to learn."

"Then why don't you teach him? You *are* his father," I spat.

Daniel locked his eyes on something immensely fascinating outside the window and didn't move.

"You spend all day with him. Why can't *you* control him?"

I glared at him until tears welled up in my eyes. His face was a stone. I wrenched myself sideways and joined Daniel in staring intently out the window.

When we arrived at the Reading station we fell into step behind Daniel as he exited the train and began to search for his friend. The platform was a jostle of passengers and the smell of soot was overwhelming. I clutched Hubie tightly as we pushed through the crowd and Henry hovered close behind like a protective barrier. It wasn't long before we heard a strong Irish brogue call, "Daniel! Over here!" and saw a young man with curly, dirty blond hair and long mustache in a gray suit and matching Homburg hat waving at us.

"Joe!" he called back, returning the wave and ushering us toward him. They shook hands heartily. "Good to see you! Thanks for meeting us."

"Anytime, a'course," Joe said graciously, extending his hand to Henry as Daniel introduced us one by one.

"This is my cousin Henry, his wife Annie, and their son Henry, Jr."

Joe delicately took my hand by the fingers, bowed his head and placed a kiss just above my knuckles. "An honor to meet ya, ma'am," he said with a wink of his glittering blue eye. I blushed.

"Come on," Daniel interrupted playfully, wedging himself in between us. "Hadn't we better be going?"

Joe chuckled and directed us to follow him. "He seems nice," I whispered to Daniel as he led us outside.

He barked a laugh. "Of course he does!"

Joe's shiny black Elmore runabout was waiting for us. Henry, Hubie, and I climbed into the backseat and Daniel rode in the front with him. Joe pointed out landmarks as we drove along, giving us a personal tour of his favorite points of interest. Henry put his arm around me and smiled. It was a tight smile but an effort all the same. I wasn't ready to forgive him for the train incident, but I also didn't want to burden the day with unpleasantness, so I smiled back.

Growing up I had been to Reading a few times with my family and once on a church outing, so some areas looked vaguely familiar, but I would have been lost without a knowledgeable guide. It was far more enjoyable to let Joe lead us around while we gawked and pointed, carefree from the backseat. High Street was bedecked with flags and star-spangled bunting and streams of revelers walking toward the park. The excitement of the day was creeping in as we rode and I could feel the mood lifting for all of us like an errant ray of sunshine peeking through a thunderstorm.

Joe parked in a lot behind Leidy's Department Store. "It's three blocks to the park from here," he explained as Henry exited the car and took Hubie so I could step out.

"His feet don't touch the ground today," Henry said sternly as he watched the traffic on the sidewalk we were about to join.

I nodded in complete agreement.

Joe led us down the street to the low stone wall and swirling iron archway that marked the entrance to the park. Large, shady maple and oak trees grew in clusters along the edges of the worn, grassy space, and in the center were a few tents with vendors selling lemonade and snacks. Beyond them there was a bandstand with a brass band playing and a good sized crowd lingering under the nearby trees, enjoying the music in the shade.

We searched for a shady spot devoid of crowd, and Henry and Daniel spread out the blanket under a thick maple tree. I set to work unpacking the picnic basket and setting out our lunch spread—cucumber sandwiches, strawberries and blackberries from our own patch, and small chocolate cake sprinkled with powdered sugar. When Joe told me, with a look of heartfelt sincerity, that it was the best picnic he'd ever had the pleasure of being invited to, Henry and Daniel practically tripped over themselves trying to outshine his compliment, much to my amusement.

"Henry, how 'bout we go take in a few innings?" suggested Joe, jutting his chin toward a baseball diamond in the distance, beyond the bandstand. "Looks like they're just gettin' started."

Henry nodded and got to his feet. "Join us?" he asked Daniel.

"No thanks. Think I'll stay and listen to the music. Not a big baseball fan."

"Suit yourself," he said amiably, and he and Joe walked off toward the game.

I cut myself another sliver of cake once they were gone and packed up the remnants of our late luncheon. Hubie tried to grab everything I picked up until Daniel noticed and began distracting him with the stuffed toy that had fallen out of the knapsack.

"So how do you know Joe?" I asked as I finished cleaning up.

"We grew up, went to school together. Then we both went into the cities to look for jobs. If I was smart I would have gone with him to Reading. He's fared well for himself. Besides, it's not often I get to see him now."

"Then what made you pick Philadelphia?"

He stopped looking up at me, watching Hubie and fidgeting with his toy instead. "I thought there would be more opportunities there. I got in with the Mayfield Company quickly and thought I would stay there."

"But you didn't," I prodded, lying down on the blanket, propped up on my elbow.

"Obviously." He grinned but the word came out sharp. I didn't dare push any further.

"What does Joe do?"

"He works at Central Bank. Don't let him fool you. His parents bought him the automobile. He's getting along well, but not *that* well. He's still only twenty, trying to work his way up."

"Oh, I would never presume—"

He shot me a look. "Anyone would. You would never say it, of course. It's impressive, and he works hard to portray that image. But for now, he's just a clerk."

I couldn't argue; of course that's exactly what I had been wondering. I didn't take offense to his honesty. I was getting accustomed to his straight-to-the-chase approach. In truth, I was starting to enjoy it. Pretenses were so tiring.

"Have you considered trying your luck in Reading next?"

"I don't know what I'll do," he replied vaguely.

"Perhaps you could apprentice somewhere, learn a trade."

He shrugged and began to fidget again.

I sighed. His reticence was frustrating, made all the more so because I knew there was more to his hesitation than he let on. "You'll have to make a decision eventually," I stated.

"All too soon," he murmured, staring off at the band on stage.

"Perhaps Joe could use a roommate? It would give you a chance to spend time with him again."

"He already has one. I probably won't see him again until Christmas."

"Too bad you don't enjoy baseball more, then. You're missing out on time together."

"I enjoy it just fine." He picked a blade of grass and began to pluck it into pieces.

"But I thought you said—"

"We'd hardly leave you sit here alone amidst a park full of strangers, and there wouldn't be much place to spread out a blanket up there. I don't suppose you'd enjoy sitting on the risers with the little one in the sun."

"Oh," I stammered, surprised. "That was very considerate of you."

He shrugged again, unconcerned. "The day is long, Annie. I'm quite content to take in the music with you in the shade. I've spent enough of my time in the broiling sun as of late, anyway."

Hubie crawled over and curled up against my breast, tired from the journey and the excitement of new scenery. We relaxed as the breeze washed over us with the lingering scent of warm mud and foreign perfumes. Cheers from the baseball game occasionally interrupted the melody from the band. They sounded like they were having a good time but I was grateful not to have to feign interest in the sport.

Daniel stretched out on his side, propped up on his elbow like me, and closed his eyes. Hubie's nap must have been contagious; I was suddenly feeling very sleepy, too.

"How is your foot?" I asked, trying to keep the conversation going so I wouldn't nod off.

"Slowly improving. The aspirin has been making it tolerable."

"How did you explain the limp to Henry? I know he must have noticed."

"I told him I turned it over stepping in a groundhog hole."

"That sounds feasible."

"Yes, that's what I thought." He closed his eyes again.

"How is it really?" I asked.

"Hurts like the devil," he said without looking at me.

"I'll give you something stronger when we get home."

"I can't take the laudanum if I'm working on the roof. Not unless I want to fall off again."

"No, not that. I have other remedies."

He nodded, settling his head into a more comfortable position cradled in his palm.

I watched the two boys sleep and let the music carry me into a restful and placid, if not unconscious, lull, drifting without thought or direction. I breathed deeply and told myself to be present. I was here in the park on a beautiful day. Not at home sweating over chores, locked up in the same old tiny rooms. Those rooms held my worries, and I was not there. I was *here.*

I drifted on a blank ocean under a colorless sky and felt warm nothing. It was almost better than sleep.

When Henry and Joe eventually returned, their noisy voices rudely rousing us, they were laughing and smiling as though they had been friends for years.

"Ya missed quite a game!" Joe informed Daniel, nudging him in the back with the toe of his shiny black dress shoe to rouse him. "Whattya doing, napping over here with the babes?"

"Of course not," he said as he sat up quickly and tried to not look groggy.

Henry sat down on the blanket. "Your friend here sure does have some stories," he said to Daniel, bemused.

"Don't believe a word of them," he warned, and Joe roared with laughter.

"Come on, Daniel. Whattya say we take your wee cousin here for a walk and give his mother a chance to enjoy herself?"

Daniel nodded. "Sure. Annie, would you mind if we took Hubie for a while?"

He was awake from his nap, in that post-groggy state that made him complacent rather than irritable. "Not at all, if you'd want to. Just don't let him wander."

Joe piped up to reassure me at once. "He shan't leave my sight, ma'am. Not for a second." A blinding smile capped his promise.

I handed him off to Daniel, who grabbed his puppy and engaged him at once so the transition was a seamless one. As they walked away I heard Joe say, "Lasses will fawn over a wee guy this cute, believe me!"

"What?" I called after them. "What are you up to?"

To my surprise, Henry chuckled. "He's just having a little harmless fun. Don't worry about him."

"But…is he using our son to—"

"No, dear. He's just teasing. Just trying to get a rise out of you. They'll be fine. Trust me."

We watched them walk toward the footbridge over the creek in the distance, Hubie giggling in Daniel's arms and Joe reaching over to tickle him every few steps.

"He seems to have taken to Daniel," Henry observed.

"He certainly has," I agreed.

He nodded. A stilted silence hung between us.

Henry turned his attention to the bandstand. I adjusted my hat and tried to think of something to say.

"It feels peculiar not to have Hubie here."

"Yes, it does," he agreed politely, turning back to me.

"I hope he doesn't have a fit for Daniel."

Henry opened his mouth to speak, then sighed. A moment later he said, "Let's not speak about Hubie. And I won't speak about work. I can't remember the last time we've conversed about anything else."

I clucked somewhat dismissively; a reflex. "We talk about plenty else."

He didn't respond immediately, measuring his words. "We disagree...often. About many subjects." His eyes softened, and they darted away. "We used to talk for hours, didn't we? We don't anymore."

"Well, we...we're not children anymore. Work consumes you. Raising Hubie and keeping the house consumes me. It's who we are now. Of course it's what we have to converse about."

He looked away again, shaking his head. "Never mind."

I sighed, sitting up, feeling my fingers clench. "No, Henry, I...what do you want me to say?"

"Nothing."

"No!" He turned sharply, and I lowered my voice. I stared down at the blanket, wanting to rip it into pieces. "I want to talk to you—I do. You're right, we used to talk for hours. But sometimes the most innocent of statements seem to make you angry. I find my words often leave me when I'm in your presence when I most wish to keep peace and not quarrel, like now."

"I'm not angry," he insisted, but it sounded like a weak argument.

"Well, whatever you are, you're not happy."

"Neither are you."

I sucked in a sharp breath. So he could tell. Here I thought it was a clever mask I'd been wearing.

"I just want to make you happy, Annie," he continued, and I could hear the earnestness in his voice. "I promised you that the day I married you and I'm still trying."

"I know," I murmured, fidgeting with the stitching in the coverlet.

I didn't know how to tell him the very fact that it took an effort on his part to discern the key to my happiness broke my heart, as he always used to know it intuitively, or the fact that he frequently missed the mark when he tried, as with Daniel's arrival. I didn't want to argue and, even more so, I didn't want to hurt him.

I realized that perhaps, if I were more open, he wouldn't flounder so. But that was a Pandora's Box I wasn't willing to open.

"I'm sorry we fought on the train," he said finally, visibly uncomfortable. "When he gets into those screaming fits, it just unravels my patience. I lose my sense. My father would never tolerate such behavior—but that's beside the point. I apologize."

"Thank you," I replied, understanding more than I'd like to admit the irritability that sprung from enduring Hubie's cry. "I'm sorry as well. I could have been kinder."

He reached for my hand on the blanket, gently tracing his fingertips over my skin. The sun reflected off his sandy hair, curled slightly at the edges where it was growing a bit long. I watched the slow blink of his thick lashes as he looked down at my hand, imagining them velvety as butterfly wings, appreciating the chance to watch him without his eyes on me.

"Sometimes I can't speak because I can't breathe," I whispered. He looked up at me, his eyes wide and soft. "I miss when things were simple between us."

His brow furrowed as he exhaled slowly. "Darling," he breathed, raising my hand to his lips and placing a kiss there, his mouth lingering gently. In his hesitation I could feel his urge to kiss me properly, but we were in public, and such a display would be indecorous. He glanced upwards after a moment, a thoughtful look on his face. "Let's take a walk," he suggested, rising and carefully pulling me with him. "I want to show you something."

My curiosity piqued, I let him help me up and we walked deep into the park. The baseball diamond had been taken over by a patchwork group of young boys playing a game that looked like it might have been baseball's second cousin. Fathers lingered near home plate, giving instruction to children who cared little more for the rules than the chance to swing the bat.

Just beyond the next scattering of lemonade stands the manicured grounds curved to the left. Suddenly I had a strange sense of familiarity.

"Have I been here before?" I asked, perplexed.

He nodded just as I heard the first strains of the music. "I want you to remember," he said with a shy smile, "when things were simple."

Around the bend and across another expanse of patron-filled open ground, my eyes locked onto a pavilion. As the jaunty melody of the band organ hit us at last, I was instantly smiling.

"The carousel?" I exclaimed in disbelief. "Is this the Brass Ring Carousel?"

"It is," he proclaimed, his face a mirror of my own enthusiasm. "You remember, then, when we came here—"

"With the church! And our families! How old were we? Ten?"

"Thereabouts."

"Oh, my. I didn't realize this was the same place. Let's go see it."

I took the lead as we hurried up to the railing that surrounded the carousel. Children and adults alike crowded at the gates, eager for their chance to ride and mesmerized by the flying animals. The band organ, crowned with bare-chested mermaids and guarded by four petite figures who adorned the front on tiny platforms, shook and vibrated in the corner of the pavilion behind a railing as it belted out a continuous tempo for the horses to dance to. Gentle brass pipes alternated with thunderous drums and cymbals as the carousel spun round, occasionally punctuated by the chime of the bells held by the tiny statues who jerkily moved their arms to ring them.

That music was a shot of nostalgia straight into my veins. The moment I heard the familiar melody I was a child again.

"Now, if I remember correctly, *my* horse should be coming up…now!" Henry pointed to a black and white spotted horse on the outside ring with a red, white, and blue saddle and the stern face of Uncle Sam tucked just under the back.

"Ha! I remember that. We used to fight over that thing. I don't even know why."

"You liked it…so naturally, I had to have it," he said with a shrug.

"Oh my. How silly."

"Yes, you were."

"Oh, was I?" I cried playfully, giving him a little shove. He beamed.

The carousel slowed to a stop and the next rush of riders swarmed through the gate.

"Hubie would love this," I said as I watched it slowly pick up speed again.

"I'm fairly certain Joe and Daniel will make sure he gets his fill of it today."

I nodded, studying the rows of ornate wooden horses that sat four abreast and trying to decide which one was my favorite now.

"Would you like to ride it?" he asked, giving my waist a subtle squeeze.

"Certainly. We could find Daniel and get Hubie—"

"No, that's not what I meant. You and I. Why don't we go for a ride?"

I chuckled, thinking he must be joking, but his face was earnest. "Really?"

"Why not?"

"Well, we're..." I looked at the people in line. Some were children with adult chaperones, some were teenage sweethearts, and some were single adult riders. All looked equally excited.

"Yes," I said definitively. "I *would* like to ride."

He turned and led the way to the ticket window. After a short wait he handed me a small yellow ticket and we got in line at the gate.

Standing there clutching my ticket in my sweaty palm, it didn't matter that I was twenty-three years old and a mother and responsible adult. This place was wonderfully bewitched, enchanted with a spell of enduring wonderment, and this afternoon had become my fleeting escape. I was going to ride the carousel and catch the brass ring and I would step on anyone who got in my way.

When the ride ended and the inner circle had been cleared, the attendants opened both gates simultaneously and we burst forth, scurrying to the right as the crowd moved to the left. The hulking, carved animals, garishly painted and bejeweled, beckoned us from the outside ring, their tongues lolling around their bits and their hooves frozen in mid-prance.

Henry claimed the Uncle Sam horse. I quickly clamored up onto a chestnut mare with green eyes directly behind him. He turned around to see that I had mounted safely and beamed proudly.

Once every horse had a rider there was a clang of a bell and we began to creep slowly forward. An attendant jumped aboard and began collecting tickets. After a few rotations, once tickets had been taken and the ride was up to speed, the bell clanged again. I wiped the sweat from my hands and gripped the pole tightly with my left hand, leaning as far as I dared off my horse and extended my right arm, poised and ready, just as everyone else did.

In the half turn just before the band organ was a mechanical arm that had been extended with the signal of the bell, and at the end of this steel dispenser was a metal ring. Rider after rider leaned and grabbed for it. I stretched my fingers as far as I could, reached for the mechanism, and felt them slip into something. With a yank I pulled the ring free.

Round and round we whirled with the steady beat, the carousel chugging and swaying as though the horses were actually galloping. Another pass, another ring. I stretched my arms out, felt the breeze in my face, and felt like I was flying.

Every time Henry got a ring he hoisted it in the air like a trophy. Occasionally he would turn back to me and hold his hand up, the rings looped along his left index finger. "Three!" he shouted, inviting me to compare my number.

"Three!" I shouted back.

A few turns later, "Six!"

"Seven!" I laughed.

He scowled and leaned farther next time.

I couldn't stop myself from envisioning him as a short, chubby, wavy-haired little boy riding the horse in front of me, waving his rings obnoxiously in my face after stealing my favorite horse, and how even after informing him I wasn't speaking to him ever again I begged my father for another ticket and chased him right back on.

The bell clanged again and the mechanical arm was retracted. I surveyed my rings; ten total, none of them brass, which would have granted me a free ride. On the next turn I joined the other riders in throwing my rings at the canvas painting of a lion with a wide "O" cut in its mouth to return them.

When we slowed to a stop and climbed off, I wasted no time in announcing proudly, "Ten rings."

"Ten?" he exclaimed as he held the gate open for me and we exited the ride. "I only got nine. I suppose you win. Oh…except for this." He opened his palm to reveal a scratched, worn, but unmistakably brass, ring.

"You got it?" I squealed in disbelief. I picked it up and examined it closely. I had never gotten the brass ring; had never even seen another rider claim it. I had my suspicions there wasn't one at all and it was simply a ruse to keep people riding and hoping. But there it was in my hand, very much real.

"You want to ride again?" he asked, wearing a smug grin that looked like it would never come off.

Without a word I hooked the ring around my finger and made him chase me to the ticket booth.

When evening set in our little group reconvened at the picnic blanket and we packed up and left the park. Joe drove us to the edge of the city to a cafeteria that he frequented for dinner. He and Henry bickered at the register when he tried to pick up the bill until Joe finally gave in and let Henry pay, but by the time we picked a table all was forgiven.

After the meal, which Joe assured me did not outshine my picnic, we drove to the edge of the mountainous border that cradled the eastern edge of Reading. Turning onto a steep, narrow road that cut through the closely gathered trees, Joe carefully navigated through a series of switchbacks as we ascended. I wrapped my arms tightly around Hubie and prayed that we wouldn't slide backwards down the mountain.

Eventually the trees became sparser and the road widened a bit. Joe pulled to the side and parked.

"Just up around that last turn is a lookout," Joe explained before we could assail him with questions. "They just finished the resort they built up here, but it ain't open yet, so there shouldn't be more than a handful of people. Bring your blanket."

As we rounded the corner, I wasn't the only one who gasped at the sight.

The lookout was a wide, flat ledge gouged into the mountain. A waist-high stone wall started at the tree line and ran along the outer edge just before the hill dropped sharply downward, terminating at the newly constructed resort. Beyond this was the entire city of Reading and the rolling hills that lay beyond it, stretching for more miles than I could fathom. The deep amber sunset backlit the clouds, ragged navy blue holes ripped across the sky, and made it hard to determine if the mountain range I saw in the distance was actually there at all or just part of the sky meeting the horizon. Tiny scatterings of light marked the city limits in the darkened valley.

A few families had the same idea as we and were gathered along the wall or spread out on blankets, taking in the view and waiting for the fireworks show to begin. As we made our way to an open spot on the wall, Joe said, "Some friends a'mine work on the construction crew up here. I expect it'll be a popular place to come by next year, but for now most people don't know they can get up here."

Henry spread out the blanket for Hubie and I, and the men sat on the wall. They chatted amongst themselves as I took Hubie's arms and danced him to a tune in my head, trying to keep him awake for the show. When the final streaks of rose and burnt sienna darkened to a deep violet and the stars began to brighten in the darkness, the first brilliant firework exploded across the sky. Daniel let out an enthusiastic cheer and I scooped Hubie up and scrambled to my feet for a better view. The sudden commotion brought him to full alert, and he was mesmerized.

I divided my attention between the display and the random groupings of people around us. They all appeared relaxed and entranced by the show. No one was lighting up their own explosives or shooting their pistols in revelry. Even so, every few minutes I scanned them again.

Halfway through, Henry slid down off the wall and stood beside me. "They seem like a quiet bunch," he observed.

"I'm hoping they stay that way."

"I expect they will. This is a rather remote place to come if you're inebriated to cause a ruckus. You'd probably get lost just trying to find it."

"Good point." I shifted Hubie in my arms. For being such a picky eater he certainly seemed to be bigger every time I picked him up.

"Is he too much?"

"No, just a mite heavy. My arm's a little tingly."

"Here. Let me take him for a bit." He took him from my hip and clutched him with one arm to his chest.

"Thank you," I said. As I stood there stretching my arms and rubbing them to restore blood flow he leaned over silently and kissed me on the forehead. Not a quick, on-the-way-out-the-door kind of peck, but a soft, lingering kiss; the kind he used to place on me when he thought I was sleeping. By the time I looked up at him he had already turned his attention back to the fireworks. I leaned closer and rested my head against his sturdy shoulder with a tiny smile.

We watched the sky rupture with color and light, the sparks falling and shimmering like confetti in the sun, and I realized, a bit sheepishly, how grateful I was for Daniel's meddling insistence. I gazed at my boys fondly, their eyes glued to the spectacle as though they were the same age. Yes, I had to admit, Daniel had been right about coming out to see this. But no one ever need know that.

That night, after we said our goodbyes to Joe and he made us promise to come and see him again, we boarded the train to return home. Hubie was fast asleep by the time I took my seat, a dead weight in my arms, and did little more than stir at the wail of the whistle and the jerky departure. Once home I laid him carefully in his crib, said goodnight to Daniel as he slipped into his room and closed the door, and basked in the warm daze of sleepiness that was quickly coming on as I shuffled down the hall. I imagined Hubie being so worn out that he finally slept the entire night through, and I would wake in the morning to the sun and the twitter of birdsong, feeling lighter and more refreshed than I could ever remember being. I embraced this fantasy with the kind of enthusiasm most people have for a beloved hobby. I could already feel the pillow beneath my neck.

Henry, however, had different plans.

The moment I stepped into the room he was on me, pulling me in and shutting the door behind me. His mouth was on my neck and his fingers worked through my buttons as he pressed me firmly against the wall with the length of his body.

We were both aware, with knowledge of Nature's timing, I was hardly likely to conceive that night. And still he reached for me, with an earnestness in his touch that was not gentle. My fatigue dissipated as I felt the sturdy muscles in his arms flex as they tugged at my clothing. I kissed him back with a burning charge just below my skin that caught me off guard.

"Aren't you sleepy?" I giggled as he dropped my skirt to the floor.

"Do I look sleepy?" he whispered hotly into my ear.

There was something in his touch that was raw, even vulnerable, as he held my face in his hands and tangled his fingers in my hair. I could feel him opening to me, letting down his walls, finding me no longer simply a wife, or a mother, or an obligation to him. He reached beyond all that and I was his Annie again. As I began to desire him in a visceral way that defied reason or sense, as I had not so long before, I caught a glimpse of the man he was beyond the husband, father, and provider that life had dictated he must be.

I pulled his nightshirt over his head and felt his broad shoulders beneath my hands. I wanted him to make me forget everything. Every doubt I ever harbored. Every disappointment I suspected he felt. Every word I locked inside me. The miles between us faded to inches as we clawingly, graspingly closed the gap.

After months of wandering through the pressing darkness, I was home at last.

I wanted to tell him, *I still love you, more than you know. Sometimes I just feel suffocated by everything we expect each other to be. But I don't want to hide from you anymore.* But I let the words be silent, and told him with my body all the things I didn't have the strength to say.

I fell asleep that night with my head on his chest and his arm around my shoulder. My slumber was deep and unbroken. Hubie didn't stir once.

FIVE

It was late afternoon and a thunderstorm had rolled in. I closed up all the windows in the house except the kitchen, where I was preparing dinner, because I couldn't bear to lose the sweet, cool breeze or the intoxicating scent of the pear trees, amplified by the dampness. I hummed to myself as I snapped green beans and wiped the sweat from my brow.

Daniel was working inside the barn to escape the rain and Hubie was upstairs napping. I was surprised when I heard a buggy coming up the lane, and concerned when I looked out the window and saw it was Henry. I looked at the clock; it was only four-thirty. He hadn't arrived home from work this early in months. Worried he was ill or injured, I took off my apron and stepped out onto the back porch.

He pulled up to the barn and unhitched the horse. After disappearing inside for a few minutes he emerged, hurrying through the rain with his head down. A man with a gray hat pulled low followed behind him, and it wasn't until they were almost to the house and the stranger finally looked up that I recognized the mischievous-eyed, blond-haired young man of sixteen.

"Nathan!" I exclaimed, fighting the urge to run off the porch and embrace him.

Henry was smiling when he reached the porch. "I've brought you a guest," he said. He stepped aside and Nathan, laughing, swept me off my feet in a hug.

"How is my big sister?" he asked, setting me down and removing his hat to keep from dripping more water on me.

"Very well!" I replied, reluctant to release him. "Are you joining us for dinner?"

He was beaming. "Yes, Henry's invited me to join you. We have some exciting news to share. And celebrate." They exchanged knowing looks.

"Well, come in! Dinner's almost finished. What is this news?"

Nathan shook his head. "Not until dinner," he insisted.

"Oh, don't tease me!" I begged, but he laughed and shook his head stubbornly.

"Where's my little nephew?" he asked, glancing about and seeing no toys in the kitchen or other signs of play.

I handed him a dishtowel and he dried his face and disheveled locks. "He's upstairs in his crib. I think he's awake from his nap—"

"I'll fetch him!" he cried helpfully, tossing the towel back to me and hurrying out of the room. Henry shook his head in amusement and retreated to his armchair in the living room to read the newspaper.

The sounds of happy squeals and laughter rose from the living room as I finished dinner and set the table. Henry summoned Daniel from the barn, as we were eating earlier than usual for the sake of our guest, and we all sat at the table and bowed our heads as Henry said grace. Nathan shifted and bounced in his seat, unable to bear the chains of his secret any longer. As soon as the food was passed and plates were filled, he announced proudly, "I've gotten a job!"

"Congratulations!" I exclaimed. Daniel echoed my sentiment with polite interest in between bites. Henry beamed like a proud father.

"Are you going to be a laborer? Will you be working under Henry?" I inquired, undecided as to whether this would be a positive development or not.

"No. I won't be working for the construction company. That's the exciting part. Mayfield wants to hire me to work in the theater when it opens! And not just any job—*they want me to be the projectionist!*" It took all his restraint not to erupt into a childish fit of excited giggles.

Daniel's interest was suddenly piqued. "Mayfield? But Henry, you don't work for Mayfield. You're with Tierney & Sons, aren't you?"

"Yes, but the owner of the theater is Mayfield. It's their project."

"I hadn't realized," Daniel muttered, lost in thought.

"Daniel, you worked for Mayfield, didn't you? Didn't they run the textile mill you worked at?" I asked.

"Yes," he whispered, then shook his head and cleared his throat. "Yes," he repeated louder, with a tight smile. "That's correct."

"This is wonderful news," I replied, bringing the conversation back to Nathan. "But, honey, what do you know about being a projectionist?"

"Nothing yet. They're going to train me. If I was younger they'd hire me on as the projectionist's assistant, but they think with some training I can pick it up straight away."

I glanced at Daniel. Doubt was written on his face but his jaw was set; he wasn't speaking.

"Nathan, I'm terribly happy for you, but…The Walt will be open before the end of the summer. Is that enough time? Don't you need years of special training?"

"Not years," Henry intervened. "Nathan's a bright boy. He can pick it up."

"I won't be alone in the beginning," he chimed in. "I'll be apprenticing with a professional until I am completely trained."

Daniel opened his mouth, then thought better of it and took another bite of roast beef.

I didn't want to be the dark spot on his sunny day, so I shelved my concerns. "It sounds like they have a good plan in place for you. You could make a real career out of this."

"You bet I can! Theaters are opening up all across the country. I could find work in any city I choose. I could board a train and set off for parts unknown, and there would be opportunity for me with a trade like this. A *good paying* opportunity once I'm a professional!" He blushed briefly at the inappropriateness of mentioning the pay. I couldn't help but grin at his unbridled enthusiasm.

"Congratulations, dear. I know you'll do well. This will open a great many doors for you."

Henry explained how he had brought Nathan to the jobsite to inquire about a menial job for him until the end of the summer. The owner of the Mayfield Company, Jonathan Mayfield, happened to be visiting the site that day and spoke with him, took a liking to him and, upon learning he was Henry's brother-in-law, took faith in him and offered the job. Henry lauded the adventures that would lie before him in his new career, and Nathan ate up every word of his fantasies. Daniel appeared strangely sullen, as though he were trying to block out the conversation by concentrating inordinately on his silverware.

It was the protective elder sister in me that worried he was too young for a job that required such skill and so much responsibility, and I chastised myself for entertaining the thought. He was almost a man, I reminded myself, and quite capable. He wasn't mine to protect anymore. But still it nagged me.

After dinner, as I cleaned up in the kitchen and Nathan and Daniel conversed in the living room, Henry appeared in the doorway. His exuberance faded, his expression was now pensive. "Are you pleased, Annie?"

"Pleased?" I repeated, drying a dinner plate. "With what?"

He took a step closer. "With the position I've secured for Nathan. You seemed a bit apprehensive."

"Oh. That." I set down the plate and waved my hand before continuing on to the next. "Just motherly concern, that's all."

He nodded, but the look of trepidation on his face grew. "I only did it for you, doll. I know you've a special place for your brother. I thought giving him a step up into a career early would be a good opportunity for him, and that you'd be pleased knowing he had a direction."

"I am," I assured him, surprised by his sudden unease. "I am. It's wonderful news. You know how I dote on him. I just worry for the responsibility it will put on him. He's still young."

"Of course." He leaned against the doorway, watching me, his thick arms crossed. The silence hung heavily in the room, pregnant with unspoken words that could have belonged to either one of us.

"You seem rather quiet about it now," I observed. "You were quiet animated at the dinner table."

"Don't mind me. I've just had a long day, and I believe it's catching up to me." The creases in his forehead cleared and his smile returned. "You'll see. Everything will be well in the end." With a firm nod of his head he turned on his heel and rejoined the boys in the living room.

Later that night, as the sun finished its descent below the horizon, I heard Henry return from taking Nathan home. I was upstairs changing Hubie into his nightclothes, singing a quiet lullaby to calm him before bedtime when the sound of low voices drifted in through the partially open window. At first I paid no attention but the volume of the conversation quickly elevated. I placed Hubie in his crib and crawled over to sit on the floor next to the window, nudging it open slightly more and trying not to be noticed.

"You don't know what they're capable of," I heard Daniel say.

Henry shushed him. His reply was inaudible.

"I worked for these people, I know…They don't care. They cut corners. They are not to be trusted —"

"You know nothing of the situation," Henry growled, finally raising his voice.

The breeze picked up and carried their voices away, and their words faded in and out of audibility.

"I've got this under control…" Henry was insisting.

"Mayfield….ran the textile factory…what I've seen…don't let Nathan get involved…"

"This conversation is over." Henry's voice was loud enough to be clear.

"Jesus." Daniel's voice was hushed, but I could hear it now. "Have they *bought* you, Henry?"

"Who the hell do you think you are? How dare you?"

Daniel refused to back down. "Do you already know they're hiding something? Is that why you won't listen? Do they pay you for your silence? Speak up—do they bribe you to hide their secrets?"

The conversation was halted by the hard sound of a fist against flesh. The sound was quickly returned and a skirmish ensued. I crawled away from the window, tears springing to my eyes, not wanting to hear any more. I turned down the oil lamp and hurried to my room, changing into my nightgown and climbing into bed. I didn't want to face either of them. I couldn't handle cleaning up whatever they were doing to each other out there.

It was a long time before I heard them come into the house. There were no voices but two sets of footsteps moving together, so at least I knew they had ceased trying to kill one another for the night. When Henry came into the bedroom I lay limply with my face buried in the pillow, feigning sleep. The cloudy night hid my deception, and he didn't try to rouse me. Once they were both in their respective beds I could finally relax enough to drift off.

I slipped into a vivid dream that was more memory than fantasy. In it I was a young girl and had accompanied my father to a fair in Reading. We strolled along the dusty midway, past the games of chance and the freak show and the men who begged for our pennies in exchange for a display of wonderment beyond our imaginations. The sun beat down on us and we ducked into a maroon canvas tent with worn, gold flaps to escape its glare. Inside the darkened room were rows of wooden folding chairs all facing a white canvas screen, filled with sweaty patrons fanning themselves and murmuring. A tall man with a dark moustache and large green top hat stood at the forefront, next to a clean-cut, elderly man crouched over a piano.

"Ladies and gentlemen, I am here today to present you with a modern marvel so captivating, so breathtaking, that you will hardly believe your eyes!" The man with the moustache proclaimed. "There is a movement that is revolutionizing the country—dare I say, the world—gaining momentum as we speak. I am here to show you the wonder of cinematography! The days when man contented himself with a photograph to capture a moment of life, one solitary flicker of memory, are over. With the advent of these modern marvels, sprung from the mind of our own dear Edison and many other genius minds across the ocean, we can now capture the living movement of our reality! Today I have for you a moving picture show all the way from France. Captured here on a strip of film, from a world away, a charming production forever preserved! If you do not believe in the wonder of magic, ladies and gentlemen…you just may soon enough."

The man disappeared, and a few moments later the screen before us was illuminated with the words "Le Voyage dans la Lune." The high trill of the piano began as the screen faded to black for just a second and then, as a collective gasp took the crowd, a group of men in long robes appeared on the screen, gesturing and waving their arms in debate. For almost fifteen minutes the story unfolded as the group of astronomers decided to build a spaceship and fly it to the moon. As the spaceship took flight toward the ever-larger orb its face became visible and they landed squarely in the eye of the man in the moon.

I, as everyone else in the stuffy tent, sat mesmerized and silent. I couldn't comprehend how something like this were even possible. Photographs, moving before our eyes! People in another country dancing before me. The man in the tacky hat was right. It *was* magic.

As the film drew to a close, my father leaned toward me and took my hand. Pointing toward the screen, he said, "Remember this, Annie. This right here…this is going to change the future for every one of us."

My father had never in reality said such a thing. It was a novelty—a marvelous wonderment, but a novelty all the same. But in this dream there hung an air of momentous importance, and as I looked into his solemn face, I realized he was right.

Then the scene was gone and Henry was rolling into me, pushing me to the edge of the bed. Groggily I shoved him back just far enough so I would not fall to the floor and immediately slipped back into a deep sleep.

Breakfast the next morning was quiet but oddly lacking the tension I was expecting to radiate from the two of them. Instead they seemed to make an extraneous effort to be polite, as though I might be ignorant of what happened the night before. It was ludicrous watching them exchange stilted pleasantries as the blotchy black and purple bruise darkened under Daniel's left eye, outshining the similar but fainter one along Henry's jawline.

"The almanac is calling for a harsh winter, heavy snowfall," Daniel informed us casually as he tempered his coffee heavily with milk.

"Hmm," replied Henry between mouthfuls. "Interesting."

I ignored the both of them.

Hubie kept me occupied, steadfastly refusing any food I offered to him. Eggs, grits, biscuits, milk—nothing was satisfactory. I managed to coax down one mouthful of each before he rejected it and refused anything further.

"Why is he fussing? New tooth coming in?" Henry asked, watching me struggle.

I sighed. "Yes, but he still at least ate the grits yesterday. He's been in a foul mood since he woke up. Now he won't eat at all." As I offered him another spoonful of grits he smacked the spoon in my hand, sending white mush all over the tablecloth.

"No!" I admonished him, grabbing him by the chin and forcing him to look at me as he wiggled and protested. "You do not do that!"

"If he won't eat, let him go hungry. When he's ready to behave, he'll eat," Henry stated matter-of-factly.

"I can't *not* try to feed him. He needs to eat."

"You need to be firm with him. Either make him eat or take away the food. Don't let him fuss."

The fuse on my temper ignited and began to glow.

"I'm not *letting* him fuss," I replied through clenched teeth. "I am *trying* to feed him."

"Well, he's not eating. So take it away."

"I can't just take it away!" I snapped, exasperated. "If he spends the morning hungry he'll only become crabbier and more difficult. How is that better?"

"You need to teach him who is in charge. If he will not eat he will be hungry. That is the consequence."

I knew this, of all mornings, was not the morning to cross him, but I couldn't stop myself. He sat there at the head of the table with a righteous countenance on his battered face and the nerve to lecture me on child-rearing. I could have spit fire.

"Don't tell me how to handle him! Don't you dare!"

He raised his voice as well, gesturing angrily with the fork still in his hand. "I am simply trying to help you—"

"What wisdom could you possibly have to impart? You are not here with him all day. You don't know."

"And obviously neither do you."

"I am not a child to be educated! You are not my father or my teacher. Don't take your high and mighty stance with me."

He ducked his head, closing his eyes momentarily with a deep breath, and his voice dropped to a pitch so quiet and measured it was more frightening than his yell. "Annie," he said as he raised his eyes to meet mine, "I am only trying to help."

"Your insinuations infuriate me. I am capable of feeding my child."

His gaze became a glare that just as quickly melted into stoic defeat.

"Do as you wish," he sighed, finishing the last bites on his plate and rising to take his leave.

Daniel finished his breakfast in silence, keeping his eyes on his food as I angrily cleared my own plate while Hubie sulked in his high chair, whimpering miserably.

As I stood at the sink washing dishes, Henry breezed through the kitchen, planting his customary kiss on Hubie's and my cheek. I turned my head to accept it but otherwise did not acknowledge him. His dry lips pecked me roughly and he continued out the door without a word.

When I finished cleaning up from breakfast I carted Hubie into the living room with me, set him up in the corner with his blocks, and set to work dusting and polishing the woodwork and furniture. My anger was gone, replaced by a smoldering frustration that radiated through my limbs and caused my scalp to prickle. I chided myself for even bothering to argue with him. What was the purpose? He didn't listen to what I had to say. I could give him twenty reasons why his suggestions weren't feasible, but he would be incapable of hearing them. All he wanted was to have the superior word. The things I said that he brushed aside, and the things I longed to say but deemed futile, burned inside me.

I was wiping down the framed family photos hanging on the wall when Daniel crept into the room, lingering in the doorway. He leaned against the wall and studied the photos without speaking.

I saw him reflected in the glass. The dark bruise under his eye was visible even from my indirect line of vision. I glanced away, trying hard not to notice.

"I remember that day," he said quietly, gesturing toward our wedding picture. "I don't know if I've ever seen Henry so happy as that day."

I nodded. "That was a wonderful day. I miss having all my family together. We don't see them as often as I would like."

"He truly loves you," he continued.

"I know," I said automatically, moving on to the next frame.

He sighed. "He loves you and I'm wrong to question whether that's good enough."

My breath caught in my throat. I refocused my eyes to avoid his reflection and concentrated on removing a smudge on the glass. Wherever he was leading me I was sure I did not want to go.

"I used to think he was a good man, Annie. I don't know if I can say that anymore."

"Because we argued? Because he hit you? He has never laid a finger on me, I swear it. He has never been anything but gentle."

He chuckled without humor. "No, not for that. I earned what I took from him last night, believe me. I pushed him knowingly; I wanted to have it out. Sometimes you have to lay your grievances to air no matter the consequences."

I moved onto the next frame, studiously wiping every groove in the ornate design. "Nothing is worth fighting over."

"You are so very wrong."

The skin on the back of my neck prickled despite the warmth of the room.

"D-Don't you have work in the barn to do?" I stammered, afraid to offend him but desperate for him to leave.

He crossed the room and stood beside me so I could not avoid him.

"I can see a change in him," he murmured, as if someone might overhear. "He's determined. He's grown hard. He's carrying a burden, whether you can see it or not, and I worry what it will do to him."

I swallowed hard and shrugged, not wanting to listen. "He used to confide in me. He doesn't anymore," I explained curtly. "I don't know what plagues him, what drives him so hard." I refused to look at him despite his inquisitive stare. I moved to the other side of the room and began to polish the mantle, gasping for a steadying breath as soon as my back was to him. I waved my hand dismissively and tried to make my words sound nonchalant. "I suppose he prefers his work to evenings in this house with me."

The moment I said it I regretted my unthinking candor. It was meant to be facetious but it rang with a hollow note of truth. I had never admitted aloud to discord between us to anyone, not even Emma. I wanted to run from the room, away from his prying conversation and intrusive concerns.

He moved to my side again and, tentatively and seemingly without breathing, laid his hand on top of mine, coaxing the frantic motion of my cleaning to a stop. His hand was hot and moist with sweat, as though he had been clenching his fist. My legs quivered, so deep inside it couldn't have shown, and the dark grain of the mantle grew blurry. I saw him begin to reach for my other hand, resting on my hip with my fingernails dug into the cotton of my dress, and when I looked into his bruised and helpless face something inside me broke.

The sob came out of me so fast I was powerless to stop it, and with it went any hope of composure. I clasped my hand to my mouth as the tears streamed down my face, trying to stifle my shameful display, but it was no use. I leaned against the mantle, trembling, overcome with the unfamiliar sensation of letting go, and wishing it had no audience.

He rested his hand on my shoulder and watched me for a long moment. "Annie," he whispered. "Would you like to talk?"

I didn't want to bare my soul to him. I knew that I should not. But in that moment, I couldn't hold it in.

I nodded, and he took the dustrag from my hand and dropped it to the floor. I carefully placed Hubie in his playpen and we walked outside and sat side by side in the rocking chairs on the front porch.

The fresh air dried the wetness on my cheeks and quelled the feeling of panic that was squeezing my heart and making it pound.

"I apologize for my argument with Henry this morning," I said, wiping the last errant tears from my eyes. "You should never have witnessed that."

"Don't worry about it," he assured me.

"I do. It was shameful. I shouldn't have lost my temper in front of you."

He shrugged. "Apologize for letting me see it if you must, but don't apologize for losing it, because to be honest, I agreed with you.

Left to his own devices that child would starve; I've seen him. You're a saint for keeping him nourished."

The corners of my lips twitched into a tiny smile.

"I thought I was the only one with the nerve to stand up to Henry," he revealed. "I underestimated you."

I shook my head ruefully. "That wasn't a display of courage. It was a petty fight, and not an uncommon one. There is just something about the tone of voice he takes with me that unravels my sense."

"What tone is that exactly?"

"That tone of superiority. Surely you detected it. He speaks as though what he were saying was the undisputed truth and anyone who would question it would be a fool. The natural inference, then, is that I am the fool for not knowing whatever it was he is educating me on." I could hear it below his words, even if he never said it. *Poor, simple child. Let me teach you these things that should come naturally to you but never will, but somehow come completely naturally to me.*

"I can't say that I've noticed that exactly," he said carefully, looking fearful of offending me. "Henry's speech is cocksure often, as he was with me at the dinner table my first night here. It's just his way. I'm certain he means no disrespect towards you. He's simply assertive."

I sighed. "This house always used to be so peaceful," I remembered. "So quiet and joyful, just the two of us. We used to sit out here on this porch and talk for hours. He would spin stories about what our life was going to be like. He would describe every detail of the house he was going to build for us one day; tell me about our future children and all the little quirks they would have. About our dog, Charlie—oh, he had it all planned out. I loved sitting here, just listening to him dream it as though it were already reality. He could see forever from here." I twisted my wedding band around my finger. "I fell in love with him when I was fourteen years old. I don't remember what it's like to have my own thoughts without him there in my head with me. Does that even make sense?"

Daniel nodded, never looking away. I sensed he was afraid to speak and interrupt my thoughts. His attentiveness unnerved me, and I suddenly felt his gaze like a spotlight on me. "I'm sorry, I don't know why I'm going on about this. It doesn't matter. I shouldn't—"

I began to stand and he scrambled to his feet. "No, please. Stay, Annie. Please."

There was an edge to his voice that told me my openness was as meaningful to him as it was liberating to me. I sank back into the chair and he did the same. My eyes wandered down the shady lane toward the road, and I thought back to the oval wedding portrait hanging in the living room; of the woman in it whose smile flashed in her eyes as the cheerful, dashing young man beside her tickled his fingers against the small of her back.

"Perhaps we are no longer the same people we were then. When we promised forever we assumed that we would grow together, but what if sharing a life is the thing that changes you? Living in such close proximity—physically, emotionally—sometimes it feels like we're puzzle pieces that don't quite fit. Maybe that's what marriage is. You push against that other person and you rub down their rough edges and you smooth away the jagged pieces of yourself until you fit together. In some ways, it's a positive thing. Necessary. Love *should* soften you; make you a better person. But sometimes it feels like we can't find the spot where we fall into place. We are caught in the continuous friction."

He was quiet for a long moment, and I did not feel a push to fill the silence between us. He rocked slowly in his chair, his eyes searching the field until, at length, he spoke. "Life is a tapestry of challenges and decisions, Annie," he began, his voice thoughtful and muted. "It is unfair to place the burden of who life shapes him to be onto yourself, just as you cannot place your own destiny upon him. Certainly, we shape each other, but it is so much more complicated than that. Please understand it is with kindness when I say this: the world is large and without the confines of this house, but I do not think you can see beyond them."

I fought the urge to immediately rebut him. He couldn't understand the weight of the responsibility I felt to make sure the people I loved—Henry, Hubie, my parents, my siblings—were properly cared for, to buffer against the very trials of life he spoke of. If my brother grew up to be a thief, or my son a murderer—or, less dramatically, my husband unhappy and sullen—how could I not hold myself accountable in some way? Life may have shaped them, but it was my job to love and guide and protect them. Perhaps this was irrational—certainly he did not subscribe to my way of thinking—but it was my purview.

"I'm sorry Henry was so short with you when you first arrived," I diverted, not wishing to turn our conversation into a debate.

He shrugged. "Why are you apologizing for him? His actions are not in your control."

"I've felt uncomfortable about it since it happened. He was inexcusably rude. He never spoke of you that way when we discussed your arrival."

"Now I know you're just being kind." He began to rock slowly in his chair, leisurely, as if we were discussing the weather.

"He didn't! Well, he didn't speak so harshly. Some of his sentiment was the same but he was much kinder." I tugged at the toughened skin around my fingernails.

"He still deemed me lazy."

"He never said you were a disappointment to your parents," I insisted.

"Until I arrived." He smiled wanly.

"I am sorry."

"Will you please stop apologizing?" he begged with a chuckle. "Guilt is a dreadful companion. Abandon it, I beseech you."

"I'll try," I promised dutifully.

"Besides, I know what that was about, and it was far less about his true feelings about me and more about making a statement." The motion of his foot against the railing lost its leisurely cadence as he jerked his ankle to and fro.

I raised my eyebrow in question.

"He was making sure I knew who was in charge but, more importantly, he was making sure *you* knew *he* was in charge."

"Me?" I squeaked, taken by surprise. "What does this have to do with me?"

"He wanted you to know our family didn't pressure him into taking me in; that it was his decision and he was in control of it. And if I displeased him, or, more probably, displeased *you*, you should have faith that he would deal with it." He looked past me as he said this, subtly avoiding eye contact without making it obvious.

"No, I think that's very unlikely."

"Every motive a man has is rooted in the woman he loves. No matter how subtly or subconsciously. When you dig down to the origins, she drives everything. It's understandable. I would have been just as stern if it were me bringing in my shiftless—what was the word? Playboy? My younger, shiftless, playboy cousin to stay with my beautiful wife and child," he said, a trace of good humor taking the serious edge off his words.

I blushed at his description of me, and at the implications of his description of himself, and couldn't help but giggle. He smiled in return, unabashedly, and I marveled at the lightness that sprung from abandoning the weight of propriety and reserve that typically governed my speech but was so often absent from his own.

"Thank you," I said, glancing down as a sudden shyness overcame me.

"For what?"

"For listening." The breeze caught loose tendrils of my hair, and I brushed them away from my face.

He leaned forward, catching my gaze, and reached out to tame a loose strand I had missed. "You will always have my ear, Annie, any time you may want or need it," he said, his fingertips lightly brushing the wisp from my cheek.

"Thank you," I whispered, feeling my skin grow flushed at his casual touch. I leaned away slightly and he sat back in his chair, adjusting his shirt-sleeves but not looking away.

"So," I began, hating to steer our conversation toward an unpleasant topic but knowing I must, "let me return the favor, then. Tell me of your concerns. I have confided enough of mine. What is your distress? What burden do you see upon Henry's shoulders?" I didn't want to let on what I had overheard the previous night; I wanted to know what he would deem fit to divulge to me.

To my surprise, his eyes darkened and became guarded. "Don't worry about that. It was nothing."

"Pish," I said. "You were eager enough to discuss it when you came into the living room."

"No. You've enough on your mind. You don't need my thoughts weighing on you as well."

"Do my tears make me too fragile for confidences, then?"

He shook his head and smiled. "Not in the least. I believe you may be sturdier of spirit than either of us men. I simply mean it is unfair to you to be burdened with my fancies and I had no right to presume. Forgive me."

As I began to object he raised my hand to his lips and placed a kiss there, rising from his chair abruptly. "Forgive me," he repeated. "I really must get to work now." He squeezed behind my chair and disappeared around the side of the house before I could continue to protest.

I lingered on the porch, confused by his hasty departure, recalling the conversation I had overheard the night before. I knew he suspected Henry of backwards dealings with the Mayfield Company but I couldn't possibly imagine what would lead him to such an idea. It was utterly impossible. Henry was the most morally unambiguous man I knew; strong and sure and frustratingly black and white. He wasn't capable of such a thing. How could Daniel think otherwise?

The sun was sliding farther and farther across the morning sky. I had cleaning to finish, and I couldn't let Hubie stay in his playpen all morning. I stretched my arms up as far as they would go, feeling the tightness in my back, and tried to rub away the knot at the base of my neck as I stood and circled the house, headed toward the outhouse.

As I sat on the wooden bench I heard Hubie call for me from inside the house. With a sigh, I pulled a piece of sanitary tissue from the nail to my right and quickly finished up.

The sight of blood stopped me cold.

A slight pink trace was there on the tissue. Small, but noticeably there.

A tiny cry of joy escaped my lips.

I wasn't pregnant!

I wanted to shout it at the top of my voice. I could have danced a jig right there in the tiny, smelly space. I hummed out loud as I cleaned myself up, feeling all the tribulations of the morning burn away like fog in the dawn. When I stepped outside again, I could have sworn the cloudless azure sky was bluer.

Henry woke in the middle of the night with a shout.

It was still dark; no trace of dawn. He threw himself to the edge of the bed, grunting and whimpering. I was alert at once, accustomed as I was to mid-night interruptions. "Henry?" I reached for him and he recoiled with an alarming twitch, disoriented, staring at me with the blankness of unrecognition. I held still, patiently, waiting for him to brush away the gauzy haze of sleep that clung to his brain like spider webs.

"Henry, it's Annie," I cooed. "It's Annie. You're awake now."

He rubbed his face vigorously and sank back against the pillow with a deep, relieved exhale.

"Are you—"

"I'm fine," he mumbled too quickly.

The night breeze had grown cool. I pulled the sheet tighter around me and settled back into a comfortable spot. "You haven't had nightmares like that in a long time."

"I know. This was…" He drifted off with a shake of his head.

"What happened?"

I assumed he would decline to elaborate, and was not surprised to receive silence as his reply. After a few minutes of listening for an answer or further conversation I began to drift back to sleep. His voice brought me back suddenly with a drowsy jerk.

"Do you suppose there's a hell?"

"Hmm?" Surely I misheard that.

"Do you believe that there's a place…that hell actually exists?"

My fatigue skittered away as I sat up beside him. "Darling, are you truly all right?"

He sat up as well, angling the pillow so it cushioned him from the headboard. "I just…can't shake this off."

It was hard to fight the apprehension that crept upon me. I recalled Daniel's accusations and felt goosebumps raise on my arms.

"Why would you ask such a thing?" I whispered.

"Because I'd like to think there's not. But I don't know."

I swallowed. "What reason would you have to fear hell?" I asked tentatively, trying to gauge the temperature of his voice.

He shrugged. "I'm no murderer, or thief, but aren't we all guilty of some sin? And isn't all sin equally damnable in the eyes of God?"

"This is a little heavy for so late at night," I protested.

He sighed. "I know. I'm sorry. I shouldn't bother you. It's just that sometimes you have a way of making things…" He hesitated.

"Difficult?" I guessed, trying for levity.

"Comforting," he said, looking down at the covers.

His words brought a warmth that took the edge off my fear.

"You're a good man, Henry. Surely you know that."

"By what parameters?"

"Well—"

He interrupted me. "I didn't intend for you to answer. I know that I can be...difficult at times. But I want you to know that your happiness means everything to me."

"I know that," I responded.

"Everything," he reiterated simply, turning his head to look me in the eye.

I pulled the folded rose-patterned coverlet from the bottom of the bed and draped it across us. "Try not to dwell on troublesome thoughts this late at night. You'll just draw yourself into more nightmares."

He nodded silently.

"It must have been an awful one," I said, still curious.

He tucked the blanket around him, shivering for the first time. "It was one of those dreams where you think you've woken up, but you still can't escape it. Again and again you think it's over but you're trapped; no way out."

I wrapped my arm around him, planting a kiss on his forehead and nudging him toward me. "Don't worry, you're awake now," I said as he slid down and nestled his head against my chest.

He wrapped his arms around me and squeezed me close, and as I began to stagger into the beginning of a dream I could have sworn I heard him whisper, "Am I?"

SIX

Large posters hung in the windows of the shops in town, screaming in large black block letters, "Opening Night—Walt Theater—August 18th!" It was only four weeks away. The summer was streaming by, trickling through my fingers faster than I could grab it. At times the whirlwind suited me fine, blurring the nuisance of continuously oppressive heat as I dreamt of cool autumn days. Other times I longed to slow it down, concerned for what would become of Daniel at the summer's end. As he still harbored a weariness of factory work and had learned no particular trade beyond the general repair work he was performing around our house, I feared for his prospects. But no matter my misgivings the days continued to rush by like an endless current.

I sat in the buggy with Henry, Daniel, and Hubie as we made the trip into town to my parents' home for dinner and a visit. Henry was in a particularly jovial mood, pointing out the theater advertisements and describing the progress on the building's construction.

"It's going to be tight making our deadline, but opening night is set and they won't hear of postponement. The films have been ordered, the furniture is being shipped, and the staff is being readied. They picked out the most beautiful damask fabric wallpaper for the auditorium. You would love it, Annie. And the woodwork! Very ornate, very beautiful. I don't doubt it will be the most impressive building this town has ever seen—and I've helped build quite a few."

"It sounds lovely," I replied. "When can I see it? I'm getting so curious seeing it week by week from the outside. Can we stop by today?"

"No, no," he said. "Not until it's finished. You won't truly appreciate the grandeur seeing it like it is. Once it's complete we'll go and see a performance. Nathan will be helping to run the projector on opening night—they have four one-reelers to show; I don't know what they are yet—and there's a stage production of 'The Reckoning' Friday evening."

"That would be wonderful. I've heard so much about it I can just picture it in my mind."

"Whatever you're picturing, it's grander," Henry promised.

We turned down Washington Street, which was not our usual route. I glanced questioningly at Henry and he explained, "Just a little detour." Two blocks later he pointed to a newly constructed, stout three-story gray stone house. Delicate iron-work window boxes graced each window and a grand porch wrapped around the side of the house. The windows were deep set and had freshly painted scrolled woodwork. A wrought iron fence lined the perimeter of the immaculately landscaped yard. It was easily the size of Emma's substantial home.

"There," he said, slowing the horse so we could gawk. "That's the house we're going to have one day."

"*That?*" I squeaked. "It's huge! It would take a staff just to keep it!"

"Then we'll have a staff!" he declared, as if it were an obvious conclusion.

"But we don't need all that."

"We don't *need* much more than a shack and a fire to keep warm. Who wants to fulfill what you need and then rest idly by? Think of what we could have. You could live in comfort and fashion, Annie. Be the envy of your friends for once."

"In our dreams!" I laughed.

His smile faded. "Why is that such a dream? Why couldn't I build a home like that for us one day?" I heard the slight offense in his voice. Daniel stiffened, watching the exchange closely like a pupil shadowing his teacher.

"It's not that," I backpedaled gently. "I'm sure you could. It's just not necessary. Our home is more than adequate. I don't need all that finery."

"I don't know anyone who wouldn't want such a palace." He quickened the horse with a light tap.

"It is beautiful," I conceded. But beneath the gorgeous architecture I saw only work and unnecessary expense.

We turned back onto the main road and Henry began to tell us about the new department store in the works that construction would begin on around the time the theater was completed. Daniel and I listened intently but did not interrupt. When Henry got to talking, rare as a talkative streak from Henry was, it was hard to get a word in.

Near the edge of town we turned down Cherry Street, passed a line of nearly identical, narrow, brick Colonial homes, and arrived at my family's home at the end of the block. My mother must have heard our approach and was on the porch before we were even stopped, greeting us and scooping Hubie out of my arms with kisses and coos and quick hugs to the rest of us. Her thin frame seemed frailer since I had seen her last and I worried that Hubie would be too heavy for her, but she waved me off as he wiggled and playfully tugged at the errant gray tendrils that framed her face. We followed her into the house with Daniel lagging shyly behind.

My father was seated in the parlor, rising only when we entered, but the smile on his face was no less exuberant than Mother's when he saw his grandson. He greeted us all—a warm embrace for me, handshakes for the men—and then coaxed Hubie from Mother's unwilling arms. Standing next to her, he was only inches taller but three times as thick, with a full head of wavy gray hair I hoped Henry would have when he reached his fifties.

"My goodness!" he exclaimed as Hubie began to wail and reach for his grandma. We laughed as she took him back with a knowing look and a boastful smile.

"He certainly grows like a little weed, doesn't he?" asked Father, nudging me good-naturedly. "What have you been feeding him over there?"

"Can you do better? You're welcome to try," I teased. "Perhaps we will leave him here."

"Then we shall take him and keep him and eat him up like a little teacake!" fussed Mother, who nuzzled and tickled him, making him giggle with delight.

"Then he's yours!" I laughed. "Henry, we've one less passenger for the ride home."

"And one greatly quieter night's sleep," Henry added, shaking his head.

Nathan trounced into the room with a book under his arm, his eyes slightly red and hair disheveled as though he had just woken. "You're here!" he sang happily, hugging me and exchanging greetings before setting the book on the end table and taking his turn to steal Hubie from Mother.

"Have John and Thomas arrived yet?" I inquired after my elder brothers.

"Not yet," said Mother, glancing toward the window, "but they should be along any time now."

Father motioned toward Henry and Daniel and they took a seat on the couch while he resumed his place in the armchair. They began to converse about troubles with the management of the local railroad, a topic I had no interest in. I picked up Nathan's book and sat down on the settee to page through it. Its hardcover looked brand new and was titled "Principles and Applications in Cinematography."

"Is this part of your training?" I asked, scanning it for any interesting diagrams.

"Yes. Well, no...yes and no," he stammered. "They haven't formally started my training yet, but I found this book and started learning what I can."

I looked up, alarmed. "You haven't started training yet? Opening night is in a month! Aren't they supposed to be sending you to classes?"

"Not formal classes, no. The original plan was for me to spend some time working with a projectionist in Reading at the Gem, but that fell through. Then they found a man who travels with a fair to come and teach me, but he was delayed when their management added another town in Virginia to their schedule. He should be here next week. They also want to send me to the Colonial Theatre in New York the weekend before the Walt opens to work with the projectionist there." His voice was restrained but his smile was exuberant.

Mother wrung her hands. "New York City! I don't see why they need to send you so far."

He shot me a look that said this conversation had been had so many times, the verses were memorized. "Mother, I'll be fine. I'm old enough to travel without a chaperone."

"I don't like it," she insisted, looking toward Father for an agreement that wouldn't come. He continued complaining about the misappropriation of some funds in the railroad, but Henry seemed to be only half listening, attempting to divide his attention between the two conversations.

"This is a great opportunity," Nathan said, a whine creeping into his voice. "I can't compromise their faith in me. I don't want them to think that perhaps I *am* too young. I can do this. I'll be fine."

Mother's eyes narrowed. "Do you know what the city is populated with? Pickpockets, murderers, and undesirable women." She ticked the items off one by one on her fingers. She looked at me. "Daniel lived in the city, didn't he? He was wise enough to leave. He can tell you. It's not a safe place."

Henry was now paying more attention to Mother's tirade against loose morals than Father's, and at the first available pause he interjected. "Are you desiring a chaperone for Nathan?" he asked, turning toward her with his full attention.

"Gerald has obligations here," she explained, her brow creased deeply with worry. "Thomas has been working for Mr. Peterson every weekend, and John and Maria have their hands full with the twins."

"Perhaps I can help," offered Henry, glancing between Mother and myself. "I could accompany Nathan to New York. I don't have any particular obligations that weekend, and Daniel can look after things while I'm away. As long as you approve, Annie."

Surprised by his sudden offer to be of service, I grappled for a response. He didn't think much more highly of the city than my mother, and I imagined he would rather have his teeth pulled without ether than spend a weekend in New York. My heart swelled at his concern for Nathan. "Of course," I agreed heartily. "That's so kind of you, darling. Thank you."

Father reached out and shook his hand. "Thank you, Henry. See there, Barbara? You mustn't worry. Everything has a way of working out."

Mother sighed and smiled and took Hubie, who was beginning to squirm, back from Nathan. It didn't look like he would get much practice learning to walk today. I felt an odd pang of jealousy as I watched him settle immediately in her doting arms. I forced it from my mind with a scathing, silent reproach.

Nathan came and sat next to me on the settee, taking the open book from my hands and flipping through it. As Father resumed his conversation and Mother carried Hubie into the kitchen, Nathan and I were left to ourselves.

"Do you want to know how movies work?" he asked, opening to the page he was seeking.

"I think I know the basics. The film has still pictures, and when the projector flips through them very fast, it looks like they're moving, right?"

"Basically. But do you know why they appear to move?"

I thought about it for a minute. "No, I suppose I don't."

He pointed to a bold heading in the book. "It's called 'Persistence of Vision.' It's the idea that when you see something—like a picture—your eye retains that image for a second—not even a second; less than that. So when you see a film, you see a series of still pictures, but your eye hangs onto that last image until it blends with the next one. That's how you perceive motion."

"Hmm. Interesting. I never knew that."

He pushed a lock of hair from his forehead which fell right back, as he continued to fidget in his seat. "It's really fantastic! Just think, everything you see—everything in the world around you—it's not just this moment in time. It's a fraction of the past, melted into the present."

"So we're seeing things that aren't there?"

"No, it's more like a flicker of something that's already gone, just so quickly that you can't even comprehend it. It really is much more subtle than I'm making it sound. I wish I could explain it better."

"I think I understand," I assured him, awed by the foreign idea.

His weary eyes were wide, his pupils alight with the intoxication of new knowledge. "There's so much that we don't understand, that we don't even realize…it's fascinating. I know this all makes Mother nervous, but I'm so excited, Annie. I want to learn everything I can. I want to see things—places—that I never even imagined. This could open up so many opportunities outside of Evansville." He lowered his voice, even though no one else was listening now. "Didn't you ever feel like there was a whole world out there waiting for you to come out and find it? I don't want to just live and die here. Mother's never even left Pennsylvania, and she never will. The railroad will take you just about anywhere now, if you've a plan and means to go. And this job will eventually be my ticket out of here."

I wrapped my arm around him in a half-hug. "You have to understand, you're Mother's last baby. It's going to be hard for her to let you go. I know because it's hard for *me* to even see you as no longer a child. You're still my little Nathan, being carried around like my own living baby doll. I have to remind myself sometimes that you don't need another mother, but I'll always worry after you—the trick is to keep that concern to myself and let you go. Mother's getting there, too, but it will take her longer."

"You needn't worry about me anymore. You have your own real baby doll now."

"If only it were that easy, dear." I grinned and brushed an errant lock of hair behind his ear. "You're looking due for a haircut, aren't you?"

He playfully rolled his eyes and turned from me to join Father's conversation, which was now centered on criticizing the local newspaper editor. I headed into the kitchen to check on Mother and Hubie.

Her kitchen was approximately the same size as mine but it felt much smaller. Sage green striped wallpaper covered the walls and delicate, yellow lace valances decorated the windows, fluttering in the breeze. A clock and various framed needlepoint pictures hung on the walls in between the two hutches and the large cast iron stove in the corner. A wide, worn kitchen table was pushed up against the wall in front of the windows, with four equally beaten wooden chairs circling the three exposed sides. This was the sturdy table I had grown up at, meant for the rigors of children and food preparation, which guests would never see.

"Is your father still on a tirade?" Mother asked, looking up from the pot she was stirring as Hubie pointed toward me happily from his chair at the table.

"Do you mean to imply they ever end?" I took a seat and handed Hubie a wooden spoon to play with. "I'm sure he and Henry will have enough fuel for the fire between them to last all evening. There's always some ineptitude or affront to his moral compass to rail against. They're kindred spirits that way."

"Well, God bless them for keeping each other entertained so we can be spared."

"Amen."

Hubie grasped the spoon with a tight fist and drew invisible patterns on the table. I blew him kisses each time he looked up, making him break into a shy smile.

"Can I ask you a question?" I asked her.

"Of course." She half turned her body toward me to signal her attention but continued to tend the stove.

"I know you have some concerns about Nathan travelling to the city for training," I began. "But beyond that, now that we're alone—what do you truly think about this new job?"

She laid down her spoon and wiped her hands on her apron, turning with hesitation to face me at last. Her brow was creased with discomfort and concern, but she looked me in the eye as she spoke. "I think it is a wonderful opportunity for him, and I am thankful to Henry for helping him to secure it. I do not know, however, if he is ready for such responsibility. He's just a bit too young. According to Gerald, most boys who go into this field work around a theater for years, learning about the trade. This is all new to him. I just don't know if he can learn it all—and be confident in the knowledge—quickly enough." She sighed and gestured helplessly with her hands. "But if this is what he wants to be, how can I not give my blessing? An opportunity like this may not come again."

I nodded my agreement, unsurprised in her answer as it reflected my own thoughts perfectly.

"Would you like me to make us some tea?" she offered.

I wasn't particularly in the mood for tea, but the breeze was so lovely and the kitchen so cozy and the conversation so intimate that I didn't dare break the spell. Soon it would be dinnertime and this tiny little woman would be swept away by the jostling for attention of her grown children in their excitement to share the latest news in their lives. But for now, in this quiet, comfortable space, she was all mine.

"Yes. Tea would be perfect. Thank you."

I couldn't help dwelling on her comment about what Nathan "wanted to be." I could recall a time when I was a child, sitting at this very same table with a tattered book of poetry that I practiced reciting while she prepared the evening meal.

"I want to be a poet," I had informed her. "I want to write poetry when I grow up."

She chuckled out loud. "Don't be silly, dear. When you grow up you'll want to be a mama like me."

"No," I insisted. "I want to be a writer."

"Sweetie, only women of leisure can spend their days writing poetry without a care in the world. Unless you marry a very wealthy man and are unable to have children, you will grow up to be a lovely wife and mother."

"I will not!" I cried, flinging the book across the table. "I'm going to do something important!"

Her voice had hardened then, her eyes narrowing as she looked at me. "Is that not good enough for you? Then you can toil in a factory, standing on your feet all day. Surely there are worse things than raising a family." At the time I had mistaken the pain in her voice for anger, but I understood now my words must have cut her.

Just as she had never asked me what I desired to be, but knew what I would be, I never asked her what she had wanted to be, for I knew what she was. She never would have answered the question anyway. She wouldn't have wanted to lie.

Nathan was different. The doors to Nathan's future were wide open, beckoning him to find his destiny. How could either of us begrudge him that? Could it be a tiny sliver of envy, buried and denied, that was the root of our apprehension? No. That was too shameful to even consider. It must simply be motherly concern.

We sat and sipped our tea, enjoying the silence as the birds chirped outside the window and Hubie mixed imaginary batter in the mixing bowl. I found myself wishing he would remember this moment, but memories slip through the minds of babes like grains of sand through the hourglass.

It was a Thursday evening at the end of July. Time constraints in the construction schedule meant Henry was at the theater until after dusk every night. Daniel, Hubie, and I had eaten dinner long ago. A plate of brisket and potatoes was made up and sat waiting in the warm stove. A haze of humidity hung in every room and refused to drift out with the cool of the evening. We sat on the front porch and watched the deep orange speck of sun slide down below the darkening horizon.

Daniel had dragged the rocking chairs so that they were facing each other, a few paces apart. A blanket in between them made a place for Hubie to play with his blocks until he grew sleepy and curled up to drift off. A glass of Irish whiskey sat on the floor next to Daniel's chair, a gift from Joe from the day we spent with him in Reading. He played a few slow, quiet songs on his fiddle and I sat with a notebook and a lantern on the porch railing.

I watched him as he concentrated on his music, enthralled. The shadows played tricks on my sight, and the flickering light made him appear to sway at times with the melody. His eyes closed occasionally and his brows furrowed when they did, creating a dimpled crease between his brows I had never noticed before.

I recalled his comment about feeling as though people could read your thoughts and was particularly grateful that he could not read mine that evening. As I studied him I found myself wondering about his past, spinning stories to fill in the gaps I did not know. I imagined him working as a spy, infiltrating corrupt organizations and rooting out the hoodlums guilty of misappropriation, until his identity was revealed and he had to flee those who would do him harm. I spun a tale about a gorgeous young redheaded woman with bright green eyes whom he fell madly in love with, and how her tragic and untimely death sent him running from her memory.

I wondered how much of the world he had actually seen. I wondered how many women he had known.

I was thankful for the music; it filled the void of silence comfortably without the need for conversation.

We stayed for nearly an hour that way, floating on the tranquility of the evening, until his curiosity got the better of him and he spoke.

"What lingers on your mind this evening, Annie? You look pensive."

I blushed and hoped he couldn't discern the change in color by dim lamplight. "Nothing of importance," I replied, glancing down at my still-empty notebook.

"I'm curious just the same. Won't you indulge me?"

I sighed and tried to think of a lie. I wasn't quick enough.

"You seem content, so I doubt it's something troubling," he surmised, eyeing me speculatively as he halted his playing and balanced the fiddle on his knee. "But you'd rather not divulge, so that leaves me to think it's personal."

I didn't want him speculating about anything he might think I held personal, so I answered him honestly to halt his inquiry. "We've spent weeks living under the same roof, but there is still much about you I don't know. I wonder about the things you leave unspoken."

"Such as?" His eyes tightened and he reached for his glass of whiskey.

I twined my fingers together, unprepared to air my private musings and questions, considering which I was bold enough to voice. "What is the farthest distance you've traveled from home?" I asked at last.

"Philadelphia. Surely you knew that."

I shrugged. "How were I to know if you'd traveled to New York, or Europe, or any such place?"

He smiled, relaxing again. "Do I seem well-traveled to you?"

"You do," I admitted. "But, as I've never travelled beyond Reading, I suppose that's not difficult to achieve."

"I suppose not. I would love to see France or Ireland, but I likely will never make the voyage. New York is a possibility, however. One day."

I doodled scrollwork in the margin of the notebook. "May I inquire further?" I asked bashfully, not looking up. "About your time in Philadelphia?"

He hesitated, and I peeked up under my lashes to see him looking out across the yard, his lips pursed. "I can't guarantee I've had enough of this to answer," he said eventually, swirling the liquid in his glass. "But I'll endeavor to be honest."

A nervous excitement tingled through my fingertips at the prospect of his candor. "Well then," I began, fumbling for a question that would hopefully not stoke his defenses too quickly. "How did you develop your taste for whiskey?"

"By drinking fair quantities of it," he replied with a cheeky smile. "Anything else?"

"Oh, come now."

He laughed. "A gentleman at the textile mill I became friends with introduced me to his brother. Until I met them, it was all drudgery—the work was filthy and dangerous, and I went home to my rented room each evening to read. I was a proper young lad. And lonely and bored out of my mind. Until I met Robert and Patrick. They decided I'd spent enough of my days holed up alone, and took me out to a dance hall with them."

He took a sip from his glass, his eyes focused on some point beyond me. "I went to Philadelphia looking for something more exciting than life on the farm, and after a few weeks at the mill I thought I had found just a new way to grow old and eventually die. But then they showed me the city, the *real* city—it isn't buildings and chaos; it's *people*. That was when everything changed."

"Go on," I bade him, mesmerized.

"They took me to a dance hall, and the place just teemed with life. It was a tiny place, down a back alley—nondescript as any other building—but inside it was alive. Musicians on the stage playing music I've never heard my parents play. Alcohol flowing—my God, I didn't even know there were so many kinds. Beautiful women everywhere, adorned in jewels that glistened in the low light. They sparkled. Everything sparkled that night. And the more whiskey they handed me, the more everything shined.

"People wanted to talk to me. Well-dressed men wanted to know my opinion on the latest politics. Women wanted to dance with me. I was *no one* and then, suddenly, I wasn't. I was one of them."

He took another sip, his focus falling back on me. "I realized that night I never had to feel alone again. That if life was destined to be drudgery, I could do something to blot it out each evening. Robert and Patrick were searching for the same thing, and it wasn't hard to find in a place like that. Not if you knew where to look."

"Did you ever visit an opium den?" I asked, wide-eyed, too absorbed in his narrative to remember decorum.

"No. Alcohol was my preference. Dens are dark, depressing places."

"Did you ever visit…a brothel?" I whispered the word.

He grinned. "There was really no need," he said, and I blushed five shades of crimson. When I could raise no further questions, he chuckled.

"I can't imagine," I stammered. "That all sounds so…intimidating."

"It was, especially in the beginning—and therein lies the exhilaration just the same. To be overcome, to have everything familiar be washed away, was liberating. There is an allure to the novelty of the *different*, whatever that may be."

Beyond the impropriety of the lifestyle he described, I could understand the appeal of its baser elements; the desire to strip free of life's confinements, however familiar and safe they may be, and revel in the freedom of anonymity in a strange land.

"I suppose it is heady to cast away that which we were to become someone else, and reinvent ourselves according to our own making," I agreed. "But that only makes me wonder—why ever would you leave?"

The change that came over him was subtle, but did not escape my notice. His body tensed, his forearms twitching with the involuntary reaction, and his eyes lost their luster in an instant. "I've made no secret of my distaste for the mill," he said by way of explanation. "And you cannot uphold the lifestyle I was living with no income to support it. Once the money ran out, my parents begged of Henry to take me in." He smiled thinly and it did not touch his eyes.

"But it has never been clear to me—did you quit your position? Or did they ask you to leave?"

"I don't see that it makes any difference."

"It does," I insisted. "There are a fair number of jobs in the city. If you left on good terms, I see no reason why they wouldn't provide you with a reference. Why did you remain unemployed?" I heard the echoes of his conversation with Henry the night they fought. *What I've seen...they are not to be trusted...*

"Because I lost my taste for work," he shrugged. "I became spoiled by the leisure." He finished his whiskey with an agitation in the movement.

"Daniel," I said quietly. "What did you see?"

His eyes widened infinitesimally.

"What happened at the mill?"

He laughed, arranging his features carefully and with intention. "Nothing that doesn't happen every day at every factory—it's grinding work, Annie, and the truth is I simply wasn't suited to it. You've seen my laboring ability. I fell off the roof my first week here, for Christ's sake. I am far better suited to drinking and debating. But I was unfortunately unable to find a way to make that a profession."

Before I could object he set his empty glass on the railing, tucked the fiddle under his chin and resumed playing. One song morphed into two, and after a time he seemed to lose himself in the melody, letting his eyes fall closed. Not wishing to perturb him and knowing any further attempt to pry would be in vain, I let the conversation lapse and turned my attention back to my notebook, fighting the desire to soothe the pain in him that lingered obviously just below the surface.

"What are you writing?" he asked as he began to play a familiar lullaby.

At the moment the page was still devoid of words, my pencil motionless. "I'm hoping your music will inspire something poetic."

"You write?" The notes seemed effortless for him as his fingers glided gracefully along the fingerboard.

"It was something I once enjoyed very much but lost the time for. I should like to discover it again."

I wished then that it were not so dark so that I could better see his face. His eyes glowed warmly in the lamplight; the music seemed to soften them. The mask he had assumed once again dissipated.

"What shall you write about?" With his chin resting against the fiddle it took a small effort to continue eye contact, but he kept his gaze cast upward.

"Whatever inspires me."

His song morphed into a low, mournful melody as he languidly coaxed each note from the bow. "The most common subjects for poetry are love, desire, and nature," he mused.

I began to shade in the edge of the paper as the earnestness of the song sent a quiver down my spine. "I don't have much of an opinion on nature," I murmured.

"No?" he teased. "No yearning for the blades of grass, no odes to the beautiful sunset we just watched?"

I giggled. "No, I am not particularly moved by the yard which requires me to toil or the sun that gives us this stifling heat."

"Hmm, no love for nature...then perhaps you can extol your passion for love?"

I waved my hand dismissively, rolling my eyes and stumbling for a retort.

"Perhaps in reminiscing you can find some inspiration."

My stomach clenched at the thought of invoking Henry, as though if he came into my thoughts he would see what lay there presently and be aghast.

"Tell me about your courtship," Daniel prodded, ceasing his music once again.

I eyed him cautiously. "Why?"

"Because I divulged to you the time that was, for me, flush with the thrill of novelty. And although we've known each other peripherally for years, there is much that remains unknown to me about you as well. I admit when I was young I was uninterested in — and, quite frankly, barely cognizant of — your relationship with Henry. Now, I'd like to understand. What did he do to make you fall in love with him?"

I vacillated between his shadowed face and the darkened trees that lined the lane. "You make it sound as though he tricked me."

"Not at all." He shifted in his chair, settling the fiddle more comfortably in his lap, drawing my eyes back to him. "I simply wonder, what did it take to turn your head? We spoke of the allure of the different, and you said yourself you understood the pull. Was that what drew you?"

In the growing darkness our solitude was palpable. I could hear the notes he played beneath the words he spoke, and my chest began to tighten.

"Why does that matter, Daniel?"

He glanced away. "I just want to know what it felt like when it was just beginning."

I took a deep breath and squeezed my hands together to stop them from trembling. "What it felt like when I first began to be…attracted?" I clarified hesitantly.

"Yes." In that one syllable I imagined I heard a tremor.

"Well…I felt like I could tell him anything. Like it was safe to let him see the parts of me I kept hidden away."

I became aware of the sound of crickets underneath the porch and cicadas singing their noisy summer songs now that Daniel's fiddle was silent. I preferred his music to theirs and was about to tell him so but he spoke first.

"So how did you know you were in love with him?"

I closed my notebook. "It's growing late. Perhaps we should go inside." I stood and he was on his feet just as quickly.

"Please. Stay." His position put him between myself and the door.

The darkness felt thick, draping the porch and threatening to creep onto it, making the space feel suddenly narrow. "Why do you ask me these questions?"

"The same reason you question me. Because I want to know you."

My eyes narrowed. "You *do* know me. You're intrusive."

"I'm curious. You needn't answer."

But I always do.

"Then I shan't," I declared.

"Why are you suddenly so reticent?" There was a wounded edge to his voice.

My answer was honest and came without thinking. "I tell you too much."

His eyes locked with mine and he watched me, wordlessly, as I felt the heat rise on the back of my neck. I glanced down at the floorboards, trying to make out the shape of his boots in the darkness. I saw them move when he took a step closer.

"Do you find our discourse too intimate?"

I nodded furiously, unable to speak, my eyes locked on the ground as though his gaze might burn me.

"Then what harm could come of discussing your husband?"

My mind raced as my heart began to hammer, echoing the frenzied and erratic chirping of the cicadas. Only his voice could make a phrase as innocuous as "your husband" sound illicit.

I couldn't bring myself to be bold enough to say the words that were in my head—*We're not discussing my husband, and you and I both know it.*

"I can't," I whispered, stooping to gather up Hubie, who moaned and whimpered but lay limp. Daniel stood still but made no effort to stop me as I gently pushed past him. As I crossed the threshold I heard him speak.

"The things you can't say become your prison if you let them."

I closed the door behind me.

SEVEN

I moved quickly and efficiently, referring many times to my checklist so I would not forget any necessity, as I folded Henry's clothes and packed them neatly into the knapsack. It was Friday afternoon and the eve of Nathan's big weekend in New York City. Henry would be arriving home from work early (or on time; however you wished to look at it) and Father would be arriving soon after with Nathan to pick him up and take them to the train station. There they would travel to Philadelphia and then on to New York. Arriving late, they would stay at the hotel the Mayfield Company had booked for them until Sunday. Nathan had supposedly been training with the travelling projectionist they had promised to bring in, and they were hiring a full-time projectionist for a six month contract until he was proficient enough to be on his own, but I was eager for him to get a taste of the nuances and pace of a real operating theater. I could only hope he would learn much in his short stay.

I checked my list one more time to make sure nothing was overlooked. I laid out a pair of charcoal trousers and a clean dress shirt on the bed and his good dress shoes for traveling. Daniel peeked his head into the room. "He's here," he announced.

"Thank you. I'm almost finished." He disappeared down the stairs. He never actually stepped foot into our bedroom once during that entire summer. The closest he ever came was to lean into the doorway, as though an invisible barrier lay just beyond. To be fair, I avoided his room as well, except when necessity dictated that it must be cleaned or fresh laundry delivered. Even then I tried to be quick, to respect what little space he had for himself in a strange house.

Ever since our conversation on the front porch two weeks prior, which was followed the next day by a precipitous visit to call on Emma so I could take my leave of the house for a day and gain some distance and distraction, Daniel had widened the margin on the respectful distance he maintained, keeping our conversations polite but mundane and busying himself ever more diligently at his chores. It didn't take a conversation to communicate to him that he had crossed a line, and he backpedaled from it deftly, assuaging my discomfort in every subtle way he could. I couldn't help but commend his efforts. He made pretending his insides didn't twist and shudder every time he looked at me seem easy. I knew better.

As I finished packing the last few items I heard the door slam and Henry's boots hurry upstairs. As soon as he stepped into the room he began to unbutton his worn, sweaty work shirt. "I'm running late," he said breathlessly, throwing it to the floor and yanking his belt loose. "Gerald will be right behind me. Are my things ready?"

"Yes," I assured him, pouring fresh water into the basin for him to wash his face and hands in before he changed into his clean clothes. He was ready for it as soon as I finished, barely giving me time to step out of the way before he splashed his face and neck, half soaking his undershirt. I handed him a towel and he dried his face, took a few wipes at his shirt, then gave up and handed the towel back to me.

"Thank you, doll," he said. He stepped into the new pants. "I'll give Daniel instructions before I leave—"

"Don't worry," I told him for the twentieth time. "We'll be just fine. He knows the routine. You just worry about keeping an eye on my brother. That's the only concern I have—praying the two of you don't end up pick-pocketed."

"No need for concern there. I won't let anything happen, to either one of us."

"Yes, but you can't accompany him everywhere."

"Did I forget to tell you? I *will* be accompanying him to the Colonial Theater tomorrow."

"You will?" My worry receded a tiny bit. "What for?"

"Well, there will still be some work left to do once the Walt opens—just a few items we don't have time to address before next Tuesday, but that can be dealt with afterwards. I should like to see how a large theater like the Colonial has handled these things myself."

"Oh." So it wasn't concern for Nathan that spurred his generosity; it was simply another duty to his job. "It was your boss's idea for you to travel, then?" I asked, dismayed.

His expression abruptly shifted to one I couldn't decipher before he turned his back to me and picked up his shoes. "Uh, no. It was mine." He faltered like there was more to be said but did not continue. He sat down on the bed and hurriedly tied his shoes.

"I'd prefer if you hold off the Saturday night bath until Sunday," he requested. "I should like to bathe after travelling."

"Very well." I picked up his bag and followed him downstairs, tired of guessing at the things he left unspoken, as we heard Father arrive. Daniel was in the living room, holding Hubie up to the window and explaining that his grandfather was coming up the lane. He turned when we entered, momentarily unsure what to do with his squirming armful, and then set him free to stumble toward his father.

Henry bent to pick up his son and kissed him on the cheek. "You be good," he said sternly, hugging him close. "Daniel…" He hesitated and seemed to think better of what he was about to say. "I'll be home Sunday afternoon. Gerald will pick us up from the train station."

Daniel stepped forward and shook his hand. "Safe trip, Henry. I'll take care of everything here."

"Good man."

He turned to me then and we awkwardly traded his bag and Hubie, who sensed his father's departure and began to whimper and reach for him. Henry took his chin in between his thumb and forefinger once he was in my arms and looked him in the eye. "None of that," he warned, to no avail. With a small sigh he looked at me.

The differences in our faces struck me, and my smile faded at the look of apprehension in his eyes. "Everything is fine," I reassured him, reaching out to embrace him. He hugged me tightly, pressing his face against my neck for a moment, and did not immediately release me. I chuckled uncomfortably, the gesture feeling too intimate in front of Daniel, and pulled away, resting my hand on his cheek. "Be safe, dear. Enjoy your trip." He nodded, finally forcing a smile, and kissed me just as there was a knock at the door.

"Off you go," I said with a fond pat on his lower back, following him to the door where my father waited on the other side, as Hubie's whimper erupted into fitful sobs. I greeted Father with a quick hug and called a farewell to Nathan, who waited in the buggy. He waved in return as Henry climbed in beside him, and the three of them hurried off to catch the train that would take my brother and my husband farther from home than they had ever been.

When they had disappeared from view, I took a deep breath and let it out slowly. Over Hubie's wailing I could hear nothing, but I could feel when Daniel came up behind me, stopping a few inches away.

"Hubie, you're going to give your mother a headache," he said, gently rubbing his back.

"Too late," I mumbled. "He's like a siren in my ear."

"Shall I take him for you while you finish dinner?" he offered.

"Would you?" The peaceful solitude of the kitchen sounded incredibly appealing at the moment.

"Certainly. Here." He took him from my arms and I stepped aside to let him through the doorway. He carried Hubie outside to the grassy field next to the porch and sat him down in the warm, swaying weeds, standing back and looking around for something to amuse him with.

I returned to the kitchen, where I had been before stopping to send Henry on his way, and finished preparing our simple dinner of dumplings and dandelion salad. An increasingly cool wind was blowing through the house and the sky was darkening to a tumultuous gray with every swirling layer of clouds that drifted in, settling one on top of the other until they seemed about to touch the tops of the trees.

I sang to myself in spite of the impending storm and the fissures of pain that were beginning to wrap around my forehead. The sweet summer air was in abundance all around, and with the room to breathe and the drunkenness it brought, it was impossible not to feel the unbridled lightness that had taken root in my step.

After a quiet and relaxing evening meal, as I gathered up our dirty plates and silverware, I noticed Daniel carefully massaging his fingertips against his temples. When I looked at him he stopped and grinned abashedly at being noticed. "Little one smacked me in the head with a stick," he explained with a shrug.

"Oh dear. Are you all right?"

He nodded once and immediately winced at the motion.

"I can get you something for it," I offered, sympathetic as my own headache was lingering stubbornly and beginning to damper my good mood.

"I'm fine," he said, but his bravado didn't mask the squint in his eyes that told me the late afternoon sun slanting through the dining room windows was like a dagger piercing his skull.

"It's no trouble," I enticed him.

"No, really, I…what is it? Is it that stuff from when I hurt my foot?"

"Laudanum, yes. It'll cure your headache, I guarantee it."

"I don't doubt it," he murmured, remembering.

"I was thinking of taking some myself, so it's really no tro—"

"Get it," he decided.

I took the remnants of our dinner to the kitchen. Grabbing a teaspoon, I went upstairs to my bedroom and retrieved the amber-colored glass bottle labeled "Poison" from the top drawer of my dresser, where it was safely hidden from any misguided or inquisitive hands. Daniel was waiting in the kitchen with Hubie when I returned, sitting on the floor in the corner with his head resting against the wall, trying half-heartedly to show him how to build a tower with his wooden blocks. His eyes lit up when he saw the bottle.

I measured out a dose onto the spoon. "It's a bad one," he informed me, suddenly uninterested in acting brave as he watched me count out the drops.

"Don't go getting ideas," I said sternly as I knelt down beside him and spooned the vile liquid carefully between his already quivering lips. He shuddered violently as it hit his tongue, shaking his head and stifling a cough. "You have to be careful with this. You only take as much as you need. Understand?"

"Of course." He leaned back against the wall and watched me take mine. I crinkled my nose in disgust but otherwise betrayed no sign of aversion. He raised his eyebrows and pursed his lips in a momentary gesture of respect. It made me grin to impress him.

I returned the bottle to my bedroom and then finished cleaning up in the kitchen. Surges of pleasant warmth like bathwater on a cold winter's day washed through my veins. My headache melted away as quickly as my will to finish my chores, but I had the presence of mind to see them to their conclusion so the rest of the night was mine for the taking.

When I finished, Daniel was still slumped in the corner, now holding one of Hubie's blocks in his open palm and surveying it from each side. He ran his index finger along the edges and then began to trace the grain in endless circles with a bemused smile on his face.

I sat down next to Hubie and picked up where Daniel had left off on the construction of his third tower. Left to his own devices, this tower leaned heavily on the wall for support. He happily handed me blocks to stack onto his shoddy masterpiece but protested with a sharp "No!" if I tried to adjust one of his. I laughed and played along. How precious to waste such energy on something so trivial.

As we placed the last available block and glanced around the floor for any more, Daniel reached over with the one he had been toying with and placed it squarely on top. Hubie squealed happily and clapped his hands, then rushed toward it with both arms outstretched and smashed it into the wall, stomping and kicking as it crumbled. We applauded his efforts with cheers and encouragement.

Then, without warning, he grew bored and stumbled off toward the doorway to find something new to do.

Daniel and I rose to follow after him. Suddenly he grabbed my wrist. "We should go outside," he suggested.

"But there's a storm coming," I protested.

"Exactly! We don't have much time until it hits. Let's go now. I can take my fiddle out and we can enjoy what's left of the evening until the rain comes."

It was irrational, but in the moment I couldn't think of anything I would rather do more.

"Get your fiddle," I replied with a glimmer in my eye.

With an impish grin he scrambled up the stairs and out of sight.

Hubie pounded his tiny fists against the front door and looked back at me impatiently. I wondered if he was wise to our plan or had simply devised his own. "Come here, little one!" I sang, scurrying toward him and making him squeal and attempt to run away. I scooped him up in my arms and covered his face with kisses as he whined in protest and wriggled like a trapped cat. "Oh, stop that," I chided mildly as I tucked him around my hip. "Or you can sit inside and pout while we have fun outside." It was an empty threat, but the word "outside" caught his attention and he inclined toward the door again.

Daniel descended the stairs with his fiddle under his arm, opened the front door, and ushered us outside. I was about to sit down in the rocking chair when he caught my hand and pulled me forward, shaking his head and leading me from the porch around to the side of the house. There, in the flowing field of yellow ryegrass he released me, and I sank down into its warm blades, letting Hubie run free the moment his feet touched the ground. The balance was shifting as the storm rolled in, and the air was beginning to cool more quickly than the earth. The humidity incited a sheen of sweat that made my thin cornflower blue cotton dress cling to my limbs, which was at once welcome and uncomfortable as the persistent breeze drew goosebumps on my flesh.

Daniel sat down near me and began to play. I didn't recognize the roaming, disorganized melody until I eventually realized he was improvising it. Then, as I drank in the notes and opened my eyes to see what he saw, it was at once familiar. He played the roll of the clouds, the stutter-stops of my child's feet, the grace of the buttercups I plucked to pieces, my peals of laughter as I swiped playfully at Hubie's legs as he ran toward and away from me. I saw the music as tangibly as I saw the world around me. I couldn't have understood it better if he had been singing me lyrics.

I lay back in the grass and stretched my arms out. A flash of lightning lit up the darkening sky farther down the field and a few seconds later there was a rumble of thunder. The wind rippled patterns in the tall grass and I closed my eyes and let it wash through me. The ground seemed to undulate beneath my back, pulsing and rocking as I drifted like a raft on the ocean.

I tried to envision next summer. Hubie would be speaking sentences by then. He would be steadier on his feet. I would bring him out to this field to play and he could truly run, pointing out objects of curiosity and wanting to understand the world. I would show him the wildflowers and explain the different kinds, try to catch butterflies and teach him to be gentle. I would do it with a tiny baby in my arms, or a swelling expectation in my belly. I would do it in silence, as Daniel and his music would have drifted away like dandelion snow on the breeze.

It wasn't so much of a daydream as it was a certainty. Even if Daniel's sojourn extended beyond the end of the summer, he couldn't stay with us forever. He had a life to live and a future to build, and as long as he remained with us he would only be running in place. Eventually he would move on and Hubie would grow up and there would be siblings. This was the natural progression of things. I knew this, but I couldn't make it feel real. My mind rejected it as one would a dream upon waking.

As my mind danced from thought to random thought of its own accord, Nathan came to my memory, and his intriguing explanation of the persistence of vision. Such a fanciful concept—but what if it applied to everything? What if this life, my family, our home, were all just remnants of something which had already died; a captured scene hanging on for a fraction of a second beyond the life of its reality? What if the life I was living was already gone, but I just couldn't see it yet?

The thunder growled again, reminding me of where—and when—I was. With effort, I pushed my musings aside. The storm was coming. We had only so much of this perfect evening left.

As I sat up slowly Daniel stopped his impromptu melody and began to play a song I knew well. "In honor of Nathan's first trip to New York," he explained.

"Oh!" I exclaimed, delighted. "I know this one!" When he got to the chorus, I joined in, "Give my regards to Broadway! Remember me to Herald Square! Tell all the gang at Forty Second Street that I will soon be there! Whisper of how I'm yearning to mingle with the old time throng! Give my regards to Old Broadway and say that I'll be there e'er long!"

Giggling, I beckoned Hubie to come to me and gathered him in my arms. I got to my feet carefully, as the ground still seemed to be moving just a bit, and we danced to the music. Daniel watched us with a broad smile, trying not to laugh at my awkward waltz. Hubie wrapped his arms around my neck and played along, enthralled by the sound of my giddy laughter.

When the song ended he segued right into another, prompting me with the first word, "Ida..."

"Sweet as apple cider!" I chanted, picking up the lyrics and continuing from there. I swayed and twirled, breathlessly trying to recall the words. Jagged shards of lightning tore across the sky directly above us. I imagined them as grand chandeliers decorating our open-air ballroom.

When he stopped playing I collapsed in a dizzy heap. Hubie crawled out of my grasp and sat on the ground, a little dizzy as well but obviously enjoying it. Daniel watched the sky apprehensively. "I think we'd better go inside," he said at last, standing.

"No, Daniel," I begged, grabbing his hand, suddenly feeling an irrational moment of panic. "Just one more. It's not raining yet."

"It'll start any minute now," he insisted, although he didn't look any more ready to return indoors than I was.

"It might go right past us. It's held off this long. One more. I haven't danced with you yet."

He chuckled. "How are you going to dance with me? Who's going to play, then?"

"We don't need the fiddle. I'll sing!"

He laughed and shook his head, pulling me to my feet as he held my hand.

"The phonograph!" I suggested, refusing to walk. "I'll play the phonograph. I can open the window. We'll hear it just fine."

He sighed, amused and contemplating, but did not answer.

"Please?" I took a step closer. "It's been such a perfect evening; I'm not ready for it to end. And it's been so long since I had a *real* dance partner." I threw a glance in Hubie's direction, then met Daniel's eyes with sincerity. "Will you please dance with me?"

His answer was a smile that caused fissures to break open in my heart as it swelled; a smile that lit up his face, creased the tiny tell-tale dimple in his left cheek and glowed radiantly in his deep brown eyes.

With a happy squeal I turned and hurried into the house before he could change his mind.

The phonograph sat on a cabinet right next to the window that overlooked the yard. I opened the window and turned the machine so that the graceful golden horn, fluted like the edges of a morning glory, was pointed outside. There was already a wax music cylinder loaded from the last time I played it, although I couldn't recall what it was. I turned the crank on the side to wind it up, lowered the needle, and scrambled back outside.

The rich sound of a full band was a stark contrast to Daniel's lone violin. It sounded like an orchestra was hiding somewhere on the property, playing to a secret party, their music drifting to us from far away as the wind caught and carried it.

He was waiting patiently for me beneath the window when I came around the side of the house, his fiddle tucked away safely on the rocking chair on the porch. His muslin dress shirt was damp in places from perspiration, his shirt-sleeves rolled up to his elbows. His dark hair was tousled and wind-blown. He extended his hand to me with a grin.

I hesitated, feeling a momentary slip in the opiate haze, then felt my worry drain away again as I took his hand. He pulled me to within inches of him, placed his arm so delicately around my waist that it more hovered than touched, and we began a simple waltz.

I could smell the faint traces of the soap he had washed up with before dinner still lingering on his neck, mixed with the musk of his sweat. Under the hand that wasn't grasped in his, his shoulder felt broad and solid. I fought the overwhelming urge to lean into him and bury my face against it. Could these arms truly be the same ones that had embraced me on the porch the day he arrived on our doorstep? He felt like an entirely different person now.

His steps were nimble and languid. We swayed to the music, my feet occasionally bumping his as my concentration drifted. I recalled my father teaching me to dance as a child, standing me on his toes as he twirled with me. I wished I could do that now; let him sweep me along so I could focus my concentration on the feel of his body near mine.

The song ended too soon. We halted our movement but neither of us stepped away. I felt his fingers fidget against the pleats of my waistband as he hesitated, unwilling to release me but unsure how to proceed. I leaned minutely closer and whispered in his ear, "Again."

He dropped my hand at once and disappeared around the house. I saw flashes of movement through the window as he replaced the needle and cranked the handle to play the cylinder again. He was quicker than I was, and returned to me before the song had barely begun to play. He didn't waste time as I had when he returned, walking right up to me and stepping into the waltz without thinking about it, taking my hand in his and pulling me tightly against him. He knew how long the music would last this time. There was no delicacy in his haste.

The heat of his arm around me was like an iron holding me against a fire. My breathing was shallow and ragged as I struggled against the sticky cage of my corset but I couldn't bring myself to pull away. I was thankful for the cool wind or else I might have fainted.

The first needle-like raindrops began to fall. I pretended I didn't feel their tiny barbs on my overheated skin, turning my face into his neck to hide from them. *No*, I pleaded silently. *Just a little longer. Please…*

The tip of my nose brushed his throat and I felt a violent shiver go through him. He leaned his cheek against the top of my head, our dance slowing. There was no resisting, no keeping him at arm's length as I gave in with weary relief to the sensation like falling that pulled me toward him. We moved as one now as his hips matched the graceful swing of mine. He was hot; he was shivering. He was family; he was a stranger. He was mine; I was Henry's.

When the music ended he pulled away slightly, releasing my hand to trace his finger gingerly across my chin. I looked up at him and saw that little crease between his eyes again, only his expression this time looked more like pain than concentration.

He looked at me for a long moment, his face mere inches from mine, and I felt the heavy weight of imminence immobilize me. If he leaned toward me, I wouldn't have the strength to stop him. Unable to breathe, I simply hovered and braced for the impact of my world shattering into a thousand pieces I wouldn't begin to know how to pick up.

He touched the pad of his thumb to my bottom lip, slowly drew a line down to my chin and sighed, the crease disappearing, the tautness in his face relaxing. He stepped away from me abruptly, picked up his fiddle, and looked toward the sky as though he had just noticed the rain.

"Come," he said, slowly moving toward the house without waiting for any more stalling from me. "It's beginning to rain."

I dutifully picked up Hubie, who began to cry when he realized his playtime was over, and followed Daniel onto the porch. He opened the door but avoided making eye contact as I passed through.

The house felt tiny and dark compared to the field. I carried Hubie upstairs to his room to quiet him and prepare him for bed, lit the oil lamp and shut the door. I heard Daniel moving the phonograph back into place. I was thankful he didn't follow me up the stairs. Somehow being inside the walls of the house made me feel thrust tighter to him than I had felt in his arms outside, and it frightened me. I was exceedingly aware of our solitude. It reverberated off the walls as though the rooms were empty.

I took a long time with Hubie, peeling off his sweat-soaked clothes and wiping him down with a cool damp rag, which helped to settle him. Then I took a nightshirt from the dresser drawer lined with dried lavender and dressed him.

We rocked in the rocking chair until he was fast asleep. Then we rocked until fatigue began to creep upon me as well. I laid him carefully in his crib, put out the light, and tiptoed out of his room. The door to Daniel's room was wide open and his bed was still vacant. He must still be downstairs. With a little sigh of relief I continued to my room and quietly closed the door behind me.

Once changed into my eyelet-trimmed nightgown I lay in bed, hoping fatigue would pay me another visit. It had disappeared quickly as I found myself straining to hear any hint of sound from downstairs. I knew that I shouldn't care; he was a grown man and would go to bed when it pleased him. But I wondered what he might be doing down there. Reading? Napping? Watching the storm?

The minutes ticked by. I heard nothing.

When I finally did hear his quiet footfall it did not have the desired effect on my psyche. Perhaps it would have, had he ascended the stairs and crept discreetly into his room. But he did not. He lingered at the top of the steps, and in the deafening silence my mind raced anew.

Sleep, I commanded myself. *His movements are not your concern. Just sleep!*

He took two steps. Having observed the length of his stride and the size of the hallway and my imagination having nothing better to do since it certainly wasn't going to obey me, I surmised he had just moved past the doorway to his room.

There was only one other door past his room. Mine.

A hesitation. Two more steps, slower this time.

My heart pounded out of my chest. This couldn't be real; I must have fallen asleep and into a dream. He would never be so brazen as to approach the room where I lie slumbering alone.

His footsteps stopped right outside the door. I wondered if he could hear my heart; my tense, anticipatory gasps. They seemed to me the loudest sounds in the world.

An eternity seemed to pass. I held my breath, listening. Then I heard his hand on the porcelain doorknob. The mortise rattled.

I envisioned him entering my bedroom and felt terror-struck at the impropriety of it. Just as quickly, I was flushed with shame at the momentary rush of exhilaration that coursed through me at the thought.

I waited, frozen in place. And waited. My skin crawled with nervous anticipation as I listened but there was no further movement. Just when I felt that I couldn't stand it for another second there was a rustle and I heard his footsteps slowly retreat back down the hall. Another moment's hesitation and his bedroom door closed. I released the breath I didn't realize I had been holding and pulled my knees up to my chest, curling into a ball. It was going to be a long night.

I was awake to witness the sky first begin to lighten with the coming dawn. The storm had blown through during the night, leaving no lingering traces in the spotless sky. When the cicadas began to complain shortly thereafter I sighed, knowing the rain had not washed away the humidity.

My slumber had been more fitful than Hubie's for once, as we had thoroughly worn him out playing in the field. He woke up crying only once. I, however, spent the night cobbling together light naps between periods of tormenting lucidity. I tossed and rolled until every cool corner of the bed had been consumed. I sat on the windowsill and counted the black, shady splotches that were trees in the dark. I strained my ears listening for movement. The house held its breath for me and there was no sound at all, until the silence grew so loud my ears imagined they heard distant music and insistent whispers coming through the windows. I whispered back but they did not invite me to join their private conversation, and they ceased to speak when I tried to discern their words. Then my foot slipped off the sill and I realized I had been sleeping, and I lumbered into bed with minimal movement so as not to scare the timid creature away.

Having the bed to myself was an unsettling experience. It should have been glorious to be able to stretch out and have all the room I wanted, but it simply felt empty and foreign, and it made me uneasy every time I woke and there was no weight beside me.

By the time dawn came I had given up on sleep and was ready to give up the pretense as well. I rose with heavy limbs but an eagerness to begin the new day.

Breakfast was nearly silent, as the moment I saw Daniel I could think of nothing but the feel of his arms in the field and a flush of shame tied my tongue. Henry's specter loomed in his empty chair at the head of the table, daring me to find a safe, mundane topic of conversation. Nothing came to mind. Daniel didn't speak either but he also didn't avoid my eyes—in fact, in the brief glances I stole in between concentrating on anything else I could find, I saw him watching me.

When he told me, just before I cleared the table and scurried into the kitchen, that he would be taking the window in his bedroom out to fix the broken ropes that held the counterweights, I decided today would be a wonderful day to work outside in the garden.

The ground had been softened but not muddied by the previous night's rain as I sat in my wide-brimmed straw hat and yellow and sage striped short-sleeved frock and endeavored to teach Hubie to pull up carrots. I dug one out, wiggled it loose, and couldn't help but be amused at his exaggerated strain at trying to pull the tiny vegetable free. When I giggled he mimicked the sound and seemed to be enjoying himself.

"Shall we pick some strawberries next?" I asked, leading him to the patch.

"Sta!" he enthused.

"Can you say 'strawberry'?"

"Sta!" He waddled excitedly ahead of me to the little red beacons amongst the green.

I didn't let him pick these, as there were not many and his clumsy, eager fingers would undoubtedly smash them and send him into a fit. The excessively dry, brutally hot summer had insured our garden struggled to survive and the crops it produced were meager. I let him point out the berry he desired and placed it delicately into his waiting hands.

I looked up when I heard the back door close and saw Daniel walking briskly toward us. He cradled his left hand against his chest. We were too far away to see the extent but I could already tell there was blood involved.

I picked up our pan of vegetables, took Hubie by the hand, and reluctantly started toward the house.

"I smashed it with the hammer," he explained haltingly as we neared. "The bleeding is slowing now, but I didn't...I couldn't find..." He was ghastly white.

"Let me see. It doesn't look too severe," I assured him, letting go of Hubie and examining his wound with my free hand. His thumb was split open along the fingernail and a solid streak of blood stained his hand and circled his wrist but it was beginning to congeal. Ugly, but nothing a bandage wouldn't take care of. I ushered them both into the kitchen and Daniel dropped into a kitchen chair, trembling. I gathered my supplies and began to clean and dress his injury.

"You don't handle blood well," I commented.

"I suppose I'm not accustomed to seeing much of it."

"Neither am I. It still doesn't make me faint."

"Well I don't exactly wish to practice my tolerance for it any more than I have, thank you."

I wrapped his thumb in a white linen bandage and tied it neatly. "Can I get you a glass of water? A piece of bread?"

"No, I'm fine...but my thumb is throbbing."

His tone took on the note of a wounded puppy and I knew what he was hinting at.

"I'll get you some aspirin," I offered, rising to retrieve it before he could object. He took the pills without a word.

"Could you possibly give me a hand getting that window back in? It's very difficult to hold it level while hammering the rope into the groove on the side, hence my accident. Perhaps you could hold it steady for me? It won't take but a few minutes."

It was a reasonable request, and one that I could not refuse, even if it did raise goosebumps on my arms. I nodded and took Hubie upstairs to his crib, then hovered in Daniel's doorway until he had everything in place and gestured me toward the window. I held it in place while he pulled the rope down, raising the counterweight in the wall with a grating, metallic clanking sound, and lined it up with the edge of the window.

"Angle it in closer," he instructed. "You're leaning away too far."

I shuffled an inch closer and stared outside.

"It's odd not having Henry here," he said, carefully tapping in the first small nail.

"Yes." My hands began to sweat.

"He'll return tomorrow afternoon, correct?"

"Yes."

"Hubie will be happy to see him." His aim went off-center on the second nail and bent it over, and he pried it out and tried again. I sighed minutely.

"Do you miss him?"

"Of course," I snapped, squeezing the window until I felt the edges make their mark on my palms.

The tapping of his hammer ceased. I knew he was waiting for me to make eye contact. I wasn't about to. I was too sober and agitated to handle his innuendos. I felt like a trapped animal in the tiny bedroom.

"Are we done yet?" I asked, my voice tight.

"One more nail," he said quietly, and began tapping again.

When he laid down the hammer and took the window from my hands I turned on my heel and bolted for the door.

"Is this the way it is, then?" he demanded, stopping me cold. "Is this where we are? Last night you were in my arms and today you won't look at me?"

I felt the blood drain from my limbs. "I don't know what you're talking about," I said coolly, turning to him. "We three had a nice evening last night. I—"

"Don't," he spat, his lips twisted with disgust. "Don't toy with me. Don't speak to me like I'm some stranger who just showed up at your door."

"No, you're not a stranger. You're family."

We stared each other down. My body felt as though it had been wrapped in ice.

He took one step closer. "Look me in the eye and tell me I'm just family to you."

I swallowed hard, trying to hide the conflict that was raging in my eyes. He scanned my face anxiously as his confidence in my answer faded with each second I hesitated. The truth was, I didn't know what he was to me. But I knew what he had to be.

"You're family," came my trembling whisper.

He stepped back, his face blank, then shook his head with an incredulous snicker. "So," he breathed. "Perhaps it's true. I keep telling myself I know you, but maybe I'm mistaken. Perhaps you're just as good a liar as he is."

"What did you say?" I demanded, incensed at his accusation. "How dare you? What are you insinuating?"

"Then you tell me, Annie, what is going on in this house? When last I saw you, you were madly in love with my cousin. I've never seen two people happier. Now you have a home, a family together, everything you ever wanted, yet you quarrel constantly. The light has left his eyes, and I think you know why. I think you know exactly why he's grown hardened and cold, and that is why you shun him, and cast your eyes at me."

In an instant I closed the gap between us and slapped him hard across the face.

"How dare you speak to me that way," I spat. "I have done nothing of the sort. As for my husband, I have no knowledge of his affairs, and you had best think twice before making accusations towards your own cousin who's given you shelter. But if you wish to discuss things that lie hidden, perhaps we should start with you. Why have you come here, Daniel? It's a very simple question, and yet one that you have eluded. What lies hidden in *your* past? What drove you out of Philadelphia? *Why are you really here?*"

He stood motionless as he absorbed my verbal onslaught. I waited for his response, close enough to feel his strained, heavy breath on my face. Meeting my gaze evenly but without a word he stalked past me, left the room and descended the stairs. A few moments later I heard the back door open and slam shut.

My heart still pounding furiously, I stormed down the hallway to my bedroom and paced around the bed before finally sinking onto the windowsill. I closed my eyes and wished fervently that everything around me — the walls, the furniture, the baby, Daniel — would simply disappear. When that didn't occur I began to wish that I would. Alas, that didn't happen either.

I cradled my head in my hands and let the tears of insult, frustration, and helplessness fall freely. For not wanting to be alone, I certainly did a fine job of pushing everyone in my life away with both hands.

So…what in the world do I do now?

I stood in the kitchen, staring out the window toward the barn, stalling. The room was filled with the rich, warm scent of vegetable soup which had been simmering on the stove for hours. I had baked a loaf of bread to accompany it which was cooling on the windowsill, and the combined aroma made my stomach growl. I poked the bread gingerly. It was slightly singed; I had been too distracted to concentrate on making something so temperamental. But it was still edible and sufficiently cool and I knew I couldn't stall any longer. I hung my apron on a nail by the basement door and dragged my feet towards the barn.

Daniel was lying on the ground, only his dark brown pants streaked with lighter dirt and his half-untied shoes visible from where he worked underneath the buggy. I got just close enough so I wouldn't have to yell.

"Dinner."

His bare arm reached out and set down the wrench he had been using, then felt around for the mallet nearby. "Coming," he replied.

I returned to the house and set the table.

We didn't speak a word during the meal. He ate slower than usual, picking through the vegetables as if searching for something. Hubie had decided he was only eating carrots so I was forced to pick through my bowl as well, feeding him pieces in between my own bites. When Daniel was finished and I was still persuading Hubie to eat, he pushed his bowl toward me and left the table silently.

It was empty save for some broth and carrots.

He spent the next few hours in the barn, laboring over the buggy. I cleaned up the kitchen and busied myself wiping down the furniture in the living room. When the shadows on the floor grew long I took Hubie upstairs to his crib and read to him from my book of poetry until he was drowsy. I slipped out quietly and tiptoed downstairs to return to the living room with my book.

When I reached the bottom of the stairs I saw Daniel standing over the phonograph, holding an Edison Gold Moulded Record canister in one hand and a tumbler of amber colored liquid in the other.

"Hubie's sleeping," I informed him, taking a seat in the armchair furthest from him and opening my book.

"Then I shan't play it." His voice was surprisingly thick. He sipped from his glass and replaced the cylinder in the cabinet.

I could smell the alcohol, and it wasn't the whiskey Joe had given him. "I see you've found Henry's brandy," I said, not looking up.

"It wasn't exactly hidden." He sank heavily into the chair next to me and set his glass on the small end table in between us that held the oil lamp.

"How much have you had?"

"Almost enough."

I studied my book, not registering the words, concentrating instead on clenching and unclenching my toes inside my boots. He watched me for a time through his thick, low eyelashes, then picked up his glass and drank again. He leaned forward with his elbows on his knees, holding his nearly empty glass between his palms and rolling it back and forth for a long while.

"Jonathan Mayfield," he said at last with a long exhale, slurring the *th's* and the *f's*. "The first time I met the bastard was the day they promoted me to supervisor at the textile mill."

I closed my book and laid it on my lap, turning my full attention to him. I was equal parts eager, curious, and afraid of what he was going to say, and struggled to keep my face from betraying any of them. He drained his glass and then studied its emptiness.

LISA GERY

"You have to understand men like him. They see only two things: money and risk. You take risks to make more money. You use money to silence bigger risks that would cost you more money. It's all a game. Everything has a cost. Everyone has a price."

He reached for the decanter, which I hadn't noticed he had stowed beside the chair, and refilled his glass.

"I needed a job and the mill was hiring. That was it. I walked in there and walked out with a job. I was seventeen. They hired me on to work a picker. It's a machine that rips up the cotton, rolls it into a sheet. Simple work. Not easy—you could lose a finger, even an arm, faster than you can blink—but it didn't take much skill, and that was fine 'cause I didn't have any. You just had to pay attention, and I could do that."

He swirled the brandy in the glass once around and gulped a quarter of it back. "The mill was hell no matter what time of the year it was. In the summer it was so musty and humid and stale you could barely breathe. Your lungs were just filled with that cotton fiber. In the winter it was drafty—right on the Delaware River—and you ended up standing there, sniffling, hacking that damn stuff up, trying not to get yourself caught up under some roller the minute you lose focus. There were huge windows to let the light in, but hardly any of them opened to get any fresh air in the place. Machinery was crammed everywhere—every corner, in front of doors; you could barely walk through the place. They hired a fair bit of children—they were cheap labor in addition to their parents. They also hired a lot of young girls. They were small...graceful...could get around in tight quarters." His eyes darkened and he took another swig.

"I worked all the hours they would give me. I ran any machine they put me on. I showed up on time every day. I did as I was asked. I was grateful for the work, even if I hated it, and I gave them everything, like I was raised to do. And they noticed.

"I'd been there a year when my supervisor pulled me off the picker one morning and said the boss wanted to see me. I was terrified. No one ever met Mr. Mayfield unless they were headed out the door and didn't come back. He never stepped foot on the floor. But he marched me upstairs and left me at this office with a big glass-front door, and there was Jonathan Mayfield sitting behind his solid mahogany desk. I always imagined he would be a large, bald, middle-aged man with a cigar. But he was older, full head of gray hair, trim, light eyes. Could have been somebody's grandfather. Probably is.

"He called me in and told me to have a seat. Said one of the supervisors had quit and they were looking at me to take his place. Said I was a good, hard worker and they wanted to give me a chance. Truth was, I was young and cheap and able to follow directions, and as far as they cared that's all I needed to be. But I saw the chance for extra money and less chance of losing a limb and took it, no questions asked." He emptied his glass and began to roll it between his palms again. I was too enraptured to worry about him dropping and shattering it on the floor.

"Not long after we hired two girls, sisters—Gretchen and Alice. Alice was young, about ten years old. Gretchen was just younger than me. Both such tiny girls, fair blond hair, these crystal blue eyes, frail like baby birds. They worked on ring spinning the cotton. Good workers, they were. They picked it up quick; never had a problem.

"I used to sit with Gretchen on her break while she ate her lunch. Told me about how her family had come from Germany; they lived in a tiny room, all eight of them, and they struggled to get by. Told me how she wanted to run her own dress shop one day in the heart of the city, buy her parents their own house with a little yard out back. She hated having her little sister work in the factory but there wasn't a choice and no better jobs available, so there they were. I told her she'd have her dress shop one day, sell them to all the rich old ladies and make so much money she'd never have to worry again." He smiled and lowered his head. "Having her there was like having the sun stream through those filthy windows; brightened the place up, just for a moment." His smile faded. He studied his glass, never looking at me.

"Eventually I noticed our workforce dwindling. Not by huge numbers, but the whole floor thinned out and they didn't hire more. They pushed who was left to work more hours. They pushed for production to increase. Jonathan offered a week's salary bonus to any supervisor who could meet his new requirements. If you couldn't, you also risked being replaced, although no one came out and said it.

"Once they stepped up production the accidents increased. Everyone was tired, overworked, sloppy. A little boy lost his hand in the picker. An inspector came out after that and looked over the mill. I overheard him give his report to my manager. He said the place was too crowded, machinery was blocking fire exits, and we weren't giving adequate break times. My manager passed this report on to Jonathan. He came back with an envelope of money. The inspector left, and that was the last I heard of that.

"The pressure kept coming, and more people quit. We tried to make do with less and less but it was getting impossible. When one of the women who attended the drawing frame left, I pulled Alice off the ring spinning and put her there. Gretchen came after me, insisting I shouldn't move her, that she wasn't familiar enough with the machine. They had both run it before—it pulled slips of cotton from these large drums and combined them into one even strand—but only minimally. I explained that I had to move one of them and she was more proficient at the ring spinning, so it just made sense to move Alice. I remember her pleading with me, 'She has trouble on that machine; please, let me do it.' But I just kept thinking I couldn't waste her agility on a machine where either one of them would be slow, so I told her to go back to what she was doing, and I walked away from her."

He sighed deeply, setting his glass on the floor between his feet and cradling his forehead in his hands. "A few hours later I heard the screams. One sharp shriek, and then these screams of absolute horror. I could hear Alice the loudest, above them all, screaming, 'No, no, no!' I ran toward the drawing frame, and before I could get close enough to see I could *hear* it...this cracking, snapping, sickening sound of bones breaking; the groaning and whining of the shaft as it began to bind up and stall; the machine grinding to a halt. The horrible vision was in my mind before my eyes could seek it out—Gretchen clawing her way toward the machine as the other women held her back, crying out for her poor sister who lay mangled within.

"But lo, standing before the machine, there was…Alice…splattered with blood, shaking, staring with vacant eyes, unable to speak. I pushed her toward the crowd of weeping women who were watching, frozen, gesturing them to take her away. 'Take her to Gretchen!' I ordered, puzzled for a moment why Gretchen hadn't already come to comfort her sister. Alice clasped her hand over her mouth and began to scream, her knees buckling out from under her."

His voice broke, and with a single sob tears began to fall from his squeezed-shut eyes. "And that's when I saw the strands of fair blond hair, staining with blood, wrapped tight around the shaft of the drawing frame."

He wiped his eyes roughly with the back of his hand and cleared his throat. My stomach turned as I watched the memory come to life in his face. "Gretchen had been helping Alice. She ran back and forth between the machines, trying to run both, and in her haste her apron became entangled. It pulled her in before anyone could do anything. I tell myself it was over quickly, before she knew what was happening. Before she felt anything."

I wanted to agree with him, but I couldn't find my voice. I was frozen, tears brimming in my own eyes, in sympathy for him and pity for the girl.

He picked up his glass and, with unsteady hands, refilled it halfway. "We made our quota," he said bitterly, eyeing the brandy with disdain before knocking half of it back. "I got my bonus." For a moment I thought he would hurl the glass across the room. Instead he squeezed its thick faceted bottom until his knuckles turned white. "The money went to help pay down our debt to mother's physician."

"I didn't realize she'd been unwell," I said at last, concerned.

He nodded. "Pain in the joints so bad she can barely move some days. No one can seem to help her. I'm sure you can see why they were less than understanding when I quit the mill and couldn't bring myself to step foot in another factory. The truth is, right now, I don't know what to do with myself."

"You never told them," I murmured.

He shook his head. "I killed her, Annie. How could I ever tell them that?"

"But you didn't—"

"Please don't," he whispered, rubbing his face wearily with one hand. "I spent months reassuring myself of my innocence as I walked by the bloodstain on the floor. But innocent men don't have to force themselves to make eye contact with the people they care about. Innocent men don't wake up shouting in the middle of the night."

My face reddened. It was a small house. I had no doubt he'd heard Henry. It had happened more than once that summer.

"And do you want to know why we all pushed so hard? Why that extra revenue was so vitally important? It was needed to fund their next venture—the Walt Theater." He sat back in the armchair, smiling without joy. "I hope the son-of-a-bitch enjoys the vat of money it brings him. I hope he drowns in it." He looked at me then, with an urgency in his eyes. "I don't want to see your brother get involved with those people, Annie. I don't know what's going on—I can't prove anything—hell, maybe it's just my own guilt making me crazy, but I know how that company works. Why is Henry suddenly so distracted? What does Nathan know about being a projectionist? It doesn't sit right. Something's off."

I sat fidgeting with the binding on my book. I didn't want to believe Henry could be involved in anything half so scandalous, or that my baby brother could be stepping blindly into the hands of such corrupt men. It was inconceivable. I also feared voicing these doubts would send Daniel into a desperate rage.

"Speak plainly," he implored. "I see the struggle in your eyes. Tell me what you know."

"I know nothing," I replied honestly, looking him in the eye so that he might believe me. "I know nothing of Henry's life outside of this house, save for the occasional rants and stories he has voiced to us both. If a secret lies within him it is hidden to me as well. As for Nathan, lucky timing and a good word can go far. How does anyone move up in the world, if not for opportunities like this? I refuse to believe there is an ulterior motive. I understand your hesitation, your mistrust, but I —"

He rose and began to staggeringly pace the room, biting his tongue, waiting for me to finish so he could contradict me.

"I do not agree," I continued. "The company is large. Jonathan Mayfield may be a despicable human being, but that does not mean everyone in his employ is. The theater is not the mill, Daniel. Its ghosts do not haunt this place. They haunt *you*."

The words he had been so eager to speak died on his lips. He quit his pacing and leaned against the mantle with his head against the wall. "I know that I am prejudiced," he admitted with a wave of his hand, "and chasing after shadows. I swear to Almighty God that I want to be wrong. I implore Him to let me be wrong. I beseeched Henry, on my knees, to prove me wrong. But he has not." Weary of standing, he slid to the floor with a sigh and sat.

"When a man sells a piece of his soul, it dies," he explained, the lines in his forehead creasing deeply. "If that man has any bit of conscience within him, it is a slow, painful death, one that leaves its mark on him. I know what a dying soul looks like, Annie. I've looked in the mirror. And nothing Henry says — or doesn't say — can hide that."

I picked nervously at a callous on my palm. He was wrong, I knew. Henry didn't have a guilty conscience. The reason for his misery was much simpler. It was me.

"Prove me wrong," Daniel whispered.

I shook my head.

He slid gingerly across the floor, retrieved his glass, and refilled it. Sitting by my feet like a dutiful puppy, he offered me the drink.

"I've told you my demons. Are yours so much more monstrous?"

I shook my head again.

He tried to put the glass into my hand and I grasped it with a sigh, if only to keep him from spilling it.

"Loosen your tongue," he bade me, "and bare your soul."

I could smell the tang of the brandy from the glass and on his breath. It was tempting. Unspoken words were so very heavy.

"You're not a sinner, Annie. You're a good woman. Pure like snow...perfect."

I snickered at the ridiculousness of his words. "And you're drunk."

He traced my wrist delicately with his finger. "Perfect," he continued, unabated. "Strong. Sure. You're everything I would strive for, if I...if I was half good enough."

"Stop," I said, agitated by his blind, foolish praise.

"It's true," he murmured, caressing my hand. "You have the biggest heart of anyone I've ever known. You've been so kind to me, so accepting—"

I remembered the fights I had had with Henry over his coming to stay with us, my bitter reproaches of him before he ever stepped into our home, and my cheeks burned. I took a draught of brandy, my nerves wound to the point of snapping. He continued to ramble incessantly of my virtues.

"So patient, so beautiful, you—"

"I am *not*, I—"

"Are so smart, so fair—"

"I'm a failure as a mother!"

It happened so suddenly I felt as though I were outside my own body. The words erupted from the depth of my being, a raging river that overflowed its banks in an instant and washed away all restraint, all dignity, all instincts of self-preservation. I was not some pristine angel to be worshiped. I was scarred and flawed and hideous and

trembling. I was an imposter in a pretty mask, an inexcusable mess —
but I would be a liar no more.

"I feel trapped inside this house with this needy child who
doesn't even like me! No matter what I do it seems we are at odds.
I'm so exhausted and every day is the same. And now Henry wants
to have another baby, and I can't do it again! Another person in this
house demanding another piece of me until there's nothing left! Ever
since Hubie was born Henry has lost interest in me. I'm a failure and
he hates me for it. I've ruined Hubie and now he wants to start over
with another baby, and I don't doubt if he'd just be honest he'd admit
he'd rather start over with another wife!"

I didn't realize I was crying until Daniel took the glass from my
shaking hands and set it on the table and, rising to his knees, wrapped
his arms around me.

"I've ruined everything," I sobbed into his coarse work shirt.
"I've ruined his life because I'm not good enough. What is wrong with
me? Why can't I do this? Every woman is meant for this. What is
missing inside me that I don't know what I'm doing?"

"Shh, it's all right," he whispered, rubbing my back and patting
my hair awkwardly. "Please don't cry, dear. Settle there, and tell me
everything."

I clutched him tightly and let the sobs wrack my body, unable
and unwilling to reign them in. I felt like I was floating with the
dizziness of gasping breaths and the intoxicating taboo of speaking
my most shameful truth. When at last they had run their course and
my eyes were sore and dry, I marveled at the boundlessness of his
understanding. He had seen the ugliest thing I kept hidden and here
he was, asking for more. It had been so easy to let go, so painless, that
I realized the specter of the reproach I feared was far more menacing
than reality. Perhaps it was the fact that he had no expectations of me
and therefore I could not fail them. Whatever it was, I craved
absolution. I was ready to drop the mask entirely and watch it float
away.

I began to speak, haltingly at first, of my darkest hours. "Henry and I were so excited for the baby to come. I had dreamed about having a family for so long. He would talk to the baby all the time, tell him about how we would go on picnics together and go to the fair, tell him about the puppy we would get...I thought it was adorably silly. I thought we were ready.

"When I was a child I asked my mother once what birth was like. She told me it was inconsequential; that once you hold your child for the first time, God makes you forget the pain that brought him into the world. Being young I took her literally, but when I got older I thought it was quite a beautiful thing to say. I expected the joy of that moment to overwhelm everything. But the second I held this bloody, wriggling, screaming baby in my arms, I was absolutely terrified. It was like a wave hit me and dragged me underwater. I couldn't move. I didn't know what to do. I had waited so long to meet him, and there he was...and all I could feel was the breath being squeezed from my lungs."

Daniel's lips pursed as he struggled to resist the urge to interject with reassurances.

"I still can't explain it. The instincts I felt certain would come simply didn't. Instead there was only a paralyzing fear and a certainty of nothing but my inadequacy. He came from me; I should know him innately. I waited for that certainty to come. But there was nothing. They could have placed a kitten in my arms for all the relation I felt to him.

"Mother said I was just overwhelmed by the birth, and that I needed time to adjust and convalesce. She stayed with us for a while, teaching me how to care for him and helping me until I recovered. But the truth is, I've never felt like the same person again. It is as though when Hubie was born I was reborn, too, and now I am trapped in this stranger's body.

"The doctor said I was suffering from melancholia. He gave me laudanum. But it merely dulls my senses, and once it has faded these feelings persist."

I reached for the glass of brandy on the table. Daniel, who had released me but remained hovering against the side of the chair, relaxed into a seated position at my feet as it became apparent I was in control of my senses. I let the alcohol settle the trembling and fidgeting in my fingers and warm a path into the pit of my stomach.

"Henry was so good with him in the beginning. He tried so hard. After Mother left, Hubie started sleeping less and less at night, screaming all evening and falling into an exhausted sleep during the day. At first I merely slept when the baby slept but she warned me I must get him back on a proper schedule or we would never sleep at night again. I tried, but soon it seemed he was barely sleeping at all, day or night.

"One night, after a particularly brutal few days of him being completely inconsolable, the lack of sleep got the better of us. I broke down crying and Henry flew into a rage. He threw himself out of bed, handed Hubie to me, and began to drag the crib out of the room and down the hallway.

" 'I can't take it anymore!' he shouted as he struggled to shove the crib into the other bedroom. 'I can't take one more minute of this! He's not staying in our bedroom anymore. Let him cry himself to sleep in here.'

" 'I can settle him,' I promised through my own tears, but all I could do was shush him helplessly as we both wailed uncontrollably.

"Henry came back and just stared at me with the strangest expression. 'Get a hold of yourself,' he grumbled as he took Hubie from me and exiled him to the other room. When he returned I was still falling to pieces.

" 'Damn it, Annie, what's the matter with you? You're as bad as the baby! Stop these hysterics this minute!' But I couldn't stop. And the more I cried, the angrier he became. We never screamed at each other the way we did that night. I don't remember half of what I said; I was so tired and distraught. I remember him asking what was wrong with me that I couldn't get the baby under control, and that I had better stop crying because he needed me to be a mother. I could see the disappointment and the disgust in his eyes when he looked at me. I already knew I was a miserable failure, but that was the night I knew he knew it, too. In the morning he apologized profusely for the cruel things he said and promised me everything would get better. I agreed, and promised myself that was the last time he would ever see me break down.

"And now he says we should have another baby and I don't think I can go through this again."

Daniel exhaled slowly, hesitating to be sure I was finished speaking. "You must know he doesn't consider you a failure. Tell me you know that, Annie. He was just as overwhelmed as you were that night, I'm certain of it."

I shook my head, wishing I could believe him, but unable to.

"Am I correct to assume you have not expressed your preference to Henry?"

"I tried. But I cannot explain it to him. He won't hear it, and even if he did, he wouldn't understand."

"He would. I'm certain he would."

"No. He wouldn't. He always respected me for my strength. How could he ever love me if he knew how I truly felt?"

"He needs to know, Annie," he insisted gently.

"He needs to know what a reprehensible, unfit mother I am? He already knows too much and he doesn't know half."

"No! Nothing could be farther from the truth. You are good with Hubie. You are patient, gentle, and kind with him, and it's all the more remarkable what you've been able to do knowing how you suffer. You are to be commended, not reproached."

"You…are still drunk," I declared, which drew a grin from him, "and, as always, far kinder to me than I deserve."

He shook his head in dissent, his lips twitched up adoringly.

"You don't understand," I went on in all seriousness. "Children…know. That first moment I held him, I…I didn't want him. Deep down inside him somewhere he knows that. He'll carry it with him forever. It's why he hates me so."

"If you think your child hates you, I don't even know how to begin to—"

"I'm not telling you this to goad you into reassuring me I'm wrong. I'm not looking to debate. I'm simply telling you how I feel."

We sat for a long time in silence.

"So what will you do?" he asked at last.

It was a question I had already spent too long pondering with no answer. I shrugged. "What will you?"

He considered this for a moment. "I will finish that glass of brandy," he decided, reaching up and finishing the last gulp. "And then I will retire to bed while I can still find my way unaided." He rose carefully, one limb at a time and with help from the arm of the chair, and reached for my hand. I stood as well, and he placed a kiss above my knuckles.

"Goodnight, sweet Annie," he murmured with his lips still pressed to my skin. He let go and stumbled backwards, regained his balance with a tranquil smile, and walked slowly and deliberately to the stairs. I extinguished the light and followed behind, watching that he did not lose his footing in the dark. He fell into his bed without incident, and I curled up in mine, slipping almost immediately into a deep and mercifully dreamless sleep.

The next morning I dressed in my nicest dress, a slate blue taffeta garment with a white ruffled bodice, and carried a freshly scrubbed and dressed Hubie outside to meet Daniel, clean-shaven and wearing his brown suit, as he pulled the buggy up to the front of the house and drove us into town for our usual weekly church service at St. John's Lutheran Church.

Stepping through the beautifully carved, chestnut double doors, I was somewhat amazed I didn't burst into flames. After everything that had transpired since Henry left town I felt as though my sins were carved into my flesh, written on my blouse in my blood for the world to see. I sat in the pew, scarcely registering the pastor's words, praying fiercely for forgiveness, resistance to temptation, clarity of mind, and strength of spirit. When I looked over at Daniel and found myself hoping he would change out of his suit once we returned home so he would not look so dapper and well-groomed I knew I had better repeat that "resistance to temptation" clause in my original request.

After the service concluded we walked to the farmers' market and the corner grocer to pick up a few items. We avoided the theater at the other end of town, now in its final days of preparation for opening night. Henry had demurred taking me by there in recent weeks since the façade had been completed, saying he wanted me to experience it in all its glory once it was fully completed. I didn't want to have to feign surprise after seeing it prematurely, and Daniel didn't care if he ever saw it at all, so we ran our necessary errands and returned home for lunch.

I was sitting in the living room working on a needlepoint and Daniel was sitting in the chair next to me—still in his suit—reading the newspaper to Hubie, who sat in his lap and tugged at the pages, when we heard the noises of arrival outside. Daniel froze, his eyes darting toward the window, and the tightening of his lips confirmed that Henry was home. He shot me a regretful look.

"I know," I said, rising and setting my work on the chair.

I stepped out onto the porch to greet the arriving party and pulled the door mostly shut behind me. Welcoming my father and brother, I invited them in for a cup of coffee, which they accepted eagerly. Nathan was a bundle of energy, split between finishing the story he had been in the midst of telling Father and trying to tell it to me from the beginning simultaneously. Henry maintained a polite smile and unloaded his bag without a word.

He looked so tired. Perhaps it was only obvious in contrast to Nathan, but it startled me. The weariness that was normally only hinted at in his eyes seemed to manifest throughout his body. When he saw me his contrived smile grew wider and he set his bag down and hugged me tightly.

I recognized that mask and it pained me that he had a need to wear it. I let Nathan's chattering fade into the background and hugged him back. I didn't need to lie when I whispered in his ear, "I'm glad you're home."

He kissed me tenderly, which was not something he was typically apt to do in front of others. I believed him when he whispered back, "I missed you."

EIGHT

On Monday morning I opened my eyes to a spotless summer day and turned twenty-four.

Henry wished me a happy birthday over breakfast which, much to my chagrin, sent Daniel into an incredulous interrogation.

"Your birthday? Why, Annie, I had no idea! Why didn't you mention it?"

"Because it is a day, like any other," I replied, more concerned with my chance to eat breakfast while it was still hot than discuss my newly completed year of aging.

"But—"

"You need to stop fussing," I admonished, pointing at him with my fork, much to Henry's amusement. "You're like an old woman, clucking away. Stop it. I don't need to be fussed over. I'm not a child."

"We'll have a treat tonight," Henry murmured conspiratorially to Daniel.

"There's no need!" I insisted, to deaf ears.

"Nothing fancy," he assured me. "I was just thinking a little sweetcake from the bakery downtown."

I stopped arguing and concentrated on my scrambled eggs, my mouth watering at the mention. "I do like cake," I admitted.

"Settled. I shall bring us dessert tonight. I'll be home early; I just have to finish some final reports on the theater. It won't be a long day."

He kissed Hubie and I on the forehead and left for work.

Daniel lingered at the table as I freed Hubie from his chair and cleaned up, lost in thought. "We should have a picnic today," he suggested as I balanced the last of the plates in my arms.

"It's washing day," I reminded him as I walked away.

He followed me into the kitchen. "Then what can I do for you?"

"You can stop trying to find ways to fuss over me," I said patiently.

He leaned against the sink and watched me, concentrating again. "I know," he said at last. "I can take Hubie while you do your washing."

"That's not necessary, and you have your own work to do."

"It would be fine. I'm not so very busy."

I shook my head. "You don't listen well, do you know that?"

"Annie." I continued washing the dishes so he touched his finger lightly to my chin to make me stop and look at him. "I care about you," he said. "I want to make this day special for you somehow, and I've very limited resources. The only thing I have to offer is a few hours of peace and quiet. Would it be so terrible if you accepted?"

"Ohh...fine," I relented. "But I don't deserve favors for aging. Everyone does that every day."

"Fine, then it has nothing to do with your birthday."

"Ok," I chuckled, unable to be stalwart in the face of his benevolent persistence. "Then what is the reason?"

"I don't know," he said with a shrug as he walked off to locate his cousin. "Pick one that doesn't annoy you."

I threw the dishcloth at him as he ducked out of the room.

Standing in the shade cast by the back of the house, scrubbing bed linens in the wash tub, I reveled in the solitude. The day was as beautiful as it had looked from inside; the morning light poured a honey-golden hue over everything, the temperature was perfectly mild, and the slight breeze was laced with the sweet perfume of nearby honeysuckle vine, steeped in dew. I was thankful it was washing day because to be cooped up indoors on a day like this would be a shame. There was something to be said for the fresh air that made the work tolerable, even enjoyable in some ways. Pristine weather such as this simply wouldn't permit a foul mood.

A picnic with Daniel would have been lovely but I appreciated the quiet morning more than I expected. The birds chirped happily and the cicadas were nowhere to be found. The rhythmic sloshing of the steamy water could have lulled me to sleep. There was no need to speak or think or analyze or feel anything except the cool breeze fluttering loose wisps of hair across the back of my neck. I could let my mind wander, daydream, or just switch off into quiet nothingness. Company was wonderful but the simplicity of solitude was delicious.

I wanted to exist in that moment forever. Forget moving through my twenty-fourth year. If I held my breath and was very still, I could pretend the seconds weren't ticking by. That moment was uncomplicated. Content. I realized contentment, like joy, is most profoundly experienced and intricately appreciated when found in small, unexpected doses amidst the mundane.

I spent my birthday washing laundry. I spent it alone. And I was happy.

Henry was true to his word and arrived home early from work. He found me in the kitchen just as I was taking the chicken out of the oven. Greeting me with a kiss on the cheek he presented me with a square brown paper wrapped box tied with twine that smelled suspiciously like bread and honey.

"Ooh, thank you!" The aroma was knee-weakening, slight as it was through the wrappings. I indulged in a few appetizing whiffs but resisted opening it as I stored it on the open lower shelf of the sink until after dinner, nestled safely next to my pastel ceramic mixing bowls. "That was sweet of you."

"It's no trouble." He dropped heavily into the chair by the window with a long exhale and watched me busy myself at the stove.

"Where is Hubie?" he asked, glancing around as he bent to re-tie his boot laces.

"He's out in the barn with Daniel."

"Not pestering, I hope."

"No—well, I hope not. I haven't heard from them since lunch. He insisted on watching him today to give me some peace and quiet."

"How chivalrous." His voice sounded dubious.

"It was," I assured him, suddenly finding I had to try too hard to sound casual. I struggled to swallow my unease.

"How have things been working out with him?"

I was deeply thankful he was sitting behind me as I felt a blush creep all the way to my ears. "Fine!" I exclaimed, stirring the beans in the pot. "Just fine!"

"I hope you're not pretending on my behalf."

The room began to spin as my breathing grew shallow. I had a death grip on the pot handle and another on the spoon. What did he know? What *was* there to know? Nothing, I reassured myself, because nothing had ever happened and nothing ever would. I floundered for words but my mouth had gone dry.

"I know we didn't exactly agree on his coming here," Henry continued thoughtfully. "I hope you're not making light of the difficulty to appease me."

Every clenched muscle in my body relaxed with relief. "No!" I said breathily with a wave of my hand, still clutching the spoon. "Don't be silly. It has been fine. He has been working very hard, he's been courteous and helpful…there's nothing more to say, really. He's been fine."

"Good," he said, seemingly pleased with my response. "I'm glad to hear it."

The silence that followed wasn't unpleasant, but I wanted to make sure the topic was closed so I brought up a new one.

"So, the Walt Theater opens tomorrow."

"Yes." After a pause he added, "I should be glad to move on from there."

"I thought you enjoyed this project," I said, surprised. "You go on about it like a proud father sometimes."

"Do I?"

"You do. You've invested enough hours in it, I suppose you've a right to be proud."

"Proud isn't the word," he insisted. "Not at all. I mean—it's a handsome building. Aesthetically it's the most beautiful structure I've ever worked on, and the prospect of having a new theater is exciting, so in that respect I'm enthusiastic. But the construction schedule was arduous and impossible to meet, and I'll be glad to be done with it."

"Isn't everything finished now? If they open tomorrow, what could be left to do?"

"There are just a few small modifications they need to make in the coming weeks. Minor issues; backstage type of stuff we ran out of time on. I'll have to oversee its completion."

Remembering the conversation we had had about this on his way out the door to the train station in light of the talk Daniel and I had confused and concerned me.

"Did you find the answers you were looking for in New York?" I asked with some trepidation.

"Not exactly," he murmured with a slight snicker.

I glanced back at him, eyebrows raised.

"Don't fret yourself, dear. It's nothing important."

"It sounds important," I countered.

"It's nothing I can't handle." He stood and looked out the window, then turned to me. "Now, smile! Put away your worries. Today is a celebration and I want to see you happy." He waited patiently until I produced a small grin, then nodded approvingly. "There you go. I'm going up to the barn," he announced, striding toward the back door before I could object.

Dinner conversation that night, which was normally reserved and polite and conducted with proper decorum, was surprisingly boisterous and thoroughly enjoyable as Henry and Daniel took turns sharing humorous stories about growing up with mutual relatives. Afterwards, I brewed a pot of coffee and served the cake as Henry bounced Hubie on his knee and Daniel told a story about his Uncle Steve and the time their pig got loose and the collective effort it took to recapture it, weaving a yarn so ridiculous he had us all cracking up. If the pleasantry took an effort on their part, it didn't show. The camaraderie in their laughter was genuine, the way I remembered it being when we were young and they were as close as brothers.

Hearing it loosened the tremulous knot in my stomach whose company I had grown so accustomed to.

Henry's sandy hair had grown slightly longer than he usually kept it and a hint of the curly waves he had as a child were beginning to creep back. One lock in particular kept falling over his left ear and it caught my notice. When he chuckled his cheeks grew flushed but when he really let loose from deep within his belly the pink went all the way to his earlobes. They were cherry red now against his pale strands.

It was easy to forget how charming he could be when he smiled. It was easy to overlook, next to Daniel's chiseled jaw and animated eyes, the strong, simple handsomeness in his features. It struck me as a revelation from time to time, when I found myself unintentionally taking him for granted.

I could still feel the cord between us, even if it was brittle. Its core was intact, struggling to bind us, surging and receding, surviving in glimpses and moments and memories. As much as I didn't know how to repair it, I didn't want it to break. It was our history, our shared past and promised future. It was a security net of familiarity in a strange and frighteningly large world.

I longed to step back in time. Before Hubie. Before the rigorous demands of Henry's job. Before Daniel had come asking questions and making me ask questions of my own. Back to a time when I actually knew what I wanted and had the means to effect such a change. Was there ever truly a time when my heart had a simple path and no obstacles in following it? It seemed an impossibly long time ago, if ever at all.

I saw a tear in Henry's eye from the strain of his merriment as he clapped a chortling Daniel on the back and felt a warm tug in my stomach. Could there be hope? We couldn't go back, but what if there was still a way to move forward? What if, deep down, we were still the people we used to be; the carefree children who had fallen in love? What if we were buried inside our selves; not obliterated with the change of growth and maturation, but waiting to be resurrected?

What if the sum of all our missteps and failings had not yet constituted a fatal flaw? What if it was just a moment *not* too late?

"Annie!"

I jumped visibly, startled from my trance.

"Annie, dear, are you still with us?" Henry asked, wiping his face with his handkerchief as Daniel looked on inquisitively.

"Yes! Yes, of course. Just lost in thought." I smoothed my skirt over my legs and tried to recall the last bit of conversation I had registered.

"I was just asking you to close your eyes. I have a present for you."

"A present? But the cake was my present. And it was delicious, thank you."

"No, I have something else for you. Something special. Close your eyes."

I sighed with heavy martyrdom. "You all have fussed over me enough today. I'm not accustomed to presents. It's not practical."

"Well perhaps you should be more accustomed to them. Perhaps that's the problem. You deserve fine things. They shouldn't be foreign to you. Enough now," he said when I tried to interject. "Eyes. Closed."

I obeyed. His footsteps thudded out of the room and up the stairs.

"What is it?" I whispered to Daniel.

"I have no idea," he whispered back.

A moment later he was back and there was a soft thud in front of me as he placed a box on the table. "Open," he instructed.

The round, brown paper wrapped package was most likely a hat box, judging from the size. I grew a bit excited in spite of myself. I only had one good hat. It would be nice to have another. Not completely unpractical, anyway. I untied the string and stripped away the paper.

"Henry..." I breathed.

There sat a brand new hat box with the signature green and beige striped pattern of Moreau's. The upscale French hat maker had a store in New York City and our quaint hat store in town carried exactly two of his cheaper designs for the local ladies to choose from, aside from many other non-designer options; the green boxes a succinct and priceless advertisement beckoning perpetually from the storefront window.

I opened the lid with trembling hands while Henry beamed from ear to ear and Daniel watched in confusion, the magnitude of the gift lost on him.

This was not a cheaper design.

I lifted the hat delicately out of the box with both hands. It was made of rich peacock blue Parisian silk, the graceful curved edges lined in matching velvet. Parma violets, blush colored tea roses, and thick white peonies adorned the crown from which sprouted an impressive plume of wispy osprey feathers. A veil of white tulle cascaded gracefully from the back.

It was the most beautiful hat I had ever seen. I sat gaping at it, turning it gently in my hands to view it from all sides. I had never owned something so fancy in my entire life. The dress I was married in was not this nice. Not by far.

"Well?" chimed Henry. "Do you like it? Try it on! Let's see how it suits you."

Henry placed the hat carefully on my head and began to fuss with the proper angle, unaccustomed to dressing me, but I couldn't move to help him. I was frozen by the price tag that had been removed and hidden but which I could only imagine. We could not afford this. Judging by the size of the ospreys alone I knew this was far out of our budget. A hat like this cost two week's salary if it cost a penny.

"Henry, I can't, this hat is far too−" I stopped myself from saying "expensive." "Much," I finished. "It's just…too much…"

But he wasn't listening. He prattled on about seeing the shop while he and Nathan were in New York and how long he had spent selecting just the right one that would complement the blue of my eyes.

"If Emma can have a line of fancy hats from Moreau's, my darling wife shall have one, too!" he declared.

His words after that faded to a hollow din in my ears. Emma? How on earth did he know what Emma wears? What did it *matter* what Emma wears? Did I mishear him?

"What did you say about Emma?" I interrupted weakly.

"What? Oh, well, I remembered how you went on about her new hat that day she came to visit. It was obvious you were taken with it. And you need a new hat, something fine—"

Something better than Emma's, I finished in my mind. It all began to make sense. His distaste for my friend had nothing to do with her husband. It had everything to do with their money. I could hear the envy dripping in his voice, something I had never noticed but which had, upon reflection, been rearing its head as of late.

Why is that such a dream? Why couldn't I build a home like that for us one day?

I didn't even remember telling him about the hat. Why had he picked that conversation among so many more important others to start listening?

I could feel their eyes on me as their joy quickly turned to concern at my stoic reaction. I swallowed and said the only honest thing I could. "It's absolutely beautiful."

Daniel and Hubie applauded as Henry laughed triumphantly. "I knew you'd love it! Come take a look in the mirror." He took me by the hand and led me from the room, up the stairs to our bedroom where my hand mirror lay on the dresser. I followed him blindly, my mind digging through its memories as I tried to recall ever implying I wished for something that was the better of Emma's. As he held the mirror up I took in my reflection and responded reflexively. "Beautiful. Thank you so much."

He heard the tone in my voice that told him something was off— I could tell by the wane in his enthusiasm—but he continued on as though it were nothing. "I'm glad you like it," he said, replacing the mirror. "Come, let's return downstairs." He took a step towards the doorway but I was closer, and I grasped the doorknob and swung it shut. He stopped and eyed me quizzically as I removed the hat and held it limply in my hands, leaning back against the door. I was terrified to ask the question that was on my lips but even more terrified to realize the rising panic in my stomach told me I already knew the answer.

"Where did you get the money for this?"

He broke into an actor's broad smile, chuckling and gesturing with his hand. "No, I won't hear a word of that. It's a gift. Don't you worry about it."

"No," I insisted, shaking my head, refusing to join him in making light of the conversation. "We don't have the money for this. We don't."

"We do," he countered.

"How? Where did it come from? That's what I want to know."

He was still smiling, still trying to placate me. "You don't even know how much it cost, darling. Don't upset yourself. It—"

"Don't speak to me like I'm a child!" I snapped, finally wiping the grin from his face. "I know you spent a great deal more than we can afford. I want to know where you got it."

He stepped backwards, his eyes hardening dangerously. "It's none of your concern," he stated.

"It is. Why won't you tell me?"

He glanced at the floor to break my stare but remained silent.

"Your silence breeds far more suspicion than a simple answer," I hinted, trying to coax him into speaking. It did not work. "Did it come from the Mayfield Company?"

His head snapped up at the name. "What is that supposed to mean?"

I opened my mouth to speak but could not get the words out. I shook my head, squeezing my eyes shut as I fought back sudden tears, wrestling with the urge to walk away and spend the rest of my life pretending everything was normal instead of looking him in the eye and asking for the truth.

My voice shook so badly I didn't recognize it. "Did they...buy your loyalty?"

I saw the surprise flash in his face as his jaw fell open. "What did you just say?" he whispered incredulously.

"Is that where the money came from?" I clarified, fighting the tremor from my voice.

"You think I took a bribe? And where did you get that idea from?" His expression was a mixture of shock and anger as he gestured downstairs. "What nonsense has he been whispering to you?"

"Daniel has nothing to do with this—"

"Bullshit," Henry snapped. "Why else would you ask me that? He's been telling you stories."

The air felt suddenly thin; insufficient to fill my lungs. "And why would he do that? What would breed his suspicion of you, if you've nothing to hide?"

"He's trifling with you, isn't it obvious? His reasons are no secret. I see him watch you, with those puppy eyes. You think I don't notice how he fawns over you? Do you think I'm blind?"

I shook my head vehemently in nonverbal denial and wanted nothing more than to throw up.

"Don't make this about Daniel," I finally returned. "This is about you—and your refusal to be honest with me."

"Annie, you're reading far too much into this. You said you liked Emma's hat so I bought you one. That is all there is to it. It wasn't as expensive as you're imagining. You're making something out of nothing."

The part of me that wanted to believe him, that was capable of believing his words in the face of so much contrasting evidence—the part of my brain that usually whisked me curtly away from dwelling on unpleasantries and strived for peace—had been steadily shrinking, and was now silent.

I glared at him. "You're lying," I accused flatly.

We stared each other down.

With a resolute shake of his head, he reached around me for the doorknob, but I refused to move.

"We are not leaving this room until you come clean," I told him.

He backed away from me, and his look took on that of a wounded, cornered animal. His eyes raked over me, softening and hardening, as though searching for a way through me.

"What choice did I have?" he said at last.

I felt lightheaded as I gripped the brim of the hat so tightly my knuckles turned white. The sensation of being outside my body, watching this scene as an unattached observer, came upon me.

"It's true," I said tonelessly; an affirmation rather than a question. "You sold yourself to those people. What did they pay you off for?"

"Annie—"

"What have you done, Henry?"

He stood silent, the clouds in his countenance darkening.

"What choice did I have?" he asked again, but this time his words had a bitter edge. "You stand there, so righteous and ignorant. The life you want has a price. I'm doing my damnedest but—"

I cut him off with a furious wave of my hand. "The life I want? What is *that* supposed to mean?"

"Emma!" he erupted, throwing his hands up. "You envy her! It's plain in everything you say about her. Ever since she married I see the way you are about her. Her children, her money, her fine things. It's obvious you're unhappy. Finally I realized—you envy her life. All I'm trying to do is to give you that."

Nausea and fury roiled in my stomach. The idea that he could know me so scantly as to think I pined for my friend's life of leisure and affluence made me sick. The fact that he used it to blame me for his decision to accept ill-gotten money made me livid.

My voice was a measured growl. "You don't know me at all. I do *not* envy her. I need nothing she has, I don't want—"

"Don't lie to me. You're simply trying to appease me."

LISA GERY

"No, I'm not!" I screamed in frustration. "You *are not* listening! Why can you not hear me when I'm standing right before you?"

"Then what *do* you want?" His volume matched my own. "I have no idea how to make you happy! Nothing I do seems to work. I work long hours to provide for us and keep you in a life of comfort and provision. I gave you a home. I made you a mother. God willing I'll give you as many children as you want. I even secured your darling brother a position in a true career, one that could open doors for him for the rest of his life! And still I cannot find your favor. *Nothing pleases you!*"

"You think I *want* endless children and a huge house I can't keep up with? You don't understand anything! I don't care about the money. I'm content with what we have, I'm not pining for something more. And I never asked you to do any favors for Nathan. You think I want him involved with those shady people? I don't trust them! That's the point of all of this!"

He snatched the hat, which I had been clutching in front of me like a shield, from my hands and hurled it onto the bed. "Fine then. You tell me because I haven't a clue. Right now. What the hell do you want from me?"

I couldn't force myself to stop and breathe, halt this unproductive arguing and be calm and honest. My blood was too heated, pumping through me like an angry river, carrying away my sense and reason, and my words were too sharp to not be cutting as razors. No one could scream this loud and possibly listen. There was no point in trying.

"All I want is a husband who can look me in the eye," I sneered.

"Damn you." He pursed his lips and shook his head maniacally. "I work myself to death for you." Without warning his hand clenched into a fist and slammed into the wall a few feet from me, sending me jumping out of my skin as bits of plaster trickled down the inside of the wall, shook free from the lath. "*I sell my soul for you!*" he exploded, mere inches from my face, the veins in his neck turning purple. His eyes were wild; his pupils dancing. "I give everything for you! And what's the point of any of it? Not a damn thing!"

He looked like he could tear the door from its hinges whether I was standing there or not. My heartbeat thundered erratically in my burning ears as I struggled against the feeling that someone was pulling the laces of my corset tighter and tighter by the moment. I reached behind me, fumbling for the doorknob and pulling it open just far enough for me to slip through without turning my back on him.

I saw the tears spill down his cheeks just before I turned and ran down the hallway and out the front door, keeping my own inside until I was in the arms of the meadow and there was no one to see.

NINE

I didn't return to our bedroom that night and Henry didn't emerge from it. I sequestered myself on the front porch, clasping my hand to my mouth as the air rushed out of my lungs and my stomach turned itself inside out. The yard before me was a barren desert and it stretched out in every direction forever.

No.

My eyes stung with the tears I had shed and the new ones that I struggled in vain to hold inside, and my body shook with the effort.

This can't be happening.

I could hear the echoes of us eviscerating each other every time I closed my eyes.

How could he do this to us?

Daniel slipped onto the front porch with Hubie and lowered himself into the other rocking chair. At the rustled sound of his arrival I opened my bloodshot eyes and stared grimly down the oak-lined path in the waning light, wishing myself down the lane and anywhere else.

"Is there anything I can do? Annie?" he asked timidly, setting Hubie down on the dusty wooden floor as the boy began to squirm.

"Please don't speak," I begged him, my mind cloudy and still reeling. "I don't have any answers. I'm empty."

He nodded and we sat in silence as the sun set. Henry's words replayed in my head in an infinite loop. But even now I was no closer to understanding exactly what had happened. What secret deed had they paid him to do? It was the construction of a theater—what could there possibly be to hide? I recalled Daniel's story of Gretchen's death and shuddered. Surely it was nothing so atrocious. But the fact that he wouldn't divulge the details terrified me.

I was bewildered that he would betray his own moral code this way, and devastated that he could risk our family's future by running afoul of the law—surely, if there was a bribe involved, it wasn't something legal he had been asked to do. But part of me contemplated his true motives. Did he honestly believe that money would fix our marriage? That our problems could be pinned on anything or anyone outside of this house? How could he be so naive?

That was exactly the heart of the problem. He was a blind man fumbling in the dark, lost and grasping for answers beneath his confident exterior. But I had no sympathy for his turmoil. He had ceased listening a long time ago. Whether or not I stopped speaking was inconsequential.

In the back of my mind, however, buried beneath the anger and the confusion, hid a shiver of remorse at the look of broken despair I saw in his eyes when he pleaded, "What the hell do you want from me?" Was it possible I wasn't the only one who had my rough edges worn away by the intensity of sharing a life with another person? Had he been broken down, too?

Eventually I picked up Hubie to take him inside and prepare him for bed. Daniel stood as I did and opened the door for me. As I stepped past him he murmured, "I could sleep on the floor in Hubie's room, or the living room, if you need a place to sleep."

I sighed and brushed him fondly on the cheek. "Thank you...but no. I will sleep in Hubie's room. It won't be the first night I've spent in the rocking chair."

"It would be no trouble; I don't mind at all," he insisted, his eyes darting into the house as though Henry might come down the stairs at any moment. I knew he wouldn't.

"I'll be fine," I assured him.

He nodded, seeming more at ease knowing I was sleeping anywhere as long as it was alone.

I did accept the blanket he retrieved from the trunk in his bedroom, and the pillow he had wrapped in between the folds that I didn't see until I was already preparing my makeshift bed in the spindly rocking chair and it was too late to insist that he keep it for himself. I slept lightly, fitfully, for maybe thirty minutes at a time until a creak would rouse me or my lower back would spasm from my contorted position. The regular groaning of bedsprings from two different points in the house told me I wasn't the only one who was going to have a groggy morning.

About an hour before dawn I finally fell into an unbroken, exhausted sleep so deep the morning light didn't wake me. What did wake me was heavy footfalls in the hallway and down the stairs. Folding up my blanket, I tiptoed to the door and eased it open just far enough to peek my head into the hall. Our bedroom door was open; Daniel's was still closed. With Henry downstairs I crept quickly to my room, washed my face and arms in the basin, and changed into a clean dress.

I cooked a pot of oatmeal for breakfast. It was simple, took little more concentration than stirring, and made for a small amount of clean-up. I stirred and stared vacantly at the beadboard, trying to keep calm while envisioning all of us sitting at the table together. I tried to plan out the rest of the day's meals but it was hard to summon an appetite and the glue-like mixture in the pot didn't exactly help.

When the front door banged shut I jumped a foot.

"Breakfast is ready," I called, my voice cracking. I quickly plopped scoopfuls of oatmeal into three bowls and carried them to the dining room.

Henry and Daniel were sitting in their usual seats at the table, each sullenly nursing the coffee cups I had set out earlier. Daniel was blank-faced, blowing the steam from his drink and sipping minutely. Henry's eyes were red, his face blotchy, his hair combed but slightly mussed on the sides. His hands rested on the table, cradling his cup, but he made no move to drink. It struck me how drastically changed this scene was from the last time we had all sat together. It felt like years had passed.

I served their food and scurried upstairs to retrieve Hubie. When I returned they were both silently picking at their bowls, staring at the pasty mush and nowhere else. I felt somewhat relieved as I took my seat and began to feed Hubie. Tense silence I could handle. I was a professional at that. It was words that were dangerous.

When our bowls were empty I stood and picked up Henry's. Daniel handed me his, looking up as he did. "Thank you, it was very good," he said as I nested his bowl into the others.

"You need to leave," came a gravelly voice from the end of the table.

We turned to look at him. Henry's hands were folded under his chin, his lips set firmly, his eyes cast downward. He didn't move or look at either one of us.

"I beg your pardon?" Daniel shifted in his chair to face Henry, and I saw his hand clench.

"Your time here is at an end. Your presence has become a disruption. You need to leave."

It felt as though time slowed to a halt as all the air was sucked out of the room. No one moved. No one breathed.

"Henry," began Daniel at last, the shock plain on his face, "I don't—"

Henry stood and walked out of the room, cutting him off before he could say another word. He continued straight out the front door, letting it swing carelessly half-closed. Daniel and I stared at each other, mouths agape, frozen.

"No," I breathed, barely an exhale.

Daniel's eyes narrowed, glaring out the doorway after Henry. His carefully controlled, unassuming features hardened into stone as he kicked back his chair and stalked after him. I dropped the bowls back onto the table, took Hubie by the hand, and hurried into the kitchen.

The windows were open and I could see Henry heading for the barn as Daniel chased after him. "Henry!" he roared, quickly closing the gap between them. He grabbed him by the shoulder and Henry whirled, shaking him off and grabbing Daniel by the suspenders and a handful of his work shirt in return.

"I suggest you walk away," Henry muttered through clenched teeth, releasing him with a shove.

Daniel stepped right back up to him. "You're a real big man, kicking me out because you had a fight with your wife. Are you going to kick her out next? Throw away anyone who sees through you?"

"Oh, I'm sure you'd like that. Swoop in and be her knight in shining armor. Is that what this is? Showing her how tough you are? Hoping she'll see you as a real man and not the clueless child you are? Why don't you take a swing; I know she's watching. Go ahead, prove you're better than me. Hit me!" He jutted his chin in an open invitation.

For a moment it looked like he contemplated it. I saw his fingers twitch as I pleaded silently for him to not take the bait. His sense returned just in time, and he stepped back. "You're delusional," he said, shaking his head slowly.

"You'd like me to believe so. But you're not as clever as you think. You think I've never been where you are? That I don't know that *look* when you look at her? Oh, I know it." He turned and continued his march to the barn. "Pack your bags," he called back. "And make some arrangements quickly."

Daniel stood motionless as the fight drained from his limbs. He didn't move until Henry had pulled the horse out of the barn and gone flying down the lane, raising a cloud of dust that would take several minutes to settle. When it did, Daniel was gone.

I fought the urge to go to him. If he had wanted to talk he would have come back to the house, I reasoned. Perhaps he was as much at a loss for words as I was. Perhaps his anger felt as helpless as my own because Henry was not delusional and we knew it.

I couldn't say that I believed Henry would never force him out. He had been clear from the beginning that if the arrangement didn't succeed it would end, which I was in agreement with at the time. If he were calling for his immediate departure because Daniel had shared his suspicions with me I could—and would—fight him with every breath in my body. As it was, his reasons were valid, his own suspicions just as correct as Daniel's, and now they were at a stalemate I knew I wouldn't be able to break.

I was so tired of feeling helpless, anchored in the middle of a war without a weapon of any value or consequence. As the fighting pulverized what shreds of our life were left the frustration of impotence only served to slowly destroy the last of my will to piece it back together.

I slipped into a suit of denial that was becoming necessary for survival. I forced myself to continue on as though it were any normal day. I heated the irons on the stove and set about pressing yesterday's clean laundry. I recited words and phrases to Hubie and tried to coax him to speak. I sang to him and planned the next day's chores, telling myself that even though it felt like the world was ending it was not; that tomorrow the sun would rise on a new day whether I dreaded it or not; that Daniel's stay with us had only ever meant to be temporary and that if this was the time of our parting that I must handle it with strength and grace; that this wrenching feeling of my heart being ripped into pieces only strengthened the argument that he should go.

"Hubie, you look sleepy. Come here, let's put you down for a nap." I picked him up from the floor where he had been lazily swinging his stuffed puppy, much to his displeasure, and deposited him in his crib. "Mama's just going to check on Cousin Daniel," I told him, kissing him on the forehead as he began to whimper. I slipped out the door, closing it behind me, and let my feet carry me to the barn.

He was there, as he always was. It would have been startling to have found the place empty; he seemed a part of the landscape, a natural fixture, like the rough hewn beams that held the structure together. He was pitching loose straw into a pile next to the remaining bales to make room for more, his sleeves rolled high and his collar loosened. He didn't hear me enter from the back corner where he worked so I stood watching him by the empty stall, taking in the swing of his movements without the knowledge of my presence to alter him. He always insisted he was clumsy because he lacked proper skill in manual labor but his agility presented itself in his lithe movements and in the way he held himself. There was an awareness of his body and the space it possessed that reminded me of a dancer, and I was quite certain he was unaware of this about himself.

The air was dusty, thick, and hot, and tinged with the sweet and pungent strains of manure. I wanted to invite him to step outside for some fresh air, to take a walk and discuss what would happen next, but I didn't want to disturb him with unpleasant conversations. He was busy and distracted in that moment and I appreciated that. I wished I could take a photograph of him there so I could remember the simple moments of that summer forever—of his rolled up shirt sleeves and toiling in the familiar barn. Nothing more complicated than that. I watched him intently, committing every inch of the scene to memory.

When he turned and saw me there out of the corner of his eye he was visibly startled. "Good God, Annie! Are you trying to kill me?" he asked, clasping a hand to his heart. "Never sneak up on a man with a pitchfork."

"Sorry. I'll remember that for next time."

"If there is a next time." He jammed the pitchfork into the straw so it stood on its own.

I nudged a stray piece with my foot. "That's what I came to speak to you about."

He shook his head in resigned defeat, squinting as he looked away toward the open barn doors. "What is there to say? If he wants me gone I don't have much of a choice. I suppose I should be preparing some telegrams for him to send for me tomorrow."

I tried to rationalize that, regardless of current circumstances, his stay with us would only have extended another few weeks, but it didn't dull the sting of the reality of his sudden departure. The thought of losing his quiet confidences in the lonely hours of the afternoon now, in the midst of the storm, left a crippling isolation in its wake.

"Where will you go?"

"If I knew that I would have written them already," he said bitterly, looking down.

"I'll try to speak to him tonight, reason with him. I'll explain you don't have anywhere to go. I'll tell him he's mistaken about you." Try as I might I couldn't manage to inject my words with anything resembling hope.

"Don't make things worse for yourself. I don't want you embroiled in another fight because of me."

"I thought you said some things were worth fighting over."

"I thought you said nothing was."

A cautious grin lit both our faces. Inconceivable that this effortless banter used to offend me. Now it came like breathing.

I leaned back against the stall, reaching for some sort of consolation. "Well, at least you won't have to witness the aftermath of last night...or deal with Hubie's fits..."

He looked back at me incredulously. "Do you think there's even one thing about life here with you that I won't miss?"

"I'm just trying to make it easier—"

"Don't," he sighed. "It only makes it worse. You have such a grievous burden and all that concerns you is easing mine. It just reminds me how much..." He trailed off, turning his back and giving the pitchfork a half-hearted kick.

"Fine then. Forget your burden," I said cheekily, crossing my arms. "What about mine? When you're gone there will be one less mouth to feed."

He chuckled. "That there will be."

"And I'll have half as many work shirts to wash." I stepped forward and picked at the fabric on his shoulder, wanting to hear his laughter chase away the gloom that hung over us and feeling an irrational need to touch him and be assured he was still there before me, not yet a phantom.

"You'll be glad to be rid of me," he said, turning to face me again, with a grin that looked partially genuine. "Tell me you will."

"So glad." I felt my chest tighten as I continued to force a smile, tears pricking at the corners of my eyes. "You've been nothing but a nuisance since you arrived."

"That has been my objective, for as long as I've known you." He stepped closer, his eyes intense. "Tell me honestly," he whispered, so close I could feel his breath. "You never wanted me to come here, did you?"

"No." The humor slipped away as I stared into his eyes. "I knew you would cause nothing but trouble." The heat radiated from him, charged like static electricity before a storm. I could feel him against me even with inches between us.

"Then tell me you want me to go."

The words stuck in my throat. I was tired of lying for the comfort of the men around me. I wanted to cease the incessant questions and considerations that crowded my mind. I was lost. I *wanted* to be lost. Gloriously lost, as long as it was anywhere but here. At least that was mine. I wanted one thing that was only mine.

"Tell me to walk away from you." He tentatively slid his hands to my waist and pulled me against him.

"No." I wanted him closer. I wanted him tighter to my body than my clothing; deeper than my skin. Already there was not a breath of space between us and it wasn't close enough.

I felt his fingers trembling as they kneaded the light fabric of my dress into tiny, nervous pleats, and everything else dropped away. In the silence, there was only him. No logic or rationality—only a need sharper than pain that blocked out all else.

His breathing grew strained as his eyes locked with mine; darting, considering. His voice faltered as he tried to form words, his plea remaining unspoken as he suddenly surrendered with a helpless moan and brought his mouth to mine.

The night we danced in the field I had struggled to keep him at arm's length. Now, hidden away in the ramshackle barn, his lips the softest, most gently urgent thing I had ever felt, the weakness in every pore of my body told me I didn't even have the strength to brace myself for the fall.

His kiss sent tremulous waves rippling deep below my stomach. He tasted like sweat and sugar and pine tar soap. His hands crept up to cradle my neck, to caress my face, to tug at the collar of my dress.

My hands worked through the buttons of his shirt with swift ease. He had always seemed rather slight of build but as I freed him from his suspenders with his eager cooperation and slipped the rough fabric off his shoulders I was surprised by the hard, graceful curvature of his arms and chest. The labor of the past few months had left its mark on him.

His lips moved to my throat as he clawed and pulled at my dress, feeling for buttons. After a quick and unproductive search he gave up trying to remove my tight layers and instead worked around them, grasping lower around my thighs where the fabric flowed more freely.

We stumbled backwards toward the bales, collapsing onto the bed of straw with a puff of dust. The edges were scratchy against my neck and arms but I barely felt it as he ran his hands up my stockinged calves, bunching my skirt up around my knees. When I pulled him against me, fumbling for the button of his trousers, he buried his head against my neck and began to tremble, his breath coming in gasps.

Freed of just enough clothing I pulled his mouth back to mine and he hesitated no longer. "Oh, Annie..." he murmured against my lips, the fervor in his touch abating, as he cradled my face in his hands.

In my imagination the moment of capitulation had been reckless and frenzied, without space for words or considerations. But he was cautious, every move deliberate and gentle as though I might break under his fingertips. He took his time, capturing every moment so that for the rest of his life his imagination would be a perfect memory.

I wanted to stay in his arms for hours, to float away from place and time to something endless and greater than myself or him or us, but soon the moment was over and we were still where we began, entangled in the shadowy corner of the barn; still, silent, breathing.

With my head nestled against his chest he began to stroke my hair, his fingers barely grazing my loosely pinned strands. They drifted down to trace my jaw, my lips, with tender reverence. I could barely hear the birds outside over the low, steady drum of his heartbeat in my ear. I clung lightly to a blissful state of suspension, afraid if I concentrated too hard it would disappear.

"You're so beautiful," he whispered, resting his cheek against the top of my head.

The stifling heat and the occasional waft of warm air felt strange against my bare legs. I pulled at my skirt but he caught it, tucking it back up above my knees and exploring the childhood scars left there with his fingertips.

My drowse began to dissipate. I felt my heartrate slowly accelerate as memory of the outside world trickled in.

"I never could have imagined what it would feel like to touch you, to hold you. It's indescribable." He brushed away a loose tendril of hair that intruded my face.

"I'm no different than any other. You suffer from the delusion that I am unique."

He kissed my ear, tickling it as he whispered, "You are. With you, everything is different."

"Oh? How is that?"

"Because," he whispered. "I'm in love with you, Annie."

I flushed with uncomfortable warmth. "Pish," I said, bristling. "I'm not one of your girls on the town. Don't whisper your sweet nothings to me."

I felt him pull away slightly. "You think I'm insincere?" he asked.

I looked up at him, his eyes gleaming and expectant. "I want you to be," I murmured against his chest.

"I'm quite serious. I'm in love with you."

"Please, Daniel. Don't say things that will make no difference. You'll wish you hadn't once you've gone."

"How can I go?" He took my hand in his, placing kisses in my palm. "How can I ever leave you?"

I felt the last of the hazy afterglow that seemed to suspend time itself slip away, and the world expanded again, pulling me from the warm scent of his skin back to my place in the barn. The straw beneath me grew uncomfortable and a slow, prickling apprehension came over me.

I stood, stumbling on shaky legs, and began to pick pieces of straw from my dress and hair.

"Wait," he implored, standing and grabbing his shirt in case he had to chase after me. "Stay. Please."

"I have to go check on Hubie," I said, stepping away.

"No. Stop." He pulled his shirt on loosely and took my hands in his, looking into my eyes with resolute determination. "Let's leave here."

I rolled my eyes and tried to pull away but he refused to release me. "I can't do that."

"Yes, we can," he insisted. "I know you care for me. I don't want to be without you. Why couldn't we?"

"Because it's not that simple and you know it. I have a life here. A family."

"I know that! You think I don't know that?" he said, finally growing agitated and dropping my hands. "But you have choices. If you want out that's your decision to make. If you want to be with me you can. But this—" he swung his arms wide as if to indicate everything around us, "can't go on like this. If this is what you want you can't look back."

The fleeting fantasy had become reality, and now I forced myself to follow it through to its wrenching conclusion. I imagined looking Henry, the man I had loved since I was a child, in the eye and telling him our marriage was over. I imagined walking out the front door into the vast, terrifying unknown with the knowledge I would never step foot in our house again. I considered myself starting again with a new husband. *New*. Never in my life had I dreamed I would be that woman. A woman who failed at marriage. In our union, by Henry's side, I was part of something tangible. Regardless of how complicated things had become, I had a place; I had a role; I knew who I was. My loyalty had been ironclad, my morals unwavering. But now I was the woman I had never even considered, and I didn't recognize myself.

I slowly backed away from the stranger I saw reflected in his eyes.

"Don't do this, Annie. You always do this. Don't run away."

"I'm sorry," I whispered, wanting to curl up in his arms and flee the property in equal measure. "I just need to think."

"No, you don't," he said, beginning to button his shirt with a helpless look. "You've already decided this was a mistake."

I looked back when I reached the barn doors. He was already back to work, strewing our bed of straw with the pitchfork, with a newfound vehemence in his swings.

Back in the house I found Hubie sleeping. I stole the pitcher that was still mostly full of water from Daniel's room and took it to mine, locking the door behind me. I filled the basin with water and began to scrub my skin with a wet soapy washcloth anywhere I could reach without the confines of my dress—anywhere he had touched me. I rubbed until my skin was red. I scrubbed until it hurt.

I had wanted this; deep down, in the moments when I felt so alone and he was there, a beacon in the dark street. Buried so deep I could scarcely admit it to myself, I had wanted this. Now, the sharp lines of my memory cut through the soft delusion of my imagination, and raised a crescendoing panic in my veins.

What did I expect to happen? Did I truly think that breaking my marriage vows would somehow undo Henry's betrayal? That the score between us would be settled in my heart? I had accused him of not knowing me, but how could I have known myself so little as to think that I was capable of such duplicity with no conscience or remorse?

Henry.

I saw his face in my mind, felt his eyes watching me from the bedroom walls, and I scrubbed harder.

I loved him. I hated him. I wanted to hurt him for hurting me. I wanted him to pull me close, block out the world and all its troubles, and never let me go.

He wasn't an extraneous part of my life I could sever like a gangrenous limb. He was braided and interwoven through every aspect of my being. To tear him out would leave me in pieces as well.

In joining my life with his I had given him a part of my soul, and with it the ability to know me more intimately than anyone else. But with this ability came the power to cut me deeper and closer to the bone than any other person could ever reach. I don't believe he ever wielded the knife intentionally but I bled just the same, and I wondered now how many scars I had left on him in return, in my blind, angry thrashing, in defense and in pain.

When my vision of the washcloth blurred into agitated color and movement, I hurled it into the corner, sank to my knees, and began to pray.

In the late afternoon bands of steel gray storm clouds slowly swept across the clear sky, obscuring the crystal blue atmosphere in strips and allowing it to peek through in scattered holes, funneling golden rays of sunlight that made an eerie contrast against the darkening billows.

The clothes were pressed, the ones needing mending sorted out and piled for tomorrow's sewing, and the rest put away. A pot of cabbage soup was cooking on the stove. Hubie wandered the dining room, ducking and weaving between the chair legs and trying in vain to move them. I paced between the kitchen and the living room, occasionally darting to stir the pot or adjust the curtains or snatch a dust bunny, chewing on the chapped, rough slips of skin around my fingernails until they stung and bled. My boots clicked monotonously across the creaking wooden floorboards, keeping time with the clock as it ticked away the seconds until Henry came home from work.

I rehearsed my plea for leniency for Daniel in my head. I muttered it to myself aloud, repeating the phrases until the words didn't make me jumpy or weepy. "There is nothing inappropriate taking place in this house. He has never crossed that line. He is just young, perhaps innocently enamored. This is all a misunderstanding. He just needs some time to secure proper arrangements. We can't put him out on the street. I swear to you...honestly...there is nothing inappropriate taking place in this house..."

I didn't know if I could say it while looking him in the eye. I conjured up every hurtful and unsympathetic word he had ever spoken, every justification that shifted the blame for this situation back onto him, shuttering away the guilt and steeling myself as best I could. The minutes dragged by with agonizing sloth.

When I heard the horse outside I didn't flinch. I was ready.

I took Hubie upstairs to play in his room with his blocks, telling him to build me something very special and I would be back to look at it, and shut the door. I hurried downstairs to the kitchen and tended the soup, trying to slow my breathing and steady my hands and look as though nothing were amiss.

When minutes passed and there was still no sign of him emerging from the barn I began to panic. Daniel would have first access to him. I hadn't even considered this. Who could fathom what he would say? He was in an unpredictable state. I assumed they would avoid each other, but if they didn't, all bets were off.

Before I could work myself up to go up to the barn after him Henry emerged, alone, and marched slowly toward the house. I took a deep breath and stepped away from the stove, locking my gaze on the doorway.

He walked into the living room first, then peered into the dining room before finding me in the kitchen. The sight of him caught me off guard.

He looked haggard, even more so than he had that morning, his face ruddy as though he had been out in a cold winter's day. A shadow of a beard was beginning to show on his cheeks and his eyelids looked vaguely swollen. He stopped in the doorway, eyeing me levelly. "We need to talk," he said quietly, stuffing his hands in his pockets.

I nodded and he turned toward the living room. I followed him and took a seat in the armchair next to him, holding my breath.

"I spoke with Daniel," he began, leaning forward and crossing his arms on his knees. My mind raced ahead of him as my stomach dropped like a lead weight to the floor. *He knew.* The look on his face, the hesitance in his voice—he was beyond anger. He looked destroyed. Daniel had told him everything; I could feel it.

"Our arrangement was until mid-September and I will honor it. I know, as of yet, he has nowhere to go."

I stared at him in disbelief, quickly pulling myself out of my own thoughts to hear his words. There was no way I heard that properly.

"I won't compound my sins by putting my own family on the street," he continued, digging his fingernails into the corner of his elbow uncharacteristically. "My outburst was unwarranted, and I apologize to the both of you."

"Thank you," I whispered, too stunned to muster anything else.

He nodded stiffly, looking away toward the window. He sighed, stood and started toward the stairs, then turned on his heel, running his hands through his hair and shaking his head.

"I can't do this anymore," he announced, throwing his hands in the air. "This is..." He shook his head again and began to pace.

I had never seen him struggle for words that way before. My knees were locked and I remained frozen in the chair, mute.

"You're not my wife anymore! You're a woman who lives here and puts up with me. You used to love me, Annie! There was a time when I could have told you about the horrible shit that's gone on at the theater. But now I just know the more you know, the more you'll detest me. And that fire doesn't need fuel; you find enough on a daily basis without my trying."

I wanted to rebut him but no words came to me. I closed my eyes and struggled to retain a mask that would hide everything that was raw within me.

"Dammit, look at me!" he yelled, grasping my chin in his hand and then quickly releasing me when I did. "Say something. Don't just wait for me to walk away. Fight for this!"

"What do you want me to say?" I cried at last, rising to my feet. "You want me to scream things at you, to hurt you? For what? We don't get anywhere! You want me to tell you you're right? That I live here and I put up with you? Would that make anything better?"

"It's better than your damned silence! It's better than watching you give up on us. I still love you, Annie. And I sit here and watch you bestow your affection on *him*," he gestured angrily in the direction of the barn, "when you didn't even want him here, and it kills me. You think I'm not jealous when you smile at him? When you have your little late night talks on the porch? I want you for mine! I want you to look at me the way you used to. I want you to *want* my touch, not turn me away—"

"When do I turn you away? I always acquiesce! I never deny you."

"Yes, you *acquiesce*. You close your eyes and fulfill your duties. I *hate* that you do that. I'd rather you tell me outright that you don't want me than make me feel like I'm forcing myself on you just because I need you."

"Need me?" I laughed without humor. "You don't need me. Need me to bear you more children, perhaps. But you certainly don't desire me."

He stopped short, his mouth agape. "You think I don't desire you? How could you think that?"

"How could I not? Months would pass before you reached for me. The only reason we're intimate now is because you want more children. You said so yourself."

"No!" He shook his head insistently. "I don't care if we ever have more children. I only said that because I missed our intimacy and could think of no other way to resume it. I never stopped desiring you. I was desperate for you."

I blinked rapidly, taken aback. "How could that be? You withdrew from me completely."

"How many times do you think you can rebuff me before I stop trying?"

"I do not!" I hissed.

"You don't now, but you certainly did. For months you turned me away. And when you did allow me to touch you it was clear you didn't want it. I wasn't going to continue to abase myself forever, so I left you alone."

My mind spun as I struggled to view my memories of that time through the lens of his comprehension. It was true, after Hubie's birth, I had pushed him away. Recovering from a difficult birth, struggling to adjust to a child who cried all night and all day, physical intimacy was hardly feasible. I thought he had understood that; surely he could see how I was struggling. Surely he hadn't taken it personally. "Well, I didn't expect you to stop trying completely," I countered.

"So you can reject me with no explanation for months and I am at fault for refusing to endure it?"

"I'm sorry," I murmured, looking past him at the wallpaper. "After the birth I was lost in my own skin; I had nothing left to give you. I was frightened and hurting. I didn't want you then but I didn't want you to give up. I thought you lost interest in me. It only made things worse."

He studied me, his breath slowing as his heart rate came back down. "Why didn't you tell me that? I would have understood that." The anger was gone from his voice now, replaced with a tired frustration.

I shook my head and turned away. "I couldn't, I just...I can't explain."

"Try."

I sank back into the armchair. Explaining my state of mind since Hubie's birth was still a complicated knot I didn't know how to begin to untie. "It had nothing to do with you. I needed you." I looked up at him reluctantly. "I'm sorry if I hurt you then."

He took his seat as well, his face softening with concern. "Why didn't you come to me?"

"It's not that simple. We were exhausted. And fighting constantly."

"It was a difficult time, a very hard adjustment," he admitted. "I kept waiting for you to stand by me, to fight through it together instead of fighting each other, but that's all we could seem to do."

"How could I? I felt like we were miles apart. I felt alone."

"You're only alone if you withdraw from me."

His deflection of blame inflamed and emboldened me. "You're not exactly easy to confide in. You're impatient. You're quick to temper. You can be impossibly frustrating."

"You're right, I am. But you know me. You know how to handle my faults, just as I do yours. We've always been honest with each other. What has changed?"

I bit my lip. I let the silence sit between us and he didn't chase it away.

"I'm not the only one who stopped confiding," I said at last.

He bristled. "No," he admitted, beginning to fidget again. "You're not."

"So tell me." There was no more avoiding last night's conversation. It was inevitable. "What did Mayfield pay you for?" I steeled myself for whatever would come.

"We've been through this already."

"No. We screamed at each other last night, accusations and vague admissions. We need to talk about exactly what happened, and why. I don't understand, and I need to."

"Very well." He sat back in the chair, fixating on the mantle before he began to speak. "We couldn't get everything done in time. The construction schedule was so tight, and we had difficulties with some of the vendors. Some of the current theater construction doesn't meet code requirements. So we...we paid the township inspector to overlook a few things so that we could procure the occupancy permit on time."

I swallowed the lump in my throat with great difficulty. "We?"

His gaze dropped infinitesimally. "I," he clarified quietly.

A tiny spasm of relief shot through me at the lack of violence or bloodshed in his story, but it was short lived. His sin was a flagrant insubordination of the law and a compromise of his very character, with potentially life-altering consequences for us all were he to be caught. This was no minor offence.

"It wasn't how I wanted to proceed. I did everything I could but there was no earthly way we could reach completion with all the setbacks we encountered and the sheer amount of work there was to be done. There was never enough time but the owner wouldn't hear of it. He offered a bonus if we finished early or even on time. And if we finished late...there would be damages to pay. Of course my boss wasn't willing to suffer that. He gave me an ultimatum — complete this project on time or the damages to be paid would be gotten from the salary he was no longer paying me. And in the middle of all of that there was Jonathan Mayfield himself...offering me a way out.

"I know it wasn't right. But when faced with losing my job, failing in this project, failing you...when he offered me a quiet bonus 'in good faith for the work I would complete' and intimated that money could fix a number of problems if I knew what to do with it...he didn't have to say the words for me to know what he meant. He assured me he had no qualms about seeing the necessary work completed after the opening but that the theater needed to earn its keep immediately and he would not be dissuaded. I tried to find another way but in the end...I took his money. I bought the permit. I achieved my goal." His tone was bitter and rife with self-reproach.

"What do you mean, when faced with failing me? Are you saying this is my fault?"

"No. Of course not. I'm sorry I said differently last night—it was deplorable of me to ever insinuate you had a role in this, and I don't expect you to forgive me. But if I failed at this, how could I not fail you? I owe you a stable, comfortable life. You deserve that and more. If I can't give that to you…I'm nothing."

"That's ridiculous."

"That's how I see it."

I sighed. I knew no words would change that. His pride was so vulnerable, so easily wounded, underneath his sure demeanor. Daniel had been right in a way. Everything Henry did was directly influenced by his desire to protect his pride, but that pride was tied inexorably to the reflection of himself he saw in my eyes. It was the only image of himself he was capable of seeing.

"But you didn't give all the money to the inspector," I concluded.

"Most…but I did keep some."

"For my gift." The word tasted sour on my tongue.

"I wanted you to see what was to come. To give you a promise of what our life could be; what I would make it." The determination in his sentiment sounded hollow and deflated.

"I never asked for that," I insisted.

"You never ask for anything. You're not that kind of woman. That's what makes me want to give you everything."

I shook my head. I could see us going around and around and never gaining traction.

"How could you ever seek to win my favor by sacrificing yourself?" I asked him, offended. "Do you honestly think the cost of your integrity could ever bring about my happiness?"

"I was willing to keep it buried to protect you. If you never knew the whole truth it could never hurt you."

No, I hissed to myself as I felt my anger waver. *It's not the same. It's not.*

"I don't want you to lie to me," I told him.

"I was not willing to lose you," he said simply. "But that seems inevitable, so I'll take the risk of truth. I don't want to lie to you anymore, either."

He turned his thick, worn hands over and around themselves, twining his fingers and picking at his uneven fingernails. He pressed his lips and squeezed his eyes shut, his cheeks growing redder until he exhaled slowly and looked over at me with lost, pleading eyes.

"I never thought I would be this person," he whispered. I blinked away as I recalled having the exact same thought not long ago.

The confident façade he had expertly donned was transparent now as he struggled to confess. I could see, at last, the moments I had not comprehended before; the diminutive hesitations and indiscernible, fleeting expressions that were so easily discarded amongst his boastful prattling. He rambled to talk through the situation in disguise. He dissected and obsessed to convince us as well as himself that everything was fine.

I couldn't hate him, as much the incredulous anger swirling inside me begged me to. He was not heartless and he was not greedy. There was no maliciousness to be found in his actions. He had erred catastrophically and he knew it. One momentary slip in judgment; one weakness in seduction. One moment to acquiesce was all it took for a regret you could never eradicate to spring forth. I was the last person worthy to sit in judgement upon him.

As I contemplated the inexplicable temptation he had succumbed to at the manipulative fingers of Jonathan Mayfield I recalled with horror that the chain didn't end with him and Daniel. "And now my brother is working for those people," I gasped.

"I never intended that," he assured me. "I tried to secure him a job with Tierney & Sons, learning the ropes of construction until the end of the summer. When Mayfield offered him the projectionist job I was as shocked as anyone. I'm as conflicted about it as you are. I don't want him falling prey to those people but in a couple years when he has some experience he can seek a job elsewhere. He won't be tied down to them. And what could they really do to him in his position?"

My eyes narrowed without my intention. "If you had misgivings you hid them well. You sold it like an expert the day you brought him home."

"I had to. The wheels were already in motion and he was so excited. I convinced myself that the benefits outweighed the risks. And I thought it would please you."

"It doesn't. Now I simply worry for the both of you."

"And so I fail again." He gestured helplessly, smiling with no trace of humor. In his face I saw no fight left—there was only sadness and a desperate, exhausted surrender. I couldn't fire one more round at him. I knew, in some way, the battle was over, but that neither of us had won.

"I'm...sorry, Annie. I am so sorry. My mistakes are egregious and I don't deserve your forgiveness. I've failed at every attempt I've made to place your happiness above my own. I've broken things I cannot fix. I would sacrifice anything for you and I will do whatever it takes now but I have to know, after everything you know, everything I've done—do I still have a family to save?"

I turned away in my chair, my legs trembling beneath my skirt. I could feel Daniel's hands in my hair, his breath on my neck, and I shuddered. How could I answer him? We had each taken a pickaxe to the very foundation of our structure. How could we possibly hope to rebuild?

I stood and made my way to the mantle, my eyes falling on a small gold and leather-bound folding picture case, propped open on display. It was an ambrotype photo of Hubie a few months after his birth that my parents had taken for us. I traced my finger gingerly over the oval edge. He was crying in the picture, his face slightly blurred from the movement. Even my parents had failed to soothe him that day.

"Annie?"

"I miss you," I said, my voice tremulous.

He rose and came to stand behind me, his hand resting on my shoulder, watching as I thoughtfully thumbed the portrait.

"I tell myself I don't but I do," I whispered, struggling to hold myself together. "I tell myself I don't care so it won't hurt when you're not here, or when we argue, but it's not true. I can't stop wondering how we fell apart." Tears began to slide errantly down my cheek and he squeezed my shoulder, bowing his head against mine. "I want to want you *now*, I can't spend my life chasing ghosts anymore. I can't do it. You're not the only one who's failed; I have too, in so many ways. So many ways."

He wrapped his broad arms around me, spinning me to face him, and I forced myself to look into his eyes, into the tears brimming there, into the sweet, familiar face I had known my entire life. My first love. My first cold taste of reality. My first tenuous hope for happiness after the child had grown and put away fairy tales as frivolous myths.

"I'm so lonely," I sobbed. "I miss you so much I can't breathe! You were this mysterious world to discover. There weren't enough seconds in the day to take you in. How did we lose that? How did you become just another fixture in this damned house?"

He held me tight against his chest. "I don't know what I'm doing here, in this marriage, anymore. It just became easier to be gone—to throw myself into work."

"So you run? Just like you scold me for doing?"

"I know I'm no better," he whispered against my hair. "I didn't think you wanted my presence."

"There were times when I didn't," I admitted, my face buried in his shirt. "But I needed it."

He exhaled slowly, his arms tightening around me. "Do you still?"

I looked up at him through my wet lashes. "I do," I said. "I still love you, Henry."

He brushed my hair away and pressed his lips roughly to my forehead, kissing me twice with my face in his hands. "There is no fissure we cannot mend, no wound we cannot heal," he said resolutely. "I promised you my life. In joy and in strife. We have much to discuss still. But we will see this through."

Charlatan, sneered a vicious voice in my head. *Playing the virtuous wife with the scent of another man still on your lips. Why do you deserve his contrition? And what will it change? Your impasse remains and he isn't even aware of it. Until you confess your sins you can have no hope of changing your path.*

Go ahead. Tell him you don't want his child. Tell him you're not fit to be a mother. Tell him you were happier when you weren't. See how long his compassion lasts.

I clasped his hands in mine, nodding and smiling, suddenly terrified inside. I wiped at my tears and fanned myself. "I need some air," I explained, side-stepping towards the door.

"Go ahead," he said, the hardened lines in his forehead relaxing. "I'm going to go wash up for dinner."

I stepped outside and fairly ran down the lane, to the overreaching protective cover of the ancient oak trees. I leaned against the rough bark and tried to catch my breath under the fluttering canopy that was growing restless with the sharp breeze of the coming storm.

What have I done?

The last few hours whirled through my mind as I stood paralyzed, desperate to reverse them. If there was any chance to mend this, it would take equal effort, and an accounting of my shortcomings as well as his own. There was no way around this; there was only a dangerous and intimidating path straight through. One I knew I wasn't strong enough to tread.

I must get out of here.

I needed time to collect my thoughts. A few hours to contemplate which of my confessions might be forgiven, and which would destroy him and must be buried forever. The naked truth would do nothing to fix this. I needed time to wrap it carefully in prettier dressings.

The theater.

It was the only excuse I could think of to get away. I could tell Henry I was concerned about Nathan and wanted to see him and wish him luck on his first day of work. I could tell him Daniel wanted to take me there as a celebration of my birthday. I longed to escape from both of them, but there was no way I could attend the theater unescorted and, the hour being late as it was, my options were severely limited. It was far from perfect, but I was desperate. I would make it work. I had to.

After a silent and civil dinner Daniel took Hubie into the living room and Henry, after remaining at the table in contemplation, followed me into the kitchen as I began to wash the dishes. Before he could speak I struck first.

"Daniel would like to take me to opening night at the Walt," I announced, raising my voice just loud enough so that Daniel would hear me in the other room. I had not informed him of my plans so this was news to him as well.

"Would he?" He tried to hide it but I saw his jaw tighten.

"Yes. As a present for my birthday. And I should like to go." I continued scrubbing the dishes with my tattered washcloth.

"Annie." He dropped his voice, looking a bit taken aback. "I don't think that's the best idea."

My stomach twisted but I remained calm. "Surely there's no harm in it," I continued innocently.

"After what we discussed…" he whispered, eyeing me meaningfully.

I reached for the one weapon I possessed. "Yes, after what we discussed about my brother…I'm nervous for him. I need to lay eyes on him. Please."

Conflict struggled in his eyes for a long moment. "Fine," he said at last. "But I will take you."

"No!" I insisted. "I—I don't want to leave Hubie here with Daniel unattended. I'd rather he stay with you."

"He's perfectly capable of caring for him. He's good with him. And I'd rather he not accompany you."

I wracked my brain for another excuse. He watched me with suspicious disbelief.

"We obviously have much more to discuss," he said carefully. "This would be a good opportunity for us to be alone, get out of this house for a bit and talk."

"I can't," I said, unable to come up with anything except the truth. "Henry, I need some time…away from you…to collect myself."

"No, you don't, you just—"

"*Yes*, I do. I can't think, I'm such a mess. I need space to breathe. To consider some things."

"You want to go talk yourself into saying what I want to hear. I want you to speak from the heart, to be honest—"

"I swear we will speak, Henry," I promised. "I swear it, but not now. Please. Not right now. Just let me get away for a little while. I can't do this right now but I promise you I will, just…give me a moment to hear what's in my own heart and consider it before I speak it to you."

He sighed reluctantly, pacing to the window and back as he considered it. I held my breath as I watched him, my hands motionless in the soapy water. After a long moment he placed his hands on my shoulders. "When you return—"

"We will discuss these matters at length," I vowed. I would have promised him the moon to take leave of that house in that moment.

He placed a soft kiss on my cheek, brushing his thumb gently across my chin. "If you must," he conceded in a whisper, looking down as he stepped away.

"Thank you," I sighed, concentrating again on the dishes so I wouldn't have to see him wrestle with his jealousy as he swallowed his pride and went out to tell Daniel to go get ready for the theater.

I took Hubie upstairs and changed him into his nightclothes early so Henry would not have to do it. He babbled as I did, not resisting or fussing. As I finished pulling his arms through the white cotton gown and was about to pick him up he suddenly pulled away, pointing his chubby finger at me.

"What?" I asked with mock enthusiasm.

He stared at me with such concentration it unnerved me. "Mama," he declared plainly.

Usually his words were slurred and unintelligible as a drunken fool's but this one rang clear as a bell. It startled me.

"Yes?" I asked, almost expecting him to follow it with a full, well-contemplated sentence.

He smiled, and for a moment he wasn't a baby. He was a tiny human being. Subtle, the difference, but a revelation just the same.

"Mama," he repeated joyfully, reaching up to touch my cheek.

I wondered how different motherhood would be when he was grown enough to express his needs and desires plainly and patiently like any other member of the family. When he was old enough to leave me for the day and attend school. When I would be expected, in the normal course of his childhood, to loosen the apron strings and begin the gradual, protracted separation between us that would allow him to grow into a self-sufficient and functional adult. When he would need guidance but not directive; care but not coddling.

Most mothers mourn that transition. But I could not summon any apprehension at the thought. Things would be so very different, surely. *Perhaps*, a tiny optimistic notion whispered in my ear, *things might get easier*. Perhaps it would be in his maturation rather than his infanthood that I would find my joy.

After the whirlwind of the past twenty-four hours I could believe almost anything possible. So I indulged the fantasy. I shuttered away my pessimistic tendencies for a moment and let myself imagine that happiness was a thing that could still be salvaged, somewhere in the coming years, with patience and effort and a stubborn grasp on hope.

My lips twitched into a smile, tiny at first, growing as he explored the contour of my chin with his little finger. I took it in my hand and placed a kiss there.

"I do love you," I whispered into his miniature palm. "Always know, beyond my failings, that I love you."

I hugged him close as I carried him back downstairs and set him to stumbling around the living room under Henry's watchful eye. Then I retired to my room to fix my hair and freshen up. I noticed the blue silk hat lying in the corner on the floor, partially hidden by the dresser, and sighed as I pulled on my old scarlet bonnet. I would certainly turn heads in that beauty, but I simply couldn't wear it.

Daniel stalled in his room until he heard me descend the stairs. Then he slipped out to the barn without a word.

I stood in the doorway to the living room watching Henry toss Hubie's stuffed dog across the room and Hubie clamor after it like an obedient puppy.

"What do you know," he said, bemused. "He fetches."

I chuckled, shaking my head.

He tossed the dog once more and stood before me. Reaching into his pocket, he pulled out a wad of cotton and pressed it into my hand. "I want you to have this tonight. You look tired."

My throat tightened as I thumbed the material. I couldn't recall the last time Henry had tended to his son's cries in the night. It was plain that after a year of sleepless nights he wasn't just volunteering to take the brunt for an evening while I slumbered. He was trying to tell me he understood.

"Enjoy your evening tonight."

"Thank you," I breathed, thinking a hundred reasons after it that did not need to be specified.

He took my face in his hands and kissed me softly, his tongue dancing lightly across my lips. It was not hurried. It was not desperate. It was sweet and it was slow and it was hopeful.

I blinked back the tears as he released me and fled without looking back into the waning evening.

TEN

"It looks like it may rain."

"Hmm?" I didn't remember climbing into the buggy or the horse toting us rhythmically down the lane but suddenly I was sitting beside Daniel in his rarely worn gray suit on the road to town and my reverie slipped away as if it were tethered to the house and I had just surpassed its boundaries.

"It's getting dark up ahead. It looks like there may be a storm."

The piecemeal clouds that cluttered the sky earlier were becoming more prevalent, funneling the diminishing sunlight into smaller, brighter channels of golden amber against blue-black. The snatches of pastel sky that remained grew paler.

"It may blow over yet. It still looks clear over that way." I pointed to a break in the clouds toward the right.

"I'd rather it rain. It might wash away some of this mugginess."

"It might." I picked at my fingernails and felt for rough edges.

He reached over and took my hand in his, twining our fingers and resting our hands on the seat in between us. I felt the phantom of his fingers fidgeting against my waist, gathering my skirt in handfuls, and a shiver went through me.

"Are you all right?" he asked.

I didn't know the answer to that question so I did not respond, instead withdrawing my hand from his grasp and turning my head to watch the grassy fields pass slowly by.

"You didn't tell him," he surmised.

"You thought I would?"

"I wondered how far your conscience would take you."

"I don't know what to do yet. That's why I needed to get away."

He hesitated. "Then what did you tell him?"

"What else is there to tell?"

He squeezed the reins tightly in his hands. "I suppose if you cannot think of anything else of consequence, then there is nothing."

He had been hoping I had at least told Henry I was in love with him, if I hadn't admitted our affair. I cringed, turning toward him. "Daniel…"

"I love you, Annie. I know I don't deserve you and I have nothing to offer. It's foolish to even think you could love me but you do feel something for me; I know that. And I cannot walk away from you if that is true."

"I know." It felt unbearably cruel to not return the sentiment but he was exactly right. He loved me and had nothing to offer in the way of a home or future or any feasible prospects. I felt *something* for him and that was enough to make him persist.

"You're not going to leave him, are you?" He said it with a resignation that told me he already knew the answer.

"Suppose I did. First off, what of Hubie? I could hardly leave him behind for Henry to raise alone. Are you prepared to raise your cousin's child? How would I explain to him why his father is not in his life? Do you think my parents would ever speak to me again if I disgraced them with a divorce? They would be cut out of my life and Hubie would lose his grandparents as well. So now the three of us are out on our own with no money, no employment, and no home. To whom shall we go for help? Who in our lives would be sympathetic to our cause? I can think of no one.

"And that's not even considering Henry himself. If I left it would destroy him. Do you think the guilt of leaving him to spend the rest of his life alone wouldn't follow me the rest of my days? That looking at his child day in and day out wouldn't poison what you and I attempted to grow between us?

"You love who I am; who this life has made me. Good or bad, this marriage has shaped every part of me, and if I became your wife I would become someone else in the process. And it would be the death of us."

He sighed, squinting against the bright contrast of the setting sun. "That doesn't change what I want," he said petulantly.

"It will, eventually, once it's too late."

The clouds grew even darker as we neared town. Simple red brick cape cods and narrow, stretching Victorians with wrap-around porches and tiny grass patches for yards became more prevalent as the fields ended and we rounded the curve where the sidewalks began.

"You still love him."

"I do," I admitted, not making eye contact.

"And you believe there is hope to mend things yet."

I hesitated. "I don't know."

"You do. Whether you say it or not, you do. And if there's even a chance you won't walk away."

"And that is the very reason you respect me at all."

He quickened the horse with a tap, his gaze locked on the road ahead.

The cobblestone streets were clogged with activity inside the town limits. Pedestrians stepped out everywhere, forcing carriages and automobiles to stop suddenly and allow them to cross. Mothers ushered their children onto the sidewalk as they skipped ahead with haste. A good deal of foot traffic was headed toward the far end of town, toward the Walt Theater.

We drove past Yuler's Cigar Factory, on the corner of the main intersection in town with its distinctive wrap-around porch overhang that covered the entire sidewalk, turned off the bustling road and took the side streets to a lot where we could park in the block across the street from the theater, tucked away behind the row of wooden storefronts and painted brick homes on Main Street. It was filling up quickly. We found a spot at the far back of the lot and he jumped down to hitch the horse. When he came around and helped me out of the cab I held his hand fast.

"You know I care about you deeply, Daniel. Tell me you know that."

"I know it," he said with a slight jut of his chin.

"And I'm sorry I—"

He pressed his finger to my lips. "Stop apologizing. I knew there would be no easy end to this the day I arrived on your doorstep. I still wouldn't change a thing. If I live to be a hundred and never touch you again I still won't regret one second of this summer with you."

My resolve wavered at his sweet and unflinching steadfastness; my emotions a violent pendulum. He coaxed my arm around his elbow, linking our arms decorously, so that my hand rested on his forearm. "Let's not be late. I assume you want to see Nathan before the show starts."

I nodded and we trekked across the weedy gravel lot, falling into step with strangers and neighbors alike, their voices rising and falling with curiosity and unbridled excitement as we all converged to get our first glimpse of the Walt Theater.

Funneled through the narrow walkway between Primrose Bakery and Grayson's Hat Boutique, we spilled out onto the sidewalk and stood in the shadow of the hulking, newborn architectural creation.

It rose three stories from its white smooth stucco foundation, dressed in multi-tonal russet brick, on the wide corner lot that had formerly housed the decrepit planing mill. Three arched French casement windows were centered above an awning lined with gas-lit swirled orbs, directly below which were three matching sets of double doors with beveled glass transoms above each. Above the casements, on the third floor, were three squat rectangle windows, perfectly symmetrical, with brick columns separating them that began at the foundation and supported the stucco frieze near the top of the building that boldly announced the words "WALT THEATER" flanked by Roman swirls and filigree. The outer two thirds of the building were recessed a few inches on each side, making the grand center entranceway even more prominent and giving the building an imposing silhouette as the flicker of the gas lamps began to glow brighter against the storm-hurried sunset.

I pulled at Daniel's arm and we stepped back from the crowd against the storefront, out of the way of patrons hurrying to continue across the street. I pressed my back against the window and lingered for a moment to take it all in.

In its façade I could see so much more than clay and mortar. I saw the evenings stolen from me before Daniel arrived, when I sat on the front porch alone and waited until dusk and sometimes beyond for Henry to come home. I saw Henry's shame as he stared silently at the ceiling night after sleepless night. I saw the blind faith and hope of my brother as he studied his books and itched to learn his new trade. I saw the pain of the momentary decision that changed Daniel's life and sent his path careening toward mine. I stood there on the street that night, stinging and reeling from the force of our collision, coin in hand ready to drop into Jonathan Mayfield's filthy, gaping purse.

I could hear Gretchen's blood pumping through the veins in its walls, giving it life and vital breath.

We stared each other down. I smirked because I knew the secrets hidden beneath its hard, calculated beauty. It laughed at me because in spite of this I had still ended up here with nowhere else to go.

The bell tower of St. John's Lutheran Church, stretching tall against the hills that buffered the town, tolled the time of eight-thirty. The show would be starting soon and I still wanted to see Nathan. One of the few men in my life who was obligated to love me in an unchanging, uncomplicated way.

"Ready?" asked Daniel.

I took a deep breath. "Yes," I said, stepping forward. "I'm ready."

We crossed the street with the next wave of patrons and followed them through the doors, each held open by tuxedoed ushers, across the threshold and into the vestibule to wait in line at the ticket booth, which still smelled of fresh paint and varnish.

After we had our tickets in hand we entered the lobby and a congenial, portly, balding man with a pink carnation in his lapel tore our tickets in two and granted us admission. Before us a single set of thick mahogany double doors stood open leading into the main level of the theater. We stepped out of the flow of traffic streaming into the auditorium and hovered against the wall, trying to figure out where to go.

"He must be upstairs," Daniel rationalized. "So let's start there."

There were two winding staircases, one on each side of the lobby. We took the one on the right, closest to us, and found ourselves in another lobby, this one narrow and more sparsely populated. Cream walls were sectioned into square and rectangle panels with gold painted wood trim, and these panels were covered with pale green fabric damask wallpaper. At each end of the long lobby was a double-hung window covered with heavy drapery. The arched windows that were visible from the street were situated between the staircases and I could see now they were taller than they had seemed from below. They stretched approximately six feet tall, more like doors than windows, and opened not onto a balcony but individual iron railings that allowed maybe six inches of outdoor space. They looked beautiful but seemed rather impractical.

Across from these windows were four doors. The two in the center were identified with black and white porcelain signs as a men's and women's lavatory. The two doors on the ends were recessed, at the end of matching ten foot hallways and were not labeled, but the occasional passing of people told us they were both entrances to the theater balcony.

"So where is the projection room?" I wondered aloud even though I knew Daniel had no better answer than I, growing anxious as the time grew late.

"Let's enter the theater and perhaps we'll see another door," he suggested. We picked the left hallway at random and by luck we saw that just before the door, on the right-hand side of the hallway so that it was not noticeable from our previous angle, was another door, again unsigned.

It was immediately obvious we were heading in the right direction as we opened the door and were faced with a steep set of plain, unfinished wood steps, more like an attic entrance than the grand staircases that graced the lobby. The walls were rough, exposed wooden lath. I gripped the railing and tried to keep my fingers from brushing the wall for fear of splinters.

"Looks like they ran out of plaster," commented Daniel, glancing back at me.

"More like time," I said, actually preferring the smell of the wood to the artificial and somewhat chemical new construction smell that lingered everywhere else.

"Is someone there?" a familiar voice called from somewhere above us.

"Nathan?"

"Annie?" He appeared at the top of the stairs just as we reached the landing, grinning widely. "What are you doing here?"

"We came to see your big debut!" I explained, melting into his hug and never wanting to let go.

"Thank you! I can't believe you're here. Where's Henry?"

Daniel and I exchanged subtle sideways glances.

"At home with Hubie," he volunteered, looking more at me than Nathan. "I wanted to take Annie out to celebrate her recent birthday."

"Oh, well, tell him 'hello' for me, then. Hubie, too."

"I will," I assured him, finding my voice again. "Are Mother and Father here?"

"No, Mother was ill with a headache. They might come over the weekend. You want to see the projection room?"

"Certainly," said Daniel, and we followed him into a tiny room a few steps away. The walls were unfinished here as well, and Nathan identified the tight clutter as a hand-cranked, single-reel projector; a wicker basket on the floor to catch the film as it dropped; a rewinder on a side table in the corner to spin the film back onto the reel; a spotlight; an exposed toilet and sink in the back corner; and a single small stool by the projector.

"Not much room to move around in," I observed, trying not to touch any of the equipment.

"No, it's tight," he agreed. "And hot. Just wait until the limelight in the projector is lit. I'll be sweating a few pounds off cranking that thing." He gestured toward a jug of water on the table by the rewinder. "That's a necessity."

I noticed something small and brown lying next to the jug and stepped closer to investigate. He looked sheepish as I picked it up and shot him a dirty look. I held the half-spent cigar in the air questioningly.

"Fine, I stole it from Father," he confessed, his hands in his pockets. "It's just for a little celebration after. There's no harm in it."

I shook my head and replaced it on the table. "He'll kill you if he finds you taking his good cigars," I warned.

"That's why I didn't take a new one. He'll just think he misplaced that one. Aw, come on, I'll sneak it back after tonight. I just wanted to try it, for fun."

He wasn't the first of my brothers to be tempted by my father's stash. He wouldn't be the first to be caught, either. The very idea he could outwit him amused me.

"So where is the projectionist?" I asked, glancing around. "It's almost show time."

Nathan laughed nervously. "Uh...you're looking at him."

My head snapped back to him. "I thought you said you'd be working with someone until you got the hang of it? You're not supposed to be on your own yet."

"I have had some training. I'll be fine."

"No, it's not fine. They promised you proper training. If you are to succeed it's not fair to send you in here unprepared."

"Annie, really, I'll be fine," he assured me with measured patience. "I've run a few reels already. You're sounding like Mother."

I bit my tongue then and tried to smile even though my heart was suddenly racing. "I'm sorry, dear. You know how I worry."

"Not you!" he exclaimed sarcastically.

I'm certain Daniel would have laughed if he hadn't grown as protective of my brother as I was.

"Just...stand your ground, Nathan. I know you're young and you want to make a good impression, but don't let anyone push you into doing something you're not comfortable with, because you'll be the one who must live with it."

He rolled his eyes. "It's just a film."

"It's not just in this, I mean—"

"Seriously, you worry so—"

"Nathan Bauman, you heed me!" I snapped, silencing him. He stared at me, taken aback. Daniel touched his hand lightly to my shoulder, warning me. I sighed and began again.

"I just want you to know it can be uglier out there than you realize. People will take advantage of your youth, your inexperience, your willingness to please. Don't let them. No one is worth compromising yourself for. I'm not just talking about running the reels tonight. You're entering the working world and it's not going to shelter you like Mother and Father, and I can't shelter you, either. I just want to know you're going out there with your eyes open."

He nodded, somewhat bewildered but understanding. "I am. I promise. I still think you worry too much, though," he said with an unassuming grin.

I remembered my mother's words about learning only happening the hard way and prayed fervently that she was wrong.

"We should find our seats," Daniel said, edging toward the stairs.

"Yes. We don't want to hold up the show by distracting the projectionist." I almost choked on the word.

"You should sit in the balcony," Nathan suggested. "You'll be closer that way. Then after the show we can meet in the upstairs lobby."

"That sounds like a fine idea. We'll do that." I hugged him close one last time. "Good luck. I mean, not that you need luck. You'll do fine. You'll—love you."

We descended the stairs and slipped into the auditorium, finding an open pair of seats on the right side by the brass railing at the front of the almost full balcony. Large panels of the same mint-colored fabric wallpaper as in the lobby covered the walls. An arched box seat flanked each side of the stage, each adorned with a relief painted with creatures from Greek mythology and Corinthian columns on each side. A narrow wooden panel decorated with maroon swags and tassels crowned the stage and connected it to the box seats, and above this soared the most elaborately decorated ceiling I had ever seen. Painted geometric borders encircled an intricate floral-and-vine-patterned fabric which surrounded a large gold and sky blue plaster medallion in the center, from which hung a teardrop crystal gaslight chandelier. I couldn't take my eyes off it.

A thick red velvet stage curtain kept the screen hidden from view. On the left-hand side of the stage was a pedestal with a large vase of cream roses, pink daisies, yellow lilies, and sprigs of fern. To the right was an upright piano at which a man sat playing prelude music.

I scanned the crowd below for familiar faces. Both Emma's and Robert's parents were in attendance, seated three rows apart and fairly close to the stage. Plenty of our fellow parishioners from church were there as well, both below and up in the balcony with us, but none I would go out of my way to greet. The number of people I would seek out for a conversation was few. I exchanged suspenseful grins with Daniel and kept to myself.

The music came to an end and I heard a low, sharp, two-note whistle. I turned in my seat, as did a few other people. Nathan was peering out of the hole in the wall in front of the projector, wiggling his fingers at me. I chuckled and waved back. He disappeared and a moment later the lights slowly dimmed. The raucous din hushed to a whisper as the curtains sashayed to the sides of the stage, unveiling a white screen.

The pianist began again and a title card flashed on screen, right on cue.

Rescued by Rover

A baby sits next to a faithful Collie, both the picture of contentment. The child is taken for a stroller ride by the nanny and subsequently kidnapped by a poor beggar woman, and it is up to the hero, Rover, to rescue her.

Nathan kept the pace steady and the black and white images flickered along to the musical accompaniment. I watched in delight as the dog raced through the streets, searching frantically for the baby.

Perhaps we should get a dog for Hubie, I mused. *It could keep him entertained while I tend to other things. If it was well-behaved, that is, like that Collie…*

Rover reunited the baby with her family and the six minute adventure came to an end. The screen went black as Nathan changed the reels. After a minute the audience began to stomp their feet on the floor and call out for the next film. "Slow on the take-up!" a man nearby shouted out, and the people nearby cheered their agreement.

"Don't worry, it's all part of the fun," Daniel assured me as I began to nervously chew my cuticles again. "They're laughing. They're just giving him a hard time."

I nodded.

"What's the worst that will happen?"

I glanced sideways at him.

"You're so afraid for him. Why do you coddle him so? He's going to fail at something eventually someday, and he'll learn from it. The world won't end. He'll go on and be better for it. Believe me."

"I know," I agreed, unoffended. "I don't know why I dote on him. I can't help it."

"Because you have more motherly instincts than you give yourself credit for."

I opened my mouth to protest, and he silenced me with a finger tracing gently over my cheek. He leaned closer, speaking quietly.

"You frighten away your own confidence with your effort and your doubt. Do you know that the first thing your little boy wants to do when I take him outside is to pick you wildflowers?"

I shook my head once, my eyes locked on his.

"You've done more right in your life than you will ever see. But I suppose we are all guilty of self-blindness."

The Adventures of Dollie appeared on the screen and the piano came to life at the same moment. The crowd clapped their approval. I clasped Daniel's hand in mine, next to my lap in the darkness where no one would see. It used to feel like this when Henry and I would talk. There was no doubt in my mind his sweet insistences of my virtue and worth would grow tiresome and clipped after repeating them for years to a woman who could not be convinced.

I was able to see myself through his eyes more accurately than he would ever give me credit for, or even admit to himself. I was a project; a broken thing to mend. A distraction from the wounds that needed mending in himself. If he succeeded in "fixing" me there would be no more need of each other. If he did not, he would accrue another bitter failure in his life, and grow weary of trying with the passing years.

I understood the pull of his conviction to try. I was mesmerized by it myself, as I was guilty of the same delusion about him. But the more I swung toward him the harsher reality's glare became. Saving a drowning person is admirable, but if you are not a strong swimmer, he will pull you under with him.

I took in his prominent profile as he watched the film, his full lips turned upward just slightly at the corners. Who was I kidding? I could no longer even tell which one of us was swimming and which was drowning.

The second film ended and I realized I hadn't watched a second of it. I resolved to stop obsessing and pay attention to the next story.

Dr. Jekyll and Mr. Hyde

I quickly failed, as a contemplation on the duality of man's nature was the last topic to have a chance at succeeding in distracting me from my thoughts.

Maybe I could slip out the back, I dreamed idly. *Excuse myself for the restroom and never come back. I'll hop on the train and just run away. Land a role in one of these pictures so my brother can still see me when he plays the film. I'll leave Henry with his stubbornness and Daniel with his driftlessness and Hubie with his petulance and tell them all to go to hell.*

I'll kidnap Emma and take her with me. We'll go to New York City and smoke cigarettes. We'll be free to do whatever we want. We'll be free...

On screen, forced to acknowledge the blood on his hands, Dr. Jekyll is tortured by pangs of conscience while the hideous monster Mr. Hyde is haunted by nightmares of repercussion. Images of the gallows flash before him as the inevitability of his fate closes down around him. He shudders away from it, hopelessness and terror setting in as he realizes he is a man already standing in his own grave.

The image shuddered and suddenly froze, Mr. Hyde jerking to a halt as he cast his eyes over the audience with a fearful gaze. Before the pianist could react, before anyone could wonder aloud if this was part of the show, the projection wavered—rippled for a moment and seemed to lift off the screen—and with a flash tore apart from the center, melting away in a black, streaking mass that bubbled at the edges and left the center of the screen blank and motionless.

The music screeched to a halt.

I whirled in my seat and saw an insidious swirl of black smoke seep from the projection window just as the smell registered in my nostrils.

The balding man who had taken our tickets clamored to the stage, adjusting his jacket and imploring in a booming voice, "Ladies and gentlemen, please remain in your seats. We are having some difficulty with the film but will have it remedied in short order. We apologize for the inconvenience." He signaled to the pianist, who quickly launched into a jaunty intermission piece.

Confused and concerned murmuring grew loud among the crowd. A few people, mostly the ones at the ends of rows and near the doors who could easily slip out without disturbing their neighbors, discretely made their way to the door, despite the manager's pleas. Others grew agitated and contemplated following them, looking around for reassurance.

I was frozen in my seat, fixated on the window, waiting for the smoke to dissipate or Nathan to poke his head through and sheepishly assure us that everything was under control. But there was no sign of him, and the trickling tendrils of haze quickly became thick, noxious wafts billowing from the projection room, blocking out the light that glowed from within. Then, in the darkness that was impossibly growing darker, a flash of illumination broke through.

"*Fire!*" a man shouted. That was when the screaming began.

All semblance of order fell away in an instant as the warning was caught up and repeated, carrying downstairs to the lower auditorium and creating a mass exodus for the doors. The manager changed his plea, but even his loudest shout could barely be heard.

"Everyone please remain calm! Move toward the exits *in an orderly fashion!* There is no need to panic!"

He and the pianist abandoned their post and slipped backstage. A few people near the front of the theater saw this and followed in search of a closer exit. There were no side exits in the auditorium; the only other way out was the way they had come in—through the lobby. As everyone rose from their seats at once and rushed for the aisles they became jammed immediately, and although people pushed and clamored and shouted and moved as fast as they possibly could, the collective crowd moved as though through sludge, funneled through three narrow walkways, clumsy with panic.

Daniel grabbed my hand and we struggled to push our way to the end of the aisle, but the balcony was just as clogged as the lower auditorium, the chaos even more frenzied as the smoke enveloped us, and as we stood and shoved we barely moved inches. When we finally began to make headway he nudged me forcefully toward the closest doorway, which was not the one we had come in, and I pushed back, throwing myself around him and trying to swim against the crush of people, clawing my way against their current toward the other door. I felt his arms around my waist and I swung at him desperately, trying to free myself.

"Nathan!" I screamed. "I have to get to Nathan!"

"You can't! We have to get out!"

"I'm not leaving my brother!" I shouted in his face, my fingernails in his neck, prepared to hurt him if he hindered me any further.

I wasn't afraid for myself, or for Daniel. We would get out. We had to. But my brother was in that blazing hole in the wall and my mind exploded with panic at the thought of leaving without him. I had to know he had gotten out. I couldn't leave knowing he might be trapped in there. There was no other thought in my mind. There was no other option.

I launched myself through the thick wall of bodies, finally making headway. When I felt arms around my waist again, they were pushing me forward rather than dragging me back.

My heart pounded as the noxious air burned a path through my sinuses, down the back of my throat, and into my wheezing lungs. My eyes watered furiously, irritated further by the sweat that dripped from my brow. I could barely see my hand in front of my face.

When we reached the point where the crowd split between clamoring for the left door and pushing for the right the fire spilled out of the projection window, seeping onto the damask wallpaper and devouring the molding that framed it. Within seconds the entire wall was alight.

I was awestruck and terrified by the speed at which the fire spread. For the first time, I pushed against the crowd with something more than a selfless fear propelling me.

The heat was like a physical entity pushing down on us with unbearable weight. We jockeyed our way through the doorway and no sooner had I caught a glimpse of the doorway leading to the third floor, Daniel was gripping me tightly and hauling me through the small hallway and toward the lobby before I could break free and run for the stairs.

I didn't fight him. The door was open, smoke billowing down the narrow stairway, flames following close behind, tearing through the exposed, unfinished lath like kindling. No patron would have cause to climb those stairs. If the door was open it was because Nathan had gotten out. If he hadn't…I was helpless to traverse the wall of fire I saw on the stairs either way. But that was irrelevant.

"He got out," I choked, doubting that Daniel could even hear me. "I know he got out, he got out…"

My legs began to feel heavy and uncoordinated. My breathing grew shallow with the sharp, searing pain of each breath that spread from my chest and radiated through each limb. I leaned on Daniel for support. He had his right arm around my waist and pulled my left arm around his shoulders as I stumbled.

I expected the lobby to be brighter and more open than the cramped maze of seats in the balcony, with room for people to flow far more quickly down the double staircases and out the front doors. I had it in my head that once we reached the lobby we would have no trouble getting out. That might have been true, had the stairway that was directly before us not been blocked by an iron gate that stretched almost to the ceiling.

"Dammit!" I heard Daniel shout, even over all the other noise.

Visibility here was only minimally aided by the presence of overhead lights. The smoke was so thick it obscured nearly everything. In the darkness it was easy to underestimate just how pervasive it was, but here in the lobby under the pitiful flicker of the waning lamps the bleakness of the situation was suddenly, jarringly evident.

Daniel's body shook as he coughed and retched. I looked around us frantically for a way out. The tall, arched windows that faced the street were clustered with people trying to escape, attempting to pull the inward-swinging windows open against the crush of bodies or break the windows apart with brute force. All of these attempts were unsuccessful.

The only viable exit I could see was the window to the right of the blocked staircase. I couldn't see far enough through the haze to tell if the other staircase was blocked or open and the other end of the lobby felt as though it were miles away. I would rather walk on a bed of nails than try to cross that expanse, fighting through the people, gasping for breath. Already the room was beginning to spin and the ground seemed to shift and grow soft and uneven.

As we staggered forward I realized with sickening horror that I was no longer walking on the floor.

My stomach lurched and I wanted to throw up. All I could taste or smell was soot.

My knees buckled. Daniel hoisted me up, barely standing himself.

"Hang in there. We're going to get out," he assured me, fumbling his free hand to feel for my face.

The room began to rock violently and it felt as though I was breathing through a straw. I wanted to tell him I was trying but my throat felt like it was shredded.

As we inched closer to the window it became apparent why the wall of people was barely moving. There was no fire escape at this window. Upon learning this, some took their chances and jumped. Some fought their way back through the crowd toward the other staircase or the other window. The situation made for hesitation, which was something none of us had the luxury of, and heightened the sense of panic to the breaking point.

"We have to jump," Daniel croaked, his voice hopeless. "There's no other way out. I'll go...I'll break your fall, just jump toward me...Annie?"

I nodded, or at least I think I was nodding, but the room was spinning too much to be sure. I tried to speak but the moan that came out was lost in the din, so I grasped at his chest with my free hand to let him know I understood.

"Hang on. We're going to make it," he promised between violent coughs.

We got close enough to the window that I could feel a slight breeze, and the hot summer night felt cool in comparison. I sucked a tiny gulp of air into my spasming lungs.

A sudden force came from behind me, and suddenly Daniel was gone and I was falling. For a moment I thought we had jumped, but I was on the ground in an instant and it was not outside. Two strong men had forced their way through the crowd, overpowering anyone in their way. They climbed through the window and leapt to their fate.

In the shuffle Daniel had been pushed forward and I had been knocked back. He found himself at the window without me and turned to find me, but the frenzied crowd was no longer forgiving of a last minute change of heart. He was in the way and they were packed too tightly around him to let him through. I heard him shout my name, once, desperately. And then they pushed him out of the second story window.

All I could think was, *He got out. Thank God.*

I couldn't know how he would fare in the fall, but he wasn't going to die inside this God-forsaken theater, and there was peace to be found in that.

I struggled to get up but the room was spinning faster and faster every time I so much as moved my eyes, to the point where I could no longer tell which way was up and which was down. The more I gasped the less air there was to be found. Each one of my limbs felt heavier than my entire body, and I felt my control over them slipping away.

I felt an odd lack of panic as I tried to rouse my body to action. All of my exertion was channeled into trying to breathe, blocking out the pain, and commanding myself to rise. There was no time to dwell on the consequence that would come with failing. There was no room for fear.

I summoned the last bit of strength I could muster and willed myself upright. I grabbed onto whatever was in my reach — A man's sport coat? A woman's bustle? — and pulled, and felt a precious separation between myself and the ground. Then the fabric suddenly jerked away and a heavy weight fell upon me, covering my legs up to my waist, and I could move no more.

Minutes. That is how long it takes for the entire world to change.

Minutes ago I held Daniel's hand as we watched the baby Dollie be kidnapped by gypsies onscreen. Minutes ago I was contemplating my future with all-encompassing obsession. Minutes ago I was imagining what would happen when I returned home tonight.

My life broke apart into tiny capsules of time and scattered out before me as far as I could see. Millions of minutes of joy, grief, confusion, epiphany; each one a snapshot of a memory, suspended in infinity, which obscured my vision as the last glow of light from the fire that was now rippling across the ceiling faded away into nothingness.

Henry and Hubie watching the fireworks from the mountaintop in Reading.

Daniel's enthusiastic embrace on the front porch when he first arrived to stay with us.

The triumphant first time Hubie accepted my breast.

Crying myself to sleep the night I gave birth.

Henry and I slow dancing in the living room to the phonograph, my belly so swollen I could hardly get close to him.

The quiet sunrise I watched my first morning as his wife.

Hearing the first thud of earth hit Henry's mother's casket after it had been lowered carefully into the ground.

Playing tea party with Emma while our mothers shared a cup of coffee in the kitchen.

Pushing my new baby brother Nathan around in his carriage even though I was barely tall enough to reach the handle, my mother hovering just behind me.

LISA GERY

I could no longer smell or taste the soot and smoke. The cramping in my lungs eased and finally ceased.

So insignificant.

All my fears, all my insecurities, all my doubts, all my transgressions. They slipped out of my grasp like the velvet wings of a butterfly; never meant to last.

I could see now, clearly, the unfathomable arabesque that was the world, laced through with every life that ever was and would ever be. How my own vine-like strand overlapped with so many others; touching, through association and chance, lives I would never even be cognizant of; interconnected in a delicate web so intricate it could not be comprehended but from a distance. How our paths intersected and merged, and how each and every different path wound its way toward the same destination, no matter the length or direction.

The blazing heat dissipated and a numb coolness washed over me. I felt it pull me under and I wanted to go.

The shouting and choking, the crackling and roaring, drained away as though the sound was reaching me only faintly through a tunnel, until it dissipated completely.

In the silence I heard my heart beat, once. And then it was still.

There on the floor of the theater, in that moment of absolute and unbroken silence, I died.

ELEVEN

Death was nothing like I had ever imagined.

Not being the type of person given to morbid fantasies and musings, I had not at length contemplated the details of my own demise, nor dwelt upon the curiosity of the journey. I imagined that when my life ended it would *end*. That was, to me, the very definition of death. It was the end of life; the epitome of finality. Then, as my beliefs led me, I would awaken in heaven as a new creature, a purified soul, in a peaceful and wispy world far removed from life and Earth and everything I had known. It would be a new beginning; an afterlife.

I was wrong on every front, the first and most surprising being that there was no end when death came. My awareness of my self in the current moment never ceased. There was a receding of my senses, an altered perception of reality, but there was no definitive end. There was only transition.

When my heart stopped beating a strange sensation came over me. It began as a prickly, pins-and-needles feeling that emanated from the center of my body and spread outward, growing more and more intense until every cell seemed to vibrate with raw energy. Then the vibration became a pulling, twisting, sucking, *moving* that was weightless as the part of me that remained was extricated from the flesh that lay with horrifying stillness, weighing me down. I was pulled upward, outward, torn to pieces and forced away, merged and lifting, hurtling through the darkness, fighting and grasping and clutching at nothing, until I felt a single point pulling me like a string on a kite. The blackness dispersed like smoke on the breeze and there before me was Nathan.

He was running up Main Street toward the firehouse, screaming for help until his voice gave out. His face was streaked with black soot, his blond hair darkened and dirty and disheveled, his burned and blistering hands stretched out uselessly before him. I was overwhelmed with relief at the pitiful sight of him, instantly diverted from the confusion and fear of my own situation. He was alive. He was alive and well enough to be running for help. I could not ask for more.

The rain that had threatened all afternoon was falling now in a steady drizzle. People came pouring out of their houses into the street to see what the commotion was about. When they saw the black plumes rising into the night sky they took off running, scrambling for ladders, tearing sheets and blankets from their beds and anything else they could use to catch people as they plunged from the windows.

The emergency bell was already ringing at the firehouse when Nathan reached it and the last of the blissfully unaware sprang into action. A team of eight men pulled the hose cart into the street and, forgoing the time it would take to hitch a team of horses up to pull it, raced it themselves down Main Street toward the Walt.

Nathan stood there on the sidewalk, the rain dripping dirt into his eyes, and watched them all funnel toward the eerie glow that was illuminating the cloudy night, lost and terrified. He wanted his mother. He wanted to know Daniel and I were safe. Now that help was on the way he was frozen and didn't know what to do.

A man with an armful of sheets rushed by him and grabbed him by the arm, not noticing his mangled hands. "Come on then, son, help out!" he exclaimed, pulling him along. Nathan ran with the man, dazed, his mind blank except for the repeating insistence that Daniel and I were safe.

A block from the theater he stopped short, clarity returning in an unwelcome rush as he saw the angry flames lapping out of the arched windows. He shrank back against the storefront, unable to bring himself to get any closer. The man continued on, stretching out his sheet to a stranger who grabbed it and raced toward the building in an attempt to help.

Someone had finally managed to break out the right-hand set of the arched windows and men and women flung themselves onto the outstretched sheets waiting below, hair and clothing aflame. Other Good Samaritans helped carry the injured to safety across the street. Mr. Grayson emerged from the apartment above his hat store and opened the doors to use his shop as an infirmary. It was filled within minutes.

Nathan sank to the ground, his knees to his chest, his face buried against his forearms. He rocked back and forth, shivering with cold as the rain soaked his shirt and stung his hands. All he could hear was the snapping of the fire and the endless screaming and wailing that came from within. "No, no, no," he chanted, louder and louder to block out the horrific sounds that filled the night. "NO, NO, THIS ISN'T HAPPENING," he shouted, over and over, his entire body shaking, tears of helplessness finally coming as he sat there and listened to them die.

It wasn't very long before the sounds coming from the theater ceased, and no more jumped from the windows. When that happened Nathan turned his head to the side and vomited until there was nothing left.

The air was acrid and thick and full of particulate. He wiped his mouth with his sleeve and covered his face with it, sickened by the thought of breathing in whatever was in the ash in the air. The one moment he stopped thinking about me and wondering of my fate was the dark moment he regretted fleeing the projection room at all.

When he released me from his thoughts I felt myself being pulled away, back towards the inferno, but before I could put up a panicked resistance I was across the street, standing over Daniel.

He was staring at the window from which he had fallen, and at the scattered pile of bodies in the street which had broken his fall and allowed him to survive. His left leg was broken and twisted unnaturally and his right ankle was swelling alarmingly. The break had occurred in the fall but the sprain happened in the frantic shuffle of neighbors hurrying to pull the survivors clear of the landing zone before they were crushed by the next jumper. They hauled him roughly across the street and left him lying against the cool stone foundation of the First National Bank.

The adrenaline coursing through his body just barely kept the pain from being overwhelming. He watched anxiously for any sign of me, knowing my only chance at escape was through that window. He murmured to himself that if he had made it, I would too, fighting back the rising panic with avowals that I would emerge any second. I would jump and be pulled to safety and he would do his best to track where I ended up so that he could find me once the doctors arrived. But when no more took their place at the window, even at the gathering crowd's hopeful pleas of "Jump, jump!" he began shouting for me, adamant in denial, as though if he commanded loud enough I would obey and appear.

Tears and sweat blurred his view of the chaos all around him. Desperate, he tried to drag himself forward into the street, pulling his lame legs uselessly behind him, and a motherly-looking woman in a nightdress and shawl hurried to his side and pulled him back.

"Annie!" he screamed hysterically, his voice breaking. "She's still in there! I have to! ANNIE!!"

The woman wrapped her arms around his chest and held him fast despite his feeble struggle. "I'm sorry," she whispered in his ear, her eyes wide and darting, watching that they would not be trampled. "You stay here or you'll get yourself killed, too."

He shook his head violently. "No," he insisted, not at her request, but at her implication. "No. She can't—"

She hugged him tightly, the boundaries between strangers meaningless. "I'm so sorry," she said, beginning to cry herself as she watched the blaze rage on.

"No." His voice was a whimper now. "No. Annie..."

He went limp in her arms, his body shaking with the force of his sobs. I ached to comfort him, to assure him the horrific images that flashed in his mind were not true, to tell him I was not gone, but I was silent, locked away, a specimen under glass.

I moved away from him, unable to witness any more. Now that I knew my boys were safe the enormity of the situation began to settle in. They had gotten out alive. I had not.

No...

It didn't feel real. I was still there; how could I be gone? If I was gone, why was I still there?

I looked around anxiously for guidance or comfort but there was none to be found. I was surrounded by people lost in their own worlds; fighting the fire, tending the wounded, pulling people to safety. All singularly absorbed in their tasks and oblivious to all else. The streets had never been more chaotic and I had never felt more frightened or alone.

There were others like me in the crowd. I could identify them from the way the people they hovered by ignored their presence. They were anxious, confused, angry. One by one many of them drifted away, simply fading until they were gone. I watched incredulously, desperate to hide so the fading would not take me. I wasn't ready to leave my family. My fear began to harden into anger as I glared at the burning building. I shouldn't *have* to leave my family. This choice had been made for me; I didn't cause this and I didn't want this.

The firemen were in place with their hose cart and a second fire company from the other end of town arrived shortly after with theirs to get another stream of water on the fire. When it became clear this would not be enough and help from a nearby town would be at least an hour coming, the old pumper wagon, which had gone into retirement since the installation of municipal water, was rushed down the street and brought back into service. Three burly men on each side pumped the handles up and down to build water pressure as two other men aimed the hose at the arched windows and a group of local men formed a bucket brigade to keep water pouring into the side troughs to be pumped onto the flames. They hoped for the rain to increase and come to their aid but it did little more than slick the road and add hazard to an already losing battle.

I was the only one not hoping for a deluge. The damage was done; all who would perish already had, all who would escape had had their chance. The building now was naught but a tomb and I wanted to see it burn. Caught in the midst of the desperate frenzy in the street, the pulsing flurry around me a discordant rhythmic beat, I was hypnotized by the sheer force of destruction raging before me. It called to something deep and primal I never knew was inside me; something violent and free that made me revel in the slaughter. I wanted to dance in the ashes as the world came to an end. I wanted to watch the brick char black and the windows shatter into sharp crystal snow. I wanted to see the proud frieze that boasted the name *Walt Theater* crumble into tiny, useless chunks. I wanted to help the fire along, tear the structure to pieces with my own two hands.

"Burn, you bastard!" I shouted with delirious glee as I whirled. "You think you're going to take me down and still stand? I will watch you come undone, brick by brick!"

I felt the pull again but I resisted, unwilling to leave my prime vantage spot to the theater's demise. I channeled all my hatred, all my fury, my helplessness and frustration into my senseless shouting at the flames, lost in the incongruous euphoria, encouraging them to reach for the sky until the walls caved in on themselves. The walls of the monster sat resolutely, refusing to bow down, even as the roof caught fire and began to collapse in sections, sending billowing clouds of glowing embers into the night sky, the glittering deadly jewels floating four stories high in one monumental rush.

The flames reached upward, twisting angrily out of the reach of the feeble jets of water, rearing up against the firemen's attempts to extinguish it with retaliatory fury. Its brightness lit up the street like day, devouring and erupting like a dying sun, untamable and vengeful. As they struggled in their work it toiled in its own, both united in the exhaustive labor of destruction, but each expending their passion on the other. And, before my ecstatic eyes, my brethren were losing the fight.

Empty nights. Torturesome dreams. Weighted secrets. Two beautiful men, lost and broken.

Precious time...fragile, finite, irreplaceable...wasted.

"Burn away," I demanded, whispering now, speaking more to myself than the structure before me. "I just want it all to burn away."

The flames crackled and groaned as they consumed all that had been beautiful and grand just hours ago. Soon there would be nothing. Nothing.

The pull came again and, as my powerless fury faded into exhaustion, I let it take me. I did not know to where and I did not care.

A moment of gray blur later I was beside my elder brother John as his horses went tearing up the lane toward my house, his buggy almost tipping as it made the hairpin turn off the road. Henry was on the porch by the time John had scrambled out of the coach and sprinted toward the house.

"Thank God you're here!" John exclaimed breathlessly.

"What happened? What's wrong?" asked Henry, visibly alarmed.

"I was afraid you were at the theater tonight. Where's Annie?"

Henry's frozen reaction made John's heart drop to his knees. *"Where's Annie?"*

"What happened?" Henry demanded in return, his voice much smaller than he intended it to sound.

"There's been a fire." He turned on his heel and hurried back to turn the buggy around. "Grab Hubie! I'll explain on the way!"

Henry was already halfway upstairs before John finished speaking. Thirty seconds later they were galloping back down the lane.

"Father's trying to find Nathan. It's chaos. The entire town is in the streets, searching for family, trying to help. He sent me to make sure you two weren't there and to tell you about Nathan." He shook his head. "None of us were there, but so many were. There's injured lining the sidewalks for blocks."

When they were still two miles from town Henry could see the clouds alight with a fiery glow. "Oh, dear God in heaven," he muttered, the blood draining from his head.

They drove to the church and left the buggy there, as the streets were too clogged with pedestrians to get any farther. Henry held a disoriented Hubie close to his chest and he and John set out on foot. Instead of heading toward the center of town John signaled up the street, in the direction of my parents' house.

"This way," he said, much to Henry's reluctance. "Maria is with Mother, waiting for news. We'll leave Hubie with them and begin searching."

He acquiesced without a fight, recognizing that John was in a clearer state of mind than he and these smoky, dangerous streets were no place for a child. They left Hubie in my mother's capable hands and rushed off into the night to search for Daniel and me.

Word of the disaster had been sent by telegram to all the surrounding towns and two additional nearby fire companies arrived with teams of firemen and hose carts an hour later to assist. Makeshift infirmaries were set up in both schoolhouses and the arduous task of transporting and cataloging the injured began. Henry and John picked through the crowds, searching everywhere for familiar faces. Henry was outwardly composed but urgent, his jaw clenched so tightly his teeth began to ache. He passed over face after blackened face, continually insisting to himself that he would find me just around the next corner.

When a train from Reading arrived with doctors, nurses, and undertakers just before midnight, the fire was still burning. The threat of spreading was a continuing battle and it would take most of the night to bring the flames under control.

"This is useless," said John, after what felt like an eternity of endless circling and weaving through crowds. "Let's check the elementary school. At least there should be some order there."

They traversed the three blocks to the two-and-a-half story gray stone school building in anxious silence. The classrooms were used to group patients of like injuries together; the mildly infirm sat up in chairs, sipping water and washing debris from their eyes, and the seriously injured lay on blankets in rows. The desks were pushed together against the walls, serving as additional temporary beds.

In the second room they found Father, crouching next to Nathan on the floor. He was lying prostrate, his hands curled in front of him, staring fixedly at a point no one could see. Father stroked his hair, talking quietly to him.

"Nathan!" John exclaimed, hurrying to him. But Nathan did not respond, only barely turning his head toward him in reply.

"He'll heal," Father said, with far more worry etched on his face than there should have been after finding his son alive. "His hands are burned but they will heal. But he's...not right."

Nathan slowly made eye contact with Henry, and whispered his first word in hours. "Annie?"

Henry swallowed hard, shaking his head once, almost a wince. "We're still looking."

Father's head snapped up at once. "She was there? But, were you—?" He was understandably confused by Henry's clean appearance and had assumed my safety by it without question.

"She and Daniel attended the show. We've been searching for them both." His face grew red with strain.

"Why in God's name was she at the theater with Daniel?" Father demanded, frightened and irrational. "She should have been home with Hubie!"

I could see the knife twist in Henry's gut as he replayed the evening in his head. "It was for her birthday," he said measuredly, without elaboration.

"She's here. We'll find her," said John, turning away and motioning to Henry. "Come, let's keep looking." He patted him once on the back as they walked away from my father, whose eyes had taken on the same glassy look as my brother's.

Three rooms later, at the end of the hall, tucked in the corner of Mrs. Peach's third grade classroom they found Daniel lying on a bed of woolen blankets. His shoes were beside him and his pant legs had been sliced up the sides, exposing his twisted and bloody extremities.

When he saw Henry he didn't call out for him. He was still, his eyes wide, darkened with pain instead of hazy with morphine.

"Daniel!" The relief was clear in Henry's voice as he made his way over to him. He knelt beside him clumsily, torn between wanting to embrace him and being afraid to hurt him. His hands hovered awkwardly before settling on his arm. "Are you badly injured? Where's Annie? Is she nearby?"

He cowered, his mouth opening and closing, unable to form words. "I...I..."

Henry grabbed him by the collar, leaning close to his face. "For God's sake, I've been searching for hours! I need to know she's safe!"

"I'm sorry!" he blurted, trembling. "I tried to get us out! She had to go back for Nathan, and the stairs were blocked, and I tried to get us to the window but they pushed me out, and I kept watching for her, but she never came—" His sobs choked off the rest of his words. "She was right there, and then she was gone, and there was nothing I could do. Oh, God, Henry, please don't kill me, I'm so sorry..."

Henry's face went blank, his fingers slowly loosening. His eyes unfocused and he stared at Daniel without seeing. Daniel gasped and tried to pull himself together but his fear of retribution in Henry's hands only served to unravel him further. He clasped his hands over his face and resigned himself to whatever was to come, guilt corroding his brain and whispering cruelly that he deserved it.

Henry felt the floor dropping out from beneath him. He braced his hands against Daniel's shaking shoulders to stop himself from falling. My pleading voice echoed in his mind.

Please... just let me get away...

He heard us screaming at each other in the living room. He remembered the softness of my lips against his before I left. He felt the brush of my skirt against his legs as I whirled and ran for the door.

He slid his hands around Daniel's neck.

And pulled his head to his chest, cradling him like a child.

"It's not your fault," Henry breathed, his throat too tight for voice, as Daniel shook and latched onto him like a man drowning.

"No," John said, backing away slowly. "She has to be here." He stalked off obstinately, continuing to search for me.

Henry closed his eyes, every muscle in his body taut and controlled. He breathed in as a blanket of hard and fast denial wrapped itself around his mind, blocking out every thought and image with cold, blank nothingness.

"I'm s-s-sorry," cried Daniel, his voice muffled in Henry's shirt.

"Shhh..." he said.

Nothing.

Henry returned home in the middle of the night, carefully closed the door behind him, walked upstairs to our bedroom, and sat on the edge of the bed. Daniel was still waiting for the doctors to set his leg and bandage him up and the infirmary was so crowded that Henry was doing more harm than good, getting in the way. Hubie was at my parents' house, fast asleep.

He recalled the tentative tremble in my mother's voice as she asked, "Have you found her?" the minute he and John had returned to my parents' house. She halted her pacing just long enough to wait for an answer.

He shook his head, not voicing his certainty of my fate. He couldn't bear to destroy the hope he saw still in her eyes. He knew it would be dead soon enough.

She wrung her hands and nodded with a sigh. "Go on up and get a few hours of sleep," she instructed him. "Hubie's upstairs sleeping in the spare room. You can stay there for the night."

"Thank you, but no. I need to go home."

"You might as well stay. You'll have to go back out in the morning. You should stay close."

"I appreciate your offer, I do, but I need to go home."

The look on his face kept her from insisting. "Go on, then," she conceded. "You'll come back and find her in one of the infirmaries in the morning. That's where she'll be, you'll see. They just have to get everyone settled. It's impossible to find anyone out there now. Why don't you leave Hubie here at least, so you can try to rest? He's already sleeping."

He agreed to this, and John walked with him to the gravel lot behind Grayson's where our buggy sat abandoned beside dozens of others, the horses restless and unsettled, as if knowing their owners would not return.

"We'll resume at dawn," he promised, and Henry nodded weakly and turned away. When he left he found it a relief to be alone.

The rain was falling hard now, the wind picking up and whipping it against the house. He stared at the bedroom closet and listened to the rain pummel the windows. He wondered idly if Daniel had fixed the window on the east side of the house that leaked sometimes when the rain blew sideways like this. He heard the clock ticking and noticed the seconds were taking longer than usual.

He pulled off his boots and placed them neatly side by side. The emptiness of the house was a tangible sensation, like dampness or cold, and it made the room feel larger than it was. He got up and shut the door, as if that would seal it out, and went to the dresser to light the candle. There his gaze fell on the peacock blue hat in the corner.

He picked it up gingerly with two fingers, holding it away from him, and ran his thumb over the delicate velvet edge. Sinking back down onto the edge of the bed, he placed the hat in his lap, worrying the trim as he stared out the same black window I watched him from.

His breathing labored as his chest tightened. He blinked furiously, rocking minutely back and forth as every clenched muscle fatigued and began to tremble with the exertion of keeping him upright, controlled, composed.

There was nothing outside the house—no trees, no storm, no sky—no floorboards beneath his feet, no plaster walls surrounding him. The nothingness overwhelmed him, in the lack of my stirring in the bed next to him; in the silence down the hall. The nothingness stretched on forever; unyielding, unbreakable.

His voice was tremulous and managed only one softly spoken word. "Annie?"

He stepped out over the vast chasm and felt himself fall.

The sobs ripped out of him violently, loudly. He crushed the hat between his shaking hands, tearing futilely at the ungiving fabric before hurling it at the window. His solid frame crumpled in on itself as he slid from the mattress and collapsed on the floor on his hands and knees. He raked his hands through his hair, digging his fingernails into his scalp until he drew blood, and screamed.

The sound pierced through me like shards of glass. This was the price. Infinitely more painful than losing my own life was watching the unbreakable man I had loved for so many years shatter into a thousand fragile pieces before my eyes and being powerless to stop it.

"I was wrong!" I shouted through the rain at his weeping form. "Henry, can you hear me? I wasn't ready to give up on us! And now it's too late and — oh God, please help me, I can't fix this — "

But it was, as I saw now, too late. My reaches were invisible and my words silent, and my tears were just another raindrop amidst hundreds sliding down the glass, unnoticed and unseen by the one who lay within, here in the darkest of all places.

It wasn't until dawn that the last embers of the fire were extinguished and the building sat silent and eerie, the windowless holes blackened and dripping and offering smoky glimpses into the hell within. Teams of construction laborers arrived of their own volition to begin the arduous task of removing the dead. Tall ladders were leaned against every window and lined with planks of wood to use as ramps to bring down the remains, hastily wrapped in sheets and blankets and bound with twine. From there they were taken to one of three makeshift morgues: St. John's Lutheran Church, the high school, or the First National Bank. Coroner Robert Matthews of Reading, an assertive, copper-haired man of middle-age oversaw the operation, giving strict instructions that no family members be allowed into the morgues until every body had been removed and accounted for. It was a painstaking process that took all day, performed under the watchful eye of the ever-growing crowd, whose numbers had swelled from devastated family members to curiosity seekers from neighboring towns who came to catch a glimpse of the carnage and marvel at the spectacle of a town in grief. They filled the streets for two blocks, kept at bay from the ruins by a rope barrier and a line of policemen so that the men had room to carry out their morbid task without intrusion.

The chief of police ordered all the saloons in town to be closed, deeming it unwise to fuel the crowd with easy access to alcohol. Occasionally a grief-stricken mother or husband broke through the barrier and lunged toward the building in an effort to reclaim their dear departed, but for the most part, the gathering milled and wept and waited as patiently as they could for the dreadful work to be done.

The streets ran with black, putrid water and the woodwork on the surrounding storefronts was coated gray with soot. The noxious, smoky smell that hung in the air was overpowering. Men and women alike breathed through their handkerchiefs and windows were shut for a mile despite the heat that grew throughout the day.

A committee was hastily formed of twenty men from the town who went door to door to get an accounting of who was missing or injured. Posters were hung on telegraph poles denoting the post office as Coroner Matthews's temporary office and a place to go to report missing loved ones or lodge a request for assistance. Children would be orphaned, elderly would require care, and money for burial expenses would be needed. The committee would work methodically to attend to all these needs.

Henry and John made another half-hearted sweep through the infirmaries. My name wasn't on any of the lists but still they searched up and down the aisles of blanket-beds and cots. John still clung to hope but was quickly losing it. Henry went through the motions of following him simply because he was as yet unable to enter the morgues, where he knew the real search would begin.

Daniel's leg was set and casted, his ankle wrapped and bound, and he was moved to my parents' house to convalesce. Nathan's burns were severe and he was transported to Reading Hospital for further care. He persisted in his muted and vacant state.

Telegraph inquiries from out of town family members came pouring into the already overwhelmed telegraph office. Henry notified Daniel's parents of his injuries and whereabouts but assured them of his safety. To his father, who was a twenty minute train ride away in Stowe with his eldest brother, he wired the following: *Annie is missing. Evansville is Hell and I am caught in the center. Don't come.*

An hour after dusk the last of the bodies had been cataloged, wrapped, and prepared for viewing, and Coroner Matthews finished his count of the dead. He ascended the second story of the First National Bank, overlooking the ruins, and announced from the window that due to the late hour the morgues would be opened to the public at first light.

The crowd, waiting all day in the heat and fetor, restless and distraught, rushed the bank in protest, pounding on the doors and threatening to break in the windows until he relented and ordered the morgues open at once for fear of his own safety. Twenty people were allowed in at a time to each one, to try to keep some semblance of order among the mob.

Both my elder brothers, John and Thomas, and my father joined Henry on the somber walk to St. John's. Entering through the side door and bypassing the safe and familiar vaulted chapel they joined a growing line of townspeople making their way through a little-used door at the end of the hallway and down a steep set of wooden plank steps into the basement. Flickering gaslight reflected off the damp, exposed stone walls and a strong smell of incense assaulted them as they descended.

"Never been down here," Thomas chattered nervously, stuffing his hands in his pockets. No one replied.

Two rows of long, white, oddly shaped objects lined the walls on the packed dirt floor, and it took Henry a long moment to realize what they were. The bodies, charred fast into their death stances, did not lay neatly as one imagines the dead in their coffins. Their bleached muslin wrappings were crooked and arched, knees bent and arms twisted, forever clawing their way out of the furnace. When Henry saw, just to the right of his boot, a tiny shroud much smaller than the others, he gagged and struggled to swallow back the bile that rose in his throat. He clasped his hand over his mouth and squeezed his eyes shut as Father patted him on the back and gently urged him onward.

At the foot of each shrouded figure were objects removed from the body to be used to identify the remains. Uniquely patterned lace handkerchiefs, wedding rings, cuff links, ornate buttons, scraps of fabric—anything that might shed light on the person's identity was laid at their feet, waiting for a spark of recognition.

"Lottie!" a woman up ahead of them suddenly began to wail as she sank to the ground, finding her daughter's monogrammed handkerchief. "Oh, Lottie, no, no…"

Henry ducked his head and concentrated on the myriad of personal effects in the dirt, steeling himself against the moment he would find mine.

"What was she wearing?" John murmured, staring straight ahead.

"Uh…" he struggled to remember. He saw my face, my eyes, and nothing else. "Um…yellow-ish dress, red hat."

"Any jewelry?"

"Just her wedding band, I think. I, uh, I don't recall."

"No," I chimed in silently. "I wasn't wearing any other jewelry, and you'll never recognize my band; it looks like so many others."

"We'll find her and bring her home, Henry," Father assured him, his voice unwavering.

But they did not find me in the basement morgue of St. John's, nor did they locate me in the maze that was the high school. I knew where they would find me, even though I had been clinging to the living and not looking after my body since I passed on. The moment I allowed the consideration into my thoughts I was standing before a prostrate shrouded form in the northeast corner of the bank with a plain gold wedding band and a scrap of singed amber fabric from the hem of my dress at its feet.

I lost track of everything else as I stared down at my body. So still, so vacant, so empty. It was surreal, and I couldn't conjure any emotion beyond a vague, numb disconnection. Standing there, in the sudden silence, the reality of the past twenty-four hours began to slowly seep through the distraction of the bedlam in the streets and the distress and insistent hopes and prayers of my family. It washed over me in minute waves—as I watched the theater burn, when I saw Henry admit to himself that I was gone, and now again; a tiny, lapping realization that this was truly happening. This was no fleeting dream. I gazed at what was left of me and I knew, in a quiet part of my mind that accepted the truth without the fruitless exertion of hysterics and denial, that there would be no waking up.

I couldn't see the extent of the damage through the wrappings and I didn't want to know. The notion that I would prefer to remember myself the way I was came to mind, and while it sounded odd, it was true, even though in that moment I was having a hard time reconciling any personal connection with the cold mass on the floor. *I* was here; I was not lying there. That hard, unmoving thing was not me. But still I wished to be found. I waited eagerly for my family to come, and eventually they did. And with slow strides up and down the aisles, they passed right by me.

I shouted for them to come back. I pointed and gestured in frustration that they had missed me but they moved along, examining each button and scrap and seeing me nowhere.

Day Two of the aftermath brought a moderate dwindling of the number of unclaimed bodies in the morgues. Caskets were ordered in record numbers and pastors from other parishes came by train to assist with the overwhelming number of funerals to take place over the course of the following week. Men hired themselves out as grave-diggers and worked around the clock in Union Cemetery and Mt. Zion Cemetery. The chief of police and his team began to dig through the ruins for clues as to what went wrong. Interviews were conducted and statements were collected from those who had escaped the theater.

I kept watch over my body, concerned now that the wrong people might mistakenly claim it. It might be useless to me but I was unsettled at the thought of it being buried in someone else's tomb. It was still *mine*, even if it wasn't *me*.

Henry and Father came again, and again they could not find me. I began to suspect they did not want to.

On Day Three, boxcars filled with empty caskets arrived in Evansville. The first burials began that afternoon. Hubie and Daniel were still residing with my parents, Mother insistent on caring for them to distract her from her grief. Daniel's parents arrived from Philadelphia, ill-at-ease until they were assured of his well-being with their own eyes. They inquired after their nephew and after me but Mother wisely kept them corralled to the house and left Henry to his solitude. Henry wandered from room to room in our empty house and gathered up every item that was mine or reminded him innately of me and stowed it in the bedroom closet with my dresses. He did not leave the house that day and spoke to no one.

On Day Four, thirty-six bodies remained unclaimed and the morgue had been condensed into the bank building. Henry reluctantly emerged from the house and made one final attempt.

I followed him as he paced around the musky, incense-laced room, his hair unkempt, occasionally rumpling it further as he raked his fingers through it. He stood in front of each shroud for a long time, fingering the mementos left behind before carefully placing them back on the floor and moving on to the next one. None of the fabrics seemed familiar to him. None of the jewelry looked like mine.

"Where are you, Annie?" he murmured to himself as he picked up my burnt amber cloth and held it between his fingers.

"I'm here," I whispered from beside him, as I knew shouting did no good.

He sighed and replaced the scrap at my feet.

One of the undertakers who was standing silently along the wall waiting to be summoned came forward and approached him. "Can I help you, son?" he asked gently.

Henry pulled a handkerchief out of his pocket and wiped the sweat from his brow. "I can't find her," he said, looking down. "I know she must be here, but I...I just don't know."

"What was she wearing?"

"I've been through that, nothing looks right," he snapped before catching himself. "I'm sorry, sir—"

He held up his hand. "No need, son. I understand. This is the hardest thing you'll ever have to do."

"God, I hope so," he muttered, shaking his head. "There are a couple scraps that look so alike I can't be sure. If I could just see them, if you could unwrap them—"

"That's not going to help," the undertaker quickly insisted.

"Anything," Henry begged. "There must be something else, some clue."

"They took the best they could off each one," the man assured him. "There's nothing left under there that would help you. I'm sorry."

"Then what do I do? What happens if I can't find her?"

"The city will bury the remaining victims in a mass grave—"

"Oh, God. No. Not my Annie. No. She has to be here." He walked away briskly, fighting back the crude, unrealistic image of my remains being tossed carelessly into a pauper's pit in a corner of the graveyard, and began to make the rounds again with renewed intensity. The undertaker stepped back against the wall and watched and waited patiently.

After another hour Henry stepped outside to clear his head and give someone else a chance to search. The empty shell of the theater across the street teemed with men digging through the debris, shoveling ash and bricks into waiting wagons. A block ahead, two horse-drawn hearses turned onto Main Street and trudged slowly toward Union Cemetery. Onlookers lingered on the sidewalk, removing their hats in reverence as they passed by. The streets were silent save for the continuous grind of the laborers in the ashes.

The town he had grown up in, lived in since the day he was born, was an unrecognizable shadow of its former self. In that moment he knew he could no longer live there.

He made his way to the telegraph office and found a message waiting for him from his father. *I have not heard from you in three days. Your brothers and I are arriving on the five o'clock train.*

That was fine. A seeping numbness had taken hold of him, taking the edge off the heart-pounding panic that had pervaded the past few days. He could face them now, if he must. He folded the paper into his pocket and ambled slowly up the side street, past house after house with shutters drawn. Black crepe bunting hung from nearly every other door, signaling a death within. This monotonous pattern was broken occasionally by a white adornment — symbolizing a child. His stomach churned even though there was nothing in it and hadn't been for days.

Outside my parents' house he stopped and took a deep breath before reluctantly stepping inside.

Hubie began to squeal with delight as soon as he glimpsed him from the living room, and my heart pulled as I watched Henry try to fix his face into something resembling a smile. He gathered our son in his arms and picked him up, squeezing him tightly with no intention of putting him down.

Daniel's parents were outside on the back porch with Father. Daniel was stretched out on a cot in the living room, his casted leg propped on a pillow, and Mother sat in an armchair nearby, reading the newspaper. When she saw him enter she scurried into the kitchen and returned quickly with a plate of biscuits and gravy, which she proceeded to thrust into Henry's free hand. "Don't even quarrel with me," she warned him. "I know you haven't been eating. Now sit down and get it in you."

He didn't have the strength to argue. "Thank you," he mumbled, momentarily appreciating her coddling. He sank onto the couch, settling Hubie onto his lap, and began to pick at the biscuits.

"Have you—" Daniel began and then paused as he struggled to finish the sentence. *Had any luck? There's no luck to be had. Identified her? Too harsh. Recovered her?* "Uh, have you—"

"No," said Henry quietly, putting Daniel out of his misery. "No, I haven't been able to."

"Excuse me," whispered Mother, placing the newspaper on the side table and taking her leave of the room, surreptitiously wiping the tears from her eyes.

Daniel picked up the newspaper once she was out of earshot. "There was an article in here," he said, flipping through and looking for it, "that said the Fire Relief Committee had purchased a large plot in Union Cemetery that they would use to bury all the unidentified, as well as the ashes from the theater. They're digging a large trench with proper brick vaults for each casket and in the center they're looking to commission a monument. They say there could be as many as fifty to bury there."

"There won't be that many. There are only thirty-some left," Henry informed him.

"Well…that's good then."

He sighed. "Annie's going to end up there. I know it."

Daniel cringed and said nothing.

"You don't know how badly I want to bring her home, but I—I just can't—they're all so—you just can't—"

"Perhaps I could."

Henry shot him a dark look.

"I was with her there," he explained carefully. "I saw her right before—her dress—maybe I would recognize it."

Henry knew it was illogical but he still felt a sharp sting at the thought that Daniel might recognize his wife when he himself could not. "You're an invalid," he said flatly. "I couldn't get you through that morgue but on a stretcher, and I don't believe you'd fare any better than I."

Daniel opened his mouth to speak but Henry cut him off.

"I've been looking at that dress for the past three years, when she made it. I know the fabric well. I am intimately acquainted with it!"

Daniel flushed and looked away quickly.

"You just—you don't know what it's like; what I've been sifting through for days. Everything is water-stained and dirty and blood-baked. I am sparing you a horrible sight, believe me, Daniel. You don't want those memories."

"I have enough of my own," he mumbled, still looking away.

"More hideous than I can fathom, I am sure."

"Henry, I'm—"

"Don't," he said tightly. "I know. I thank God you got out alive, Daniel. I truly do."

"I tried." His voice broke and he choked back his emotion.

Henry turned his head, not wanting to betray his own.

"Do you want to know...how it...?"

"No. I don't want any more visions in my head than I already have. I don't ever want to know. Not one second of it. Do you understand?"

Daniel nodded, biting his lip hard, a few tears escaping. "It wasn't—"

Henry shook his head and silenced him with his upturned hand. Daniel nodded again and said no more.

"Our lives will forever be divided," he said, staring vacantly at the wall, more musing out loud than addressing Daniel, "between what happened before this moment and all that happened after."

Daniel did not respond. He stared at the cheerful, oblivious, motherless child on Henry's lap and felt the darkness he had been sheathed in for the past four days creeping up to pull him under once again.

On Sunday morning thirteen glass hearses, their accompanying horses bedecked with black plumage, slowly marched up Main Street to the First National Bank. Four white gloved and impeccably suited pallbearers walked beside each coach and entered the morgue one group at a time, returning with a simple casket draped in black velvet that was carefully placed in the back of each hearse. They secured half of the twenty-six who remained unidentified; once they were interred they would return for the rest. They were men who had been recruited by the committee who were willing to assume this place of honor — firemen, store owners, pillars of the community — in place of the grieving families who had no way of knowing which loved one was theirs to accompany.

A cacophony of clicking hooves and grinding wheels on cobblestone echoed through the streets, eerily quiet despite the horde of people who lined the way. Already flooded with onlookers, the town swelled by several thousand people more on the day of the mass funeral. The sidewalks were packed full from the morgue to Union Cemetery; men with their hats removed, women with their heads bowed, couples gesturing and pointing, onlookers straining for a better view. The press jockeyed for position on the corners, endeavoring to capture a photograph and record the spectacle for the newspapers.

I knelt beside my casket, my hand lain protectively over its velvet shroud, as the procession trudged forward through town. I scowled at the gawking outsiders, mingled among the truly grieving. This was no place for them. This was a private affair. This was not a circus, for God's sake — this was my funeral.

I tore my eyes away from the offending crowd and gazed down at my casket. My body. The skin that had felt the sting of the rain, the warmth of the sunshine, the touch of a lover. The body that had created a life. The infant that had grown through a blessed childhood into her own person, who had laughed and struggled and cried and *lived*. I lived. Regardless of how much I had failed or succeeded or tried...I lived. I wanted those words carved into the wood. I traced them into the velvet with my finger but left no mark.

I wasn't ready to let go. Everything and everyone who had been an integral part of my life was still here, still continuing on, so how could I let them go? My life still existed around me, just without me. There was no other place for me. No angels singing me home. No deceased relatives showing me the way. There was nothing, and there was here. So I clung to my casket as the coach bore me to the cemetery where everyone I loved was waiting for me.

Along the hills, between the white headstones and newly dug graves, throngs of people stood and watched our arrival. Beside the trench that would be my tomb was a roped-off area for the families so that they would not be pressed out by the crowds. I saw my brothers except for Nathan, who was still in the hospital at my parents' insistence. My parents stood side by side, watching anxiously as the horses made their way into the cemetery. Henry's aunt, uncle, two brothers and father, tall and frail and relying heavily on his cane, were bunched together next to them. Henry stood behind Daniel, who was sitting in a wheelchair after having fought tooth and nail before my family relented and concocted a way to get him there. It hadn't been easy, given the crowds, and the transport had been horrendously painful, but he would not be dissuaded. Maria remained at home with Hubie, and for this I was deeply thankful.

A seemingly endless line of ornate hearses crept up the lane into Union Cemetery, spilling out through the gates and into the street. The pallbearers formed a dignified brigade between the mourning and the dead, standing motionless in their top hats and tails until the procession came to a halt and they somberly removed the first casket.

A pastor from each church in town was there to represent all possible denominations. As the pallbearers carried the first casket to its grave and carefully lowered it down, Reverend Jones from St. John's, my own church and the largest congregation in town, read a traditional passage from Ecclesiastes, his booming voice hoarse from reciting the same words so many times in the last few days.

"For everything there is a season, and a time for every matter under heaven: a time to be born, and a time to die; a time to plant, and a time to pluck up what is planted…"

I wished his words would have held some personal resonance. If only he could have spoken a sentiment about each of us, or chosen words that provided some greater measure of comfort to my family. But I doubted words existed that could have reached them in that moment.

Nearly every person in the bereaved section, man or woman, wept openly as the caskets were interred one by one, holding each other as if they were family. My mother was crushed between my father and John as they held her up. Daniel's face reddened with the strain of control, hurriedly swiping at any tears that escaped, his fingers trembling furiously. And there stood Henry behind him, motionless.

His eyes were blank depths of nothingness, his arms hanging lifelessly by his sides. He stared at the grave as each casket went into the ground, hardly blinking, his cheeks dry. He didn't look up to see them being carried. He simply watched intently for the fleeting moment as they appeared in his line of vision and then sank from view.

When the first three coaches had unloaded their precious cargo the procession lurched forward, allowing more into the graveyard. When coach number six moved to the front of the line the honor guard opened the glass door behind me and gingerly pulled my casket from the hearse.

I clamored after it, feeling a sudden panic. This was it. The moment of my death had been so harried, so distracting and intense that I could not recognize it for what it was but this—I was fully cognizant of this. I was watching it happen with clarity and awareness. I was being lowered into the ground for all time. What would become of me? Is this what I had been waiting for? Is this what all souls wait for—their moment of closure? When my body was taken, would I disappear? I stole one final glance at my family and steeled myself for the unknown.

They lowered my casket on straps into the front right-hand corner of the trench, the last brick tomb before it turned the corner. Henry blinked slowly as it sank.

I felt nothing.

I was still there, still watching them. I wasn't whisked away; I didn't suffocate. The work continued behind me as Reverend Jones continued to recite. It was as though nothing had happened at all.

There was no connection. My body was no longer mine. All this time I had been clinging to it through sentimentality and apprehension but now I saw how completely the ties had been severed. It was no more a part of me than a dress I discarded that no longer fit.

The funerals carried on, and when the last of the thirteen were interred the hearses departed and returned with the rest, and the scene replayed itself again. Granite slabs were slid into place over the brick walls and as the crowd slowly funneled out onto the street and the families reluctantly turned away, the grave diggers began to fill the trench with cool, moist earth.

Emma made her way out of the crowd to my family just as they turned to leave. Even in grief she was well-manicured and gracefully composed but her eyes gave her away. She had been in the cemetery the day before to bury both Robert's parents and he had been too distraught to return again with her. Mother hugged her warmly, flooded with memories of our shared childhood, and insisted she return home with them for a visit. She needed people to cook for and Emma needed a distraction. She gratefully accepted.

The graveyard never completely emptied because there were more funerals to conduct throughout the day, but it stilled once the majority left. I waited patiently as the workers finished smoothing the crude square earth mound at the top of the hill. From my vantage point there was a breathtaking view of the entire town, the rows of houses and church steeples colorful interruptions in a vast, rolling ocean of green hills in every direction. Beyond Evansville was an unbroken expanse of foliage and then, just before the hills rose up to meet the horizon, the steeples of the next town broke through. I had never seen it from up so high before and I was stunned by the sheer magnitude of the countryside compared to our tiny little hamlet. Such a pebble in that endless ocean.

So insignificant.

It saddened me that in twenty-four years I had never come up here to see the view.

The grave diggers finished their work and moved down the hill for a much-needed break, their day far from over. In the stillness of the morning I felt my fear, my anger, and my helplessness slipping away. It was all out of my control. All that had transpired, the injustice of my present state, the suffering of my family; it was all absolutely and unequivocally out of my control in a way I had never experienced. The realization was liberating in a strange way. I did not know what was to come but the unknown no longer frightened me. What else *could* happen to me? I had already faced the most terrifying aspect of mortal life — death. If hell was looming at my feet I imagined I would have caught a glimpse of it by now. I supposed hell could be this very place; being forced to watch my family grieve and eventually move on without me while being powerless to intercede, but frankly, if it was, I expected much worse based on the sermons at church. I was caught here and grieving for all I had lost. It was hell in a way, but an endurable one.

"What now?" I asked aloud, to the sleeping monuments at my feet; to the trees that ushered the wind across the hill.

There was no answer. Because there was nothing.

It was at an end now — the road that could have led anywhere, laid by my design and traversed with stumbling feet; the path that was molded by the exquisite and simple fact that I had choices, and time, and willful desires. It ended here, in this silent place, and it wasn't the death of me that struck me so much as the death of *it*, for the loss of possibility and change was the true epitome of death more than the stilling of my heart or the ceasing of my breath. I could have become anyone. I could have grown. Now I was frozen, still…lacking.

And what was the purpose of it all? To have borne a child, or loved another human being? If the road led here, to the silence and stillness that reached with inescapable grasp at the end of every road, what was the purpose in traversing its treacherous peaks and plunging valleys?

And now that it was over, did it matter at all?

And now that I was gone, did I matter at all?

The answer lay within the eyes of the crowd who mingled between the headstones — the desperate and the curious. We who were lost left tears in the family fabric, left love unrequited, and made orphans and widows. Beyond this we made strangers hold their children tighter, spawned introspection of priorities and choices, and prompted contemplation of the frightening and shadowy mysteries of fate. We would be held fast in memory, our histories recounted in reverence, our deeds elevated to mythical proportions. We would live in this way, in our lasting effect, in their memories and the reflection on their lives, forever.

The living glowed with an incomparable light, their souls ablaze with vital energy. Gloriously imperfect, they were granted the opportunity to learn with every painful decision, every stabbing regret, as they all shared the common folly of humanity's inevitable fallibility. But they could grow. Growth was not a thing for children, to be achieved at adulthood. It was a thing for humans, to be concluded at death, when the true nature of all things would present itself in graceful clarity.

The chance to have bathed in that light, in that priceless gift of growth and experience, was an honor. To have known the souls who crossed my path, complex and beautiful in their frailty, allowing me into the embrace of their sacred trust and granting me a role to play in their futures, was worth the strife and confusion of navigating this meandering road. To see how my own triumphs and trials would shape the paths of those I loved, teaching and enriching them as much as myself, humbled me. I was not born solely for myself, to fulfill my own desires. I was born for the ripple I sent out into the world, to brighten their roads with my light as they illuminated mine in return.

For all of this my body deserved more for its parting than a rote recitation. I knelt down in front of my grave, placed my unfeeling hands on the lumpy earth, and began to speak.

"Annie Bartolet was a wife, and a daughter, and—" I stopped. I was censoring myself even now, when there was absolutely no one to hear. With a reproachful shake of my head I began again. "She was a considerate daughter, an overprotective sister, a fallible wife, and a reluctant, unskilled mother. She was a liar. A graceless charlatan. She was, at times, selfish and quick to cast judgment. But, she believed that she could be better. She tried to be patient and warm. When she loved, she loved whole-heartedly. She squandered too much time in arguing but not speaking, in longing but not acting, but in spite of this, in spite of brevity and ignorance and imperfect humanity…she lived."

TWELVE

Mother opened the door to a stranger standing on her front step.
"Good afternoon, ma'am. I am—"

"I know who you are," she interrupted him brusquely. "I see your little badge. You're from the committee. You've come to speak to Nathan. I told the gentleman who came yesterday that he is resting, and he is doing the same today. And if you come back tomorrow, he'll be indisposed again."

The man removed his hat with a patient sigh and spoke softly but with urgent conviction. "Ma'am, I mean no disrespect, but if he doesn't speak to me, Coroner Matthews will come down himself to interview him, and frankly I'm much more congenial company. We need to gather all the information we can to get the inquest underway. I understand he's convalescing but if he could entertain me for just a few minutes I'm sure I could gather the information I need and leave you to your business."

Mother pursed her lips and shook her head. "You don't understand; he won't be able to help you."

"I need no exertion on his part save for his recollections of what happened that night," he assured her.

She regarded him wearily. "Fine. You might as well come see for yourself so maybe then you'll leave him alone. If he gets upset I'll have to ask you to leave. I hope you understand."

He did not, but he followed her into the house with growing trepidation.

She led him up the stairs and into the bedroom at the end of the hall. Pushing open the door, she gestured him inside and shut the door behind them.

"He's having a rough day," she explained as she pulled a chair up next to the bed. "He wouldn't get out of bed today."

He took a seat in the proffered chair as Mother sat on the edge of the bed next to Nathan, who sat propped up against a mound of pillows, his bandaged hands resting on top of the light coverlet, staring away from them out the back window. From what the man could tell he was still in his pajamas.

"Darling," she cooed, "there's someone here who would like to speak to you."

Nathan blinked but did not move.

She tucked a wayward strand of his blond hair behind his ear. "He needs to speak to you about what happened at the theater. Can you tell him something?"

Nathan brought his gaze to hers, looking silently. She patted his cheek and nudged his face toward the man in the chair.

His breath caught in his throat when he saw my brother. His face was gaunt and pale, his lips chapped and peeling. Dark circles prevailed under sunken eyes that stared vacantly through him, seemingly searching and finding nothing. He chewed absently on his bottom lip, his teeth tugging at the loose skin until Mother brushed it free with her thumb.

"Tell the man what you can," she coaxed.

"It's all my fault," he intoned, his voice hoarse as though he had just woken and spoken his first words.

The man scrambled for the notepad and pencil in his jacket pocket. "Uh, tell me, son, you were running the projector that night, am I right?"

Nathan watched him, his eyes fixating on the tattered leather-bound notepad in the man's hand. Mother nodded in answer.

"And..." He flipped through the pages. "It appears the fire began in the projection room. What can you tell me about that evening?"

Nathan pulled his bottom lip in and began to chew again. "She came to see me," he whispered.

"She? Who?"

"His sister," Mother said quietly, and the pain on her face answered the man's next question without him asking.

"I'm sorry," he murmured, jotting a note in his pad. "I need to know how the fire started, son."

He stared at Mother, and she smoothed his hair back away from his face.

The man sighed, frustrated. "How did you get the burns on your hands?"

No answer.

"Was it from helping people get out?"

No answer.

"The firemen said they saw him by the firehouse as they were bringing the pump cart out. He must have gotten out fairly quickly and run for help, not long after they raised the alarm," Mother volunteered, not taking her eyes off her son.

"So how do you think he got burned?" he asked, desperate for answers, even secondhand ones.

"It must have been when the fire started. He would have tried to put it out. That's the only thing I can imagine."

"Did you get these burns from the projector?" the man addressed him, raising his voice as he carefully enunciated each word and leaned closer.

"He's not deaf or imbecile," Mother snapped, "just half mute. Those two sentences are all he's said since he came home from the hospital two weeks ago."

The man pointed to Nathan's hands. "You don't have to speak. Just nod your head. Did you burn your hands on the projector?"

Nathan's head nodded slightly, once. Mother's eyes widened. They had tried this method last week; it hadn't worked.

"So, you were burned by the projector. Is that where the fire started?"

A slight nod.

"Did it malfunction?"

Nothing.

"Did you try to put the fire out?"

Nod.

"Was someone else with you up there?"

Shake.

The man turned to my mother. "How old is he?"

"Sixteen."

"How much training did he have?"

"He worked with a traveling projectionist for two weeks and he spent a weekend in New York at the Colonial Theater."

"That's *it*?"

Mother hardened under his accusatory tone. "I wasn't in charge of his training schedule," she snipped. "Perhaps you should speak with his employer."

"Christ," he breathed, sitting back in his chair with his mouth agape. "He's just a baby and they sent him in there with *two week's training*?"

"This was supposed to be a wonderful opportunity for him!" Mother insisted. "And he wasn't supposed to be alone. He was supposed to still be in training. They never should have left him alone!"

Nathan began to shake his head, tears pooling in his eyes. "It's all my fault," he whimpered, gesturing uselessly with his wrapped hands.

"No, darling, no," Mother said, quickly calming her anger and taking him by the chin. "You look at me. This is not your fault. You did everything you could do. This is not your fault."

The man shifted uncomfortably in his chair. "I think I have enough for now," he said, tucking his notepad away and standing. "Thank you for your time, ma'am. If you learn anything else—"

"I'll show you out," said Mother, rising and escorting him to the door.

As he stepped onto the front porch she spoke low and quiet. "I'll not have my son pay the price for this when those sons-of-bitches who run that theater are responsible. He's paid enough. We all have."

The man replaced his hat, tipped the brim at my mother, and with a sympathetic nod, left them in peace for the rest of the day.

Henry saw a figure of me standing in the living room by the front window, my back to him, my hair falling down in waves around the shoulders of my honey-hued and blush-flowered dress. He came up behind me and wrapped his arms around my waist, pulling me close and resting his chin on my shoulder.

"What are you looking for?" he asked, following my gaze out the window.

"You," I said simply.

"Well, you've found me." He placed a soft kiss on my cheek.

"I need to tell you." My posture was stiff, distracted, and I did not look at him.

"Tell me what?"

"What it was like."

He swallowed. "What *what* was like?" A nervous edge crept into his voice.

"I need to tell you what happened."

"What are you talking about?" He loosened his grip, pulling away.

The twisted dream-version of me Henry's psyche had conjured turned around in his arms. "I need to tell you what happened to me. I need you to know what it was like."

He shook his head slowly, his limbs stiffening in fear. "No, no, I don't want to know."

I smiled placidly, my gaze detached and distant. "You already do."

"No," he begged. "Please don't do this."

"He tried to get me out," I continued unabated, a calm and eerie smile still fixed on my face. "But the people were everywhere. The fire

moved so fast, there was never a chance. We knew that soon enough.
There was never a chance."

"Please…no…"

"He collapsed against the wall and I knelt with him. I couldn't
leave him. I took his face in my hands like this." I gently placed my
hands on either side of his head, my fingers nestling just into the edge
of his hair. "He held me the same. We just looked into each other's
eyes. I knew the fire was coming. I could feel it lapping at my skirt,
but it didn't matter. We were together at the end. Nothing else
mattered."

"No, Annie—"

"Because I love him. I could never leave him. Now none of it
matters."

"It does, it does matter!"

"We're buried together forever, a part of each other."

"No, God—"

"I want you to know it's okay. I was with him at the end."

"Stop it, stop!" he shouted, breaking away, burying his face in
his hands and shutting out my serene face with blackness.

The darkness swirled around him like a current, twisting faster
and faster. In his resistance he caught a moment of lucidity—*This is a
dream. This can't be real.* He clung to this conscious awareness,
struggling to throw himself back into waking reality as he had done
so many times before in the throes of a nightmare. He shook and
thrashed but could not break free from its grasp.

"Wake me!" he shouted in his head, summoning energy from
every inch of his body to break from his slumber. His lucidity grew,
his control over his actions increased, but his body lay paralyzed with
sleep, unable to respond. He could feel the nightmare looming just
below him, ready to swallow him back the moment he conceded the
fight to wake up.

Darkness surrounded him on all sides as he floated in an ocean
of bottomless depth, rising ever closer to the surface but unable to see
its light. He screamed and writhed as hard as he could, hoping for one

twitch of movement to resonate in his body that would break the cycle and allow him to wake. Still he lay entombed.

"Wake me!" He jerked his body hard, twirling weightlessly. Panic seized him as he felt himself falling deeper. He saw a second's flash of my face; my cold, dead eyes.

"Annie! Wake me! Annie!" he sobbed in despair. He struggled to force feeling through every nerve ending, desperate for a spark of cognizance.

Then he heard the moan. He screamed again, from the depth of his stomach. Another moan echoed it, somewhat louder. He kicked, and gasped, and suddenly the darkness beneath him consolidated into something thick and soft. Another sound and a rush of air flowed into his lungs and his eyes flew open.

He woke with tears already running down his face; the moans had been his own. Instinctively he reached for my side of the bed and when he found it empty his mind began to frantically claw through its store of memories in an attempt to separate reality from dream. I was not there to wake him. I was gone. I was truly gone. Daniel…was Daniel…? No. Daniel was not gone. Daniel was down the hall. A flood of relief swept through him before the tears came harder as the dream played unbidden through his mind.

I need you to know…

"No," he cried. "No, she didn't suffer, she didn't love him, no, no…"

Down the hall, Daniel pulled the pillow tighter around his ears and tried not to hear.

I could tell the end of August without a calendar, without grasp of the passage of time. The pendulum of temperature swung farther, bathing the nights in a biting, sweet, cool breeze that wicked away the sweat of the daylight hours. The sunlight grew more golden in color, catching the tiniest yellow flecks in the leaves as they were first born.

Sunset marched slowly ever earlier. And amongst the smells of baked earth, honeysuckle nectar, and freshly shorn grass crept, on occasion, notes of the pungent wet sweetness of decay that signaled the first hint of autumn.

In life I had always favored spring and autumn for their temperateness. Now, as I sat removed, ensconced in the sedated numbness of separation, I knew more than anything I would miss the frenzy of summer; the heat exciting my senses, racing the blood through my veins, even the thickness of the humidity making my lungs breathe deeper and my heart thrum louder. To experience the summer is to truly feel alive.

I tried not to dwell on thoughts such as those when they came to me. The list of things I would miss was endless, as was my time to linger over it. I contemplated instead what was to come now that my journey in the physical realm was over, but with no conclusions. I kept waiting for a sign, an epiphany, but it seemed I was utterly alone and without direction, caught between the living and beyond. I knew there must be something more, some place waiting for me, or I would not be alone here, but the only pull I felt was the one holding me to my old life so that was where I remained, tethered to and watching over the ones I loved.

Four weeks after the fire I lingered in the back of the Town Hall and watched a stream of subpoenaed witnesses file into rows of wooden folding chairs for the inquest. Coroner Matthews's auburn beard was longer and a little scruffier than usual and light gray bags hung under his eyes. He was seated at the front of the room at the long meeting table that was stacked on one end with four piles of folders stuffed with reports and notes on each witness. He was joined by Attorney Ivan Harding, an alarmingly short, stout man with a ring of dark, curly hair circling the back of his head like a laurel leaf crown, whom he had appointed to lead the questioning. To their left sat a jury of six townsfolk, four of whom had served on the Fire Relief Committee.

The room buzzed with quiet conversation as everyone took their seats. I saw elderly Mr. Grayson, one of the first merchants to offer his store as an infirmary, among the crowd. Henry sat in the third row from the back, hunched forward with his elbows on his knees, his eyes locked on his clasped hands. He was flanked by his father and my parents. Mother fiddled with a folded piece of paper and murmured occasionally to Father and Mr. Bartolet but none of them spoke to Henry. He was a man of few words these days.

One by one they were called up to relive the night of August eighteenth. Mr. Grayson recalled smelling smoke and throwing open his window to discover the source. "When I saw them staggering out the front doors, I raced downstairs to open my shop and see if I could be of any assistance. The first ones needed water, fresh air, rinse for their eyes. I could provide that. Later they came with broken limbs, skin hanging in tatters from their forearms…I could do nothing for them."

The testimony went on for two hours, witness after witness. When Harding called for Nathan to testify, Mother, trembling, stood and took a seat at the front of the room, clutching the worn paper in her fist. Father watched, irritable and protective after she refused to concede her testimony to him and instead took her place before the jury. Harding eyed her speculatively, and there was something in his look that made me prickle.

"My son, Nathan Bauman, the projectionist on the night of the fire, is unable to testify before you this evening," Mother stated, her voice clear and strong.

This was not news to Harding or Matthews, but rather a formality for the jury and the record. "What keeps him from giving his testimony here tonight?" Harding asked.

"He was struck mute as a result of the horrors he witnessed at the theater and the severe burns he sustained on his hands and arms while trying to extinguish the flames."

"How old is your son, ma'am?"

"Sixteen."

And so they painstakingly recounted the story of how my brother had secured his job with the Mayfield Company, his qualifications (or lack thereof) to assume the position, and the extent to which he had been trained, to the best of my mother's knowledge.

"What details can you give us regarding the cause of the fire?" asked Harding.

Mother unfolded the paper she had been clutching and smoothed it out against her lap. "After weeks of gently pleading my son for answers, he was recently healed just enough to grasp a pencil, thereby affording him the ability to scrawl some answers to my inquiries. I have that information here." She held up the paper, covered in light, uneven script.

"Please continue."

"He states that the fire began during the *Dr. Jekyll and Mr. Hyde* film when the reel suddenly grew tight and then jammed. He struggled to loosen it but he was unsuccessful and the heat of the limelight ignited the film. In a panic he tried to tear the film from the projector but the fire quickly spread through the rest of the reel and into the wicker basket at his feet, which also held the previous film, uncoiled, ready to be rewound. He tried to extinguish it with two canisters of Kilfyre, which was ineffective, and finally with a jug of water, which he states seemed to actually increase the smoke and did nothing to diminish the flames. Fearing the situation was hopeless and crazed with panic and fear, he fled the building before most of the patrons realized the danger and ran for help straightaway."

"So he escaped the theater safely?"

"With burns to his hands, but otherwise, yes," my mother concurred.

"Because he fled the premises before the fire completely overwhelmed the projection room."

"Yes."

"He didn't stay and try to extinguish the fire to protect the hundreds in the theater, then. He ran," Harding surmised.

"He did try, I just stated that. He did the best he could but he was unable to bring it under control."

"Well, fortunate for him to have comprehension of the situation and be able to escape to safety. I imagine if those in the balcony had cognizance of the danger they were truly in they might have endeavored to escape a few precious seconds sooner."

"Is that a question?" Mother snapped, struggling to maintain her composure.

Harding shook his head, his eyes narrowed as he paced before her. "You stated that the reel jammed. Does Nathan admit this was a mechanical failure or an operator error?"

"I—I couldn't tell you. He didn't elaborate."

"Could the fire have started another way? Say, from a cigar?"

From the back of the auditorium, I winced.

"Nathan doesn't smoke," Mother informed him haughtily.

"He doesn't? Then may I ask why the hospital staff found a half-spent cigar in his trouser pocket?"

She shot a desperate glance at Father, who grimaced.

"I don't know anything about that, but I can tell you I have never known my son to smoke."

"Perhaps there were many things you never knew of your son. Right now he is the only one who can explain to us what really happened that night, and conveniently he is struck silent! He is hiding behind you, sending you in here to speak on his behalf. Now, I am not without a heart, and I do not think he acted with malicious intent. I do believe it is entirely possible he is simply a reckless young man who made a mistake, but that mistake has cost one hundred and eighty-two souls their lives! And we will not rest until these answers are uncovered!"

The audience voiced their agreement with cheers and grunts of approval and scattered applause. But my mother was not about to be their sacrificial lamb.

"Let me tell you something, Mr. Harding. I thank the good Lord I *am* here instead of my son in his fragile state, because the last thing that poor boy needs to endure after everything he's been through is a *witch-hunt*." She spat the words and pinned him to his spot with her glare. "Reckless? The only substantiation you have of the recklessness of his nature is his age. Not one person has testified to Nathan's character or ability and yet here you stand ready to hang him. His very own dear sister was in that balcony! My daughter! Whom he loved more than anything! Do you dare to tell me he would be reckless with *her* life among the audience? He has suffered just as greatly as you all have; more, even, for with the weight of his burden of grief is that of blame and self-reproach. He tears himself to pieces over his role in this disaster. But that burden of blame is not his to bear. What of the ones who hired him? Who trained him? Who promised him proper education in his trade and then sent him along unprepared? Let the blame lie with the guilty, not my innocent son!"

As quickly as they had unified against my mother they cheered her impassioned pleas now, shouting for the next witness to be brought forth. And so he was—Timothy Bensing, the projectionist from the Colonial Theater who had trained Nathan in New York.

"When I met Nathan Bauman he had a proficient, if basic, knowledge of theater procedures and how to run the projector," Mr. Bensing stated to Harding, looking a bit bored and eager for his testimony to be over so he could return to New York.

"And you worked with him for how long?"

"One weekend."

"Do you think this was a satisfactory training period?"

Harding's snarky tone did nothing to flap Mr. Bensing. "That wasn't my business or decision," he replied.

"And why not?"

"Because he doesn't work for me. I wasn't even paid to train him. I took him on for the weekend as a favor to Mr. Mayfield just to make sure his rough edges were worked out. Nathan told me he'd be working as an assistant to the projectionist down here, which is what I'd expect with someone so young. I figured they just wanted him to get a taste of how things were done in a real theater, not that gypsy setup he was trained on with the traveling carnival, so I told him to come on up. "

"And who was the projectionist at the Walt to be?"

"He didn't know who it was."

"Did you ask Mr. Mayfield?"

"No." He shrugged. "Twasn't any of my business."

"What was your opinion of Nathan's character and work ethic?" Harding asked pointedly, glancing sideways at my parents.

"Real good kid," he replied without hesitation. "Eager. God, that kid could talk a leg off a stool. Wanted to know everything. I thought he'd do real well. I'm...sorry to hear of his present state." He nodded in my mother's direction, and she closed her eyes in acknowledgement. "Anyway, he and his brother-in-law were eager to learn everything they could about the theater."

Henry bristled in his seat and folded his hands tighter until the knuckles turned white.

"His brother-in-law?" prodded Harding, unable to hide his intrigue. "What did he want to know about the theater?"

"Nathan said he was involved with the construction of the theater down here. He chaperoned him, spent his time poking around the theater, observing the architecture, asking questions."

"What about?"

Mr. Bensing sighed as though he regretted broaching the topic. "About the difference in safety codes between New York and Pennsylvania," he admitted, glancing apologetically at Henry, who met his gaze passively and without blinking.

Harding picked up a folder from the table in front of Coroner Matthews. He shuffled through the papers quickly. "That will be all, Mr. Bensing. Thank you. Henry Bartolet!"

Henry rose stiffly and made his way to the front of the room, to the plain wooden chair that sat between an audience of townspeople looking for someone to crucify and the jury that would decide who, if anyone, would have formal charges brought against them in a trial. Whispered musings and comments followed him up the aisle. My parents held hands, looking downward. Mr. Bartolet's countenance was one of steely determination and unwavering faith.

He heard Nathan's detached, tortured voice whisper in his ear. *It's all my fault.*

He took a seat in the chair, planted his feet firmly on the ground, and braced for the onslaught.

"Mr. Bartolet," he sneered with a smile.

"What do you want to know?" barked Henry, whose clenched fist was trembling in his lap almost imperceptibly.

"Well, to get right to it, I want you to explain the structural deficiencies we found in the ruins."

"What exactly are you referring to?" he asked carefully.

"Where to start? How about with the missing fire escape? There were supposed to be two, one from each side window in the upstairs lobby. There was one. Where was the other?"

"It had been ordered but hadn't arrived in time. It was going to be installed the following week."

"I'm sorry, I'm not understanding. Did it or did it not meet code requirements in its current singular state?"

"It did not," Henry admitted through clenched teeth.

"What about the missing exit signs at those same fire escape exits? Why were they not properly signed?"

"There was a mix-up in the order. They sent the wrong ones. We were instructed to return them and procure the correct ones."

"The wrong ones? What was wrong with them?"

"They were the wrong style."

Harding snickered without humor. "The wrong *style*? Do you think it was so imperative—"

"That wasn't my decision *or* my preference," Henry interrupted him.

"Ok. Let's move on. I've quite a list. Were these unmarked emergency exits at least free and clear of any obstructions?"

"Yes."

"So you don't consider heavy, flammable drapery to be an obstruction in a fire situation?"

"I — they were just drapes, I didn't — "

"Can you attest to the presence of code-mandated fireproof shutters on the projection room openings?" Harding continued on relentlessly.

Henry sighed, wiping the sweat from the back of his neck and closing his eyes momentarily. "No."

"Were there any fireproofing measures at all in the projection room?"

"There were fire extinguishers."

"Were there? According to Mr. Bauman's written testimony there were only two canisters of Kilfyre, which is more commonly used for small residential fires and would be inadequate for a theater of this size."

"His testimony is correct. When I say 'fire extinguisher' I am referring to the Kilfyre," Henry explained.

"Do you believe two small canisters of powdered chemical was adequate protection against the highly flammable nature of nitrocellulose film?"

Henry floundered for a response.

"Why was there not a proper fire extinguisher present?" Harding inquired.

"It was argued that the Kilfyre was a comparable product and cheaper."

"Agued by whom?"

"By the owner. And it was not an argument I was a participant in, so I would prefer not to speak to it."

"Noted. There is mention of a sprinkler system in the original plans but nothing was in place. Why was this changed?"

"The owners did not want to spend the extra money on a sprinkler system. They deemed its need unlikely," Henry said, his voice faltering.

Disgusted snickers went through the crowd at his words. Harding continued without pause.

"You were responsible for the completion of this project. Everything went through you. So in the unfinished state of the Walt Theater on the night of August eighteenth, how did you get an occupancy permit from the township inspector? How did you get the fire official to sign off?"

Henry's throat tightened as his mouth went dry, trying with all his might to force out the words he knew he must say and being unable to look at his father sitting in the audience and speak them.

Harding, quickly tiring of waiting for an answer, offered his own. "I have a theory as to how it occurred. I believe money changed hands behind closed doors to make this happen." He eyed him brazenly, daring him to rebut.

I watched the last bit of indignant fight go out of Henry as his shoulders slumped in defeat. "Yes, it did."

Harding came to stand two feet in front of him and looked him squarely in the eye. "Why?" he demanded, his voice hard and emotionless.

I saw the glint in Henry's eye; the first tiny spark of life I had seen in weeks. I recognized it from the night I whirled in front of the flames and shouted for the walls to crumble. If he was going down, he wasn't going alone. "Because I feared for my job," he stated, returning his stare with weary determination.

"Did you ever fear for the hundreds of lives entrusted to your word when you constructed a shoddy theater?" Harding retorted mercilessly.

He blanched, the sweat on his forehead beginning to run down the side of his face. "This was never supposed to happen," he whispered. "It was all supposed to be rectified in a few weeks. I would never have just let it go, but they had to open; they wouldn't postpone. I was going to see that every deficiency was corrected, every one. Who the hell could have imagined it would burn down on the first night?"

Harding hesitated, expecting an explosive defense from Henry and momentarily thrown by his remorseful admittance. "What made you fear for your job?" he asked, pacing back toward the jury.

Henry took a deep breath, wiping his face with his handkerchief. "Our deadline was impossible from the beginning; improbable at best. This being the first project I helmed, I was…overly confident. But once things got underway I found myself clashing with the owners at every turn. The sprinkler system. The backstage dressing rooms weren't finished. The fireproofing measures for the projection room. Hell, even the *walls* in the projection room and the third floor. Open lath and exposed gas lines were everywhere. If it wasn't visible to the patrons they didn't seem to care if it got finished. The fire escapes. They didn't want to spend the money on them and I was told they didn't fit the 'aesthetic ideal' for the building. They installed the one on the interior of the block where it faced the neighboring building but they resisted putting one on the other side. They said one was sufficient; I argued it was not. They said they didn't want to mar the beauty of the building with an additional unsightly metal fire escape. By the time I convinced them we couldn't get it ordered and installed in time. And those impractical windows that opened inward in the second floor lobby. It was like this on every front. Aesthetics were valued over practicality every time. They were far more concerned with spending their money on features that would make the building impressive, and therefore draw attention and fill seats, than they were with meeting code requirements.

"Eventually Jonathan Mayfield came to the site to check on its progress and I had a meeting with him. I explained my concerns and the resistance I was getting from his company's reps. His response was, 'I spend money where I get a return. Right now, in its current state, the Walt is not earning its keep. I need this building to be open to make money and all these changes you want us to make are going to delay our opening. There is no return there. So what do we need to do to get this theater opened on time?'

"We argued...I insisted the work must be done properly, that there were no shortcuts, but eventually...he offered me a sum of money with the intimation I pass it along to the township inspector to obtain our permit with the agreement that in the weeks after opening they would work on making the changes to bring the building up to code."

A growling of indignant outrage spread through the audience.

"The intimation?"

"He didn't explicitly instruct me to do so," Henry admitted. "But his implication was obvious and his intent clear by giving me the money. There was no other reason for it."

"Can you explain why you feared you would be terminated if you did not accept a bribe?" Harding inquired. "The Mayfield Company was not your employer; according to records you work for Tierney and Sons. Surely they didn't have the power to terminate you."

"There was a stipulation in our contract that if we failed to meet our deadline we—meaning Tierney and Sons—would be forced to pay damages to Mayfield. My boss made it clear if that happened I would find myself unemployed."

"Did you pay off the fire official, too?" Harding asked bluntly.

"No," Henry answered, "but someone must have. I suspect it may have been my boss."

"You suspect?"

"Well, we didn't exactly have an open conversation about it," Henry snipped.

"You allege Jonathan Mayfield paid you to pay off the inspector. Why involve you? Why not just pay him off himself?"

"I would say it was to keep his hands clean. I think he's too smart to do what I was gullible enough to fall for. The blame lies on me. I made the payment."

"Will you please explain to us what your business was in New York?" Harding probed.

"I accompanied my brother-in-law to the Colonial to observe the safety measures in another theater, to reassure myself our deficiencies were not so imperative that the corrections could not be delayed, and also to take note of the procedures in place in an operating theater, for my own knowledge."

Harding looked over his list of questions, whispered to Coroner Matthews, and made a few notes. "Thank you, Mr. Bartolet. You've been very forthcoming. I believe that's all for now." There was the slightest lessening of disdain in his voice as he motioned for Henry to return to his seat.

Henry stood and turned to face him and the jury. "I'm aware of my guilt and I have nothing to hide," he addressed them. "My family has been destroyed by this, and by my actions, and I don't ask for mercy. I ask only that you bring charges against *all* those who are responsible. Whoever you may find that to be, please know that Nathan Bauman is an innocent victim as much as those who have been taken from us. He is a victim of the Mayfield Company, of his youthful ignorance…and of me, and I beg forgiveness of you all."

With that he resumed his seat in the audience, followed by muttered expletive insults and furious, accusatory stares. My mother sobbed quietly into her handkerchief and my father refused to look at him, his eyes fixed ahead in shock. His father leaned toward him and murmured, "They're going to hang you."

"So be it," he muttered back, resuming his hunched stance with his elbows on his knees.

"You didn't have to give them all that. You're not required to divulge everything; this isn't a trial."

"I know."

"So why did you?"

"I've kept enough secrets. One day I'd like to be able to sleep at night again."

He nodded gravely, understanding. "If you owe it, own it," he said matter-of-factly.

"I'm trying, Pop."

Harding pulled another folder from the pile and called the next witness. "Mr. Jonathan Mayfield!"

All eyes scanned the room anxiously for the one face most of them did not know. Jonathan Mayfield's withered, gangly frame rose from the back of the room and ambled slowly to the inquisition chair, aided by an ornately carved wooden and ivory-tipped cane. He wore a finely tailored light gray suit which accentuated his frail physique and matched the paleness of his full head of wispy hair and gray-blue eyes.

Pale they may have been, but those eyes were far from cloudy. They were sharp and alert, moving continually in contrast with his aging body.

He eased himself into the chair and kept his grip on the cane, running his fingers along the grooves in the handle.

"Mr. Mayfield," Harding addressed him.

His hand shot up and he began to speak immediately, his gravelly voice carrying boldly and clearly. "Let me begin by expressing my utmost sorrow and deepest sympathy to the families and the entire town for this unspeakable tragedy. It fills me with dreadful grief that my company has unwittingly played any part in these terrible events, and rest assured I will be conducting my own investigation into how these lapses could have possibly occurred."

"Thank you, Mr. Mayfield. Your sympathies have been dually noted," Harding stated dryly, and for the first time I felt a glimmer of affection for the angry little man. He could see through him just as transparently as I could.

Jonathan pressed his thin lips together and nodded once.

"What say you to the allegations that you paid Mr. Bartolet to pass along a sum of money to obtain your occupancy permit on time?"

"That is a fabrication. Nothing more."

"So Mr. Bartolet took it upon himself to pay off Mr. Harp, the township inspector?"

"He received no direction to do so from me," Jonathan replied.

"So the personal gain in insuring the theater opened on time was his alone?"

"Speaking strictly in a business sense, and in common sense, I stand to profit more from an open theater than a closed one. But I would hardly consider this huge loss of life and my business burning to the ground 'profitable.' So no, there was no personal gain to be had by me short-shifting safety codes to rush opening night."

"Would it be more beneficial to you to receive damages from Tierney and Sons for a late opening or to meet your deadline of August eighteenth?" asked Harding.

"To meet our deadline, naturally, although I don't appreciate your implication. I speak only of my own actions and I don't care to speculate on the motives of strangers. What I can tell you of my own knowledge is that I trusted the inspector to report any deficiencies to the site supervisor so they could be corrected. This is why I have supervisors and inspectors—so I don't have to be involved in the daily activities at a construction site sixty miles away when I have a textile mill to run."

"So you're asserting that neither Mr. Bartolet nor Mr. Harp ever addressed the deficiencies at all."

"I'm sure you've read the reports. They speak for themselves."

"So while you were giving the top managers on the project early bonuses before it was clear if the theater would open on time or not, code inspectors and fire officials were falsifying reports stating that the theater was ready to open, and there is no correlation between the two."

"If they used my money for ill purposes they did it without my knowledge. I don't care what Mr. Bartolet has told you. He acted of his own volition."

Harding stood close in front of Jonathan Mayfield and met his indignant stare squarely. "It just seems odd...everyone with a motive doesn't have the means, and then suddenly there you are with both."

Jonathan's steel gaze met his evenly. "That man is lying. What he does with his money is his business and none of mine. I paid him for the work he did and nothing more. If you want to understand his motives for dragging my name through the mud with his I suggest you interrogate him further."

Harding smirked. "People generally lie to make themselves look better. I don't think anyone is looking favorably at Henry Bartolet right now." He stepped back, turning to face the crowd. "Please explain to us why one of the staircases was gated and locked, thereby preventing the escape of over one hundred souls from the balcony."

Jonathan's hand tightened on his cane. "The gate was in place to prevent patrons from moving between the balcony and the orchestra seating during a performance. By blocking off one staircase an usher could be stationed at the other to ensure no one passed through. In the event of an emergency he was to unlock the gate to facilitate the evacuation of all patrons in the balcony."

"And what became of the usher on the night in question?"

"He panicked and ran for the exit."

"Without unlocking the gate."

"Correct. The poor boy is beside—"

"Why would one need to ensure the balcony and orchestra patrons not mingle?" Harding interrupted.

Those long, crooked fingers worked themselves into the spiraling wooden grooves over and over. "To ensure someone who paid for a cheaper seat didn't slip into a more expensive one once the show began."

"Weren't all the tickets the same price?"

"For live performances there is a difference. This was a policy we were implementing across the board."

"For simplicity's sake?"

Jonathan hesitated, objecting to the phrase but unable to substitute another. "Yes."

"So it was simpler to lock the patrons into their seats rather than risk them stealing a pricier, unsold seat."

"I wouldn't—"

"Who hired Nathan Bauman on to be the projectionist?"

The interruptions ruffled him, causing his soft, grandfatherly features to harden into angry offense. "I did," he snapped. "As an *assistant*."

"So where was the full time projectionist on opening night?"

"We were unable to secure one. Nathan had been trained; I believed he could handle the job himself for a few nights in the interim."

"Did you believe he was qualified to take on the position after approximately two weeks of training?"

"I saw a young man with great potential and an eagerness to learn. I wanted to give him a valuable opportunity."

"The valuable opportunity to provide you with cheap, unskilled labor?"

"You had better watch your mouth, young man!" Jonathan erupted, clutching his cane so hard it shook against his thigh. "You disrespect me!"

"You disrespect the young man you pledged to train and left to fail alone, the child of *fourteen* you entrusted with the sole gate key in the event of a deadly stampede, and the workers whose weaknesses you exploited for your own personal gain. You disrespect this town with your denials and your excuses!" Harding gestured sharply, punctuating each point with his thick fingers, but Jonathan did not shrink away.

"I have broken no laws. The truth is that everything that could go wrong that night did, to the misfortune of everyone who ever stepped a foot inside that God-forsaken theater, in building it or attending it. Shipments were delayed; people made mistakes. You want someone to blame so you look to me for your pound of flesh. But look amongst yourselves. I didn't train the projectionist. I didn't jam the reel. I didn't send the wrong provisions. I didn't authorize an inadequate building. My only mistake was trusting those who failed me. But you need someone to shoulder the burden of guilt, so you look to the name at the top of the roster and you choose me."

Harding turned and paced slowly between him and the jury, contemplating his words for a long time before he spoke.

"How fortunate you are...to have your wisdom...to be the only innocent man in a room full of the guilty."

Jonathan glowered after him, furiously planting his cane and struggling out of the chair. "I am finished answering your questions," he spat, making his way down the aisle much more steadily than he had made the journey the first time.

"Yes, we are quite finished," Harding called after him as he limped out of the room and slammed the door behind him.

He picked up another folder from the table and paged through it. "Yes, well, moving on..."

Caught in the center of the storm, adrift in the tumultuous ocean, was Hubie.

At first, distracted by the doting and persistent affections of his grandparents, he did not miss my presence. But as the days wore on and he was passed between his uncles and cousin and father and my face did not reappear he grew anxious and fitful, his old-man scowl becoming a permanent fixture, demandingly shouting "Mama!" every time someone entered the room. They gently explained to him, in hushed whispers, in moments when he wasn't crying, "Mama is not here. Mama has gone away." But he would have none of it. He went on insisting, and I watched my family crumble inside as they contemplated how many years they would have to explain my absence to him before he would comprehend it and ask no more.

He would see flashes of me in his memory; fragmented moments of me singing to him as I beat the laundry or busying myself at the stove. Through the kaleidoscope of his remembrance I was a towering presence, equal parts kind and furious, but nonetheless essential. I was the center of nearly every memory he conjured; good, bad, or indifferent. He viewed me most often with necessity, but he did at times regard me with great fondness, like when we spent twilight in the field spinning round and round.

He would recall my voice sometimes in the night and it would set him to crying for it.

Henry returned to work after the funeral as the town struggled to resume its previous routines and ground was broken on the new department store a few blocks away. After his admissions at the inquest, however, he found himself quickly unemployed, and scrambled for new work. There were no shortage of positions available in almost every industry but it took weeks for someone to recognize his name and still offer him a job. The family who ran the planing mill finally agreed to employ him, in Christian charity, to enable him to support his crippled cousin and motherless child. At first he took Hubie to stay with Mother during the day, until Daniel was well enough to maneuver around on crutches. Then Daniel looked after him and did what chores he could manage around the house, until the evenings and weekends when he and Henry worked together to do the more physically intensive tasks, like laundry. They pulled Hubie's crib into Daniel's bedroom so Henry could try to rest enough to get up for work in the morning, but no one in the house ever slept for more than two or three hours at a time.

My dear, shattered Henry. I watched him hide the decanter of brandy in his room so he could attempt to drown the nightmares that plagued him but his remedies had little effect. I sat with him in the open doorway of the closet after Daniel retired to bed, as he worried the lace of my dresses between his fingers, feeling the rough pattern of it on his skin and drinking until it felt like silk. Some nights he fell asleep there, propped up against the jamb, his head against my empty skirts, imagining we were sitting by the fire together in the living room on a late autumn evening. Then, in the morning, he would shut up the closet and swear to himself he wouldn't open it again.

Once Henry left the house for the day and they were alone, Hubie kept Daniel busy. His new discovery was the stairs, and he tried to climb them every time Daniel's back was turned. Tortured by visions of him lying on the floor with a broken neck, he spent more time keeping him occupied and safe than he did doing anything else.

Hubie was, even in his limited vocabulary, a vehement critic of Daniel's fledgling cooking skills. This was not necessarily a bad thing, as Henry said little positive or negative and he was in dire need of the criticism.

Poor, sweet Daniel. He struggled to force himself through his daily routines, especially at first when he spent his days alone in the house without Hubie as a distraction. His injuries added to the debilitating helplessness he waded through, reminding him every second of what had transpired. He could not find one moment where he could function as he did before, losing himself in a familiar routine, as my absence pervaded the house and his casted leg greatly impeded his mobility, and every task he performed reminded him that I was not there to do it myself.

He would sit on the front porch sometimes when Hubie was napping and speak to me in the empty rocking chair, and this was cathartic for him. There was no one he could commiserate with, after all, for no one knew the depth of his feelings for me but I. The weight of the secret pressed on him, spawning the fear that one day he would slip in Henry's presence and express a sentiment he ought not to have or regale a memory of me he had no right to take notice of and give himself away. It made him withdraw further but Henry, lost in his own fog, didn't take notice.

If Daniel idealized me in life, he canonized me in death. The flipbook of memories he played through each day became more specific, more optimistically twisted and vivid. In his mind our dance in the field had taken an hour, the music stretching on and on without end. Our interlude in the barn lasted all afternoon and our conversation afterward never occurred. I was forever frozen in a heady combination of tragedy and romance, my youth expatiated and my faults minimized. But he was not alone in this folly. As I watched, below Henry's silent and temperate countenance, his nightmares and his wayward thoughts, I knew I was undergoing the same falsified transformation in his mind.

I held tight to the little house, observing them all with new eyes.

I watched fondly as Daniel barricaded himself and Hubie in the kitchen with chairs stacked in the doorway so that he would not have to chase after him as he struggled to decipher my chicken-scratch handwriting in the family cookbook. With mixing bowls and ingredients everywhere and Hubie pounding fiercely on the beadboard with his trusty wooden spoon, Daniel mopped the sweat from his brow with a flour sack towel and muttered to himself. " 'Fill a glass with milk and add half of it to the mixture.' Which glass? How much is that? Are you kidding me? What the—?" With flour-caked fingers he flipped roughly through the book for elaboration and found none. He leaned heavily onto his crutches and sighed, then hobbled to the cupboard to paw through the glasses. By the time he noticed the banging had stopped Hubie had already crawled halfway through the chair maze on his way to explore the dining room. Cursing softly under his breath, he hurried to disentangle him. Upon being wrangled, however, Hubie let his flailing limbs go limp, nearly toppling Daniel in his tenuous balance, and howled with all the breath in his lungs as Daniel lowered him awkwardly to the floor by his quivering arms.

Perhaps it was because I no longer had need for sleep and therefore no longer felt the interminable weight of its absence hanging over me every hour of the day, but this scene felt so different than when I had been a part of it. I could see the stressful creases at the corners of Daniel's eyes, could hear the familiar exasperation in his breathing as he endeavored to distract Hubie with a dancing ball of light on the wall reflected off the back of a shiny spoon, but as I watched them I found myself appreciating my little boy in a way I had never felt before. In this moment, to Daniel, he was simply being a noodge. But in Hubie's stubbornness and voracity I saw a strength he would desperately need in the coming years. He was hard and self-sufficient. I had always felt he did not cling to me the way I expected my child to. How vitally useful those traits would be to him now.

He was a sturdy child who would survive infancy to carry on his family's name. He refused to listen to anything which did not suit him; a skill that would no doubt be useful when he was of the age to hear the things people would inevitably say about his father.

He was the person he was always meant to be, the person he would need to be, even if I could never comprehend the reason before, and I didn't want him any other way. I didn't want a memory of him adoringly hiding in my skirts, lighting up with joy at the sound of my voice. I wanted him strong and independent, fighting me every step of the way. He needed to be strong more than I needed him to need me.

How murky the waters had been when I had been drowning, but now I could see the ocean had been a lake and I had only ever been inches from the shore.

He thrashed his little fists and screamed in indignation at the injustice of life, and his screams were a whisper and my tears were a smile.

THIRTEEN

Dear Annie,

I feel foolish writing to you but in my idleness I do not know what else to do. I am not allowed visitors but I am allowed post, and now written correspondence is my only tether to the outside world. Eastern State Penitentiary is a penitentiary in every sense of the word, designed to evoke penitence by alternately working its inhabitants and secluding them; the idle hours plenty and filled with naught but the word of the Lord and the echoes of conscience. Its Gothic arches and imposing stone walls remind one of the great cathedrals of Europe that one hears about but never has the fortune to see. Well, I have had the fortune, and it is a cold, bleak place, indeed. Its halls are a labyrinth, seeping out massively from the central rotunda in every direction. If I had to guess the size I could not. Even in the exercise yard those stark stone walls continue, ten feet high, so you are always miniscule and insignificant in scale to this monster, even outdoors.

The solitude is a heaviness that hangs about one like a cloak, blocking out the warmth of companionship or compassion. It sets the mind free to wander down darker roads than I've ever imagined. But I dare not complain. My treatment here has been adequate; I am not starved or beaten, and that is all the luxury I could dare to ask for. We are given oatmeal in the morning and bread and soup in the afternoon. I spend my days assembling shoes, brought the materials and made to work alone in my cell. The drudgery suits me fine; it is more than I deserve.

If they are seeking my penitence they have it; they had it the moment I was sentenced to spend the next five years of my life behind these walls. They had it the moment I destroyed our family—the moment I drove you to your doom—the moment my conscience first objected to the dirt on my hands that was, even then, too late to scrub away. They have it, but they want more, and I have no doubt they will take it from me.

The five year sentences I, my boss, the township inspector, the fire official, and Jonathan Mayfield received were more lenient than I expected, but due to the circumstances being that none of us directly caused the tragedy (as opposed to arson) and our previously spotless records, we avoided harsher punishment and were found guilty of bribery and negligence. Plenty were outraged by the outcome but that is what the court decided, and their verdict we must all abide. Other cases not so different from ours in recent years in other parts of the country dragged out in the courts for years with no prison time ever sentenced. I suppose they were not willing to let that happen here but still did not have a precedent for harsher punishment. It was, nonetheless, an insulting slap on the wrist compared to what we deserved and a mercy I was shamefully grateful for just the same. I was amazed justice grasped Jonathan tight enough to incarcerate him at all, but as owner of the theater he fell with the rest of us. Perhaps his influence was not as far-reaching as I believed it to be.

Daniel promises he will write to me and keep me abreast of any current news but I do not expect his kindness to continue now that I have been removed from his life. He was civil to me when we shared a roof—as necessity dictated, no doubt—but now that I am gone he will certainly leave me to rot without a second thought. That is his right, as it is the right of your parents and my brothers and everyone else who has declared as much save for my father, who has assured me of his love and support despite my failings and who I believe will, through some unfathomable miracle, continue to stand by me in whatever small way he can.

I only say it is unfortunate in the case of Daniel because he retains sole custody of our dear Hubie, and is my only connection to the childhood I shall now miss. Your parents continue to be burdened by Nathan's ongoing care, which has lessened in intensity as he has finally begun to speak again but remains too traumatized to attempt schooling or entertain any thought of employment. A two-year-old's upbringing was far too much to ask of them. My own father is too frail for such an undertaking, and just as I was about to beg of my brothers—or yours—to take him on, Daniel surprised me by insisting that the responsibility go to him. He had become a surrogate mother to him, if you will, in your absence, and as such formed a bond I could not deny. He secured room and board with his friend Joe from Reading, and as I had met the fellow on our excursion for Independence Day and could not object to his character, I felt this might be the best solution for Hubie. It wouldn't be a detriment to raise him out of town, away from those who would seek to inflict injury on our family.

I don't know how your parents stayed in town after the committee decided not to bring charges against Nathan and the mob nearly took the door off its hinges trying to get to him. If it weren't for the position of respect your father held in the community (and the shotgun he held as he took his stand on the porch) and the congregation backing him up against the small but furious sect of people who blamed Nathan for the tragedy, things might have ended badly. But they were the minority and were quickly put down, not to rise again. Still, if they hadn't sent me away, I would have left anyway. I know I can never go back.

I had to sell the house as there was no one willing or able to take over the mortgage and keep up the property once I was gone. My brother William took what furniture he could, at my father's insistence, along with a few boxes of personal effects, both mine and yours. They will hold these and what money is left from the sale of the house that didn't go to pay for my legal defense so that I may have something with which to start anew when I am released.

I gave the blue silk hat to Emma. It was the only item of yours I could bear parting with, and it meant a great deal to her to have something that belonged to you, even if she did not know the true story behind it. I couldn't bring myself to sell it as I did not want a dime of that money back in my possession.

I kept the hat box though, as a reminder, so I would never doubt the reality of that horrible night when you learned the truth or trick myself into the soft delusion that those memories were false. I see your slender hands upon it when I look at its gay green striping. Inside I keep the ambrotype of you your parents had taken when you were fifteen; the only likeness I have of you save for our wedding portrait, and a bouquet of dried roses and carnations from the funeral that I took from your grave the following day. They allow me to keep it in my possession here in my cell, and it is the only item I have beyond my clothing, a Bible, and a metal frame bed and blanket. I suspect they know it is more a source of torture than comfort and that is why they allow it.

The irony is, if you were here to receive this letter I would not bother writing it, for you would undoubtedly have left me by now and refused my correspondence. But now you are the only one I write to, even though you have cause to hate me more than any other and will never see my words, because you are the only one with whom there is so much unspoken that can never be dispelled. To everyone else I have made my repentance and expressed my sorrow. To you I never can.

~Henry

August 18, 1909

Dear Annie,

How is it that we have come to be here?

You are a tattered box of memories I fill with letters and I am an outcast.

Why did you have to run away from me? You never should have been there that night.

YOU NEVER SHOULD HAVE BEEN THERE THAT NIGHT.

YOU NEVER SHOULD HAVE BEEN THERE THAT NIGHT.

WHY DID YOU LEAVE ME?

April 6, 1910

Annie,

His name is Joel Fitzgerald and in the exercise yard three weeks ago I punched him in the back of the head. He is the largest inmate I've seen here and he was bent down, tying his shoes when I ambushed him. One hard blow to his skull. I felt my knuckles crack when I hit him. He whirled and I punched him in the face, and it felt like my fist was on fire but I swung again and he blocked me and clocked me right in the jaw, splaying me out before he leaned into me and landed blows everywhere. I felt my ribs breaking, the blood running out of my nose, and the numbing rush that spread everywhere made me fight back and urge him on.

In the two weeks I spent in the infirmary it was all I could think about. The feeling of my body deservedly breaking down into pieces, one at a time with each blow, and the blood and the fury running out of me in torrents. When it was over I felt empty. Nothing. Glorious nothing.

My yard and mail privileges have been revoked indefinitely.

~Henry

February 8, 1911

Annie,

The guard has just informed me that Jonathan Mayfield is dead. They found him stiff in his cot this morning, just the way I always imagined. A blizzard blew in last evening and it was a colder night than I ever remember it being. I imagine it will be a day or two until they dig away enough snow to take him out of here. I would love to lay eyes on him before he goes, just for one minute, to see him helpless and still and empty like the frozen rat in the corner of my cell, but there's not one chance in hell of that happening.

I expected to feel something when I received the news but I am numb. I envisioned there to be some sort of relief, or exultation, or sense of justice or *something* but now that the moment is here it simply doesn't matter. My day will not change because of his death save for the two sentences the guard spoke to me as he passed my breakfast through the door. The years will still crawl onward and drag me with them and nothing will be altered by his absence for onward is the only direction we can move and his destruction lies in the past. Locked in this jail he was impotent; his future never mattered. Therefore the ending of it matters not.

Nothing changes the fact that I am here. Or that you are not. Nothing that can ever happen will change that.

I have spent every day wishing for his death, blaming him, hating him. Now it feels a fruitless exertion; a disappointing anti-climax. That in itself makes me angry. Even in his death I feel his debt is unsatisfied. It makes me question the purpose of our incarceration, as I know others will feel the same about me. No amount of penance can erase our sins. So what is the purpose? Why didn't they simply hang us and save everyone the trouble?

~Henry

August 18, 1911

Dear Annie,

I miss you with everything that I am.

~Henry

November 1, 1911

Dear Annie,

The guard delivered a package to me today. My mail privileges have been reinstated. I thought I might receive a letter from Daniel, but no—I received a year's worth of letters. An entire bundle from my persistent, faithful cousin. One every month, without fail, without word or encouragement from me for ages, without knowledge if I was even receiving them. As I ceased to respond they increased in frequency, imploring me to remain strong and keep faith, and reassuring me that when I was at last free there were those who were waiting to welcome me home.

He humbles me with his devotion, and it confounds me. I have done nothing to deserve it. I took him in, yes, but I was nothing but hard on him. I sit here telling myself our relationship has been to his benefit, that I have so much to teach him. What a pompous ass I am, thinking I have ever contributed to the man he has become, while he raises my son and shows me compassion I cannot even begin to fathom or put forth myself. His constancy makes me want to be worthy of it.

And then, as if to illustrate his promises, enclosed in one of the letters from this past summer is a tintype of Hubie. He turned four years old this past spring. I admit I did not recognize him at first. It is unbelievable how he has grown. He is not the baby we left behind. Daniel is taking good care of him; he is far from scrawny and he looked happy. His thick curls remind me of my own when I was a boy.

I have never felt the passage of time more acutely than when I look at his image. I know, forevermore, my life will be measured out in the passing years of his, for a year to me is barely the blink of an eye but for him it is an eternity of growth and change. Before him, you were the cornerstone the years of my life hinged on. But now that is changing. In your absence, here in the void, I am reminded that there is something beyond all this, untouched and waiting.

Our son.

Daniel keeps him safe and connected to me, away from the recriminations of Evansville and the tarnish on our name. He is able to scrawl his name in this letter, and Daniel assures me he asks after me and sends his love, wishing me home. I thought he would forget me; I truly did.

It is so easy here to forget the outside world is still a real place and that the people in it continue without me. I think of them like fragments of my own imagination, locked inside my mind, like you. But he is real and he is out there and the realization makes me feel for the first time that redemption isn't a useless endeavor. I just still don't know where to begin.

~Henry

August 18, 1912

Dear Annie,

I feel the need to write to you diminish as the years go by, but on this day my thoughts are always singularly focused on you. Daniel writes that he has gained employment as a bank teller at Central Bank in Reading, and your brother is doing well and has recently secured a position as an ice delivery man. As he still harbors an apprehension of being indoors anywhere save your parents' house, a job consisting of solitary driving and outdoor work suits him well. I am thankful to see him slowly rejoining society. He is apparently such a timid, skittish creature now that I wonder if he will ever have a family of his own, or rather live with your parents until the end of their lives. His progress is a hopeful sign, however, and I will continue to pray for him.

Daniel says he visits your grave on occasion and takes Hubie to see it, but never on this day. I think it still unnerves him how close he came to lying in the ground beside you. I think it probably always will and I don't blame him. He assures me it is quite beautiful on the hill in the autumn, when the hills are ablaze with colored foliage. Someday I will go to see it again, but only for the view. I do not feel the need to visit you where you rest to feel your presence any more than I feel the need to search for you in the place where you left this earth. You are in neither of those places. You are here with me, and in our child, and in the memory of our families and your friends. That is where I will seek you out.

~Henry

LISA GERY

April 5, 1913

Dear Annie,

The weather was unseasonably warm today. You could taste the earth in the air and know that spring had arrived. My outdoor privileges have been reinstated due to productivity and good behavior. Seth, a fellow inmate I have become friendly with, and I walked in the courtyard this morning and talked about his life before his incarceration. When we heard sudden shouting we both ran for the source, without discussion or contemplation. We were only about twenty-five yards away and saw the scuffle as soon as it broke out. One of the inmates whom I was not familiar with had lunged at a guard, Brian; the one who delivered me the news of Jonathan's death. Brian is a kind, quiet man, and generally well-liked. He administers no beatings and rarely utters a harsh word, garnering respect instead through the respect he pays out to everyone in equal measure. I could not fathom why anyone would have a quarrel with him.

The inmate, whose name I later learned was Harold, had him tackled to the ground when we charged at him, knocking him off and pinning him down. Only then did we see the crudely-made, bloody knife clutched in his hand. He swung it at us once before Seth pinned his wrist and wrestled it away. It took the two of us to hold him down as he screamed and ranted.

Others began to shout for help and came to Brian's aid, applying pressure to the wound in his side. Five guards were on us in no time, lifting Brian and carrying him to the infirmary and shackling Harold's arms and legs.

He wailed pathetically as they hauled him to his feet. "I'm sorry, I had to...you can't let me out...they'll kill me...I owe them so much money...this is the only place they can't get me, don't you see...I had to, you can't let me out..."

Once it was clear what our role had been and that we had not been involved in the attack, only in breaking it up, the warden actually shook our hands and thanked us for our bravery. I explained there was no bravery in it; that we hadn't seen the knife when we tackled him, but he said we had probably saved Brian's life nonetheless and commended us for it.

I bristled at the praise, but the thought that we might have saved a life brought a sort of drunken high with it. After years of self-recrimination and punishment and shame, the first glimmer of true redemption was intoxicating. It made me feel hopeful. It made me want more.

In stark contrast, I can still hear Harold's terrified pleas to remain locked up. No doubt he will get his wish now. Blessings come in subtle ways, and how great are mine that I am not burdened with fear of my own freedom. Daniel assures me there will be no pitchfork-carrying mobs waiting to greet me when I am released and while at one time I might have doubted this and while I will never reside in Evansville again, I know he is right. I will have a chance to move on; to rebuild my life. I could not ask for a greater mercy, and I am beginning to think one day I may even succeed in earning it.

~Henry

August 18, 1913

Dear Annie,

Five years to the day since the fire. I have paid my debt, and I am willing to pay the interest for the rest of my days. But I want to go home. I want to live again. Eight more months until I breathe the air of a free man. Eight more months until I hold our son. I am ready. I am ready...

FOURTEEN

On a breezy Saturday morning in late April, 1914, Henry shook the hands of the guards he had become familiar with over the course of the past five years, was wished every success and good will from all and especially Brian, and stepped out of the shadow of the imposing stone labyrinth that had been his prison and his shelter. He stood just outside the gate and felt the warmth of the sun on his face, squinting against its brightness but not looking away. He twitched his shoulders, readjusting to the feel of wearing his own clothes. They were looser than they had been the last time they hung on his body; the last smell of home washed away with the harsh soap of the penitentiary laundry kettles. He smiled as he imagined changing his clothing that afternoon, burning his shirt, and never smelling that scent again.

"Henry."

Daniel stood next to the runabout parked several yards away, in a sharp brown suit, his hat tipped back, watching him. He stepped forward with a tentative grin, extending his hand. When Henry closed the distance between them and shook it they pulled each other into a tight embrace.

"Welcome home, cousin," Daniel exclaimed, a joyous chuckle in his voice.

"God, it feels good to hear that," Henry admitted, pulling away and looking him over. "You look well."

Daniel floundered to return the compliment, eyes skimming his scant frame. "You look…pale."

"Incarceration will do that."

"But otherwise well."

"Don't flatter me. I've seen a mirror. I know I look like shit."

"You just need fresh air and some good food."

"Aren't you just the little clucking housewife?" Henry teased dryly.

He shrugged. "It's the mother in me coming out. All that time spent with Hubie."

Henry's smile faded. "Thank you for not bringing him here."

"He's waiting at home for you," Daniel assured him. "Along with your father."

He nodded. "I don't ever want him to have a memory of this place."

"I know that. Why don't we get going? We have a long drive." He motioned toward the passenger door and he and Henry climbed in, stowing his one possession, the striped hat box, carefully between his feet. With the top down his first dose of fresh air was plentiful.

"This is nice," Henry admired, running a palm over the dashboard.

"Bought it off Joe. He bought a new one."

"Oh, is this his? I didn't recognize it."

"Well, it's been awhile."

"Yes. It has."

A long but not uncomfortable silence fell between them. Henry marveled at the prevalence of automobiles versus buggies and how much the ratio had shifted. He shivered slightly as the wind had a bite to it but was enjoying the ride and the constant flow of blessedly changing scenery too much to complain.

"How are you enjoying your work at the bank?" he asked eventually, even though Daniel had discussed his satisfaction at his promotion to loan officer in his letters.

"Very much. I find it very easy. I've an aptitude with numbers; it all comes very naturally. The people are congenial and I'm meeting new faces all the time. It's a rather pleasant environment."

"I'm glad to hear it. To find something you truly enjoy to earn a living at…I'm so thankful to hear you're doing well. You deserve it."

At one time he would have flushed with pride at the compliment, turning pink all the way to the tips of his ears. Now he simply smiled graciously and said, "Thank you, Henry."

A few more miles passed, bearing them ever closer to home.

"So you have the apartment to yourself now, then?"

"Yes," Daniel explained, "Joe got married three months ago and purchased a house downtown. There will be plenty of room for all of us."

"I shouldn't need to impose on you for long. As soon as I can secure employment I can—"

"Henry, you're welcome to stay as long as you'd like or need, I've told you. There is much to sort out. It may take you awhile to find employment, and then to save up enough to get started. I don't want you shorting yourself to make it easier on me. I'm fine, and glad to have you."

"I still have some money from the house; I can use that. It shouldn't take long to get set up."

Daniel's jaw tightened. "We don't need to go into all this now. We'll have plenty of time to work through a plan; discuss how things will be."

"I just want you to be assured we will not take advantage of your hospitality for a moment longer than necessary."

A plummeting disappointment overtook him. "So you plan on taking Hubie with you, then?"

"Of course, he's my son. What did you—"

Daniel shook his head and sighed, removing a hand from the steering wheel to rub at the nape of his neck. "I didn't want to have this discussion here, now, so soon."

"You'd rather he stay with you?" Henry exclaimed.

"I've raised him for five years," he said calmly, keeping his eyes on the road. "He's like a son to me, too."

Henry was struck silent, dumbfounded. "I...assumed you'd be ready to move on with your life," he stammered. "Finished with cleaning up after me, wanting your freedom."

"It's not like that," Daniel insisted. "Caring for him, raising him, he's *become* my life. I know he's not mine, I know you have a right and I don't want to keep you from him, but I was hoping we could find some way to move forward that won't completely disrupt the life he's grown to know."

"What are you suggesting? You want to *share him*?"

"I don't know what to do! That's why I didn't want to get into this now, because it's too complicated. I don't know what will be best for him and that's all I want, in the end. If handing him over to you and bidding you both goodbye is it then I would do it but you have to understand, you will be a stranger to him. I know you are bonded to him but he doesn't know you anymore. This will take time. Life is different than what you left behind, for all of us, and you can't force it to be any other way."

"I hear you. I didn't say I disagreed," Henry said, much to Daniel's surprise. "I just...you caught me off guard. I know you're right, but I need him. I've left him behind for too long already. I *will* be a part of his life now."

"I know. Let's just take this one step at a time, and start with you *seeing* him again. That's enough."

"You don't need to coddle me," he grumbled, but it was intentionally too low for Daniel to hear.

Five miles passed in silence again.

"What is it like to be out?" Daniel inquired gently, glancing sideways at his passenger.

Henry thought for a moment, unwilling and unsure how to express the myriad of emotions that crashed through him. "I can breathe," he said at last, drawing the warming morning air into his lungs again. He stared out the windshield at the scraggly weeds that had sprung up along the edge of the road, his face relaxed and softened. "It feels like I can finally breathe again."

When they turned off the main road and drove two blocks into a quiet neighborhood, coming to a stop in front of the large orange brick home that had been converted into four modest apartments where Daniel resided, Henry struggled to force his legs to carry him from the vehicle. It was one house that sat in a row of many of similar size and shape, all slightly different and built in different decades, some single family dwellings and some apartments. A few were falling into disrepair, paint peeling from the window panes and wet rot on the eaves, but most were fairly well kept. The street and the neighbors' porches were devoid of people. He clutched the hat box to his chest like a shield, commanding his hands to be steady.

"Hubie is so excited to see you," Daniel reassured him as they made their way up the concrete walkway. Henry nodded, even though he was walking behind and Daniel wouldn't see it.

They entered through a battered and gouged front door into a communal hallway and traversed the stairs to the third floor. The comingled smells of last night's dinner and this morning's breakfast from multiple households lingered in the air, converging into a vaguely greasy and oddly savory odor. It made his stomach growl and lurch at the same time.

With a small sigh he resigned himself to the fact that nothing would ever smell quite like home again.

In the third floor hallway the woodwork changed from dark varnish to an antiqued white paint. Daniel fished the key from his pocket, slipped it into the lock, and stood back, swinging the door open wide.

Henry stepped into a small but very clean kitchen with a gas range, a tiny icebox, a hutch, and a walnut drop leaf table with three chairs, two of which matched. Beyond this was a living room with two large curtainless windows that let the light pour in, furnished with two armchairs and a side table he immediately recognized as his own. The wall between the windows was hung with family portraits and in the center of these was our wedding portrait.

Before he could be drawn to the sepia and pastel memories behind glass his sight settled on the two guests waiting anxiously to greet him.

"Pop," he breathed, his smile so broad it was almost painful.

His father leaned heavily on his cane, his eyes misty and his face tight. His wrinkles were deeper than Henry remembered them, and his stoop harsher, but he was familiar in a comforting way that called to something deep inside Henry's brain, long lost in the abandonment of childhood, that made him want to run to him like a boy and cling to him forever. What stopped him—besides dignity—was the small, wide-eyed child hiding bashfully behind his father's arm. His tight, sandy curls and ocean blue eyes peered from behind his shield; his smooth, porcelain face a cross of curiosity and apprehension and excitement. He stumbled between the three, peeking out, leaning to and fro, trying to catch a glimpse of the man they called his father without chancing to expose himself entirely.

Henry dropped to one knee and called out as one might to a frightened kitten. "Hubie?" He leaned to force eye contact with the boy. "Do you remember me?"

He stepped out from behind his grandfather's arm, still clutching his hand, and observed Henry from a distance.

"Hello, Father," he spoke clearly, his sweet bell voice unwavering.

"Hello, son. Do you remember me?"

He knew he shouldn't ask, knew he probably didn't want the truth, but he couldn't stop himself.

Hubie thought for a moment, looking up at Daniel hovering in the kitchen for guidance. "I think I do. I remember a train ride. I was frightened and you carried me. I don't think it was Uncle Daniel. It must have been you."

Henry broke into a trembling smile, remembering the train ride they had taken to Reading, thankful his clouded, youthful memories were so much kinder than reality. "Yes, that was me. I carried you.

And we went on a picnic, us and your mother and Uncle Daniel and Joe. And you rode the carousel."

Hubie grinned. "I remember the carousel. We go there sometimes."

"Do you? That's wonderful. Uncle Daniel has taken good care of you."

"Yes." He beamed at Daniel affectionately.

Henry sat back on his heels, feeling unsteady. "I've missed you so much," he whispered, as Hubie stepped forward and his shape began to blur.

"I've missed you too," he replied, spreading his arms and wrapping them carefully around Henry's shoulders.

With that he crushed Hubie to his chest, openly weeping, and with his face buried in his little neck he smelled of pine tar soap and lavender and home.

Late that night, after Henry's father had been taken home and Hubie was sleeping soundly in his bed, Henry and Daniel sat up at the kitchen table with a decanter of brandy between them, half empty. An oil lamp on the hutch lit the room softly, making the liquor glow like golden honey in their glasses.

"This is nice," Henry said, tilting his glass as he swirled the liquid. "It's been forever since I've had this, here."

"Yes, you've mentioned."

"Have I?"

"Twice."

"Mmm. Well, it has."

"Well then, have some more. You're almost empty."

"Thank you, sir. That's good." He tipped his glass in salute and sipped again, and Daniel did the same, but smaller.

"Your father seems to be getting around fairly well," Daniel observed, leaning back comfortably in his chair with his legs outstretched, crossed at the ankles.

"Yes, I was surprised to see it. His doctor has him on some new opiate. All they can do is dull the pain but at least it helps."

"He's a very stoic man, your father."

"Always has been," Henry agreed.

"Man of few words."

He nodded.

"Runs in the family."

Henry laughed out loud. "Eh," he conceded with a shrug and a grin.

Daniel shook his head in amusement.

"I'm not so much like him," he insisted, growing serious. "Am I?"

Daniel raised an eyebrow and deferred his answer by taking a sip.

"I don't think I am. No, I don't think so."

"Would it be so terrible if you were? He seems a fine man."

"Well, I mean, he was always a good father; he provided us everything we needed, taught us how to work hard and have a sense of accomplishment, but…after Mom died, once the funeral was over, she was just gone. He didn't speak of her, didn't keep her effects around, didn't let us mention her. Like he tried to make her disappear from memory." He drained his glass and Daniel sat up and filled it again immediately. "I don't think he could live with her ghost. He just couldn't. So none of us could, either. And I never thought I'd be in the same position but here I am and I—I don't want him to forget her."

Daniel knew he was talking about Hubie now. He wanted to reassure him but didn't want to interrupt his flow of thought.

"I don't want it to be like she never existed," he rambled on. "Hell, at this point, to him, it's almost like *I* don't exist. And I want him to know her. Because she was such a damn good woman. She was. I know that now. She was."

"Yes, she was," Daniel echoed, fingering the rim of his glass but not drinking.

"I probably am a man of too few words," he reflected sullenly.

"Not in the company of drink, you're not," Daniel offered.

"Too few and too late," Henry continued, paying no attention. "There was so much we never said."

"Don't do that," Daniel pleaded, sitting forward. "It's been too long for that. Don't rouse that specter."

"Rouse it? It never leaves me. Not really. It's always hiding, waiting to creep back in. Just...waiting."

Daniel said nothing, unsure how to respond.

"You know...there was a time, not too long after Hubie was born...that I wondered for a moment if we hadn't made a mistake. Just a moment. I know it's horrible to say it, but, you don't realize how completely your life is going to change. You know, but you don't *know*. You can't. I love him to death, but after all the sleepless nights and the constant...I'd just look at her, and I wondered...is this worth it? She was so sweet-tempered and patient and by the end we were just screaming at each other and it's not his fault, I'm not saying it is, but I don't wonder if that's where we started to unravel. Now I look at him and I can't believe I ever entertained the thought—it must have been the delirium—because I would give up anything for him, *anything*, but in the moment when it was all going to shit I had those thoughts, when I missed when the world was just her and I."

"Did she ever know?"

"No!" He laughed as though the thought was preposterous. "I could never tell her that! I know she struggled with him at times but she was always steadfast. She would have thought me a traitor if she ever knew."

Daniel sighed. "You two were more alike than you realized."

Henry's eyes narrowed slightly. "What do you mean?"

"Both people of too few words, or at least, the ones that mattered."

THE PERSISTENCE OF VISION

"Was she, now?" He sniffed and tossed back the rest of his brandy. "And what exactly was she not saying?"

Daniel swallowed carefully. "I don't know. That's my point. She was never one for confidences."

"No. She wasn't." His eyes softened as he stared down at the table. "Although, at the end, on that last day...she told me that she missed me."

Daniel laced his fingers together around his glass. "If she said it then I'm sure she meant it."

"Yes. I believe she did." He nodded, looking up. "There's something I need to ask you."

Daniel's breath caught in his throat but he did not flinch.

"I don't even want to voice it after all you've done for me, but it's always been...I don't think it ever did...there are things you could put to rest for me that I don't want to know, but this I just have to."

His tongue felt heavy with the effect of the brandy and his mind ambled slowly from thought to thought but the question lingered and refused to leave him so he asked it.

"I accused you once of being in love with my wife," he said, still finding it painful to utter my name aloud. "And now, after all these years, I don't care if you were. I just need to know if she returned it."

Daniel understood, as he looked into Henry's tentative face and pleading eyes, the subtleties and nuances of the human psyche that had been a mystery to him in his early youth. He knew the difference between praying for what you desired and receiving what you needed. And he grasped, where I had failed to, the difference between the merciful lie that protects another person from a truth which can do naught but damage and the secret that masquerades as mercy, whose purpose is selfish and protective only to the speaker against the risk that honesty brings.

"No," Daniel said, shaking his head slowly. "She was ever faithful to you, Henry. She never stopped loving you."

He met his gaze without regret or shame, recognizing half of what he said was a compassionate and necessary omission of truth and half of it was not a lie at all.

"Thank you," Henry whispered, exhaling deeply.

"I don't let Hubie forget her," he continued. "It's why I have your wedding portrait in the living room. I explain to him constantly who those people are and why they are important to him. He may not remember everything but he knows who you are, who she was."

Henry studied his empty glass without filling it, rocking it on its bottom rim. When Daniel offered to pour he declined with a wave of his hand.

"I'm sure I'll never understand why you've done all that you've done for us," Henry said at last.

"You're family," he said simply.

"I have plenty of family who won't speak to me. You don't need to be the exception. You don't owe me anything."

"You didn't owe me anything, either, when you took me in."

"This is entirely different. I gave you a room in exchange for a few months of labor. You've *raised my son* for five years. You kept in constant communication while I was away; kept me tied to everything I left here. That was…I cannot tell you what that meant to me."

Daniel shrugged, taking a sip.

"I just want to thank you," Henry said earnestly. "There were days when an encouraging word from you was all I had. I lived on it. I had no other hope. You've done more for me than I can express and I just want you to know how grateful I am, for everything."

"You don't need to thank me."

"I do. You have no idea what it's like. I can't blame anyone for turning their back on me. No one could hate me as much as I hated myself."

"Henry, you and I…you don't need to explain it to me."

Henry's eyes, hazy with brandy, began to sharpen with burgeoning questions.

Daniel considered his words with care, as visions of the sweet girl he lost to the mill all those years ago danced in his vision, perfect and timeless. "I know your hell. I've stood within its walls. I know what it is to make one mistake you can never take back."

"You do?"

"You and I...we're the same person."

Comprehension glimmered in Henry's mind at last; years of puzzle pieces suddenly converging to paint a vague but recognizable portrait. "Mayfield," he breathed, mouth agape. "What the hell did they do to you?"

"Nothing I didn't bring on myself."

"No, what di—"

"It's in the past," Daniel said with finality, and Henry knew he meant to leave it there. "It's just...caring for Hubie, helping you...it's my redemption. I haven't done it for you half as much as I've done it for my own absolution. So don't look upon me as a saint. I'm not one."

Henry nodded, reeling, his curiosity burning but his respect for his cousin outweighing it. He poured another draught of brandy into his glass and held it above the table. "To sinners and criminals alike," he toasted, clinking it against Daniel's glass as he raised it up.

"*Sláinte*," Daniel chimed, taking a sip.

They relaxed in their chairs, watching the decanter grow empty in the flickering light as the night drained slowly from the clock on the wall, second by ever-passing second.

I watched the years dissolve beneath my feet, breaking down into fleeting moments worth remembering amidst thousands of mundane and utterly beautiful trivial seconds lost in the torrent. The years eroded as they passed, each one growing shorter and more brittle, crumbling faster into the sands of an hourglass which were already funneled into its glass coffin, measuring out the life gone by.

It frightened me, the haste with which the time passed. I watched my family advance with every breath toward the inevitable culmination of their era on earth and I knew that no matter the length it would not be enough. I was greedy for them in their obliviousness, too distracted to recognize the death march they were on. I wanted them to have all the time I left behind and more. Even witnessing my demise did not diminish their expectation of a long life; the assumption that was never guaranteed or even implied but that which every human grasps with both hands and demands with childlike insistence is forthcoming.

They marched along and I followed them, sometimes in their midst and sometimes from afar, never missing a moment of their fascinating and fragile vitality. They kept me in their hearts, sometimes pulling me close with their memories, and I was helpless and unwilling to turn away.

When Daniel climbed the hill one autumn morning to lay a bouquet of daisies on my grave I watched him from my perch at the marble angel's feet and wished he would not spend his time lingering in this place of vacuous, silent tombs.

"Hello, Annie," he said aloud, laying his gift at the base of the monument. He touched his fingertips to my name engraved in the stone, as he always did, tracing it with tentative swipes and wiping any dust or dirt away.

"Henry said he would come to see you soon. I know he hasn't yet but I think he's almost ready."

Henry was not ready, I knew; I watched him lie to Daniel when he promised he would come. Perhaps he could hear me when I whispered in his ear not to dwell here. Daniel did not listen, but then, Daniel never did.

He sat down in the grass with one leg curled under the other, half facing toward the valley, alternately glancing back toward me and out over the town. "He's doing well," he went on. "He volunteers with the West Reading Fire Company. He loves his work there. I think he's finally found his purpose. I worry for him—he's downright fearless sometimes. I worry he'll leave Hubie an orphan, but I can't say a word to him. He seems happier than I remember seeing him in...I don't know how long. At least, I suppose it's happiness. It can be hard to tell with him. Peaceful, anyway. I think he's working through some things, doing what he's doing. I think the only way he can right it in his mind is to actually go out there and save lives. It's that black and white for him, to try to tip the scale back. I suppose I can understand that.

"Through getting to know one of the other firefighters he got in at the lumber mill uptown. Finally making his own money. I *know* he's happy about that. It kills him to take a cent from me for anything; that's always been and it will never change. Even just in board. When he does it for someone else, it's 'family duty.' When he must accept it, it's 'charity.'

"Hubie is well. He has just entered second grade. You would be amazed how smart he is. He just catches on to everything, instantly. You would be very proud. He's still stubborn though—he gets reprimanded by his teacher every few weeks for sassing her or refusing to do his assignment. We're working on that, but that boy's like a mule when he sets his mind to something. Rather like his parents. Knowing you both, I don't think he stood a chance of being any different."

He plucked a long piece of grass and shredded it with his fingernails. "It's so quiet here," he muttered, gazing out over the luscious valley that dipped and rose up again on the other side, streaked with yellow and amber and chartreuse foliage.

"Quiet enough to hear every thought you've ever had," I said.

"You can see forever up here."

"Exactly."

He turned toward me with blind eyes. "I still miss you. I don't think that will ever go away. Just knowing I can't see you makes me want to more than anything."

"Seeing doesn't make you miss someone less," I observed, wishing, as always, that he could hear me.

"I've asked God to punish me instead of you so many times, but of course nothing will bring you back. And then sometimes I think maybe He is, and that's why I'm here and you're not."

His words broke my heart. "Oh Daniel, don't you see it yet? Your life is by God's grace, not His wrath. We each made a choice that put those events in motion and put us where we were that night; where we all are now. God didn't punish you, Daniel. He wept beside you."

He breathed deeply and picked another weed from the ground. "But I know you wouldn't want me to think like that. You'd scold me and tell me not to dwell. And I'm trying not to, which is why I'm here. I want to tell you that...I've fallen in love. I want to tell you about Erin.

"I think that you would like her; I truly do. I met her at the bank. I helped her get some things in order for her father when his health began to decline. She's so easy to talk to. The first time we met I felt so at ease with her; I can't even explain why. It just felt as though we had known each other for a long time. She understands my sense of humor, and I can speak my mind around her and she never reproaches me or finds me odd. That is so rare.

"She adores Hubie; she gets on well with Henry; she understands our unique living arrangement without question. She's so patient and soft-spoken. I believe you would have been fast friends.

"You told me once you wanted me to know love and honor, and believed you'd shown me otherwise, but it is because of you that I recognized love when I found it. What I feel for Erin helps me put things into perspective. Helps me to keep moving forward instead of looking back. Except sometimes, as today, I find myself wishing I could speak to you. I know rationally what I'm ready to do, and what you'd want for me, but I wish I could hear you say that it's all right to let you go. I feel like I'm betraying you in some way for moving on, like I'm forgetting you by trying to live." He sighed, lowering his head. "But you're gone and I can't live in that little house in the country with you in perpetual summer anymore. That time is over."

I rose and knelt before him, watching his face flicker with conflicting emotions as he struggled to bring them under control, and placed a kiss on the worrisome crease between his brows. "Live," I whispered, reaching with all my might for the energy to make him hear me. "Live, my sweet boy. You got out for a reason. Don't waste your precious years crying for me."

The crease disappeared, his face relaxing as a tear spilled from the corner of his eye. His lips quirked upward at the corners.

"I know it's time," he said, wiping his face with the back of his hand. "I wish I could hear you say it, but I know. You tried to let me go years ago. I just never wanted to hear it. Now when I'm ready it's too late." He chuckled softly. "You always said I didn't listen well. I can just hear you saying that now."

"Some things never change," I agreed with a smile.

He looked up, his eyes shining, the decision finally settled in his mind. "I'm going to ask her to marry me," he confided in a whisper. "I want you to be the first to know. She makes me happy, Annie. In a way I never thought I would be. She makes me love you in the way that I should — as a dear, beloved cousin; as a kindred spirit; as a best friend. And that is how I will carry you with me."

He stretched his legs out, the one which tended to ache occasionally stiffening already from his awkward position on the ground. After beginning to get up he thought better of it, settling back into a more comfortable stance. We sat together in silence, observing the gauzy wisps of clouds meander by above the minute scurrying and bustling of the town below, the automobiles and people like ants on a mission of the greatest importance and us on the hill above it all, watching with the clarity and perspective that comes only with distance.

Back at the apartment, Henry and Hubie were sitting at the kitchen table finishing their lunch of leftover beef stew when Daniel returned.

"Would you like some?" Henry offered, gesturing to the pot on the stove. "There's a bit left. We weren't sure when you were coming back so we ate."

"No, thank you, I'm not hungry. You can have it." He pulled up a chair and joined them. "I think this one here would lick the pot if we'd let him," he teased Hubie.

"It's not my fault I'm always hungry," he responded with a mischievous grin.

"No, you're just growing," Daniel agreed. "Continuously. You're almost ready to have the hem on those pants let out, aren't you?"

Hubie stretched his leg out and wiggled the trousers around his ankle, showing a generous amount of sock. "Maybe."

"I can take care of that," Henry offered. "No need to take them to a seamstress if it's just a hem."

"Papa, you can sew?" Hubie giggled, amused.

He smiled tightly. "I used to make shoes when I was away. I think I can handle a hem."

"I could ask Erin to do it, too. She wouldn't mind," said Daniel.

"That's fine. I just don't want to waste money on a seamstress."

"Understood."

When they cleaned their bowls, Henry excused Hubie from the table and took their dirty dishes to the sink.

"It's beautiful up there this time of year," Daniel told him, his voice lowered so as not to catch Hubie's attention in the next room. "So peaceful."

"I've seen it."

"This time of year?"

"It looks the same. Just more colorful." He scrubbed and hastily rinsed their bowls.

"I think you would like it."

"I like it fine. That's why I bought a plot there."

"You did?"

Henry nodded as he wiped his hands on the dishtowel. "Not long after the funeral. I bought the closest plot I could get to the memorial before they were all bought up."

"I didn't know that."

"I didn't see a reason to discuss it." He tossed the towel on the counter and turned to him with a sigh. "So you can stop badgering me to visit. I'll have plenty of time to rest there when I'm dead. All right?"

"All right," he acquiesced, not wishing to annoy him.

"I just don't need to go there to feel her," he murmured. "I don't know why you do."

Daniel shrugged, looking away. "I feel her when it's quiet. It doesn't get quieter than up there."

"I suppose," he grumbled. He cleared his throat. "So what are your plans for today? I was thinking of going out for a drive with Hubie."

"Yeah? That's nice. I, uh...I'm going to go see Erin. Today would be a good day for a picnic."

"Yeah, it would be," Henry concurred as he started for the living room.

"And as good a day as any to ask her."

Henry halted. "Ask her?"

Daniel nodded, his lips a thin line. "The big question."

He stepped back towards the table, his face lit up with a surprised smile. "Well, congratulations, man!" He reached out and shook Daniel's hand as he rose and they embraced with one arm and a pat on the back as Daniel chuckled bashfully. "It's about time! She's a sweetheart and you've been a bachelor far too long."

"Thank you. I'm sure she would agree with your assessment of my bachelorhood. I think she's known all along and has just been waiting for me to come around and get on board. But I shouldn't speak yet—I'll look a fool if she says no!"

"She won't," Henry assured him. "She'd be the fool to say no."

"Aw, thank you, Henry, really."

"Well, we should get out of your way then. You've got quite an afternoon to prepare for. Hubie, get your coat and goggles if you want to go out for a drive!" he called toward the bedroom.

"Coming, papa!" came the squeal from the other room.

Fifteen minutes later Hubie was wrapped up warmly and tucked in the wicker sidecar adjacent to Henry's 1912 Indian V-Twin.

"Where are we going?" he asked as Henry mounted the bike and the engine chugged and growled to life.

"I thought we'd ride up to Schuylkill County; take a drive through coal country."

"That's far, isn't it?"

"Uncle Daniel's going to be busy for a while," he explained as they pulled out.

Up into the mountains they drove, winding their way along the long, lazy switchbacks, the gravel road beneath the tires carrying them away into a land of vibrant, streaking color and crisp, occasionally woodsmoke-laced air. The hills wrapped around them, sometimes pulling in close and sometimes dipping away into swift ravines flowing with sparkling creek water, crossed with makeshift fallen log bridges. They were soft hills, downy with the last of the cascading curtain of leaves that would soon slip away to reveal the bare, twisted winter branches hiding beneath. Sunshine slanting through the breaks in the trees bathed them in pockets of warmth as they traversed between the light and the shadows, chasing away the chill in the air in welcome, intermittent bursts. The steady rumble of the engine between Henry's legs was like a soothing melody; the constant vibration lulling his joints into numbness for a time before they would start to ache and force him to take a break and stretch.

"Look!" Hubie shouted, pointing to an eagle soaring lazily overhead.

"I see it!" Henry said, glancing upward.

"It's very pretty up here," he added, his head swiveling constantly to take in his evolving surroundings.

"I like to ride up here. It's peaceful."

As Hubie nodded and beamed up at him, he knew his son appreciated this place as much as he did. It was a place of simple beauty and no memory. A place to get lost in, but not to hide. To soar.

He marveled at the sweet nepenthe of an unspectacular moment in the open air with the child who bore his name. The child who was a promise of so many untold joys and unconditional companionship, and the story in himself of the great love Henry felt blessed to have known. He caught a glimpse of the days that stretched before him and they were not draped in shadows as the ones that had passed. They glistened with the promise of laughter, of hope, of familial love and loyalty, of work and of purpose. He could have shouted with joy at the chance to breathe without the pain that lived in his heart like an iron weight, darkening every moment of his existence with its presence. He looked up into a sky so blue it looked like a watercolor painting, the bluest sky he had ever seen or perhaps just ever noticed, and knew a part of that weight was finally gone. Its marks would always linger on his heart but the lightness in his soul told him that he was still alive. And that he wanted to be.

He rolled on the throttle, a serene smile on his lips, the sun warm on his body, and drove onward.

EPILOGUE

It was a few moments before the earliest hints of dawn first began to appear in the sky, when the world was still dark but the sky lost its blackness by a few shades along the horizon. Hubie marched along the sidewalk, his hands stuffed deep in his pockets, his back hunched with his hurried pace. The early June air was refreshing and cool, and it cleared his head a bit. He sucked the air deep into his lungs and blew it back out harshly, trying to settle the jittery current that tingled through his limbs. It had been with him for a week now at its current intensity and he still was not accustomed to its presence.

He let himself through the low, cast iron gate that surrounded the familiar white house with green shutters and followed the brick pathway around to the back of the house. Making as little noise as he could, he opened the door to the kitchen and slipped inside.

"How's Pop? Is he still here?" he whispered into the dim room.

"He's here. You know I would have called you if anything changed. Have a seat; I'll get you some coffee."

"Thanks, Aunt Erin." He pulled out the kitchen chair closest to him and sank into it, watching as she took the coffee pot from the stove and poured some into a mug. Her blue gingham apron was cinched tight around her waist, even at this hour. He couldn't remember ever seeing her without it. He wondered if she slept in it.

"I suppose Uncle Daniel never joins you for coffee in the morning," he commented as she handed him the steaming cup and he sipped it, black and strong.

"Not this early. You know he's never been a morning person. I don't know how he stays in bed that long. Five hours and I'm finished. Any more than that and I'm just wasting time."

"How long do the boys sleep? Do they take after you or him?"

She smiled, tempering her coffee with cream and stirring it into a whirlpool. "Willie sleeps late. I always have to wake him up. But James gets up early. When he was quite small he liked to 'help' me in the kitchen. But now he just comes down and reads or tells me about what's happening in school. It's nice, quiet time." She studied him, the faint crow's feet on her face crinkling further as she narrowed her eyes at him. "You, however, are *not* an especially early riser, and you need your rest now more than ever. And yet you're at my door every morning this week before dawn." She tsked her tongue at him affectionately. "You need to be getting your sleep. Not that I don't appreciate your company. But you won't be getting any once the baby comes; you'll see."

Hubie sighed, rubbing at the tightness in his neck. "If he ever comes. Ethel's past due now. How am I supposed to sleep when I'm worrying so?"

Erin wisely glossed over the concerns she'd heard every day as of late. "He'll come. And who's to say he's a he? I'm betting on a girl. We need a little girl around here. Too many men, you lot."

"I don't think Ethel cares one way or the other right now. She's just wants him here."

"Her."

"Whichever." He grinned, his wavy blond locks falling boyishly over his forehead as he lightly shook his head. "I'll settle for healthy."

"That's the right attitude to have. None of it's in our control, anyhow."

His smile was short lived. "So Pop made it through the night?"

She nodded, taking a sip from her dainty porcelain cup; the special one ringed in gold filigree and rose blossoms that was not part of a set and that she alone used for her coffee. "He's weak, but he's been weak for days. He could last hours or weeks. We really can't know."

"He's strong," Hubie insisted. "He keeps hanging in there. Every time it looks like he's going to go he just…fights back."

Erin replaced her cup on the saucer and took his hand in hers. "I just want you to be prepared—"

"He *could* get better. He looked stronger the other day."

"And then yesterday he wouldn't eat."

Hubie winced.

"I'm not trying to be cruel," Erin assured him. "But the doctor agreed it's a certainty now. Denial is only going to make this more painful and I wouldn't wish you pain for anything in this world."

"He's too young to have a heart attack," he muttered petulantly. "He's only forty five."

"He abuses that body of his like it's twenty. I told him he should stop going on the fire calls after the last episode. But damned if he'll listen." There was a motherly frustration in her voice that kept it from being outright angry.

"I'm glad he always had you guys. Especially now."

"Of course." The praise ruffled her, made her fidget like an itchy garment.

"The older I get, I see...I think he's the type who needs looking after. It makes me wonder why he never remarried."

Erin shook her head. "Too stubborn, that one. He'd have to admit he needed someone."

"Right. Not going to happen," Hubie concurred.

"Besides, he always had you. I think that was enough."

"I would have taken him in, too, if not—"

"No, no, don't even think it. You can't handle this with Ethel in her condition. You've enough on your plate. He's fine here."

"You *are* a better nurse than I would be. I can attest to that."

She shrugged. "He heeds me somewhat. More than anyone else, anyway. He's always been like a brother to me." There was sadness in her voice, even though her eyes didn't betray it.

"I always felt I was lucky growing up that I had you both. That I had two places to call home."

"Your Uncle Daniel was always concerned you'd grow up missing something. He never wanted you to feel like that. He wanted you to have a family."

"And I did. Having you right down the road from our apartment, being able to come and go as I pleased, being shuffled off over here every time Pop went on a fire call—those are good memories. Growing up it just seemed like a normal thing because I didn't know any different but now that I'm older I can really appreciate everything you did for us. I just...wanted you to know that."

She smiled fondly, cupping his chin in her hand. "You were my first son before I had children. I've always loved you like one of my own." She stood and turned to the stove, taking the coffee pot and refilling their cups. "Have you settled on a name yet?"

"I think so, but Ethel keeps changing her mind on the girl's name."

"Well, you're going to need that one, so you'd better decide."

He didn't grin this time at her little tease. She rejoined him at the table.

"I'm afraid to wish away each hour," he admitted, staring down at his hands around the mug. "I can't take this waiting but I know what's coming and I just don't—"

"There's no doubt this baby is your father's grandchild. He—or she—is just as stubborn as he is. It's a Bartolet family trait."

"I know. They both keep...lingering. Every day I wait for word that the baby is coming or Pop is going and they just linger. It's excruciating, this waiting. Why does this all have to happen now?"

She thought for a moment, sipping her coffee. She had often wondered herself why terrible things happen, or why good things happen at terrible times. And most of the time the catalysts and reasons of life's defining moments remained a mystery no matter how thorough the investigation. "Because when the world changes it's not a subtle transition," she said at last. "Sometimes everything has to be torn away so we can find our new path."

The sun had risen enough for them to see each other clearly in the dim kitchen; its orange rays catching in the translucent curtains. The floorboards above them creaked as Daniel fumbled out of bed and made his way to the bathroom.

"And so the day begins," she murmured.

Hubie picked up his mug and stood. "I think I'll go up now."

"Go ahead." She waved him toward the stairs, as if he didn't already know the way.

His father was drowsing in the little bedroom at the end of the hall that had once been used as a nursery. His frame should have looked larger in the twin bed but it seemed to grow smaller every time Hubie looked in on him. His hair was disheveled on the pillow, a pale gray rather than blond but still thick, the creases on his face prevalent even in the relaxation of slumber. His skin had a bluish pallor to it, growing darker around his deep-set eyes. Hubie sat in the wooden chair next to the bed and sipped his coffee, keeping watch over the unsteady rise and fall of his chest under the thin coverlet.

When he shifted his gaze to the window to look for the source of the trilling birdsong he heard coming from the tree just outside, Henry stirred in the bed.

"Pop?" he whispered. "You awake?"

"Hmm." He moved slightly and opened his eyes. "I smell that." His voice was faint and breathy and Hubie knew it wasn't an attempt to whisper.

He leaned forward, setting the mug on the floor by his foot. "I keep telling Aunt Erin you just need some of her good, strong coffee and you'll be good to go but she won't listen."

The corner of his lip twitched up. "Typical."

"She's always underestimating you," Hubie teased.

He raised an eyebrow in mock agreement.

"You're looking better this morning."

He murmured something that sounded like "bullet."

"Well, you're sounding more like yourself, anyway."

Henry gestured toward his throat, and Hubie took the glass of water from the windowsill and held it awkwardly to his lips. He raised his head for a sip and then slumped back onto the pillow. "Had a dream," he said, his voice a little clearer from the drink.

"Yeah? What about?"

"Your mother." He licked his tongue over his dry lips. "She was making me a sweater...couldn't get it the right size. She was...getting so mad...it was funny." When he tried to smile this time, a bit of it touched his eyes. "We were in the old house in Evansville. You remember it there?"

"No, I don't think I do. The earliest place I remember was the apartment."

"Ahh. Shame. It was...nice there."

Hubie picked up his coffee for a sip.

"You don't remember her, do you?"

He sighed. He could see in Henry's face the answer he wanted but he couldn't bring himself to lie.

"No, I don't. But it's okay."

"I wish you did."

"Don't, Pop. What good would it do me? It would only make me miss her. This way, I can't miss what I don't know."

The stress in Henry's face was immediate. "But—you—"

He patted his arm reassuringly. "I didn't say I don't love her. She's my mother—I'll always love her. But I don't carry around a void for her. She's a story and a picture to me. That's all she's ever been. And that's fine. I'm fine with that."

The pain was still evident in his face. "She...should have been more. She would have...loved who you became."

"Please don't get yourself upset. Everything is fine. I know her through you. You've told me wonderful things about her. I have memories of the stories you've told me."

This seemed to placate him, and he relaxed with a shallow exhale.

"Nothing to be done about it," he sighed.

"You're exactly right," Hubie murmured, reaching for his mug again. "Nothing to be done about anything, really."

"Took me years to learn that. You're smarter than me."

"Nah. You just taught me well. Some things you just have to let go."

He nodded, barely.

Hubie considered him for a moment. "But you never really did, did you?"

He looked up at him, eyebrows cocked in question.

"I was talking to Aunt Erin about why you never remarried. She said you're just stubborn and proud. But that's not it. It's because you never let go of Mom, isn't it?"

He didn't answer. He closed his misting eyes and pretended to drift off.

"Why couldn't you move on? You could have been happy." He didn't mean for it to sound accusatory but it did.

"I was happy," he responded, but did not open his eyes.

"But all these years, hanging on to her—it's not healthy. You should have figured out a way to let her go."

Finally he looked at him, his cloudy eyes focused and steady. "How do you let go...of a piece of yourself? I couldn't...but I did move on. I raised you. I lived. I *was*...happy. But I couldn't love another woman...as much as I loved your mother. And...that's fine. I'm fine with that."

Hubie grinned in spite of himself at his words being used back at him.

"You'll see," he continued, struggling to draw breath but sounding stronger. "Ethel. She'll be the easiest and hardest person to ever love. She'll give you things you didn't know to ask for...take things you didn't know you had. And then the easiness wears away...and you'll doubt everything. Because you have to tear something down before you can build. And once you question it...and push it away...and it's still there, you'll know what real love is. It's what runs so deep you can't touch it...no matter how much you destroy...once the rest falls away."

Hubie blinked, taken aback. "I've never heard you talk that way."

"Well this is important, dammit." He signaled for his water again, and Hubie quickly obliged. "Love just happens," he breathed. "But forever's a decision. Forever...you have to try. Trust it's strong enough to pull you through. And when you see it's still there...you'll know it was worth it. Anything that strong is worth fighting for."

"Yes, Pop." He patted his hand, concerned by the urgency he saw in his eyes.

"Remember that."

"I will. Trust me, I will."

"Hubie?" came Erin's soft voice from the doorway.

He looked up, suddenly on alert. "Yes?"

"Come here, please." She stepped back into the hallway, and Hubie exchanged anxious glances with his father and went to her side.

She pulled the door mostly shut behind him and spoke in a hushed tone. "I, um...I think you should say everything you need to say to your father this morning."

He caught himself from rolling his eyes at her unnecessary concern. "He's stronger this morning; did you hear him in there? He's having a good day. It's not going to be today."

"Honey, sometimes people get stronger just before the end."

"Stop it!" he snapped. "I know I'm going to lose him. I don't need a constant reminder. I'm making the most of my time; that's why I've been here every day. But he could last through the weekend yet. We don't know."

Erin looked flustered, which was not an expression Hubie had ever seen her wear. It spurred a nervous quivering in his stomach that felt like dread.

"What, Aunt Erin? What's wrong?"

She took a deep breath. "Henry's not going to make it through the weekend, dear."

"And how do you know that?"

"Because Ethel just went into labor."

He froze for a split second before springing into action, lunging past her and barreling down the stairs. "When?" he called back, knowing she was following close behind.

"She just called. She's been laboring quietly all morning. She didn't want you to know until it was time to go to the hospital."

"I have to go. Tell Pop I'll be back when I can."

"Hubie!"

He stopped with his hand on the doorknob, tears brimming in his eyes. "This has nothing to do with him! He'll be here when I return!"

She stepped forward and wrapped him in a tight hug. "I can feel it, Hubie. I know it sounds crazy and I can't explain it but I just know. He's been holding on. But all your waiting is over now. It all ends today."

"That's nonsense," he spat, but he hugged her back, unwilling to acknowledge the deep, calm sensation of imminence in his own bones; a vague awareness of something larger than his comprehension.

"I'll call you when I have news." He pulled himself from her matronly embrace and ran out the door, the three blocks between their houses disappearing in seconds.

Daniel emerged from the living room and wrapped his arms around her. Only then did a whimper escape her lips and her own tears begin to fall.

I stood at the foot of Henry's bed and watched out the window as the light began to change and the evening drew near. Downstairs I could hear the boys listening to the radio. Daniel flipping through the newspaper. Erin tapping her foot against the carpet while she waited impatiently for the phone to ring.

Henry slipped in and out of consciousness. His periods of sleep had become something deeper than that in the last few hours, his heart rate slower, and his breathing shallower. Daniel and Erin had taken alternating half hour shifts watching over him for most of the afternoon so that he wasn't alone. Then the phone had rung and Erin raced downstairs only to discover it was one of her friends calling to gossip. After a curt explanation the line was cleared and Daniel, seeing the strain in her eyes, suggested they all sit together for a few minutes and try to relax as though it were any normal afternoon. In fifteen minutes she would be back upstairs, but for the moment she tried to pretend she wasn't crawling out of her skin.

Henry had grown handsome as he aged, until his health began to decline. Too little sleep and too much work had aged him prematurely. It began to show five years ago, in an onset of arthritis that made his firefighting duties increasingly difficult to handle.

"You need to stop this," Erin had clucked at him at the time. "You're ruining your body. You're not a young man anymore. You're going to end up like your father did, barely able to move around and leaning on a cane!"

"Probably," was his brazen retort.

I wished he had listened but I knew why he didn't. He wasn't working himself to death to run from anything anymore. He was living hard to make up for lost time. He was doing the things that made him feel alive, even if they were slowly wearing him down.

He lived to see Hubie grow up and fall in love with a pretty little girl from his high school class. He watched Daniel and Erin establish their own home and become parents. He counted the number of lives his crew saved from burning buildings until the number exceeded one hundred and eighty two. He raised a well-adjusted and happy son. He gave back to society for the terrible debt he had accrued. And now he was tired.

I could feel it emanating from him in the moments he roused. His limbs felt heavy—each one heavier than the weight of his entire body. His chest was tight when he gasped for breath. It grew harder to discern waking reality from the dreams he slipped into and out of each passing minute. He closed his eyes again. So very, very tired.

In all the years of watching his was the face that never seemed to me to age. Perhaps it was because I had watched it the closest and had not allowed the clarity of distance to set in. Even now I scarcely saw the wear of years on his body. I felt the essence of him as strong as ever. My Henry. My strong, faithful, fallible, industrious Henry.

Why, after all this time, after all that had transpired, could I think of nothing but the man who was still my husband and the son who bore his name? Why, after all that we had wrought and all we could not change, did I still linger here? Why could I not let go?

Because he was still here. The piece of my soul he kept inside himself, holding fast to, kept me tied to him. The love that remained after all else had burned away bound us. It had always been. The pain we caused each other had been our love struggling to hold us together when we tried to turn away. If I truly never loved him it never would have hurt. There would have been nothing to lose.

When I was a child I wanted to spend forever with him. When I was a young woman I promised him I would. But it wasn't until now that I knew what that meant.

"I've been waiting for you," I said to him.

His eyes fluttered open, their hazel depths widening as they fell on me. "Annie," he breathed.

I was not a hallucination. I was not a fragment of a dream. I was a flash on the retina of his mind; an insistence in his memory; a persistence of his vision.

I walked around the bed, placed a kiss upon his forehead, and whispered into his ear the thing he had been needing to hear. From downstairs he heard a ringing, and a few moments later the pounding of feet on the stairs.

Daniel stumbled into the room with the grace of a man bursting with exhilaration and barely the mindset to control it. Finding him awake he wasted no time in his delivery. "Henry, Hubie just called. The baby's here and they're all well."

Henry was already smiling before he made it in the doorway. "I have a grandson," he murmured tremulously, tears glistening in his eyes.

He sat down at the foot of the bed, chuckling. "Yes, it's a boy. How did you guess? They named him—"

"Henry."

He patted his foot on top of the coverlet, trying to contain his exuberance. "Yes. They did. It's a fine name. And he's a fine boy, with blond curls. He came fairly easily when he finally made up his mind to come. Ethel did wonderfully; Hubie's so proud. He's—Henry? Henry?"

On the top of the highest hill looking down over Evansville I watched the sun slide toward its nightly resting place. The sky sang with streaks of rose and violet and blazing umber; the world turning golden as it does in the dawn. At the base of the marble angel's feet I waited. I watched. And I waited.

He came walking across the cluttered expanse of half-occupied graves and lush, green grass. His sandy-haired waves bounced lightly as he strode; his cream work shirt and charcoal pants were clean and crisp. His cheeks were smooth and young and his eyes twinkled with some mischievous secret. He laughed out loud when he saw me—a carefree laugh, unweighted by the strains of the world—and quickened his pace, folding me in his arms as I stood and rushed to greet him.

His lips found mine, his fingers knotted in my hair, and all distance between us was lost. There the years fell away. There the reasons didn't matter. There nothing existed but us.

I felt his face in my hands, real as nothing had felt in so long. I caught the scent of an old cologne on the breeze, long forgotten.

"Oh, Henry," I whispered, my forehead pressed to his, unwilling to pull away. "I've been waiting for you for so long."

He beamed, and he was the dashing young man in our wedding portrait—sure and vivacious, his face an open book. "I knew you would be. I knew."

There, with him in the fading light of the evening, there were no apologies to be made, or excuses given; no explanations unearthed or questions to be settled. Our fractured roads—different lengths, different patterns, like scraps of ribbon cast away—were at an end, knotted together by their final strands. It was finished. And for the first time since I left his side to exist in the shadows, I didn't feel like an incomplete work.

The binding pull that held me to this place was gone now, as though the invisible walls that had imprisoned me suddenly crumbled. From somewhere beyond the pull called me now. Somewhere I had never been. Somewhere I would not travel alone.

"What happens now?" he asked, his eyes shining with curiosity.

"Let's find out," I said, looking toward the horizon.

With a fearless smile I took his hand in mine and we walked off in search of the forever we had promised each other so very many years ago.

ACKNOWLEDGEMENTS

First and foremost, I want to give thanks to God for all His blessings and mercy. My passion, my drive, my gifts—all come from Him; the Father who loves without question and never fails to provide.

My husband, Zac, is my rock and my balance. The encouragement to my doubt. The plan to my dream. The toast to my butter. The filling to my pie.

Thanks, Mom and Dad, for always believing in me without question. You didn't think it was silly when I tried to write a novel at age 7 (that turned out to be a paragraph). You simply said, "Go. Do it. Of course you can."

Maria Matthews is one of my biggest cheerleaders and my reminder to be fearless on a daily basis. Thanks for educating me on good music, philosophy, and snake bites, and for answering my midnight cries since the day I was born.

Thank you, Martha Gery, for hanging out in the cemetery with me on a drizzly Saturday afternoon and bringing my vision for the cover art to life with your beautiful photography.

Keith Gery, I'm sorry this book doesn't have any explosions or Iron Man in it, but I hope you'll like it anyway.

Thank you, Mr. Charles Byler, for all your editing and advice, for believing in my abilities since I was a student, and for never letting me stop believing in myself. And thank you to Linda for being one of my earliest beta readers.

Without Jack Oberleitner and his valuable insight into the workings of a turn-of-the-century theater, I wouldn't have known where to start. His knowledge and advice were priceless and gave me the confidence to begin the journey into 1908.

Erin Harding has been, and always will be, my muse.

Tom Bensing: Thanks for motivating me when the road was long. (Check out his book, "Silas Soule: A Short, Eventful Life of Moral Courage.")

Thanks to Kelly Foreman for always being there with an encouraging word.

Joe Hughes nursed me through plenty of rejections with a glass of Irish whiskey and a sympathetic ear. Thanks for reminding me why the art matters. I look forward to many more glasses with you—in celebration this time. *Sláinte.*

Anita, Lauren, Bill, Cindy & friends: my fellow writers and "critters" who gave me hours of their time and their critiques. I would not be here without you.

Finally, these books detailing the fires that were the historical precedent that inspired this novel were my resources in understanding what was plausible and what occurs in the aftermath of a tragedy—*Midwinter Mourning: The Boyertown Opera House Fire (Vol 1)* and *A Town in Tragedy: The Boyertown Opera House Fire (Vol 2)* by Mary Jane Schneider, and *Chicago Death Trap: The Iroquois Theatre Fire of 1903* by Nat Brandt.

Book Club Discussion Questions

1. How does the setting of a rural suburb in 1908 play into the plot of the novel?

2. What would you consider to be the key causes of discord between Annie and Henry?

3. If each of the main characters (Annie, Henry, and Daniel) suffers from a fatal flaw, what would you say each character's flaw would be?

4. How does the epigraph apply to the novel? What events, if any, does it foreshadow?

5. At one point, Annie describes Daniel as "just young, perhaps innocently enamored." Is this an accurate description of Daniel? Why or why not?

6. How would you describe Annie's relationship with Hubie? What are some of the factors at play that contribute to this dynamic?

7. What does the blue silk hat that Henry buys in New York for Annie's birthday symbolize?

8. What were the elements/decisions/events that set the domino effect in motion that led to the fire at the Walt Theater and determined who was present that night?

9. How would you describe the progression of Annie and Daniel's relationship? What is it based on? Are their feelings mutual?

10. Toward the end of the novel, Daniel explains to Henry that "caring for Hubie, helping you…it's my redemption. I haven't done it for you half as much as I've done it for my own absolution." What is Daniel trying to atone for? How does the theme of redemption factor throughout the story?

ABOUT THE AUTHOR

Lisa Gery resides in southeastern Pennsylvania. She finds inspiration in old buildings and historic landmarks. This is her debut novel.

To read more, please visit LisaGery.com